KU-763-727

The Ghost Lover

Gillian Greenwood

JOHN MURRAY

First published in Great Britain in 2009 by John Murray (Publishers)
An Hachette UK Company

First published in paperback in 2010

1

© Gillian Greenwood 2009

The right of Gillian Greenwood to be identified as the Author of the Work has been
asserted by her in accordance with the Copyright, Designs and Patents Act 1988.

All rights reserved. Apart from any use permitted under UK copyright law no part of
this publication may be reproduced, stored in a retrieval system, or transmitted, in
any form or by any means without the prior written permission of the publisher, nor
be otherwise circulated in any form of binding or cover other than that in which it is
published and without a similar condition being imposed on the subsequent
purchaser.

All characters in this publication are fictitious and any resemblance to real persons,
living or dead, is purely coincidental.

A CIP catalogue record for this title is available from the British Library

ISBN 978-0-7195-6873-2

Typeset in Monotype Sabon by Servis Filmsetting Ltd, Stockport, Cheshire

Printed and bound by Clays Ltd, St Ives plc

John Murray policy is to use papers that are natural, renewable and recyclable
products and made from wood grown in sustainable forests. The logging and
manufacturing processes are expected to conform to the environmental regulations
of the country of origin.

John Murray (Publishers)
338 Euston Road
London NW1 3BH

www.johnmurray.co.uk

For my sister, Jane

DUNDEE CITY COUNCIL	
C00617247X	
Bertrams	14/07/2010
	£7.99
:LR	823.91

NEVER DID I DO ANY EVIL THING AGAINST
PEOPLE. AS FOR THOSE WHO WILL DO
SOMETHING AGAINST THIS, IT SHALL
BE PROTECTED FROM THEM. I HAVE
CONSTRUCTED THIS MY TOMB WITH MY
OWN MEANS. IT IS THE GOD WHO WILL
JUDGE MY CASE ALONG WITH HIM WHO
DOES ANYTHING AGAINST IT.

*Text on the false door of the tomb
of Redi-ness at Giza*

One

In that very first instant, I felt the information merely as a matter of shocking fact. But that's how death so often comes, or rather the news of it. The telling hardly carries the words and in this case the words said that my employer (and best friend in all the world), Toby Haddeley, had been killed, along with my darling girl, Alice, and I felt nothing but a coldness that seemed quite external, a chill that seemed to settle over me, as a part of me passed away too.

The report that came through, on the telephone, was unclear, but it seemed that they had been flying over the Crimea in a light aircraft, along with four others. All on board were dead. Sometimes at night in the weeks and months afterwards, I couldn't stop myself from imagining the sensation of those last minutes in that small plane, the plummeting, the speed, the smell of fuel, the imminence of death. And I wondered over and over why they had taken the plane. After all, I had made the arrangements myself. They had been due to travel by train, from Moscow down to the archaeological dig on the Black Sea coast, a newly found site in one of the Greek colonies. The trip was a birthday present from Toby to Alice, his god-daughter, though no doubt Toby had also been hoping (though he didn't admit it to me) that the trip might yield something special to bring back for sale.

When the news came, that's where I was, working at the gallery, as I had done for almost twenty years. There had been a time when I might have gone with Toby myself, but our business, Haddeley Antiquities, had grown to such an extent that one of us had to stay behind to see to its smooth running. Toby's nephew, Kit Haddeley, was there, of course. He was working with us by then. But he was too recently out of the Army and regarded as still too green to leave on his own.

It was Kit who took the call. I was in the secure room, which we used as a vault, and I heard him call out my name. His voice was clear above the radio play I was immersed in, but of which I now have no memory at all. There was nothing obvious in his tone to alert me, as I remember, yet I stopped what I was doing at once. I had been happy, cocooned in the small steel-lined room. I had been unpacking a block of inscribed Egyptian stone, a section of a false door, the type of thing found in the better sort of tomb from the Third Dynasty and built as a threshold between this life and the next. It was the charm of proximity to such ancient artefacts that had kept me in the business for so many years, but when Kit appeared in the doorway of the vault, stiff and soldierly in his shock, and he told me that both his wife, Alice, and his uncle Toby were dead, I had wanted to take a hammer and smash the stone to pieces.

It was worse for Kit, of course. He had lost his wife, and

it was natural in some ways that he should want to cling to me as someone whom Alice had loved. And so I stayed on at Millbury Street, in the big house he inherited from Toby along with the gallery. I stayed to keep him company and because I could not bear to leave Toby's house, the place where we had lived our odd lives together and where, I suppose, if I'm honest, I had acted as a sort of surrogate wife and unofficial housekeeper. It was a role I had taken upon myself, for good or ill, and one I chose to continue with Kit. And so we helped each other through the first terrible year, when grief would render us, alternately, desolate, and after that, well, it seemed to suit us both to continue the arrangement.

Over the years, I have felt, from time to time, that I went to live at Millbury Street against my better judgement, that it was a sort of mistake, but I have always loved the house. It backed on to that stretch of the old canal to which time has lent a strange beauty, a remnant of an industrial past, softened by its proximity to Regent's Park and by foliage which the years had layered over soft warm brick. The garden swept down to the water's edge, the border a convex curve. It looked on to a small island in a wide basin, a sort of artificial lake where the painted longboats turned, an oasis fringed by willows and inhabited by geese and moorhens and an occasional swan. It was tall and white, four storeys high, and was set just out of reach of the gaze of the tourist boats that cruised around the far side of the island when summer came.

*

3

I can think about them now, about Toby and Alice, without wanting to cry, or without feeling angry, or feeling nothing, which can be worst of all. It's been more than ten years since their deaths, and life has moved on. I'm in my fifties, and Kit is forty-two and he no longer lives alone, alone apart from me, that is. It was me who introduced him to Isobel Whaley. She was the daughter of an old acquaintance, Jack Whaley, a man I hadn't seen since before his short-lived marriage to Isobel's mother, an American who, after the divorce, had gone back to the States with her daughter. And yet after Toby died, Jack, like several others, contacted me to offer condolences. It was a strange paradox of bereavement, I discovered, that people who had been strangers for decades felt compelled to get in touch, while those more familiar were sometimes too embarrassed even to telephone.

When Isobel accepted Kit's proposal I had assumed that I would finally have to move out. I offered to go. I didn't wait to be asked. But it was Isobel who wanted me to stay. The house was so big, she said, and it made her nervous to be on her own when Kit was away, as he sometimes was.

So after they married, I moved into the annexe at Millbury Street, one which Kit converted specially. I still had a small flat of my own in Victoria, rented out to a nice young woman who worked at the House of Commons and the money she paid me provided me with a supplement to the salary I received at the gallery. The annexe was over the garage, like a mews house in itself, with its own entrance, but it was also possible to go into the main house through a door on the first-floor landing. There was a small door in the outside wall of the garden which I sometimes used if I wished to be private, rather than going through the big gates. Back in the old days, the early Toby days, there would be a white peacock or two striding across the lawn, their long tails trailing behind them, but I was always rather afraid of them, of their ghostly whiteness and the terrible cries they made as they sat, grotesque and outsized, on the roof of the garage. But now, of course, the birds, pale and eerie even in life, are long dead, along with all the rest, along with Toby and with Alice.

I liked Isobel, on the whole. She was her father's daughter, and the fact that she was so very different from Alice was a good thing, I always thought. It wasn't just the physical contrast, though that was striking. Alice had been tall and dark, rather like Kit in fact (they say, don't they, that people often marry their mirror image). Isobel, on the other hand, was small and curved and blonde, and as such gave an impression of soft simplicity. It was an impression which deceived. She was a clever girl who had all her wits about her. There was a stability about her in contrast with Alice's more mercurial moods. And I believe she loved Kit and made him happy again, and for that we all loved her in return, or at least I did. There were those who had some reservations, Kit's mother Margaret for one, though it is hard to know who could have satisfied her.

The day the whole business began, or rather didn't begin exactly, but began to make itself felt, I bumped into Isobel at the tube station, on the way home from work. It was early April and raining and we huddled together under my umbrella as we walked towards Millbury Street. It was Isobel's birthday and her father Jack and his latest *amour*, Helen, a GP he had met through his work as a clinical psychologist, were coming over to help us celebrate.

As we reached the gate, Isobel tugged at my arm, insisting that I come straight in with her for a drink before either of us thought about starting dinner, with which I was going to help. I still did a great deal of helping, continuing to look after them both, just as I had done for Kit, and for Toby before him. I didn't need a lot of persuading to accept her invitation. I don't like to drink alone, though I do, quite frequently, and although it was only five thirty, the glass of wine she was offering would go down well. I would have preferred whisky, of course, a taste I shared with her father, but at that time of day, Isobel might disapprove.

I watched her as she let us both in. She stood inside the doorframe, her short raincoat riding up her legs as she mouthed the numbers of the alarm to herself, pressing the buttons high on the inside wall. Then she stopped in her tracks and held up her hand.

'Listen,' she said, her small childlike face turned up and to one side. 'Listen to the noise.' I could hear only the birds on the nearby water, the geese and the moorhens, their cries rising above the slow rumbling of a car on the far side of the wall.

'What?' I said. 'What noise? The birds?'

'Yes,' she said. 'They're noisy today, don't you think?'
No more than usual, I thought, following her down the
stairs to the large family kitchen, and she turned her head
back to me. She was thoughtful. 'It made me think of the
peacocks, the ones you told me about that used to be here.
Just for a moment, I fancied it was them. That I could hear
them.'

'Just the geese,' I said firmly. It struck me as an absurdly
fanciful thing to say, geese sounding nothing like peacocks,
and it was uncharacteristic. Isobel was an artist, it was true,
but she was a portrait painter and, though expressive, she
was rather pragmatic in her American way, certainly not
given to whimsy.

Reaching the bottom of the stairs she kicked off her
shoes, and still wearing her coat, walked straight to the
fridge. She took out an open bottle of wine and poured me
a large glass, and herself an apple juice.

'Maybe I'm hearing things,' she said.

'Aren't you having a drink?' I said. 'I can't drink alone.'

'Please,' she said. As she handed me the glass I could see
paint on her fingers that she had failed to remove. She had
been to her studio in Paddington. For the portraits she did
on commission, she preferred her sitters to come to neutral
territory. 'Drink. It's my birthday.'

'Many happy returns then,' I said, lifting my glass.

'I want to tell you something, Josie,' she said. 'Kit
knows, but no one else, yet, because . . . well, you know
why.'

I waited politely, knowing what was coming.

'I'm pregnant again.' Isobel almost whispered her news

7

as if to utter the words aloud might invite in something malevolent.

I put down my drink and kissed her, squeezing her hand.

'Congratulations, Isobel,' I said. 'That's wonderful.' And it was, of course, but it came with a shoal of complications.

'Yes, it is, isn't it?' Isobel looked down and for some reason I felt embarrassed for her. She seemed not at ease with her news. 'So no drinks for me, even on my birthday.' Isobel pulled a face. 'It's a small price to pay, I suppose.'

'Well,' I said, 'it must be a bore for you, I can imagine.' I couldn't imagine, in fact, going nine months without a drink, and I was relieved that by this stage in my life I was unlikely to have to do so. 'But wonderful news, Isobel. Really.'

She nodded, but again she seemed reticent.

I thought it best, for the moment, to leave it be. Getting pregnant had not been easy. They had had to turn to IVF and then there had been two or possibly even three disappointments prior to this pregnancy, so I could understand Isobel's uncertainty. And then there was a secret, one that Kit had confessed to me late at night when, anxious, he had come to my flat for comfort and whisky as he had so often done in the past. It was all his fault, he said. His sperm count was very low, and he had had to agree, reluctantly, that they would use a donor. Any baby they might manage to have would not biologically be his.

Isobel picked up the pile of letters that the daily help had left on the kitchen table. Most of them were for Kit, but

8

there were a couple addressed to her. One envelope was handwritten and addressed to 'Isobel Haddeley'.

'Boring,' she said. 'It's from that small gallery near the bookshop. I bought a picture there a couple of years ago and now they send me stuff all the time.' The other looked more formal, typed, to 'Mrs Kit Haddeley'. She threw it down on the table. It was the sort of thing Isobel disliked, hating the etiquette that reduced her to being a mere adjunct of Kit's. It was a view with which I could only partially sympathise. It seemed a small price to pay for everything else that marriage to Kit had delivered.

Isobel pushed the letters aside and picked up a third. She stared hard at it, then held it up in front of me. It was in a small blue envelope and the name was printed in neat block capitals: MRS ALICE HADDELEY. She reached, without thinking, for her glass of juice as she examined it again, turning it over, looking at the postmark which appeared to be unidentifiable. She pulled out a chair and sat down. By now she seemed almost to have forgotten I was there, and I found myself thinking how odd it was that we were both still wearing our coats.

'What do you think, Josie?' she said. 'What do you make of this? What could it be?'

There had been letters for Alice Haddeley before, very occasionally, and they were always slightly shocking, especially for Isobel. I suppose they were a reminder of Kit's existence prior to this one that he shared with her, a reminder of the wife who had preceded her. But the other letters had been formal, typed. They had been bureaucratic glitches that had conjured a dead woman's name from an imperfect system. This one was different. The letter's firm address and the compactness of the folded paper seemed to reach out to the living.

'It will be an oversight,' I said. 'Some unfortunate muddle of names.'

I could see that she was tempted to open it, not just out of curiosity but as if under a sort of compulsion. But she didn't, of course. It was for Kit to open, not her, and even had I not been present, I'm sure she would not have done so.

We sat at the table, not speaking; it wasn't unusual for us to sit in companionable silence. It had become clear to both of us, soon after Isobel moved in, that we would have little problem living at close quarters. Neither of us worried about such things as pauses in our conversations, and I was naturally accommodating. I have had to be.

Isobel continued to stare at the envelope which lay now between her elbows, her hands flat on the table.

'I don't usually think about her much, you know,' she said. 'About Alice. Is that wrong of me? Even though she's everywhere. In the house, at the gallery, in you too, Josie. But it's as if she's something quite separate. As if we all lived other lives that don't impinge on hers. But this sort of thing . . .' She picked up the letter and put it in the pile addressed to Kit, slipping it under the largest so that she couldn't see it. 'This sort of thing makes me . . .'

I could see that she felt that to hold on to the letter further would be an admission of some kind. I couldn't remember the last time I had heard her mention Alice. I had, in fact, always rather admired the way she sidestepped the subject when other people referred to it. And I had always assumed that it was something she and Kit had resolved before they married. Certainly he no longer talked about Alice, or not to me.

It had become harder and harder to recall her. There were photographs, of course, and I had a strong sense of the last lunch we had had together, just before she and Toby left for Russia. Alice had been bright with excitement that day, almost too bright; I had been a little concerned at her over-elation. But her plans had been clear, and her preparations thorough and I had been mesmerised by her, as always. I had promised to look after Kit, and she had hugged me to her as we went our separate ways. And now, I thought, I could hardly bring to mind her lovely face. We hadn't forgotten her exactly, I knew that. We had simply put her away for the time being. We had wrapped up her memory and interred it. And we were surely right to have done that.

I could hear the wall clock ticking as Isobel continued to stare at the spot between her arms where the letter had been a moment ago. Her hands were still spread flat on the table. Her mobile face seemed almost to ripple in its confusion. It was this inability to conceal her feelings on occasion that ruffled her mother-in-law, Margaret Haddeley. Margaret was an old-school type who distrusted expression of feeling, and she distrusted her artistic, American daughter-in-law on principle. 'That girl needs more backbone,' she had said to me one day, when

I remarked on Isobel's sensitivity. 'She's far too emotional. I'm not surprised she appears not to be able to carry a child.'

Even for Margaret, whom I had known and tolerated now for over thirty years, such callousness was shocking, but she had loved Alice very much and she had found it hard to accept Isobel in her place. Now as we sat together, looking at the letter, Margaret's words formed in my head once again. I felt protective towards Isobel, and I reached across the table to put my hand over hers.

'It will be something and nothing, the letter, I promise.'

Isobel turned to me and smiled. 'I know,' she said, 'you're right.' The concern had faded quickly from her face. 'Must be the hormones,' she laughed, delighted, it seemed, at the very idea. 'You're coming over later, Josie?'

'I'm going to start supper here, then change,' I said.

'Come early and have a drink before dinner, won't you? Dad would like that.' She hesitated for a moment. 'Do you mind me leaving supper to you?' she added. I shook my head. 'Then I think I'll go and have a bath,' she said.

Half an hour later I made my way back up the stairs to the ground floor, then on up to the first floor and through the interior door to my flat. It was quicker than going all the way outside again and across the courtyard. And it was still raining. I liked to use the outside entrance on principle, but neither Kit nor Isobel ever appeared to mind me using the first-floor connection, so on days like this I took advantage of it.

I hung up the raincoat I was carrying in the small hallway. It was a recent (and fashionable) purchase which I was delighted by, and which had satisfied my attachment to new clothes for a month or two. I switched on the radio to fill the silence and poured myself a small glass of whisky from the bottle I kept in the kitchen cupboard. I couldn't get the memory of Margaret's cruel remark out of my mind and I recalled a conversation I had had with Isobel's father, Jack, one evening, here in my flat. He had been holding forth about Margaret, about her inability to accept the idea of a second wife for Kit.

'You'd think she'd be happy for him,' he said. We had both drunk too much whisky, a *sine qua non*, of course, of our relationship.

'It was easier for me,' I replied. 'Even though I was so fond of Alice.' And then I heard myself say, 'You know, I think that at the back of my mind, I always felt that Alice might die young, though not in that way, of course. That was unexpected.'

I'd never said such a thing before, but Jack was a man who elicited secrets, with no apparent prompting.

'Ah, so you wished her dead?' he said. Jack had retired from the clinic where he'd worked, but he still taught, and saw private clients for analysis, and he was still given to gnomic utterances, especially when tipsy.

'I didn't wish her dead,' I protested. 'I said I had a feeling that she might die young, that's not the same thing.'

'Sounds like it to me,' he said. 'And not so surprising.'

'Stop being provocative.' It was an idiotic thing to say, for there was nothing Jack liked more than provocation.

Two

The drawing room on the first floor of Millbury Street was a marvellous space. It ran the length of the house, stretching from front to back. Kit had kept it more or less as Toby left it. It was very much as he was, tasteful though unsubtle, dramatic but never camp.

I can clearly remember the party we held not long after we moved in. It felt as though the decorators had only just left and I recall the exclamations and laughter as our friends took in the mirrored and gilded opulence of the grand first-floor room, and that everyone got tipsy, and someone sang an aria from *Traviata* in homage to its operatic pretensions. As I took my glass of birthday champagne from Kit that evening I was struck by the contrast between uncle and nephew, by the measured, restrained life that Kit and Isobel led in comparison with the one indulged in by Toby and me.

Isobel was standing by one of the long south-facing windows from which you could see the water. She seemed preoccupied, though not by what she was looking at. I went over to join her and together we watched the eddy of a longboat that had already disappeared from view, and which had left its wake to fan across the surface of the small lagoon. It was a view that I knew she was fond of, but I also knew that this house was not really to her taste and that she hankered for something simpler.

Perhaps it was the news of the pregnancy that made me reflective that evening, but I found myself thinking, as the three of us stood together, that the time had almost certainly come for me to leave Millbury Street. Indeed, I thought, it would probably be best for us all to go. I'd always assumed they would sell up at some point; that Isobel would eventually persuade Kit that the house was too big, too dangerous for a young family with the water so close. As I stood looking out of the window through the fading light, I told myself that if I gave notice, and went first, it might give them the impetus they needed, and that then Isobel might be happier. But I surprised myself by this conclusion. It had not occurred to me before that she might be less than content.

If I went, they would miss me, I knew. Or at least they would miss the role I played in their lives. It had become second nature for Kit to consult me, not only about business, but on the many details of domestic life which he couldn't be bothered to deal with himself, and this had continued, even after he remarried. I was glad to help, and Isobel didn't seem to mind at all. On the contrary, she was happy to take advantage of my living so close. She preferred being in her studio to managing a household.

I was aware that any residual guilt she felt was assuaged by her conviction that I was only doing what I wanted, and that by letting me help, she was shoring me up against my loneliness. But I liked to look at it another way. I regarded myself as a sort of inheritance. It was as if Kit had inherited me, I thought, along with the house, and that like the artefacts in the gallery and the furniture here, I was a valuable family asset.

'Well?' Isobel said. She was smiling at Kit who was standing over by the empty marble fireplace, watching her, as he so frequently did, with an almost reverent affection. It was early spring, cold outside, but not enough to light the fire, and the grate was concealed by a large bouquet of flowers. Kit was standing as I had so often seen Toby do, an elbow resting on the mantelpiece, his profile reflected in the mirror. Kit is dark, as Toby was, though Kit is an inch or two shorter. As Kit ages, I notice more and more the similarities between them, as if they had been father and son rather than uncle and nephew. For example, Kit took the same great delight as Toby had in offering up surprises, and both Isobel and I knew that there must be one about to come. His face was excited and he now fetched something from behind the sofa and placed it on the small inlaid table that stood next to it. The package was green, a square box made of some sort of stiffened silky card. Isobel raised her eyebrows at me and moved towards it quickly. Any earlier uncertainty that I had witnessed seemed to have vanished.

'No wrapping paper?' she said.

'It didn't seem the right thing,' he said. He was watching her closely. I could see that he was admiring her, and she did look very fetching. She was casually dressed in jeans and a pale blue cashmere sweater, her short blonde hair pushed back behind her ears. I recognised the look on his face as something more than simply admiration for his wife. He was, after all, a connoisseur of form and there was a bit of him that could stand apart and admire her as a pleasing piece of modernity in this formal room. There was an element of dispassion in his look. Kit had a good eye. No doubt he was born with it, but Toby and I had taught him well.

Isobel lifted off the lid and set it aside. Feeling inside, she pulled out a cloth-wrapped object.

'Gently,' Kit said. He was hovering about her. I was standing a few feet away, keen to have a full view. 'Here,' he said, 'open it on here.' He indicated a tall side stool that supported a lamp which he now whipped off and placed on the floor.

'It's something old, isn't it?' Isobel said, and I was surprised to detect a slight anxiety in her voice.

'It's special,' Kit said. He had not noticed her hesitation. 'I know I don't usually give you old stuff. It's too close to business. But this was too special to resist.'

He had now caught my attention. It was indeed very unlike Kit to give an antiquity as a gift, especially to Isobel. And I was surprised that he hadn't consulted me. I watched her as she unwrapped the object, turning it over and over in her hands with great care, as the cloth which was wound around it hung down like discarded swaddling.

'Oh,' she said. Her voice was puzzled. She lifted the box's contents up to the light, then placed it on her palm, supported by the fingers of her other hand. It was a statuette about six centimetres high.

'Oh. He's extraordinary. Is he a he? I think he is. He's very cute.'

'Cute?' Kit laughed. 'He's a she and she's a god, a goddess.'

'Of course,' Isobel said.

I knew at once what it was, of course, and I found myself feeling apprehensive. Sometimes Kit could display his mother's lack of tact. This piece he had bought for Isobel did have a kind of ugly beauty, but it was a strange gift.

'It's a Tawaret,' I said.

Isobel looked round at me and I smiled in an encouragement neither of us felt. She turned back to Kit. 'And?' she said. 'I know there's more.'

Kit seemed quite unaware of any reservations.

'Yes, it's a Tawaret. It came up for auction at Christie's last week. It just seemed . . . you know . . . well, it's a god of childbirth, that sort of thing.'

Isobel looked away from him and back at the creature in her hands.

'A little premature, perhaps,' she said. Her voice was low and I wanted to put my arm around her and comfort her. I wondered what Kit could have been thinking, and if this oddly tactless present was a gesture of optimism. It certainly wasn't what I had been expecting when Kit had confessed to an antiquity. I had assumed that it must be jewellery, or perhaps a small alabaster jar, some exquisite container that had once housed the cosmetics of a Greek or Egyptian noblewoman.

'Not just childbirth,' he was saying now. 'Pregnancy, the whole deal.' He reached towards her for the creature. 'May

I?' he said. He lifted it up, as if to appraise it for sale. 'Not that I'm superstitious,' he went on, and then he suddenly looked puzzled as he began to register Isobel's discomfort. 'Oh God, have I been insensitive?'

Well, yes, I wanted to shout, *you have been profoundly insensitive. She lost her last baby, and the one before that. She didn't need this reminder, from you of all people.* But then I found myself wanting to defend him against my own accusations, just as I had always done with Toby. And I persuaded myself that perhaps his point of view was quite comprehensible. Isobel was pregnant. It wasn't so strange for Kit to bring home this talisman. It was surely just a symbolic way to offer his protection.

'You surprised me, darling, that's all,' she was saying now. 'It's a beautiful thing.' As I watched her stroke the Tawaret with a finger, she reminded me of a child with a pet mouse.

'Tell me all about it,' she said. She knew that that was what Kit liked best, to paint a picture of his own, to imagine his finds as they had once been, before they were snatched away by grave-robbers and history.

'This Tawaret,' he said, 'has the head of a hippopotamus, there, you see.' He indicated the long fierce jaw of the statue. 'They were known as the guardians of the Nile. But look, she's standing up, like a human, and she has these lion's feet.' He pointed to the long strange claw-like base. 'She's swift and fierce. And then,' he turned the object round, 'look, she's got a crocodile's back. I wouldn't want to cross her, would you?' Kit laughed.

'May I see?' I said.

'Please.' He handed me the Tawaret which I inspected with a practised eye.

'It's hardly museum-quality,' Kit said. 'But I wanted one we would be comfortable having at home.'

I had handled many like it through the years. It was made of faience, Egyptian faience, a ceramic which in this case was glazed a greeny blue. It was in decent condition, if not particularly fine. I wondered what he had paid for it, maybe fifteen hundred pounds or so. It was a generous present.

'It's a good example, Isobel.'

'Tell me more,' she said. 'It's growing on me. Go on, Josie.' Kit nodded, happy for me to take up the story.

'Well,' I said, careful in the selection of my material. 'She protects pregnant women, and safeguards them through childbirth which I imagine could be quite daunting in Ancient Egypt.'

'I'll say,' Isobel said.

'You find the Tawaret all over the place, don't you, Josie?' Kit said in encouragement.

I nodded. 'Yes,' I said. 'You find them as little charms, statues, in pictures, tomb paintings.' I handed him my empty glass. 'She was very popular.'

'She's in good condition,' Kit said, pouring me a refill. 'Look at the detail on her face.'

Isobel and I leant in to inspect the bulbous blue head. 'She looks as if she's blind,' Isobel whispered, but Kit didn't hear her.

'And the fact that she's associated with the Nile makes her a life-giver, as you know, darling,' Kit added.

'The inundation,' I said, and the word suddenly carried with it a stream of sadness. It made me think of bleeding, of miscarrying, of drowning. It seemed to be death mixed with life, and I was reminded that there had been another Tawaret long ago, a pretty blue creature, far smaller than this, one that Alice, as a child, had begged to play with each time she saw it.

'I love it,' Isobel said. Her face suggested this was unlikely. She was trying hard.

Kit kissed the top of her head. 'It is remarkable,' he said, placing the Tawaret back on the table. 'Let's hope she protects us.'

'From what?' Isobel said.

Kit looked confused. 'I didn't mean that . . .' he said. 'It was just a way of saying . . . I don't know . . . that she brings good luck.'

I watched from the hallway as Jack Whaley and Helen climbed from his ancient Renault and were ushered into the house by Isobel and Kit. Isobel's father moved stiffly, his movements more constricted than the last time I had seen him, only weeks before. It upset me more than I would have anticipated. I was fond of Jack but the depth of my concern surprised me. I could see that Isobel had also noticed this apparent sign of ageing.

'What's wrong, Dad?' she said. 'You're limping.'

'He tripped over a chair,' Helen said, kissing Isobel on the cheek.

'It was an accident,' Jack said. 'I wasn't drunk.'

'I didn't say you were,' said Helen. 'Not for one moment have I implied any such thing.'

'Hello, Josie, old girl. Good to see you, Miss Price. How's tricks?' Jack seized on my presence as a distraction from the subject in hand.

'Don't squabble,' said Isobel. 'And there's no such thing as an accident, Dad, or so you always tell me. I thought the unconscious dictated everything.'

'But sometimes a cigar is just a cigar,' Jack pronounced, leading the way past Isobel into the house, kissing her en route.

'A quote from Freud,' Helen explained to us, and much to my irritation. 'You know the sort of thing,' she went on. 'Not everything means something else.'

'They all know that, Helen,' Jack said in a tone of exasperation. 'This is an educated household.'

Helen was a kind woman, a fraught and overworked GP, but one under-endowed with a sense of humour, something I was surprised that Jack had overlooked when he chose her. But perhaps he didn't choose her, I thought, perhaps she chose him. Perhaps, I found myself thinking, that is why I never married. I was waiting for someone to choose me. But I pushed the idea away.

Jack now sat himself on one of the high-backed drawing-room chairs, having insisted on hauling himself up the staircase. 'Come and sit down here, Josie, next to me.' He patted the chair beside him. I found myself, as always, flattered by his attention, though I ought to have known better.

'I should really go down and help Isobel,' I said. I had,

of course, cooked the supper but it was my custom to let Isobel put the final touches while I assisted.

'No, no, let me, Josie,' Helen said. 'I'll go. I'd like to. Let me for once.'

The words felt like a rebuke. She was jealous, I supposed, of my friendship with Jack's daughter. She and Jack had been together for a couple of years, though they felt oddly impermanent.

'I'll have a scotch,' Jack said.

'Jack . . .' Helen frowned.

'You're driving,' he said. 'A couple of glasses won't do me any harm.'

'A small one.' Helen's instruction to Kit felt almost impertinent, though Jack showed no sign of resentment. I saw that Kit was laughing as he turned towards the ornate silver drinks tray; it was an object that looked as if it had been standing on the side table since at least the 1930s, though I could remember the day that Toby brought it home, wrapped in newspaper, pleased to have found it in the Portobello Road.

Kit poured out the whisky. He was tolerant of Jack, and even though his father-in-law could be tiresome when he had had too much to drink, Kit rarely tried to limit his intake. If Jack wanted to kill himself it was his prerogative as far as Kit was concerned.

'There you are, Jack,' he said, handing his father-in-law a heavy crystal glass. Jack looked down into its bottom.

'That's a bit mean.'

'I just thought . . . dinner will be ready soon,' Kit said.

He picked up the bottle to add another measure but Helen stopped him.

'Drink that one first,' she said. 'I'm going downstairs.'

As she moved towards the doorway, I couldn't help but speak up. 'And then, Jack,' I said, 'you can tell us what you've really been up to.'

Helen turned and glared at me, but thought better of it and smiled. She picked up the glass of champagne that Kit had poured for her and walked out of the room.

Helen was tall, a big woman, rather capacious now, though photographs we had seen at her house showed that she had once been less so. There were some fragments of an earlier sensuality that had remained with her, around the mouth and the sway of the hips. I had to admit she was handsome. She didn't dress with the care that I took, but she had a certain style. Her hair was shoulder-length, rather untidy but an arresting tone of grey. She was prone to a uniform of similar loose-cut dresses in different colours and fabrics, depending on the time of year. Today's garment was a slate blue, which suited her.

Jack watched her leave us with a puzzled expression, as if he was unsure as to what she was doing there, and I wondered if the impulse which had drawn him to her might be fading. He was a striking, vigorous man. His hair was thick and white, and had been so since the age of forty. He was now sixty-seven and still unconventional, in every sense. Kit and I had once joked that his features reminded us of a lion head of Roman limestone that Kit's father had bought from Toby, and which still stood on the landing in Margaret's house at Fleet on the Norfolk coast.

'Cheers.' Jack raised his glass to me and then to Kit. 'How's the grave-robbing going?' This was Jack's standard opening gambit.

'It's going rather well, Jack,' Kit replied. It was a game between them that Jack would attempt to chip away at Kit's well-mannered façade.

'Anything interesting come in?'

Kit thought for a moment then looked at me. 'I think I'll show him Isobel's present,' he said. His tone was conspiratorial and I felt a moment of apprehension at the idea. Surely, I thought, he should ask Isobel first, but it wasn't for me to say so.

The Tawaret was in its box down by the side of the sofa. As Kit walked across the room to fetch it, his back to us, Jack reached for my hand, and squeezed it, and to my annoyance I felt myself start to blush. But I had no time to wonder at his gesture for he began to cough and splutter, as if he'd swallowed something the wrong way. I quickly fetched a glass of water but he was still wheezing when I gave it to him. Kit and I stood over him, Kit clutching the green box under his arm, looking as worried as I was.

'I'm fine,' Jack said, his breathing easing. He nodded towards Kit. 'He won't be robbing my grave for a while, will he, Josie?'

'I wasn't aware there would be anything in it worth stealing, save your good self, of course,' said Kit.

'*Touché*. Let's see what you've got.'

'This is a birthday present, to Isobel,' Kit said.

26

'From you?'

Kit nodded. He handed the Tawaret to Jack who held it in front of him at arm's length. He turned to me and said, 'It's a god, I suppose. Egyptian, yes?'

I nodded and Kit still said nothing. We both knew that Jack would find it irresistible not to suggest some interpretation of the gift, and I wondered what had prompted Kit to offer such a hostage to fortune. To keep Jack amused, I supposed. But first Jack would have to find out more about it, something he liked to do slowly, like a guessing game.

He turned it over, carefully, in his large hands. 'A hippo, something to do with the Nile inevitably. But look at its feet.'

'They're claws,' I said.

'And these breasts, milk, Nile, nourishment, fertility, and so on. Nothing human?'

'Well, that's not strictly true,' Kit said. 'It stands upright. That's human.'

'Yes, I suppose that's right,' said Jack. 'That's what makes this Egyptian stuff so sinister, the upright posture and the animal heads. Our animal nature, the repressed part of us.'

I rolled my eyes at Kit and Jack caught my expression, reaching for my hand again and laughing.

'Nothing wrong with a bit of repression, eh Josie?' he said.

'It's a goddess of pregnancy,' Kit interrupted.

'Why's it not fatter then?' said Jack.

'It's protective. The claws are lion's feet.'

Jack lifted the object higher and ran his fingers over the

27

disproportionately long talons. 'I see. And why did you give this to my daughter, Kit? Is there something we should know? Beyond the fact that she is pregnant again, I mean.'

Kit took the Tawaret from him. There was a pause, a silence. Then Kit said, 'No. I saw it at Christie's and I thought she would like it.'

'It's a very good example,' I chipped in.

Jack ignored me and looked at Kit.

'Go on then,' Kit said. 'Spit it out. I'd rather you said it now than in front of Isobel.'

'It's a remarkable creature,' was all Jack said, and picked up his drink. 'And what does Isobel make of it?' he added.

'She loves it,' Kit said. But he didn't sound convinced.

The kitchen at Millbury Street extended over a large area of the lower-ground floor. A long refectory table ran down the middle, and at the far end the room extended round into a cosy L-shaped alcove where a large television, an old blue sofa and a couple of chairs offered a refuge from the overblown formality of the other parts of the house. On the south side, the kitchen opened out, through a wide conservatory, on to the garden and the water beyond. That evening, the five of us were seated at the small round table in the bay, its windows screened by heavy pale cream and blue striped curtains which kept out the chill.

Jack was sitting in Kit's customary seat, holding forth on his favourite topic after Freud, the evils of capitalism, a subject to which he could, and did, return on many occasions and at any historical point, without ever entirely repeating himself. I sometimes thought it would be possible to go away for years and come back to find Jack in mid-sentence where he had left off. Indeed, that was almost exactly what had happened, when Jack and I met up again a year or so after Alice's death, though strictly speaking he was the one who had disappeared.

My attention wandered into the past as I listened to Isobel and Kit, and to Jack and Helen as they talked across the *boeuf en daube*, eating the crisp potatoes, the carrots and leeks that grew, under my supervision, at the east side of the garden. I could still see in Jack the young man who had seduced me, briefly, until I took fright at his intensity. He had seemed, back then, far older than me, restless, putting the world to rights, handing out his socialist news-papers, a prophet at factory gates. These days, he still looked the part, with his white hair swept back from his large forehead. I watched him, and then I watched Helen watching him, patient and smiling, and I wondered if I could ever have been quite the sort of handmaiden he had always seemed to require.

Helen's voice pulled me back into the present.

'You're right of course, my darling,' she was saying, in response to an outraged blast from Jack. At the same time, she was rising from the table to clear the plates.

'Don't do that, Helen,' Isobel said. 'Let me.' But Helen, of course, carried the plates to the side, still talking, oblivi-ous to her status as a guest, while Isobel sat by, helpless, though happy to abdicate, as always, any domestic chore. It was a reassuring reminder of why she seemed to welcome my presence in her home life.

'But how many years have you been right, Jack,' Helen went on, 'have we all been right, and nothing, absolutely nothing has changed.'

How many years, I thought. *She's known him for less than two.* It irritated me, it was as if she was blurring the demarcations between us all, but Jack shrugged and raised his hands in mock despair. Isobel caught my eye.

'I'll take those now, Helen,' Kit said, jumping up to take the plates from her though he was much too late. 'And Jack, have another glass of that claret.'

'Good idea,' Jack said, reaching for the bottle of wine. 'Excellent idea. One thing I'll say for you lot, you keep a good cellar.'

'And you're happy to drink it dry,' I said.

Jack looked at me as if he had just remembered I was there, and laughed.

'You always were sharp, Josie Price.' He raised his glass. 'To my beautiful daughter and her charming husband, even if he is a bit of a toff. Happy birthday, sweetheart.'

'Thanks, Dad.' A momentary frown appeared on Isobel's face. She had picked up, as I had, the cavalier tone in Jack's voice, a sign that he had drunk more than he probably should have done.

I studied him as he drained his glass. There was something in his posture, in the way he was now holding himself, that suggested he was about to change tack.

'Kit showed me what he'd bought you, Izzy, for your birthday,' he said. 'Very unusual.'

'Oh really.' Helen's voice was inflected with a sudden curiosity. 'What did Kit give you, Isobel?'

Isobel looked at her father. She sensed the presence of the troublemaker.

'It's a Tawaret,' said Kit.

'A what?' said Helen.

'It's a fertility symbol.' Jack's voice seemed to get louder with each syllable. 'A fucking fertility symbol.'

'Not really,' I jumped in. 'It's more complicated than that.'

'It's beautiful,' Isobel said. 'I'll show you after dinner, Helen.'

'What I want to know,' said Jack, 'is why Kit chose that?'

And I'm sure you're going to tell him, I thought, but Kit just raised his eyebrows at Jack and smiled.

'Jack. Please,' Helen said. 'Don't drink any more wine.'

'It suggests to me,' Jack said, ignoring her, 'that it may be a warning, albeit unconscious.'

'A warning?' Isobel was on full guard now. When drunk, her father was capable of saying the unsayable. 'Come on, Dad. We're not your patients to be challenged.'

'It's not a fertility symbol exactly, Jack.' Kit tried to press on, but Jack was not to be stopped.

'Something fierce and predatory from the depths of the Nile? To protect the dynasty? What would you do, Kit, to protect your dynastic interests?'

'I haven't got any,' Kit said. 'There is no dynasty, as you put it.'

'I was speaking of your class interests, something more general.'

'Oh so we're back to politics now, I see.' Kit managed to

31

laugh, his tone easier. Jack's class-baiting was something he understood. I too was relieved. Isobel had not told her father about the donor insemination. She deemed it too sensitive a matter, for the moment, Kit had said. Jack had no idea how close to the truth, in fact, his words had been.

'So you're suggesting,' I said, unable to resist discovering what Jack was up to, 'that Kit has brought home his own household god, as it were?'

'Kit *is* the household god, aren't you, darling?' said Isobel, setting down plates of apple tart in front of her husband and father. 'There's cream in the jug.'

'Don't have the cream, Jack,' Helen warned, reaching for the jug and passing it to Kit.

'I thought you said a good straightforward heart attack would be the best way to go,' said Jack. 'Bloody doctors, can't make up their minds.'

'Your father's blood pressure is a little high,' Helen said.

'It's no fun having a GP for a girlfriend,' Jack said. 'You get no sympathy on the one hand, and too much instruction on the other.' He was quiet for a few moments, distracted by his pudding, but after a mouthful or two he was off again.

'The household gods, Kit,' he said. 'We all look to those in some form. Potency. Fertility. Prosperity. The question is, what do we worship these days? You can bring home a hippo's head, or you can go for something more contemporary, like a bread-making machine or a power drill.'

'I'd rather have a hippo head,' said Isobel. 'I love my hippo head.'

'You are the hippo head, dear daughter,' said Jack.

'What?'

'You're the one doing the protecting.'

I observed this interchange with a certain glee. Jack's bright mischief excited me, but he was dangerous, and I felt the situation now required me to become a protector myself.

'With respect, Jack,' I said, 'you know nothing at all about the Tawaret, or anything else Egyptian come to that. You're talking bollocks.'

Jack smiled at me, delighted, like a small boy, and opened his mouth to reply.

'No,' I said firmly. 'You'll just run us ragged with your riddles and loops.'

He returned quietly to his apple tart, and from the corner of my eye I caught a glance from Helen that contained both respect and fury.

That night I found myself lying half awake in the early hours, in and out of a troubled sleep. I could hear Jack Whaley's voice which seemed to be sounding the end of the world as we know it, and then it was more tender and I felt him beside me. Not Jack as I had just seen him, but the Jack I had known all those years before, a ball of indignant energy and contempt for the world in which he found himself. The Jack in my half-dream was a man I had been too young to love, a man whose passion had scared me.

Awake now, I stared up at the old-fashioned ceiling fan, a legacy from Toby's time, my eyes tracing the cornice which I could just make out in the spill of the ever-present city light. In the half-dozen years since we had met again, I had been haunted by thoughts of how Jack Whaley must disapprove of what I had become. I could hear him now, chastising me for my lack of seriousness, for the poor choices I had made; and at the same time, I could hear him tell me that these were my thoughts, not his, his voice half drowned by the sound of the birds outside as the light from the street lamps faded with the faintest hint of dawn and I fell back into a shallow sleep.

Three

I have made it a habit, ever since I first arrived in London, to spend time in the cathedral in Victoria. Not Westminster Abbey with its queues of tourists and noisy guides but in the Catholic cathedral, that red-brick afterthought of faith, tucked away behind busy Victoria Street. I often go in at lunchtime and sit in a pew in one of the side chapels, sitting up close to the wall away from the visitors and the more visible penitents. I'm unsure of my own belief, but having been born a Catholic I feel a sense of ownership. I have a right to be there.

It is a place to think, to reminisce and remember, as I sometimes feel I must. And it helps me to remember Alice. When I see the pictures and statues around me, I see them through her child's eyes, and it lends them a potency long lost to me. I sometimes feel it in the gallery too, when some special piece comes in, though then I am reminded of Toby.

I first met Toby Haddeley at a party in the early seventies and the evening is preserved in my memory in a sort of memorial aspic. If I'm honest, looking back, I think I knew at once that he was homosexual, even though the general ambivalence of that era sometimes made it difficult to tell. It was the attention to detail of his dress which gave him away. He could have been a dandy, of course, but he didn't have the right testosterone swagger.

That first night he made love to me, but even in my inexperience I knew there was something experimental in the act; it was quickly over, and he had fallen asleep, saying he was sorry, he was drunk and it was all a bit confusing. The next morning he didn't refer to his inexpert assault on my person, but got up and made coffee, then sat on the bed and said that although he was attracted to young women, and liked to make love to them on occasion, it was men he preferred, and yet how very much he'd like us to be friends.

'Don't worry,' I said, wanting to reassure him. 'I did think you were probably queer. I was surprised that we . . .'

'One lives in hope,' he said, 'that things might change. But they don't and one must make the best of it. But you're so pretty, Josie, and so very young, and I wanted to. And I thought you did?' He laughed, and I blushed. But despite this odd beginning, something had happened between us, some connection had been made. It was almost, on my part, a falling in love.

Sitting in the busy quiet of the cathedral, I have often thought about my life before Toby and the life I have lived since his death, but neither have the charm or the vibrancy of existence that I felt when I was in Toby's orbit. I'm no longer unhappy. In fact I have been feeling quite content in my late middle age. But lately there has been a restlessness, a low throb of anxiety which has taken me back to a time before I knew Toby, before I knew any of them.

Ever since I was a child, I have had the feeling that there was some secret to life that was unknown to me. I usually blamed this mystery on my mother, whose obsession with her divorce and my father's infidelity had left her cold but clinging. If only I could escape her, I was sure that the secret would be mine. But it had been hard to leave the corrosive familiarity of the London suburb where I had grown up until a miracle happened: someone knew someone who was looking for a nice girl to rent a small flat in Victoria.

The prospect of a place of my own in the middle of London was so exciting that I couldn't have cared less what the flat itself was like, but its compact charm and view over the red-brick cathedral were breathtaking to me. The suburb where I had grown up was a mere fifteen miles away, but it might as well have been two hundred, such was the contrast I experienced. The landlady seemed old to me then, though she must have been younger than I am now, and as I sit here, my back aching against the pew, I can see her, standing on the steps of the mansion block holding out the keys.

'Don't be lonely, dear,' she said. 'It's a nice little flat but you might have been better off sharing, don't you think, at your age?'

I can feel the cold weight of the keys now, in the palm of my hand. I didn't want to share, and easily irritated as I was, even then, I thought it none of her business. But I smiled at her politely and assured her that I would be fine. I was running not just towards my future but away from the misery of home, and also from disappointment. She couldn't know, after all, about the guilt I brought with me, about the marks left by a man I hadn't known was married and who had paid, only months before, for a hurried abortion. I was just nineteen.

From an advertisement in the evening paper, I found a job as a receptionist at a language school above an umbrella shop, just off Regent Street. I had no idea what such a job might entail but it turned out to be a stroke of good fortune. The place was full of people of all ages, though many, like me, were young. There were not only the students but also the teachers, so-called, out-of-work actors and aimless graduates and all kinds of bohemian creatures who weren't much good for anything else.

I was a pretty girl, and even if I hadn't been, the mere fact of my youth would have made me attractive to many of the men with whom I found myself surrounded. I was suddenly in possession of a ready-made world which differed so greatly from the one I had left behind, that sometimes I felt as if I were running to catch up.

On Friday evenings a gang of us would go to the White Horse, one of several pubs in the vicinity that we took turns to patronise, on various nights of the week. But Fridays were special. Some of the teachers were already drunk, having persuaded their pupils that it was a fine tradition on the last day of their course to have an extended lunch in the Spaghetti House, or too many cocktails in the Novello across the road, a bar whose pink-and-green décor contributed to the queasiness its drinks could induce. After smiling sweetly, taking cheques, checking flights and saying goodbye to the week's intake, I too could finally leave the front desk at the top of the stairs at six thirty, and join the others who had been hanging around since five, waiting for the pubs to open. We would pile into the White Horse and stake our claim to the long table at the back, under the over-bright polished brasses, a gesture to some coaching past. We drank lager and cheap red wine and ate salty crisps and I laughed as the others performed gross and mocking impressions of their foreign pupils, until one by one we all peeled away or, if still standing, a few of us went off to find a cheap dinner.

Sometimes I would get the bus home down Park Lane to Victoria, and sometimes I would walk, though it was often hard to remember which when I woke fully clothed, stretched out on my bed the following morning. Looking back, I can't remember ever feeling badly hung over. That was youth I suppose. These days it's more likely to be morning exhaustion that a hangover brings and which requires an act of will to struggle through. But what strikes me now, as I contemplate my younger self, is the ease with which we all made friends, and how the young, hormone driven, will always seek each other out, in a sort of extension of children's playtime, fooling themselves into thinking they are all grown up.

I can observe it as I sit here, watching the visitors walk up and down the aisles. I can see a party of Scandinavian girls and boys in the centre. The girls look older than I suspect they are, and only moments ago they looked bored and eager to be somewhere more exciting. But now they are whispering and pointing at what I always think of as Alice's statue, an ugly, homunculus Jesus, held by Mary above a row of candles. Two of them are convulsed with laughter but trying not to show it, and the boys are circling, drawn by their hysteria. I can feel a silent, sympathetic spasm rising from my ribs and I find myself covering my mouth quickly with my hand as if it might emerge as a snort or a snigger. I do mourn the loss of silliness that ageing brings. I'm not old, really, but old enough to be obliged to retain my dignity most of the time.

It was at the Purnell School of English that I met Christopher, Toby's brother. It was him I met first, and that was how my real life, this life, began. He had recently been employed by the dubious management of the school, which each Friday paid my wages in cash. Christopher was older than many of the other teachers, older even than Jack Whaley who worked there too from time to time. He was all of thirty-one, and appeared rather scholarly, both of which endeared him to Graham, the harassed, sweating Director of Studies who felt he could trust him with the more exacting German students. Christopher was also unusual in that he was married, with a child, though his wife Margaret, eight or so years his senior, and who lived close to her parents, in Norfolk, was never to be seen. He told me that he shared a flat with his brother during the week and joined his wife at the weekends. On Friday nights, it was Christopher who often led the charge to the White Horse, where he would down three pints quickly, as if needing courage, before rushing off to King's Cross to catch his train.

I had never met anyone like Christopher before. He wore

old tweed suits that looked as though they might have belonged to his father, and affected a manner that seemed to me to belong to an era I had only encountered in films on television. He had a rather bony face, and ill-assorted teeth, like walnuts, and he enjoyed teasing me each morning (he was always at least five minutes late). Despite his old-fashioned manner, he liked to shock, and he had constructed for me, or rather for himself, an elaborate fantasy in which I lived with an older man who asked me to beat him each night with a hairbrush.

At first I was embarrassed by these constructions of Christopher's. I would blush as he leant over my desk and asked me if I had brushed my hair that morning, but as the fantasies grew more surreal, I began to see the joke and even to join in. My sexual experience so far had been limited to losing my virginity at seventeen to a dull boy at the teacher training college I had attended for just one term, and then the sad business of the married manager of the restaurant where I had worked the previous summer. It was an affair that had consisted mainly of clandestine, unornamented sex in the wine cellar, not wholly instructive, certainly unsatisfactory, and with tragic consequences. Up to this point, as I told Christopher, my only experience of hairbrushes had been purely for use on my head.

One Friday evening, Christopher pushed in next to me as we sat in the White Horse and whispered in my ear, 'Come to dinner next Wednesday at my brother's. I'm only inviting you from here so keep it quiet. Eight o' clock,' and he pushed a piece of paper into my hand. By the time that I pulled out the piece of paper on a trip to the loo, tipsy and

41

happy after a week of eccentric mayhem, Christopher had long ago left for the station. *11 Elgin Square, W.11,* he had written in black pen. He always used a fountain pen, I had noticed that. I wasn't sure exactly where Elgin Square was, but I was excited about the invitation.

I had been to other friends' flats, new friends I had made at the school. There was Peter Wright's, for example, a young man whose lack of ambition was spectacular and who preferred to teach only in the late mornings to accommodate his drinking habits. He had recently been sacked. He lived in Islington, which I hadn't much liked when I'd visited him, but now he was off to try his luck in Spain. And then there was Jack Whaley, who lived, or rather squatted, in Brixton. He had joined the school rota at about the same time as me, and though I had been to a party at his tumbling-down house, I had not so far accepted his confusing invitation to stay there overnight.

I knew that my anticipation of Christopher's dinner was out of proportion to the event. After all, he had no money, none of them did. But his 'Come to dinner' had conjured up something formal, something that required me to reposition myself, to be something new. On the Monday I went out shopping in my lunch hour to buy clothes, much to the annoyance of Graham, who had to field the avalanche of queries from the first day's intake of new students.

I have always had quite an eye for fashion, if not the cash to go with it, and even back then I would brave the style mavens of Browns' emporium in South Molton Street, to see what was on offer. I coveted the fabrics, of course, which the cheaper shops could not replicate but then I would trawl through Richard Shops and Dorothy Perkins to put together some semblance of what I had seen. I had always been able to spot quality. It was a family joke that I would, unknowingly, choose the most expensive item from any selection on offer.

In Oxford Street, I found a cheap dark red velvet skirt which, worn with an old belt that had belonged to my grandmother, and a pair of black suede boots which were my pride and joy, would take me through the coming Wednesday evening whatever I found it to be. When the day came I left the school as promptly as Graham would let me. I had a leisurely long bath in the chipped white tub in Victoria, then spent quite some time in front of a large gilt-framed mirror, carelessly left by the previous tenant and now propped up against my bedroom wall. As I set off to catch the tube, I pulled my old but insubstantial raincoat around me, against the March wind. I could hear my mother's voice, defeated and sad, asking why I would never wear what she regarded as a proper coat. But I liked to feel the cold. It made me feel alive, and that night I felt vibrant. This was what I had come to London for, to find a new world, to shed the grey dry film that overlay my mother's pinched life, like a snake its skin.

The large crumbling houses on either side of Kensington Park Gardens were mainly dark by the time I found myself walking down to the bowl of Notting Hill. There was an odd light at a window but they seemed quite uninhabited. The decadent peeling grandeur of the houses, even the smaller ones, appealed to me, though the rubbish that spilled out of their lower floors made me sad. I would take greater care of such a house if I lived there, I thought, just as I did of my own dear little flat, transformed since my arrival, now loved and polished and fragrant. I had buffed the mirror frame and repainted the dingy bathroom, and I had found lengths of fabric, rich remnants, to cover the battered furniture. There was, and is, a pleasure for me in caring for inanimate objects. Each thing, small or large, carries its history, and I had already begun to select small objects of desire, boxes mainly, from the dingier antique shops in Pimlico or the few stalls that were springing up among the fruit and vegetables on Portobello Road.

I turned into Elgin Square and climbed up the steep stone steps to number eleven. Even in the porch I could hear music playing, the sound of soft mellow voices from California singing through a breeze of cannabis smoke which I could smell as I approached the red front door. It was flung wide, not by Christopher but by an equally tall, infinitely more handsome creature, whose face contained a hint of Christopher, a sleeker, more modern version of Christopher, and whose dark hair curling on to his shoulders and deep-set black eyes made an immediate and romantic impression on me. He was holding something in his hand, a joint I quickly realised, its end burning fiercely in the cool evening air. He held it out to his side as if his arm and the home-rolled cigarette were somehow not a part of him.

'Josie, I presume?' the tall man said.

'Yes. Who are you?' I guessed he must be Toby but I didn't like to presume. The directness of my tone surprised me, but I had come determined not to be made shy by the unfamiliarity of it all.

'I'm Toby. Come in. You're the first to arrive. Christopher said it would be you.'

I remember blushing. Was it good or bad to be first? Was Christopher mocking me for my punctuality? I suspected he was, but in a kindly way.

As I followed him up the stairs and into the flat it seemed plunged into a semi-darkness out of which strange, attenuated sculptures loomed at me from every surface. It smelt of joss sticks and hash and somewhere in the miasma there was also a strain of curry.

'Christopher's in the kitchen. He's making his *Rogan Josh*,' Toby informed me.

I tried to negotiate the geography of the flat, aware that the kitchen was some distance from the room which we now entered, separated by a narrow corridor which seemed to traverse a back yard of some sort.

'Did you make these?' I asked, as I stood in the middle of the sitting room, not small in itself, but made so by the dozen or so creatures that flanked its walls, reaching out towards the inhabitants like importuning spirits.

'Christ no. They're Godfrey's, Godfrey Marr – he's a friend. I'm looking after them for him. He's in Madrid for an exhibition. What do you think of them?'

The question frightened me. I didn't know who Godfrey was. I didn't have an opinion, or not the sort I thought was suitable.

'They're . . . strange.'

Toby laughed. 'Fucking strange, I'd say. But I love them.'

I went up to one and examined it more closely in the dim light.

'It's hard to see,' I said. But there was no attempt from Toby to shed any further light. I could make out the form and as I looked more closely and observed the creature's outstretched arm I experienced a moment of tenderness.

'Oh,' I said. 'It seems quite sad.' I turned to Toby who was looking at me with some interest.

'Have some of this,' he said, offering me a joint which I took and puffed a couple of times, holding in the smoke.

As it took effect, I sat down opposite Toby who was now stretched out on a low divan that served as a sofa. I saw that his features were indeed those of Christopher but scaled in a more pleasing proportion to one another. His legs were stretched out towards me and I noticed that he was wearing dark blue satin trousers covered in tiny stars and I couldn't help but stare. I was used to flamboyance but these were the most exotic thing I had seen off a stage.

'Do you like them?' he said, indicating his knees. He seemed to be anxious for my good opinion which surprised me.

'I think so.'

Toby lifted his right leg and stretched it out in front of him. There was something about this attitude which struck me as not quite masculine, though at the same time he exuded a confusing sense of male power. I searched my memory to see if Christopher had made any reference of this kind, but I couldn't remember what, if anything, he had said. He must have talked to me about Toby because I definitely knew of his existence, just as I knew about

Christopher's wife, Margaret, but it must have been on a long Friday night for I couldn't bring it to mind.

'I'm not quite sure myself,' Toby said, putting his leg down and pulling himself up. 'You haven't got a drink, sorry.' And he disappeared down the corridor in the direction of the curry smell. Moments later he returned, followed by Christopher who was carrying an open bottle of red wine and several glasses. He bent to kiss me on the cheek.

'I'm sorry about my brother, Josie. He has no manners. Have a glass of this.'

I'd noticed that Christopher often mentioned manners. Someone had 'beautiful manners', or, as in this case, 'no manners', or even 'bad manners'. It seemed to me as if it were something his parents might say, and rather absurd, but it made me anxious all the same, making me wonder how he perceived my own manners and why it should matter so much. It seemed to me to have little to do with real human comfort, apart from making sure that a guest had a glass of wine.

The doorbell rang and three more people, arriving together, filled the small room. Suddenly the evening became an event and there was from the start a sense that it might be memorable. Toby had taken charge of the drinks and he recharged our glasses at a rate that only seemed to encourage us all to drink faster. Everyone seemed to know each other, except for me of course, but the wine and the music and the banter seemed to override the awkwardness I had felt at the beginning. The latest guests were two girls who had come with a young man, Nigel, a schoolfriend of Christopher's and Toby's. One was his sister Miranda, a creature so thin she looked like a foal on top of her high platform shoes. Her friend was rounder, 'more generous', as Toby was later to put it. She was certainly friendlier, lying on the cushions close to me and putting her hand on my leg each time she giggled, which was frequently, a pleasant sound that cascaded through the room but with an overtone of self-consciousness. I guessed that at some point in her life, Clara had been told how charming she was when she laughed.

It took me a while before I realised that some of the laughter in the room came in response to something I had said. At first I was uncomfortable, wondering what faux pas I had made, what embarrassment I had brought upon myself and then I understood, through the easy haze of the hashish smoke, that they found me amusing, or rather they found what I said amusing, and that they liked me, and perhaps that was why Christopher had invited me. It was a true and wonderful moment of discovery. I was revealed to myself as someone other than the person I had thought myself to be and I felt anointed. I felt one of them.

It seemed only minutes later that I was in the kitchen washing up plates and Christopher was trying to stop me.

'You don't have to do that. Leave them.'

'I want to do them.' The soap bubbles rose in front of us and for a moment we were both silent until Christopher lifted a fork and popped one.

'Christopher! That was mean,' I said. I could hear my new self speaking.

48

'You make it sound as if it were alive,' he said.

'It was, sort of.' I laughed and plunged my hands back into the plastic bowl. 'I won't do the saucepans,' I said.

He kissed my cheek, then moved around to try to kiss my mouth but I pushed him away with my wet hands. He had taken me by surprise.

'Stop it, Chris. You're married. You've got a baby.' The words were out of my mouth before I could calculate how prim they might sound in this new, louche setting in which I found myself.

'So?'

I didn't know what to say. In the world I had grown up in, married men were off-limits, and the cause of pain and problems as I had reason to know myself, and in any case I didn't find him attractive.

'I wouldn't like it if you were married to me and you kissed someone else,' I said.

'No, prissy miss, I don't suppose you would.' He kissed me again, but with affection, on my cheek, and then he put an arm around my waist and hugged me to him. 'I'll dry up the plates,' he said and laughed, though whether at me or himself I wasn't sure.

Yet another hour or so drifted by and I found myself half lying on the low divan, next to Toby whose arm was now around me. More people had arrived during and after dinner and there were at least twelve people crammed into the small space. I no longer felt I could make my voice heard but I was happy to lie next to Toby. I felt like a small cat and I found myself playing with the curls that lay on his

49

shoulders, rubbing the hair between my fingers and thumb. Its texture was silky and I wanted to rub it against my face. My leg lay against the blue starry satin of his trousers, and though I couldn't feel the fabric through the velvet of my skirt I could imagine its coolness against my skin. I changed my position to enable me to see Toby's face. He was lying back against the cushions ranged against the wall, pulling on a joint, and the inhalation made his sharp cheekbones even more prominent. He blew out the smoke and coughed, laughing, and passed the joint to me but I waved it away. I had had enough. I could see that Toby was beautiful, and more than that I could feel it. His beauty reached into me and further dissolved the stale inheritance I felt I had been carrying. Just his presence seemed to promise my future.

It was only about eleven o'clock but I could feel my eyelids closing. The wine and the hash had made me suddenly sleepy. I felt Toby nudge me and I sat up very straight, forcing my way into the present, into the gathering, afraid I might slip back at any moment.

'Here,' he said. 'You should have one of these.' He put a small black pill into the palm of my hand, and I saw him put one in his own mouth and chase it down with a large slug of wine.

'What is it?' I said, although I knew that I would follow his lead.

'It will keep you awake for a while,' he said. 'Don't worry. It's nothing. Go on, do it and I'll take you dancing.'

The offer set my adrenalin racing long before the small pill took effect. The conversation in the room seemed to grow louder and I wondered if they had all taken the little black pills while I had been dozing. I looked over at Christopher who was now sitting with his arm around Clara who was laughing and stroking his thigh. I saw him laugh in response to something Clara said and then to my astonishment I watched him squeeze Clara's breast. Christopher didn't look as if he had taken a pill, but then neither had Christopher drunk as much as the rest of us. There was a detachment in his character which had little to do with his being older. It was a more quiet calculation, a cool estimation of the possible.

❧

The club was much smaller than I had imagined it to be. In my mind I had conjured up a dance floor of ballroom proportions, like the discos of my adolescence, in halls or theatres. The Sombrero was crammed into a basement, underneath a shop in Kensington High Street, an area I recognised immediately as we approached in a cab. I was a regular visitor to nearby Kensington Market, a cornucopia of street style and fabric which I found irresistible. The club was busy that night, full of men who, like Toby, were dressed at least a shade beyond the dictates of current fashion. It took me a moment to realise that the club must cater to gay men, and I wondered why Toby had omitted to mention it. Perhaps he assumed that I knew.

There were several women scattered about, solitary muses in chattering groups, some sitting at the tables that flanked the brightly lit dance floor, others at the bar, admiring themselves in the mirror that ran behind it. A man detached himself from one of the small parties and came up to us.

'Toby. Good to see you.' The man standing before me was an altogether more conservative figure than most of the club's clientele. 'And who is this?'

Toby shook the man's hand with both of his and pulled him forward, planting a kiss on his cheek. The man flinched slightly but smiled.

'Josie, meet Roddy,' Toby said. I found myself staring at Roddy for no particular reason other than that the chemistry I was experiencing made everything and everyone shimmer a little, as if there might be a depth to fathom. He was wearing a suit and tie and his hair was cut in a fashionable but discreet style. He was a good-looking man who seemed out of place in the Sombrero, though after a moment or two, when I had become used to the strange combination of light and gloom, I recognised the same attention to detail in his dress that I had noticed in Toby's, the same grooming despite the difference in style.

'How do you do?' I said. It sounded absurdly formal in that setting but it was what I had been taught to say. The words felt oddly separate from me and I wondered if they qualified as manners and whether I cared.

'How do you do?' he said in return, inclining slightly towards me as if he were going to bow. He looked me over in a way that made me wonder what he was doing in a club such as this one, then he looked at Toby and winked.

'I'm off now, dear boy,' he said. 'But perhaps we'll see you at the weekend?'

'Not this weekend,' Toby said. 'I have business.'

Roddy raised his eyebrows. 'What now?' he said.

Toby pushed back his hair. Small droplets of sweat were collecting at his hairline. I felt hot too. There seemed to be very little air in the club and I suspected that the pills we had taken were contributing to the heat.

'Antiquities. It's my new thing,' Toby said.

'Antiques? Surely not.'

'Surely not. You're right. Definitely not antiques. *Antiquities*. Egyptian, Graeco-Roman, that sort of thing. Much smarter.'

'Who'd want those, apart from the British Museum?'

'You'd be surprised,' Toby said and now it was his turn to wink and I wondered what all the winking was about. I suspected it made reference to something clandestine and therefore, since the epiphany of this evening, of increasing appeal to my sense of curiosity.

'I take it there's a black market,' Roddy said. 'I can't see you being interested if there weren't. What are they, stuffed with drugs or something?'

'Don't be stupid, dear boy. I don't deal in drugs.'

'Not what I've heard.'

'You don't often refuse when I offer,' Toby said, and he put his hand in his pocket then clasped Roddy's, and something passed between them. 'There's a nice "mandy" for you,' he said. 'Give my love to baby Alice.'

Roddy smiled without looking down. Whatever it was he had taken from Toby, he put it in his pocket and clapped Toby on the back. 'Don't see her much since the divorce. See you soon, dear boy.'

I looked on, a little stupefied, as Toby waved and Roddy backed away from us.

'Watch him, Miss Josie,' Roddy said, his eyes suddenly upon me again. 'This man is dangerous.'

'Rubbish,' said Toby. 'I just have a talent for life.'

'Who's he?' I asked, as Roddy finally turned his back on us and strode up the staircase.

'He was married to my friend Anne,' Toby said. 'But it was . . . complicated.'

'What's a mandy?'

'We'll have one later, to relax us,' Toby said, and he pulled me on to the dance floor as the music swelled into a current favourite and there was a sudden upsurge of bodies rising from the chairs and bar to fill the little floor.

Four

The morning after Isobel's birthday, I felt old and hung over. I had, of course, drunk more than was good for me but I couldn't imagine a life without the pleasure of doing so. I got up, drank a large glass of mineral water, showered and made myself some breakfast in the small square room which served as kitchen and dining room, and which overlooked the quiet street.

It was an odd contrast to walk from my flat into the main house, and vice versa. Millbury Street felt so sumptuous, its wide rooms and staircases dressed and draped, whereas I had given my accommodation something of a Scandinavian feel. Not modern exactly, though modern in comparison, and certainly in its comforts and warmth. I liked the Northern colours, the pale light they gave off, the wood and the slight austerity were all soothing after the dressy textures of the house, and the fragments and forms of the gallery's ancient world. I liked to come home to clean lines and the light from the big uncluttered windows. I could occasionally glimpse something elusive in myself there, as if I too was stripped back to the core against its simplicity.

I was sitting at the pale oak table, looking down at the empty road. Few pedestrians ventured through, only the postman, and it was too early for him. There was the occasional sound of a car engine starting up, or an engine running as a taxi came to collect a neighbour. Getting up to refill the teapot with hot water, I noticed that there was a message on the telephone's voicemail. It hadn't occurred to me to check for messages, the previous evening, as I fell into bed. I pulled my dressing gown tighter around me, a smart blue cashmere robe (a generous gift from Isobel last Christmas), and reached over to press the button.

'*Hello, it's Jennifer Parsons here.*' Jennifer was our nearest neighbour and even in the phone message her voice carried an habitual nervousness, its tone apologetic. '*I feel like some dreadful old biddy ringing you up, but I thought you ought to know that there was a boy, a young man, hanging about outside your house yesterday afternoon. I saw him from my upstairs window. He was inside the gate, at your front door, but he didn't knock or ring the bell. Just sort of hung about for a bit. Looked through the letterbox. He must have climbed over. I was going to ring the police but he disappeared so I thought there was no point. I just thought I should mention it. Do ring me if you want to, but that's all there is really. Sorry to bother you with this, Josie, but I didn't want to frighten Isobel . . . Goodbye.*'

I filled the teapot, thinking as I did so that I must seem a tough old boot to Jennifer, not easily frightened by a passing thief, and the idea made me feel a bit sad, as though I had mislaid some aspect of femininity. Then again, I thought, perhaps Jennifer imagined me as someone who might take a shotgun to an intruder, and I found that an altogether more glamorous and acceptable picture. I sipped my tea for a moment and went back to my bedroom to pull on a pair of black corduroy jeans and an old sweater then I went down the stairs, walked round to Kit and Isobel's front door and rang the bell. I didn't like to barge through the connecting door first thing in the morning.

I found Kit in the kitchen cutting up fruit, part of some new, healthy food regime he'd adopted. The pieces of banana and mango and melon were neat and symmetrical in size. He comes from a long line of soldiers on his mother's side, fit and disciplined men, meticulous but romantic, soldier-poets, or that is how I liked to picture them. Not that Kit, as far as I knew, had ever written any poetry. Isobel had followed me downstairs after letting me in, and now she was offering me decaffeinated tea, which I refused in favour of a cup of Kit's espresso. The sun was flooding in through the east windows. I do love the big kitchen in the mornings and, much as I like my flat, it is a small sadness that my own kitchen is on the other side of the house.

'That's odd,' Kit said, as I repeated Jennifer's story. His voice was tight but his manner breezy. He was, I thought, trying not to look too concerned. 'Casing the joint, I suppose,' he continued. 'I'll give the police a call, though I don't suppose there's much they can do. I wonder why the alarm didn't go off.'

'Maybe I forgot to put it on,' said Isobel. 'But I don't think so. You came back, didn't you, Kit? At lunchtime yesterday? I thought you said . . .'

'I'm sure it was on,' said Kit. 'Though I suppose it's not beyond the ability of a young criminal to disable it.'

'That's not very comforting,' said Isobel, who liked to think of the house as impenetrable.

I suspected that Kit had forgotten the alarm. He often left the house mentally, long before he closed the front door. I'd observed it many times. He could be vague. It was hard to remember, sometimes, that he had once been a soldier, an officer in charge of men. But just as I had the thought, he seemed to take command.

'We'll get the security firm round, to check everything out,' he said. 'It's probably due for a service. Will that make you both feel better?'

Isobel nodded at him and I made a mental note to ring the security firm myself, in case Kit forgot.

'You know what, Josie,' Isobel said, changing the subject, 'I dreamt I heard the peacocks again last night.'

'It's the geese,' I said. 'It's the time of year.'

'If it was a dream you'd better check it out with your father,' Kit said. 'He was certainly on form last night.'

Kit's attitude to his father-in-law was indulgent. They were fond of each other, though Kit found Jack quaint, someone who existed beyond his view of the world, like a figure on the edge of a painting. Jack was exotic to Isobel too. It was only as an adult that she had got to know her father at all. She had grown up with her mother and grandparents in upstate New York.

'You shouldn't get on his case, sweetheart,' Isobel said.

Kit picked up the large plate of perfectly cut fruit seg-ments. 'I didn't stir him up, did I, Josie?' he said.

This small flare-up was familiar to me and I held up my hand to indicate a refusal to be drawn in. It was one of those domestic grooves that they repeated endlessly, one that seemed to be almost comforting to them, a ritual of their married life.

'If you really want to stir him up,' Isobel said, 'just mention your mother.'

'A low blow,' Kit said, but he smiled at her now, and I wondered if he, like me, hoped that if Isobel's pregnancy was successful, it might bridge the tension between Isobel and Margaret Haddeley.

'I wouldn't dare do that,' he said.

Jack could be fierce in defence of Isobel, his only child whom he had got to know so late in his life. He had once called Margaret a monolith. She was 'a standing stone', he had said to her face, when drunk at dinner, 'approachable only for worship or sacrifice'. It had taken even Kit some months to forgive him, but the memory of it made me smile, even as I wondered if a child in the family might finally dispel the shadow of Alice that clung about Margaret still.

The gallery, Haddeley Antiquities, was just off Belgrave Square. The front was discreet and all that could be seen from outside was a brass plate bearing the Haddeley name. Our ground-floor rooms were quite compact: a narrow space which served as a gallery and a small office at the

59

rear. From the office we had access to a small private basement which we used as a vault.

That morning, Kit and I had made our way there separately, which was our usual habit. We took it in turns to open up, allowing us each to have some time to attend to other things. One of us might have a client appointment, or something personal to attend to, like a trip to the dentist.

We were both a little delayed that morning and I was the first to arrive. Kit didn't come in till noon, having been first to look at a Coptic terracotta pig which had appeared for possible sale through some acquaintance of his mother's. He was sitting now at his uncle's old desk, in the back room where we worked together.

Kit was a very different sort of man from Toby, but like Toby, he had a head for business, and his passion for the artefacts themselves was even greater than his uncle's. Certainly he had more time for the details and the history of the objects that came through our hands and this enthusiasm was something we shared. My own education had been adequate but limited. I hadn't been to university and the world of antiquities had opened up my intellectual life. Toby had encouraged me, seeing himself as some sort of Svengali, and I had studied part-time for a degree in ancient history. I had proved a good scholar, and Toby enjoyed presenting me as his resident expert. It was far from the truth but like many of his exaggerations it was flattering.

I had been looking forward all morning to Kit's arrival, for I had news which I was keen and excited to share with him.

'There was an inquiry this morning about the bronze head,' I said when he arrived. I enjoyed being the bearer of such information and I liked then to anticipate what would be the sequence of events. I liked especially to speculate and guess at the odds on a sale. My excitement was a selfish one, and Kit seemed distracted though he tried to look interested for my benefit. Toby had been much more fun at playing this game. He had been a natural gambler, a maverick. But then he hadn't been required by his times to be as conscientious as Kit. Our business was now beset by issues of provenance, the history of any object's ownership, and constant suspicions as to where it had come from. Everything must be clear and clean, which was just as it should be, of course, but sometimes it felt as if some of the old excitement had been whitewashed too.

'Who from?' he asked finally.

'Brett and Lyon,' I almost whispered.

'Ah.'

'On behalf of a major client,' I said.

'Of course.'

'Just an inquiry as to whether we still held it.'

'And whether,' said Kit, 'we'll go to auction or private sale?'

'Not specifically,' I said, and tucked my hair behind my ears, waiting for him to go on. My hair was going a little grey, but it was still sleek and I paid good money to a fashionable hairdresser to keep it so.

A scuffling noise interrupted us as a dog rushed into the room followed by our book-keeper, Rita, who came in three times a week for a few hours. She was in her mid-forties and still rather pretty in an ageing sort of way, although every time I had the thought, I was aware that the same could be said of me with knobs on. No doubt it was, along with the universal view that it was really a shame that I should have wasted myself on Toby. As if in response, Rita's small Jack Russell now trotted towards me, jumping up and pawing my lap.

'Basket, Frank,' I said. 'Basket.'

Frank was indulged at the gallery, mainly by me. I had bought him the basket and a smart green wool rug, insisting when he first arrived that if he were to be a regular feature he must look the part.

The dog turned and sped back to its spot, turning twice before sitting down and gazing up at me in adoration.

'Not like old Frank to be soppy,' said Kit, though this clearly wasn't true. 'Hello, Rita. I've left the invoices out for you.'

Rita spoke little. In this instance she said a quiet good morning and went through to the small alcove which was devoted to finance.

'So,' Kit continued our conversation. 'Not specifically said.' He seemed to be losing heart for our banter and I wondered what was preoccupying him. His lack of interest seemed to go beyond any disdain for my fun. His thoughts were definitely somewhere quite other.

'No, but we both know who it was, and an offer might be made within the week. That would be my estimate.' I brought the game to an end, but on a positive note.

'Let's hope you're right,' said Kit.

The pink limestone head had been sitting in the vault for

some months and it was time for it to move on. We had both grown fond of it, but its sale would release cash for the big New York auctions in a month or so. It was the head of a woman, eighteenth dynasty, almost certainly an *amarna* princess, a daughter of Akhenaten, and her provenance was impeccable. Whenever I looked at her, I shuddered at the memory of a similar-looking piece, a brilliant fake, that had almost fooled Toby years ago. Toby had rejected it as soon as he spotted it, but all the same, it had ended up, via a foreign dealer, in an American museum.

Every few weeks, Kit would bring the head out of the vault and place it on a plinth in the gallery. He liked to trace the curve of the princess's cheek and her fine nose and he told me that he imagined her sitting for the sculptor's sketches, her neck erect, while being fanned by her slaves with peacock plumes. He liked to wonder how many children she'd had and how much time she spent with them.

'So let's see if we can find out just a bit more about her,' he said to me that morning, not for the first time.

'There is no more,' I said. 'I've checked it all out as far as it goes. We have the provenance more or less, certainly nothing suspect in the last century.' I felt I was repeating myself. It was time to sell. The princess was worth over half a million to the right buyer.

'I meant more about HER,' he said.

I looked at him in a way that meant, politely, that I thought this would be a waste of my time. But the look passed him by.

'I wonder if she ever owned a Tawaret,' he said, to no one in particular.

'I could write you a page or two more about the customs of the period,' I said, 'though I don't think that this particular collector is unaware of the details.'

Kit leant back in his chair and stretched his legs. He seemed to be finding concentration difficult and he looked around the room as if seeking a focus. His eyes seemed to rest on one edge of the security gate which was peeping out from behind the folds of the heavy curtains which were designed to conceal it.

'I rang Hammonds Security for you,' I said. 'I thought I might as well. They say they could check the house over this afternoon if anyone's in?'

'Thank you, Josie,' Kit said. 'That was kind of you. Isobel's out all day. I could go back. But tomorrow or the day after would do.'

I found his attitude odd. Surely, I thought, he would want to check things out as soon as possible. Yet despite his politeness, he seemed uninterested in the security arrangements.

There had been a bad incident, after all, years earlier. Margaret and Christopher Haddeley had come from Norfolk to stay for a week at Millbury Street while Toby and I were away at a trade fair in New York. Kit, too, had been absent, with his regiment in Northern Ireland, while Alice had remained behind in their Fulham flat. It seemed that Christopher had been called back to Norfolk suddenly, to oversee some flooding on the farmland, and Margaret had been left all alone. Returning early to the house from a social event, one that doubtless involved playing bridge, she had steered her car through the gates and getting out to lock them behind her, she had been attacked by a mugger, hit on the head, her skull almost fractured. It was nearly an hour later when Alice found her, having previously arranged to keep her company for the night.

The attack shocked us all and its consequences reached further than I had understood at the time. There had been evenings later on, after the deaths of Alice and Toby, when Kit and I had huddled together in the kitchen at Millbury Street, drinking ourselves to sleep, holding on to what we could of our earlier life. Sometimes, I would find myself crying, and occasionally I would see that Kit was crying too, manly, desiccated tears, squeezed from his eyes, his chest shaking, seeking a reluctant relief. One night, as he went over the past yet again, he told me that it was the attack on his mother that had made him decide to leave the Army. He talked of the telephone conversation he had had with his father, Christopher, formal and distant, so unlike the man I had once known. He had assured Kit that his mother was recovering and there was no need to ask for special leave. Kit was due home within the month, after all.

Kit had sat in his room in the barracks a few days later, reading his mother's letter, a typical missive which made light of the mugging, and then he read another, in the same post, from his father, full of technical terms and classical allusions to Trojan horses. But it was the one a day later from Alice that had disturbed him the most. He had talked to her on the telephone, of course, and she had seemed fine, shaken but stable. But in the writing that trembled on the page, she admitted to him how afraid she was that the attack might trigger her own potential for disturbance, that she might start to hear the voices which had been silent for some time, and that if so she would now feel unable to turn to poor Margaret for help.

The revelation had upset me deeply, even though Alice was dead. I knew, of course, that Alice had had some kind of breakdown in her teens, but at the time of Margaret's attack, she had seemed to have left any instability behind her. She had been vibrant, full of plans for the future, plans to have children and to go on studying and working part-time in the gallery. But now, to my surprise, Kit told me that there had been other 'bad patches', and that it was Margaret who had seen Alice through them. They had happened in the first two or three years after she and Kit were married, the period before she had rekindled her interest in the ancient world and come to work for us. It was a time when I had seen her infrequently, just for an occasional lunch or a family party, as she settled into her new and seemingly happy life.

Kit told me that he had known nothing of these brief, manic episodes. He had been away, on military exercises in Cyprus, and he was furious to find that they had been concealed from him. It made him all the more determined that this time, he must act. He had asked at once for compassionate leave from his colonel but was refused. There was an intelligence threat and he was needed, by his troops and his superior officer. He told me, as he sat cradling the glass of whisky that I knew he wouldn't finish, and that I would later polish off, that he had almost disobeyed orders. Instead, he had complied, but had made his decision there and then. He would retire from the Army as soon as possible and find another life. He would put Alice first.

Five

My life changed direction irrevocably when Toby Haddeley recruited me to help him in his new business. I had been helping him out on Saturdays with the stall of antiques and bric-à-brac that he ran in Camden Passage. In addition to a small inheritance, Toby had by now accrued enough money, wheeling and dealing, to buy a rundown mansion flat in Chelsea where he planned to live, and from which he would do business. After several wild evenings and fantastical imaginings of an exotic future in the world of ancient art, he persuaded me to think about leaving the Purnell School of English and come and be his assistant, his 'Girl Friday', as he chose to call me.

We were well suited. Like me, Toby had a keen eye, only in his case it was for a deal, a bargain, or a person who might be useful to him; and I was one such person. I thought about his offer for a day and a night, then said yes. I was untethered and up for adventure. My short friendly affair with Jack Whaley had come and gone, and been followed by a couple of others that had also come to nothing. I had little to lose. Christopher was right, I knew, when he said that Toby was the sort of person who would get very rich, or go bankrupt, or possibly both. But hadn't I come to London to escape dull expectations? I was still young, and if Haddeley Antiquities went horribly wrong, I could always get another job.

In later years, when Toby and I had become so slick in our dealings, so professional, I would recall our beginnings and feel a nostalgia for the old times, when the business was still just a couple of rooms in the Chelsea flat, through which a few treasures would pass. Then there had been no extra locks on the doors, though it was true that there was a small safe for the sometimes large amounts of money that changed hands. It was strictly a cash business then. Nothing much was accounted for, and very few questions were asked. Strange men, both buyers and sellers, would ring the doorbell, which I was sent to answer, and they would wait, depending on their status, either in a small room off the kitchen, clutching the parcels they had brought with them, or else in the grander drawing room, the one space Toby had decorated to impress, with its Regency striped wallpaper and furniture on loan from an antique-dealer friend. Here Toby would bring out his wares one by one, while sipping tea from a china cup, like the charming souk salesman that he was fast becoming.

I would sit in the narrow office, once a small bedroom. My desk was next to the window which overlooked the communal gardens where the fashionably dressed children of the new bohemians played hide-and-seek in the shrubberies. Against the wall there was a pair of old filing cabinets, full of photographs and decaying sections of archaeological magazines. There were a few bits of paper claiming provenance of artefacts, half of them worthless. When I think about it now, our system was laughable, but it was our first Aladdin's cave.

Unlike Christopher, Toby had a talent for making money, though, as Toby often pointed out, if he had felt able to marry, and for money, he, like his brother, might have taken that route. But I never believed it. Toby liked to deal. He liked everything about it from the opening gambit to the sharp close, however friendly. And if sometimes not everything was quite aboveboard, if sometimes an accompanying document looked less than authentic, or what looked like a reproduction figure was in truth a smuggled antiquity, crudely painted to conceal its value, well, so much the better. It was just another part of the clandestine life that Toby relished.

I rarely saw Christopher any more and it was to be a decade or so before Margaret and I began a friendship of sorts. He had left the language school before I did. Margaret, together with her forceful parents, considered it unsuitable employment for him, and he was persuaded to study accountancy at a firm in the City. It put him beyond my reach in some way. He had crossed a divide from the more bohemian world that his brother and I inhabited and it depressed him, I suspected, to look back.

I remember, not long after meeting Toby, asking him about Christopher and Margaret. I was curious to know what their marriage was like, what bound them together. Toby shrugged and told me he thought that Margaret was probably good for Christopher, and that they rubbed along all right. He seemed uninterested in his brother's domestic life, except when he spoke about his nephew, Kit. Then he became surprisingly tender. He even carried a photograph of Kit in his wallet, a smiling eight-year-old boy in a striped school blazer, along with one of Alice.

About two years into my new life with Toby Haddeley, he fell in love. It was the long hot summer of 1976 and was to be our last year in Chelsea, just before Toby took on the smart new premises off Belgrave Square. From the window of my little office, I watched the lawns below turn brown in the drought as the weeks went by. We had parties in the warm intoxicating nights; Toby's bath was full of ice cubes to keep the wine cool. We would spill from the flat to the gardens, turning down the music as it got late to stop the constant complaints from the neighbours, those casual bohemians whose *laissez-faire* pose was abandoned at the stroke of midnight for the sake of a full night's sleep.

The object of Toby's passion was Ilya, a young man of indeterminate nationality who seemed to speak a Babel of languages. Toby claimed he was a dissident from the Soviet Union and was constantly angling, among his gay diplomat friends, to get Ilya some sort of long-term visa. Toby's claim seemed to me to be nonsense. Ilya, if that was his actual name, was many things, a rent-boy perhaps, a grave-robber for the antiquities trade, a con man according to Toby, when he was feeling displeased with him. A dissident he was not, other than in his opposition to any kind of fair exchange of labour. I suspected, however, that he knew how to cross a border unseen with a stash of ancient artefacts which he would later claim were purchased legitimately and for which there was always a sheaf of suspect papers.

I did wonder on occasion what else he sold, drugs perhaps, information even. There was something of the spiv or even the spy about Ilya. He was seedy enough and I supposed the seediness was part of his attraction for Toby. Ilya was always very careful to be polite to me and my suspicion didn't actually extend to dislike. I rather warmed to him, in fact; he was an amusing companion, though quite why Toby had fixed on him as a love object, I found mysterious. I wondered sometimes if Ilya performed some arcane sexual practice for Toby. I couldn't even establish where they had met. And I suppose I was jealous, of course.

I arrived at the Chelsea flat for work one morning to find Ilya lying on Toby's sofa in a pair of boxer shorts. His narrow Slavic features and close-set eyes had never charmed me, even though he made me laugh. But this morning I was surprised at how beautiful I found him, as he lay nearly naked in front of me. Most Englishmen of my acquaintance, without their clothes on, were pale and almost soft, as if they never saw the sun or took any exercise. Ilya by contrast had a small but well-defined muscular body. His shoulders were broad in relation to his waist and his skin was smooth and lightly pigmented. I found myself wanting to reach out and touch him. He looked like a Greek statue, I thought, and I understood a little better the nature of Toby's desire.

'Josie,' Ilya stretched his arms above his head, 'I am so pleased you have come this morning. Today I go away and I have present for you.'

I had no idea where Ilya was actually supposed to live, let alone about his comings and goings. I wondered briefly why he was announcing his departure to me and why he should be pleased that I had come that morning when I came every morning. As for a present . . .

'Come,' he said. He had thrown on a scarlet silk dressing gown which I recognised as belonging to Toby and he led me to the kitchen.

'Sit down,' he said. 'I make coffee.'

'Where's Toby?' The morning was well advanced. I had been to the dentist and by now it was almost half past eleven. It seemed a little late to be lying around in underpants, even for Ilya.

'He's gone to pick up friends. One is Anne and one is Alice?' He seemed to be proud of his memory or his pronunciation, or both. 'You know?'

This was news to me. I guessed it was news to Ilya too. I had met Anne, a childhood friend of Toby's and Christopher's, but not Alice, her five-year-old daughter and Toby's godchild. They lived close to Margaret and Christopher up in Norfolk, and rarely came to London, as far as I knew.

'Oh,' I said. 'They're coming here?'

Ilya had started to make coffee in a small long-handled pan which he had bought for Toby from a shop in Soho, along with real Turkish coffee. As soon as he was satisfied that the process was under way, he stood back and lit up an elegant oval-shaped cigarette, first offering one to me which I refused. I liked to smoke but the tobacco was too strong.

'I think, yes, here,' Ilya said. 'But Toby ask me to ask you something, Josie. A special favour. He promise to Anne to look after Alice for afternoon, but as I go, he wish to drive me to boat, so he ask if you mind to look after Alice? Please?' His accent was as unclear as his origin, somewhere between Russian and Greek, but it was the content of his speech that baffled me. Such a request had never been made before. And I found the thought of looking after a five-year-old alarming. Why couldn't Anne look after her own child? I supposed there must be a reason, one which Toby would tell me about, when he got round to it.

'Well, I . . .' I began, not knowing where the words would take me. But he quickly interrupted me.

'You are very kind, Josie, and very wise.'

I thought it was more likely that he thought I was very stupid if I was going to give credence to his flattery.

'So you think I'm wise, Ilya. Why would you think that?'

'First, kind, then wise.' I wondered what the significance was of this ordering of my qualities. I did feel a little flattered in fact. It was nice to be described as kind, which I thought was probably true, some of the time. I didn't know if I was wise. I was often able to understand things about people that they didn't seem to understand themselves, though it was a quality that I failed, I knew, to apply to myself.

'So,' Ilya went on, 'I have, not exactly a present, that is not the truth, sorry, but something I would like you to take care of for me until I come back and in exchange for this I will bring a gift with me.'

I laughed. Ilya was so predictable and yet he continued to surprise me.

'I'm disappointed,' I said. 'You said there was a present.'

'I bring. I promise. But while I am gone, keep this for me. Please?' He reached into the deep pocket of the dressing gown and pulled out a scruffy newspaper parcel which he placed on the kitchen table in front of me. I picked it up and looked at him, smiling.

'Why so mysterious?' I said.

'It's not possible to take with me,' he said. 'And Toby might sell. By mistake, of course.'

So Ilya didn't trust Toby, I thought. Poor Ilya. Whatever had happened to him that he thought that Toby would sell him out? And why did he think I wouldn't?

I pulled apart the dirty paper, inky smears appearing on my fingers from the newsprint. Inside, wrapped in a bit of old dishcloth was a small blue creature, a tiny statue, or rather amulet, with a tiny loop at the top of its head so that it could be worn around the neck. It was a Tawaret, a strange hybrid Egyptian creature, a goddess of childbirth with a hippo's head, a lion's feet, and a crocodile's back. Not beautiful exactly, I thought, but, though small, its features were clearly defined, as if they had been carved quite recently. But there was something about the surface of the stone that suggested otherwise. I pulled it out and stood it on the table.

'I take it it's real,' I said. He nodded.

I looked closer. It was a fine piece, except for the lion's claws which had once been damaged and then quaintly

75

restored into a sort of webbing, as if they belonged to a wading bird.

'The feet are damaged,' I said.

'Yes,' he said, 'a pity, but it is still good.'

'It's made of lapis,' I said, surprised. I was still a relative novice and I had never seen a Tawaret made from lapis lazuli before. But I knew that because of this its value would be so much greater. 'Where did it come from?'

He shrugged and smiled.

'You mean I don't need to know,' I said. I wasn't sure what it was worth, but quite a lot. Apart from the feet it was in excellent condition and these figures were very collectable. 'Why do you think Toby would sell it? And anyway, surely he would give you the money.'

'He may have other boy by time I get back.'

'Toby loves you.'

'Maybe.'

'Why do you think I won't sell it? Or give it to Toby?'

'I know you will not. If I ask you to keep for me you will keep.'

'So you trust me, but not Toby.'

Ilya shrugged again. 'Yes. And you should not trust Toby. Toby cannot trust Toby. Maybe you waste your life.'

I was astonished, and cross at his disloyalty. I couldn't quite believe that I was having this conversation with Ilya. I'd thought of him as full of cunning, but I hadn't allowed him intuition. I sat at the table, defensive, disturbed at the collusion into which I could feel myself being drawn. But all the same, I knew that there was truth in what he said

76

about Toby. It wasn't something I wanted to think about, and certainly I didn't want to discuss it with Ilya. Still, I found myself fascinated. Ilya, it seemed, knew Toby as well as I did, possibly better.

'What do you mean?' was all I could find to say.

'You are a pretty girl. Find yourself man who love you.'

'Not that,' I said. I blushed and frowned at him, allowing my irritation to cover my embarrassment. 'I meant the other thing. What do you mean, he can't trust himself?'

Ilya stubbed out his cigarette on a plate on the draining board and poured the thick viscous coffee into two small cups.

'Toby think he is special person,' Ilya said. 'He is vain. Not only about face and body.' Ilya gestured to his own attributes with a theatricality that made me think of a dancer or a mime artist. 'But here.' Ilya tapped his chest. 'This mean that he love, but he love Toby more.'

There was something comic about his performance and I laughed, no longer cross and taking the cup he handed to me.

'See, you also think.'

'I didn't know you were a philosopher, Ilya.'

'I see people true. Like you, I think.'

I pursed my lips and shook my head.

'You are faithful person, Josie . . .' He picked up his own cup and downed it in one. I was mesmerised by the fact that he appeared not to feel the boiling liquid as it slipped down his throat. 'Toby is lucky to have you for friend. He know.'

This revelation of Toby's gratitude, or so I took it to be, produced a sense of satisfaction and I knew that I had proved Ilya's point.

'So you will keep little hippo for me, Josie?' Ilya picked up the Tawaret. 'Till I return? When I return, I may sell it or no. But I like to think of it here with you.'

'You mean I'm acting as your bank. It's valuable, isn't it?'

He smiled, crossing his legs, the dressing gown parting to reveal his almost hairless shins. 'Yes. More than one thousand, I think, more than two perhaps. You are my bank. In case I have not cash when I return.' He picked up the statuette. 'And she is lucky for me, Nile god.'

I took the little statue from him and held it close to my face. I would keep it in the safe, I thought, but Ilya had a point; then Toby might sell it.

'She's much more than a Nile god,' I said. I had already begun my own passionate exploration of the ancient world, and was keen on these animal talismans that promised a safe passage in an alarming world. 'She couldn't be more scary. I hope she's lucky for you. I'd want her on my side.'

It was past two o'clock by the time that Toby, Anne and Alice arrived back from the station. By then Ilya was fully dressed and almost ready to leave. Anne, dressed, I noticed at once, in Yves St Laurent, seemed distracted, ignoring Ilya completely. She quickly handed Alice over to me, as if I were the hired help, imperious with her instructions. I was struck by the bright-looking child who stood in front of me. Alice's hair was dark and held back with a ribbon in an old-fashioned style. Her eyes too were dark, slanted and slightly hooded, exuding intelligence above her pink cheeks and eager smile. She was quiet at first, but then seemed determined to explore Toby's flat.

She spent the first part of the afternoon marching up and down its long narrow corridors, with me chasing after her, perplexed as to how to entertain a five-year-old. There was a growing hysteria in the air as Anne redid her make-up, sitting at the kitchen table, talking loudly to Toby who was waiting for Ilya to finish his packing. And then suddenly all three of them were gone and there was peace.

I'd known of Alice's existence, of course. Toby had talked about her with almost the same enthusiasm he exuded when he talked about Kit, whose parents occasion- ally brought him in to see us. But Alice was younger, and had stayed at home in the country until now. I knew that Anne and her second husband lived not far from Christopher and Margaret, and that Toby often saw her when he went to stay with one or the other, which was most weekends. I had discovered, to my surprise, quite early on that Toby liked children. It was their natural anarchy that appealed to him, I think; he was always keen to encourage it, and as a consequence, they adored him.

I settled Alice down with milk and biscuits in the kitchen, and watched her eat them slowly. She was such a lovely little thing, her skin olive, her face framed by her curls. I was pleased with myself so far. I seemed to be handling this small child well, I thought, but then, without warning, she began to cry, strange long mournful sounds which made me think of some village women I had seen in Greece the year before, following a coffin to the cemetery. I looked quickly in the bag that Anne had left me. There was a picture book along with some juice, a change of clothes and a small velvet monkey. I pulled out the monkey and handed it to Alice.

'Ssh, sweetheart. Look. Here's your monkey.' I made the monkey dance across the table and Alice stopped crying in mid-wail, and stretched out her arms. It was as if I had performed a small miracle. I watched the little girl's face transform as she pulled the toy towards her, taking it by its arms and moving it up and down as if it were jumping.

'What's his name?' I asked.

Alice looked at me. Her face was serious but then she smiled, certainly not for the first time that day, but in a way that sent a ripple of unfamiliar maternal love through my body.

'Unky,' Alice said. 'It's Unky.'

'Unky,' I said. 'I've got an Unky too. Do you want to see?'

Alice nodded slowly, holding the monkey by the waist, still jumping it slowly up and down on the tabletop.

I felt inside my big leather shoulder bag for the ball of newspaper in which I had rewrapped the Tawaret. I pulled it out and unwrapped it, showing it now to Alice who looked uncertain.

'Unky,' she said. 'Unky,' and reached out her hand.

'This Unky is only for looking at,' I said. 'Not for touching.' Alice continued to grasp in the Tawaret's direction. To my horror her face contorted and there was no doubt about it, she was going to cry again. I shifted my seat close

80

to Alice's and put my arm around her. Keeping a firm grip on the Egyptian amulet, I let Alice touch it.

'Just gently,' I said. 'She's a bit frightened. Just stroke her.'

Alice's free hand, small and fleshy, descended on the hippo's head, the fingers flat and extended so that just her palm touched it. There was silence in the kitchen. She looked closely at the Tawaret and then at me.

'He's not real,' she said.

'Is your Unky real?'

'Sometimes he is,' Alice said. 'And sometimes not. It all depends.'

It was then that I decided that Alice was a great deal more interesting than I had thought it possible for a child to be, and when Anne rang the flat, with promises of payment and eternal gratitude, to ask if there was any possibility that I could look after Alice for the evening, I didn't object. In fact I volunteered to take Alice home with me and put her to bed at my flat. Anne was thrilled to bits. She would pick Alice up the next morning, she said, if I was sure it was no trouble. And so our routine began.

Ilya didn't return that summer, as he had implied he might. And the last that we heard was that he had gone to Jordan in pursuit of an illicit archaeological dig. And then a contact told Toby there had been a rumour that he had been shot by security police while looting. There was a further report claiming that the story was false, and that he had been out in the desert, that much was true, but that he had died from peritonitis. Whatever it was, the shady world he inhabited was convinced he wasn't coming back. I tried to comfort Toby. I showed him the Tawaret which up to that point I had kept a secret, and said it was his now, that he should have it. But Toby gave it back to me. He didn't want it. He said he didn't want anything that reminded him of Ilya.

Six

It must have been about a week or two after the first sighting of the boy outside Millbury Street when our neighbour Jennifer rang me again. I was up and ready to leave, keen to get off to the gallery, anxious to see if there was any movement on the sale of the Egyptian head and also to make a start on research for the new catalogue we were putting together for the Basel Fair later in the year.

'Josie, I'm so sorry to bother you so early. It's just that that young man, he's here again.'

'What?'

'The boy. The one who was hanging around your drive-way last week. I can see him in the street. He's looking up at the house.'

'But he's not in the drive?'

'No.'

'Wait. I'll run and look.'

Clutching the phone, I went to the kitchen window. Gazing down, I saw him. He was tall, with dark hair, slightly curly but which looked as if it had been cut properly. It was hard to tell his age, but maybe twenty or so.

'I can see him,' I said into the phone. 'Thank you, Jennifer. I'll get Kit to deal with it.'

I rang through quickly to the main house and Kit picked up the phone.

'Where are you?' I asked.

'In the bedroom.'

'Go to the landing window. The boy is in the street, the boy Jennifer told us about. She just rang me. I'll come through the connecting door, if that's okay.'

'Fine.'

A few moments later I was walking towards him across the soft wool carpet. Kit put his hand out to beckon me over.

'Isobel's gone already,' he said. 'She went to her life class.'

'It's him,' I said. 'The boy that Jennifer saw.' I wondered why I was repeating information I had already given him.

We stood together watching the young man below, standing back slightly in case he looked up. But he seemed uninterested in the house as a whole; his attention was fixed on the closed gate. The boy put his hand to the bell but then he seemed to hang back.

'Perhaps he's a gypsy or a beggar,' I said. But we both knew he could not possibly be either.

'I don't think so,' Kit replied. He sounded anxious. 'Perhaps a Jehovah's Witness or a Mormon, or something. I'm going down to speak to him.'

'Is that wise?' I said. 'Don't.'

'I have to,' he said. 'I have to find out what's happening.'

He was right, of course, I thought. Better to see what was up. Now I saw the boy move forward and press the bell and its sound seemed to resonate not just through the house but right through my body in a way that left me feeling afraid though why, I couldn't say.

'Good,' Kit said. 'He's invited himself in.'

'Don't let him in,' I said.

'I didn't mean literally,' Kit said, on his way out. 'I'm going to find out what he wants.'

As I heard Kit go downstairs, I wondered for a moment if I should call the police, but the thought seemed premature, if not foolish, and I felt it wasn't my decision to make. I walked back to the window, telling myself that I was overreacting. It was an unusual situation but not, this morning at least, a threatening one. The boy was alone, in broad daylight. Kit was a former soldier, still fit and strong. Now the boy was speaking into the intercom on the gate and there was something about him, as I looked down at his figure, tall but slight compared to Kit, that told me that whatever it was he had come for, he too was afraid.

The gate opened and I watched Kit stride out. He stood a metre or so from the boy and said something to him. The boy was staring at him and then raised one hand to push back his hair from his face. I could see Kit's body relax a little. The boy looked down at the pavement and said something. Kit seemed to recoil. And then, to my astonishment, Kit seemed to lose his temper, and though I couldn't hear what he was saying, or rather shouting, he seemed to be dismissing the boy. It was impossible from this dumb show

85

to work out what was happening. There was a momentary stand-off and the boy turned, as if to leave. Seconds later, he seemed to change his mind and pulled a piece of paper from his pocket, thrusting it in front of Kit's face.

There was something about this gesture, about the insistence of it, that made me decide to go downstairs. It had begun to rain, light drops that were now falling fast, and I was scrabbling for a raincoat in the cloakroom by the front door when my phone rang. It was Kit.

'I'm taking the young man to the Turkish café, Josie,' Kit said. He paused, but then before I could speak, he said, 'I think you should come too. Would you mind? I need someone there. I need a witness.'

I knew better than to ask a question.

'I'm on my way,' I said.

We must have looked an odd trio to the other two customers, one of whom pretended to read his newspaper while casting glances in our direction, the other appearing to be occupied with her phone. The three of us sat in the almost empty café, its Formica-topped tables recently bleached and shiny, our cups of coffee untouched on the gleaming surface in front of us. Kit was straight-backed, next to me, trying to look as if this were a perfectly normal morning coffee break. Opposite us both, the dark-haired young man was hunched over, an unlit roll-up in his hand. He was wearing jeans and a black zipped top with a striped T-shirt beneath it. It was a fashionable but student type of look, I thought, though the clothes were good. In front of him on the table was his pouch of tobacco and papers and his mobile phone.

I tried to make eye contact but he avoided looking at me and when I pushed the sugar towards him, without speaking, he shook his head. He did, however, accept a biscuit from the packet that I had insisted on buying, though he seemed embarrassed to eat it. He looked fearful but at the same time determined. There was a strength about him, I thought, and I was curious to know more about this boy and the bombshell he had come to drop, but no one seemed to want to be the first to speak.

Kit sat with his palms flat down on the table. He was waiting, though for what, precisely, neither of us knew. The boy's name was Luke, he had told us, Luke Tyler. We sat for a while in the silent aftermath of the earlier heated exchange in the street until Luke stood up, the unlit cigarette still in his hand, and made as if to leave.

'I'm off,' he said. 'I can't deal with this. I'll be in touch.'

Kit looked incapable of restraining the boy, even if he had wanted to, but I sensed it was important that we should establish some sort of dialogue with this strange young man.

'You can't go yet, Luke,' I said. 'Please. Sit down. Kit . . . Mr Haddeley . . . well, it's a shock for him, and for me too.'

'Yes. Please. We must sort this out,' Kit said, asserting himself. 'I'm sorry. I didn't intend to be rude. I'm just . . . speechless.' For the moment he did indeed seem almost to have lost the capacity to form a sentence, but his words, now that he'd found them, had an effect, and the boy sat down.

*

Luke Tyler's story had rocked us both. It seemed that he had come to Millbury Street to tell us, or to tell Kit rather, that he was the son of Alice Haddeley. The paper he had produced from his pocket was an adoption order, and it did indeed state that his mother was an Alice Wearing, as she then was. It seemed to imply that our very own Alice, at the age of sixteen, had had a child who had been put up for adoption and that he was now sitting in front of us. For once, Kit's sang-froid had deserted him and it seemed he could barely bring himself to speak to the young man, or even look at him.

'I'm sorry,' Kit said again. 'This must be a mistake. Of course, if you are who you say you are, which I very much doubt . . . not that I'm implying dishonesty,' he said quickly, as the boy moved to jump up once more. 'I just think it must be, as I say, a muddle. But it can all be . . . sorted out.' He took a pad and pen from his inside pocket. 'Now look . . .' he said. I saw him force himself to try and smile at Luke. 'I'm going to give you the name of my solicitor. I want you to give me your telephone number in return and I will get him to ring you. And I will give you his number, too, so that if for any reason he doesn't contact you, you can contact him.'

Luke nodded, and then he spoke. It was the first time that I had really been able to listen to his voice rather than concentrate on the content of what he said. His tone was pleasant, his accent educated but with a slight overlay of street credibility, a little northern or Scottish perhaps. It gave the impression, I thought, of someone who was reluctant to be placed.

'Thanks,' Luke said. 'I didn't know who else to ask about it. Once I knew she was dead, I mean. There was only you. But you didn't contact me, so I had to come.'

Kit nodded. I was struck by the simplicity of the boy's statement. It seemed heartfelt, and I felt myself softening towards him. I could see there was a shy charm making itself apparent.

'And I think you're right, Mr Haddeley,' he went on. 'I think both parties should have the phone numbers.'

'Both parties,' Kit repeated, seeming almost to smile. I too was struck by the formality of Luke's words, and it made me check my assumptions. It sounded as if this young man anticipated some sort of legal wrangle, or perhaps, I thought, someone else might have already done so, on his behalf.

'I do understand your desire to find out about your real mother,' Kit said. 'And I'm sure Miss Price and I would both want to wish you well in your endeavour.' *Miss Price*, I thought. *Endeavour*, that wasn't a word I had ever heard Kit use before, and I wondered where it had come from. Now Kit was speaking again.

'I can assure you,' he said, 'that I will treat your claim with all seriousness, I promise. But this is an upsetting situation for me, as you can imagine.'

Luke showed no sign of what he was feeling. But he looked relaxed, patient even, as if Kit's reluctance to accept him were something that would simply fall away soon enough. He looked at Kit almost without blinking, as if he were drinking him in so as to know how to proceed.

'And I have my wife to consider, my second wife,' Kit

was saying. 'So if you will forgive me, we'll wait until things are settled before we talk again.'

To my surprise, Luke fished in his pocket and handed us both a card. *Luke Tyler,* it said; nothing else, no designation or address, just a mobile telephone number. It struck me as an odd thing for a student to have, if indeed that was what he was. I wasn't sure why I had made that assumption. I would have liked to ask. I would have liked to ask him all sorts of things, but it was clear that Kit did not want to advance our acquaintance.

'You'll be in touch then,' Luke said, standing up and offering Kit his hand. His movements were confident now. He had done what he came to do, I sensed, and his words were a statement not a question.

'Of course,' Kit said.

Luke turned to me and nodded. He smiled at me, a shy smile, conspiratorial, as if it were my responsibility to make sure that Kit did as he said. I found myself responding, smiling back, wanting him to know that I wished him well.

'You'll need this.' He turned back to Kit and pulled from a pocket the document which I had seen him hold out in the street, and which Kit now accepted.

They shook hands outside the café. They were about the same height, I noticed, though Luke was thinner. He would be twenty-four, if . . . I thought, and as I did so, I realised that part of me must think that his story was true. Luke turned to me and inclined his head a little as he shook my hand. In the café, he had seemed almost adolescent, withdrawn and silent, but now he seemed quite adult as he looked me in the eye.

'I'm sure we'll meet again,' he said. His occasional formality was surprising. It was almost comical.

'You can find your way back to the station?' Kit asked.

'Yes.'

'I hope,' Kit said, so quietly that I almost failed to hear, 'that you find what you are looking for.'

'And I'm sure that I will,' Luke said.

We stood at the corner of Millbury Street, watching as Luke headed off towards the tube station. And then Kit began to repeat, quietly and slowly, the details of the scene I had just witnessed, as if he was committing them to the memories of us both. He refused to believe Luke's story. The boy must have targeted him. Why? Because he had money, he said, answering his own question. And perhaps there were others involved. It was a scam, a con trick, and the boy's evident charm, which he too had noted, was simply proof of that.

But as we watched Luke turn the corner in the distance, at the end of the long street, I stopped him.

'You'll need to check it out, Kit,' I said. 'As soon as possible.'

He looked at me as if I were a stranger, and then spoke as if I had wounded him. 'How could you think such a thing could be true, Josie?' he said. 'How could you think it for a moment? I knew her all my life. We all did. You knew her too. She couldn't just have disappeared and given birth.'

I said nothing but simply hooked his arm in mine and pulled him gently in the direction of the house.

*

It was only later, as I sat on the bus which was making its way slowly down Edgware Road, past the carpet shops, travel agents and small grocers advertising halal meat, that I understood that Kit had known that this boy would come. He had been expecting him. It was why he had been so unconcerned about the security for the house, and why Jennifer's initial phone call had failed to faze him in the way I had thought that it might.

I wondered how long he had known of the boy's existence. Only a short time, I guessed. Kit was tight-lipped in some ways but he would have felt unable to keep such a secret for long. I tried to recall at what point this could have come to light and then I remembered the letter that Isobel had shown me on the day of her birthday. That must have been from Luke. 'You didn't contact me,' he had said to Kit, and I had misunderstood.

The bus was making slow progress, sprinting briefly when not standing idle in traffic paralysis. The world outside looked to me as it did each day from my upstairs front seat, and yet I was aware that it had shifted in some way. For one thing I now knew that Kit Haddeley was a better liar than I had ever thought. He had given nothing away.

On the seat opposite, a young boy was focused on his telephone, texting or playing a game, oblivious to the streets outside from which he had come. He looked up for a moment and stared at me, conscious of my gaze, then went back to his phone. I checked my own mobile yet again. Perhaps there would be a message from Kit. I wondered again if I should in fact get off the bus and go back to the house, or even ring Isobel, against Kit's express instructions, and tell her to drop everything and go to him.

The next stop approached, but I did nothing, I might as well get on with things, I thought, go to the office and wait, as he'd told me to do. We had parted outside Millbury Street, Kit still adamant that Luke's story could not be true. He would phone the solicitor, he said, as soon as he got in and fax him the paper that Luke had given him.

The bus halted once again behind a long queue of traffic. I could see that the journey might be a long one and I tried to distract myself by pulling from my bag the notes I had received the day before from our British Museum consultant, Roger Morton. I liked to arrange our catalogues by theme and these were his careful reactions to my first attempts at an introduction.

I found the thought of Roger oddly comforting in the wake of the morning's cataclysm. He was like nursery food, a very nice man who took me out to dinner occasionally in a vague, but fruitless hope that one day we might collate catalogues together. The notes I had in front of me on the bus that morning were typical of him. There was the usual irritation at my tendency to generalise from the particular, but then his corrections settled down and the little marks he made on the page were quite generous. He seemed excited by the beautiful objects that we had collected for the forthcoming sale and was more gracious than usual in his approval. On any other occasion I would have been thrilled but it was increasingly hard to concentrate. The image of the boy, Luke, and the words he had spoken had only temporarily been put aside, and now they were buzzing round my head once more and I began to feel dizzy and sick.

It was raining with some force now and as I watched the world from the top of the bus, people below in Park Lane began to scatter or raise their umbrellas. The sky was suddenly dark and cars put on their lights for the duration of the brief spring storm. I saw a boy skid on his bicycle, avoiding the wheels of a car by moments. I needed air, I thought, and decided to get off the bus and walk, despite the rain, down to Westminster Cathedral. I would sit quietly for a while to try to recover myself, to allow myself the time and space to search my memory and attempt to make some sense of what had just occurred.

Kit arrived at the gallery after lunch, and I noticed at once that he smelt slightly of drink. He wasn't a big drinker, not like Toby had been, but clearly he had felt the need for alcohol. I myself had had a large whisky at a discreet mews pub round the corner, on the way back from mulling things over. I had felt a similar desire to soften the shock of the morning. It wasn't every day, after all, that we were visited by ghosts, or not in living form.

'I've rung Peter Southgate,' Kit said. 'We're to fax over the so-called adoption order this afternoon. I couldn't get the damn thing to work at home.' He fiddled with the clasp on his briefcase but then sat down, suddenly overcome, it seemed, by the effort. I stood up and went over to him and picked up the bag. I looked at him and he nodded and I fished inside, finding it almost immediately.

'I'll do it straight away,' I said. 'Would you like a cup of tea? Or perhaps some coffee?' Kit nodded but he put his head in his hands. I felt fortified, by the scotch perhaps or by his vulnerability, but I found myself saying, 'Don't you think you should tell Isobel after all, Kit? I think she might be very hurt at you keeping this from her. I would be if I were her. She'll want to help.'

He gave me an odd look, a look that suggested surprise that I might understand anything about the relationship between husband and wife. Then, once more, he slowly nodded, stood up, and taking out his phone walked out of the office and into the main display room to make his call. Not long afterwards, and without further discussion, he ordered a taxi to take him home.

I saw neither of them that evening, keeping discreetly to my quarters, but at about eight thirty the following morning, there was a knock on the connecting door and Isobel came into the flat.

It was difficult to tell how she had taken the news. She looked tired, her blonde hair in need of a good brush, I thought. But she assured me she was fine, though of course she was worried for Kit.

'What are you worried about exactly, Isobel?' I said.

Her face looked puzzled as if she hadn't before asked herself this question.

'This whole thing,' she said. 'These people. Taking advantage.'

It was clear that Kit had expounded his conspiracy theory and that she had taken his scepticism at face value.

This surprised me. She was a reasonable person on the whole, and far more worldly than Kit. That a woman should have had a child adopted prior to her marriage, and say nothing about it, was something she might condone, if not entirely understand.

'I'm worried about the strain it's putting him under,' she said. 'It's too cruel to bring up the past in this way.'

I said nothing. It was hard to speak to Isobel about the past though I sensed that she wanted me to. As she left, she turned at the door.

'What do you think, Josie, really? You must know. Could it be true?'

Her face was sad and curious but I could see she was ready to do battle, if necessary. She was dressed in her painting clothes. She would go, I knew, to her studio and forget all of this for several hours, and I envied her.

'I have no idea whether it's true,' I said. 'But as to whether or not it is possible, then, I think, yes.'

Seven

Alice was still a small girl when she told me about the voices she could sometimes hear. She began to visit us regularly, first at the Chelsea flat and then, later, at the new Belgrave Square gallery. She would come through the door and run up to Toby first, hug her godfather, then sidle up to me and sit on my lap and stroke my hair. She always seemed to be happy, despite the chaos of her home life where she was neglected and spoilt in turn. She was an engaging, if eccentric, child and her nature was, if anything, over-generous. She would offer up her toys without hesitation and lavish hugs and affection on whoever she was with.

Her mother Anne, Toby's friend, rarely gave us much notice of them coming. It was her habit to arrive with Alice in the late morning, having caught a train down from Norfolk. Bored by the idea of business, she would walk around frowning at the exhibits, impatient to be off for lunch and a drink. She would rearrange her hair, observing her socialite slimness in the mirror or in the reflection from one of the glass cases. She liked to tease Toby. The gallery was only a gallery, she said, because it was smart and sold

97

things you could see in museums. It was really a shop, she said, pronouncing the word with distaste. And Toby would laugh, but I knew how much her baiting irritated him and how unforgiving he could be. In later years, as he grew richer, I would hear him muttering sometimes, when he was tipsy after lunch and surveying his domain, 'Not so much of the shop now, Anne, you old lush. More like a bank these days.' And he would smile to himself like one of the sacred temple monkeys that came through our hands from time to time and graced the gallery with their oracular presence.

Sometimes, if we weren't too busy, I would go with the three of them to Fortnum & Mason for lunch, and then, in the afternoon, Anne and Toby would disappear on their separate adventures, leaving Alice to play in the gallery with me. When I look back now to those afternoons, I see an innocence in our ritual which even at the time I treasured. It was a sanctuary from the ever more dissolute world I seemed to have immersed myself in. I would lead Alice by the hand, around the long, narrow showroom, its floor covered with a thick pale green carpet which muted the busy sound of London and subdued the shrillest voices.

The room was furnished with plinths and glass cases, and I would lift Alice up so that she could see the shelves where the smaller ancient objects were displayed. She showed little interest in the Greek statues or the Egyptian stellae, those large slabs of inscribed stone suspended in brackets on the walls. By contrast she would stretch out her small rounded arms towards the rows of tiny pieces that stood or lay in the glass cases, as if they were toys.

Sometimes I would take one out for her to hold, something simple that wouldn't break; an animal, of course, was the favourite, a cat or a baboon or a crocodile. Then we sat together on the floor while I told her tales about the creatures of the Nile, and the people who worshipped the animals as gods, and who had lived such a very long time ago.

One day, Alice interrupted my story. She was usually silent, hanging on my every word, her dark eyes fixed on my face. But that afternoon, the account of the crocodile god, Sobek, and how he came to the aid of the troubled Pharaoh, provoked a protest.

'God's not a crocodile,' Alice said, 'and crocodiles can't talk.'

'The gods don't really talk,' I said. 'Not like you and I talk.' As I spoke the words, I wondered quite what I meant myself, and quite how I should approach such matters of philosophical dispute with someone so young.

'Yes, God does talk.'

I was struck by Alice's determined monotheism. I supposed it must have come from the small village school she attended. As far as I knew, Anne and her current husband, Alice's stepfather, Gordon, had no particular religious affinities. There was no church-going.

'Well, in that case, what does he say?' I asked. Alice stayed silent for a moment, and I could see that she was trying to decide whether to confide in me.

'It's not just God,' she said. 'There are others. They say things.' She paused, assessing my reaction.

'Oh,' I said. 'And who are these others? Are they your

friends?' Her trust touched me, but it sometimes made me sad to think that the two of us had been thrown together, both unsure of our position in the lives of those we cared for. I was proud, however, to be admitted into Alice's world, and enchanted by the richness of her imagination. I liked the idea that I could feed it with the stories we shared together, and I was excited by this latest development, this new panoply of invisible friends. It was a child's imitation, I thought, of the ancient cosmology that surrounded us in the gallery.

'I don't know,' Alice said. 'But what they tell me is secret.'

'Does that mean you can't tell me?'

'I'm afraid so.' Her tone was grave, adult even, but her face held a childlike expression. She was distracted by the creature which lay in her hands and she pressed the tiny crocodile amulet to her face. 'Can I keep him?' she said. There would be no more about the secret friends that day, I thought, but I looked forward to the next time.

'No, Alice,' I said, taking her hand and leading her into the office. 'You know you can't keep him. He belongs to Toby, he's part of Toby's work. But you can hold him while you have your nap.'

She lay stretched out on the worn velvet of an old chaise longue we kept in the back office; it was part of our routine. I could see her watching me, as I worked at the desk by the window, until her eyes closed, and then I would get up from the chair and creep across to rescue the crocodile, or the dog, or the ibis, or whatever it was that Alice was clutching. By the time I was ready to close the gallery, she was up and awake, full of questions and energy, and we would go home together on the bus, to my small flat behind the cathedral where, after her supper, I would put her into my bed. Three or four hours later I would climb in beside her, her small warm body soothing the upsets and anxieties of my daily existence.

The next morning, we would be up and dressed and waiting for Anne who usually arrived at my flat a little later than specified. A taxi would be waiting, its engine running, as she rang my bell. Anne always greeted me as if she had not seen me for weeks and then thanked me in such a fulsome way that I was embarrassed and didn't know where to put the envelope she thrust into my hand. I didn't like taking the crisp notes for looking after Alice. They felt like guilt money, an act of betrayal towards a child whose love and trust were freely given.

I was always impressed by how well groomed Anne looked on these mornings, chic and smart, if still smelling faintly of gin, all ready for their return home to the Norfolk countryside. There was never the slightest sign of the real purpose of her overnight stay, about which Toby and I would certainly gossip later in the day. The truth was that Anne came to London to meet a man. As for Alice, her presence was all part of the fiction of visiting Toby. No one would think that Anne would take her child to London to meet her lover.

Anne's affair lasted for almost three years, during which I continued to look after Alice. Looking back, it seems odd now that I had the patience. I was young, after all. But I suppose I took love from wherever I could get it. The two of us were happy in each other's company, mesmerised by each other's imagination, sharing, if only for an afternoon, a childlike world of animals and magic where wrongs were righted and fathers, if absent, were gods, and away on some divine and important duty.

Alice only once told me what her voices said. By then she was almost seven years old and, had we known it, almost at the end of that early time together. We were eating toasted teacakes in the small office in the gallery, sitting by the little green gas fire with the creamy old-fashioned vents that glowed blue then red. She had woken only minutes before and her body was still loose and her face dreamy.

'Do you think,' she asked, 'that when I grow up I could be a queen, like Hatshepsut or Nefertiti?' It was always a surprise to me how Alice could absorb the complex names, and how well she understood who each was and where they stood in the multiplex hierarchies of the ancient world.

'Well,' I said, caught off guard, 'that's a grand ambition. Perhaps you could be. Who knows? You might even marry Prince Charles one day, though you'll have to hurry to catch him up.'

'I don't think I will marry Prince Charles,' Alice said. Her face was serious. 'He's too old. But I would like to be a queen or a princess.' She looked up at me as if making some kind of assessment, and then she said, 'But best of all I would like to be Mary.'

The name Mary seemed to interrupt the cosy intimacy of the winter afternoon. There had been no Mary that I could remember in the stories at the gallery, but Alice spoke as if it was something known between us.

'Tell me about Mary. Who is Mary?' I said.

Alice looked at me, puzzled that I didn't understand.

'You know. The Virgin Mary,' she said. 'Our Lady, she's called. We saw her in the cathedral. You showed her to me, last time.'

It was true, and I was shocked to realise that Alice's sudden leap into Catholic iconography was entirely of my making. I had taken her into the cathedral one evening on our way home. I had done it by way of a lesson, wanting to show her that it wasn't only the ancient civilisations that had statues and deities. But I hadn't allowed for the idea that Mary was altogether closer than the ancient gods, and that her currency might be more potent to a seven-year-old.

'You showed her to me,' Alice repeated. 'And then I asked Mrs Durden about Mary because I knew Mrs Durden had a picture of her, and Mrs Durden said she was Our Lady and that she wasn't to be spoken of in the same breath as the Egyptians.'

I was aware of Mrs Durden. She was Alice's mother's daily help, and she often appeared in Alice's conversation since Alice saw a great deal more of her than she did of her mother. So that was where Alice's smattering of faith had sprung from. It had never occurred to me that there was any danger of us stepping on spiritual toes, but I had been wrong.

'Well, Alice,' I now heard myself saying, 'that is perhaps true. We must respect Mrs Durden's religious beliefs.'

'I didn't tell Mrs Durden what Mary said,' she replied. I felt a sense of relief at this dispensation. 'But she did speak to me,' Alice went on. 'And I didn't tell you either, Josie, because I thought you might be jealous.'

'Jealous?'

'Yes,' she said. 'I thought you might be sad that she hadn't spoken to you, too.'

I had never pressed Alice on the voices. I had decided they were best left alone, to fade with childhood in the usual way, but in this instance, I thought it might be better to head off trouble.

'Can you tell me what she said?' I smiled in encouragement. 'I would very much like to know.'

Alice leant forward and lowered her voice, although there was no one else to hear.

'Mary said she would give me a baby like hers.'

For just a moment I experienced a tug of superstition, and I felt frightened.

'A special one with stars around its head,' Alice went on, putting out her hand as if to touch the stars she could see in her imagination. As I watched her make the gesture, I understood, and my feeling of incipient panic subsided. It made sense to me. The statue of Mary she had seen held a doll-like figure of the baby Jesus, an odd little creature with a halo of stars. I remembered now how taken she had been with this homunculus; she had wanted to touch it, just as she loved to hold and nurse the animal creatures in the gallery. Relieved, I held out the plate of teacakes to her, smiling, and it seemed that her recent vision was forgotten at the sight of the butter running over on to the plate.

*

And then, suddenly, we lost each other. Anne got pregnant. She stopped coming to London, stopped Alice's overnight visits. Toby told me that the lover, a German diplomat, didn't want to know about the baby, and that Anne's husband, Gordon, believed it was his. Little Alice never came to stay at the flat in Victoria again, although I saw her from time to time. As far as I knew, the voices faded from her consciousness. It had been a phase that I assumed she had grown out of, just the soundtrack of imaginary friends who fell out of favour as the real world impinged.

It became my habit, after Alice's visits stopped, to light a candle whenever I went into Westminster Cathedral. I suppose at first the candles were for Alice, but now I think that they were also for me, for my receding hopes for a bright and shining future. And then I began to light candles for poor drunken Anne, who lost her lover's baby and began her own steep slide into darkness and death. And as the years have gone on there have been others, and when I light the little flames, I often feel I encompass them all: Anne, Alice, Toby, even Christopher of whom I had once been so fond, and, of course, there are still more, and then more to come. Sometimes I mouth their names as I stand back and watch the flickering lights.

Eight

I hadn't wanted to go up to Norfolk with Kit and Isobel. My feeling was that they should go on their own to talk to Margaret about Luke Tyler, but Isobel begged me to come along. She didn't much like going to visit Kit's mother at the best of times; she said that her stomach contracted each time she and Kit drove the last few miles to the house. It would begin, she said, as they turned off the dual carriage-way, on to the road lined by crooked trees, crippled by the east wind, an avenue of grotesque shapes against the cold spring sky.

It was just a couple of weeks or so after we had first met Luke Tyler, and now the three of us were sitting in Kit's old Saab on our way to Fleet. I was sitting in the front of the car. This privileged position was by way of a thank-you from Isobel, but none the less I was feeling martyred. I had planned a weekend at home in Millbury Street, with the run of the whole house. I would have got up late, caught up with the novels that sat on my bedside table. I might have gone alone to an afternoon film, always a secret pleasure, and there had been an invitation to dinner at Jack's which, despite Helen's presence, I had been looking forward to. Worst of all, when I phoned to cancel, Jack had sounded tipsy, and, to my disappointment, indifferent as to whether I was coming or not.

I knew that I should not be so harsh on Isobel. She was pregnant after all, and now she was facing a curious conundrum from a weak position, but still it seemed unnecessary of her to make quite such a fuss about going. I couldn't understand why we both hadn't stayed at home and let Kit go on his own. Isobel didn't even want Margaret to know about her pregnancy yet. She had wanted to wait until she was more certain of its duration, which I could see made sense. That alone would have been a good enough reason to let Kit talk to his mother by himself. I knew that Kit had suggested it, she told me so. But she refused to allow Margaret Haddeley the satisfaction of inquiring why she wasn't present at such a time.

Perhaps, I thought, I had been wrong about Isobel's toughness. Perhaps it had been harder than I had guessed for her to ignore her husband's past, as she'd stood at her easel these last two weeks. It was more than just the business of Luke's existence. There was the spectral presence of Alice in the uncertainty which seemed to be growing in her, and I wasn't sure, in that case, that I was the person to bolster her up.

But there was little need for her to be so anxious, I thought, as we got out of the car at last, in front of the big Georgian farmhouse. After all, Margaret was unlikely to be very concerned with her presence when she heard the news they were bringing. But it was a relief, all the same, to hear that the moment was to be postponed. Margaret, it seemed, was not at home.

Mrs Sutton, a woman almost as old as Kit's mother, and all that was left of the staff whose numbers had dwindled through the decades, opened the front door and came out to greet us with this news. She was a pleasant woman, dressed in tweed and a twin set, cast-offs of Margaret's, I guessed.

'You're to have lunch without Mrs Haddeley,' she said. 'She's been held up in King's Lynn.'

'Will lunch keep, Barbara?' asked Kit, pulling out our bags.

'Yes, Mr Haddeley. It's only cold cuts.'

'Then I think we might go and have a pub lunch at the beach if that's all right with you? What about you two? Fancy that?'

'Why don't you and Isobel go on your own?' I said. I was thinking of the P. D. James novel in my suitcase.

'But you must come to the beach, Josie,' Isobel said. 'You spend too much time cooped up with all those dusty old things in the gallery. You need some air, you need spring cleaning.'

'Go on, come with us,' Kit said.

I interpreted this to mean that the two of them were reluctant to be alone together; they didn't want to have to talk about what was to come.

'You all go and enjoy yourselves,' Barbara Sutton said now, seeming to make the decision for us. Perhaps, I thought, she wanted to put her feet up too. I seemed to have to accommodate everyone that weekend. And perhaps, I remember thinking, it wasn't just that weekend. Perhaps

I'd had enough; it was time to draw a line. Perhaps it had all gone too far.

'Do you want to take the dog?' Mrs Sutton's voice was hopeful. 'He needs a walk.'

Kit looked at Isobel who nodded. She was fond of Margaret's old lurcher, rescued years before from some unspeakable deprivation. It was an acceptable joke between them that Margaret's affection for Nobby was the nearest she came to a general humanity.

'I'll bring the bags in first,' Kit said, looking at his watch and then at us. 'We'll leave in five minutes, okay?'

The Haddeley house was just outside Fleet, a village five miles from the Norfolk coast, which was the one great compensation for the country weekends I had endured from time to time over the years with Toby and his brother and sister-in-law. The path through the estuary landscape to the dunes and the sea had been a refuge from the tensions that the Haddeleys seemed to thrive on. It was a mile or so of shifting landscape and birdcalls, until there was a sudden gentle sandy rise and then the expanse of deserted North Sea shoreline. As the three of us walked through the familiar marshland, deserted apart from a few cows in the salty fields to our right, we were quiet, each of us, I guessed, speculating on our own version of a changed future. Kit was a few yards ahead but then stopped and waited for us to catch up. As we approached, he said, 'I just don't know what to do. I just don't know.'

Isobel put her arm on his shoulder. 'Just give it more time, Kit,' she said.

'Yes.' I found myself repeating her words, like some chorus in a Greek tragedy. 'That's all you can do. Give it time.'

We had all repeated this mantra so frequently in the last couple of weeks that the words had become estranged from us. They felt almost duplicitous. I didn't know myself what they meant. Did they mean, time to absorb the information that had opened up a catacomb of skeletons? Or time for Kit and Isobel to adjust to a maverick family realignment? Or did they mean, just wait and see, as if somehow Luke Tyler might vanish as suddenly as he had come? As we began to walk along the sea path, I watched as Isobel set her face against the chill wind. She, I thought, especially, would hope that he might.

Kit was now bringing up the rear. I turned to smile at him but his hands were in his pockets, his head bowed. I had watched him struggle these last two weeks, and this mood was familiar to me. Waiting for the lawyers' conclusions had been a strain in itself, but whether true or false, right from the start I could see that the idea of Alice's son had stirred up something in Kit. Until Luke's appearance, he had managed to stop thinking about Alice, he had suppressed the memory of her. But now a new and upsetting possibility had brought her back, not as we liked to remember her, the vibrant young woman embarking on a Russian adventure, but more of a struggling soul in torment. I didn't care to think too hard about it myself.

Three days after our meeting with Luke, Peter Southgate, the solicitor, had phoned to confirm that what he had said was true. We had been going through the inventory for the return of some goods that had been sent out for sale with another dealer. I knew at once, from Kit's set expression, what Peter must be telling him.

My first reaction was to be practical. I started to talk about the law about obligations and inheritance, but Kit hardly heard me. He was concerned with none of that, none of the practical matters that might rear their head. For him, this thing had opened up a Pandora's box beyond facts and certificates and orders. It had opened a wound, one that it would be beyond poor Isobel either to locate or heal, and I felt afraid for them both. I heard myself speaking, but as if to myself, though I knew that Kit must be asking himself the same question.

'So who then?' I said. 'Who could it have been? Who was the boy's father?'

He sat down opposite me, pale and confused. He tried to speak, and when he finally did, once again he said, 'I don't know. The birth certificate doesn't say. There were boy-friends, I suppose. She knew people. You might know more than me.'

But I didn't. And I was ashamed that I didn't.

'She was only sixteen,' I said. 'Fifteen when she conceived.'

'I just don't know,' he said. But this time I knew that he was talking about the unspeakable, about the ripple of aftershock that was about to shift our daily realities. He looked at me, asking for help. 'I don't know what to do,' he repeated and put his head in his hands for a moment, then sat up again, bracing his shoulders. He took the coffee and the brandy that I gave him and as I watched him drink, I knew he was thinking back, struggling, as I had begun to do myself, to make the past cohere, forcing himself to admit that his and my knowledge of Alice's life was more limited than we had thought.

∽

It was a strange situation we were in, I thought, as the three of us walked through the dunes, protected from the cold wind as we looked out to sea. There were a couple of boats tacking at speed across the wide expanse in front of them. I had tried sailing once, with Toby and his brother who had grown up in boats, like Arthur Ransome boys, but it was no use, it made me too anxious. I loved the sea, to look at and swim in, but seen from a boat it made me jumpy. Its surface troubled me; it felt as if it was pulling at my soul, reflecting whatever darkness was lurking there, until I felt any sense of ease evaporating into the salt air.

'I'll tell Ma this afternoon,' Kit said, 'I've been thinking.' We huddled together to be able to hear what he said above the whistle of the wind. 'I think, if you don't mind,' he said, looking at Isobel, 'I'll get her on her own. Let her absorb it for a bit?'

I had already assumed that he would want to tell his mother the news alone. I hardly thought that Isobel would want to be present.

'Good idea, sweetheart,' Isobel said, then after a moment she added, 'But how about you have Josie with you. Just in case. It will be a shock for Margaret. It might be good if you were there, Josie, don't you think?'

I wasn't too sure that good was quite the right word.

'I think Kit might like to tell Margaret by himself, Isobel,' I said.

Kit was staring out to sea. He turned to me.

'Actually,' he said, 'I do think that's a good idea. You will be able to tell better than me how she takes it. If you're willing, Josie, that is?'

I shrugged my shoulders. I was happy enough to be present, rather curious, in fact, to see Margaret's reaction, if truth be known. Isobel was smart though, I thought. She wanted a more objective account than the one she would get from Kit, and she could rely on me to deliver it.

I don't believe in ghosts, but to imagine one is a way of overlaying memory with a benign veneer, a way of making light of the shadows that gather. Looking down at the beach below, I found myself able to picture Alice for a moment, as she was before she died, a little over thirty, tall and graceful and starting to lose the girlishness she had long retained. She was running towards us, just above the sand, but she disappeared from my imagination before she could reach the foot of the dunes where we sat, sheltering in the marram grass. I liked to think of her playing here with Kit as a child, and I had mentioned it to him once, years before, but he dismissed it. They had never played together as children, he said. Alice had been just a little girl, four years younger than him. It wasn't till much later that he had noticed her at all.

It was about four o' clock when we finally got back to the house. Margaret Haddeley was standing in the doorway, waiting to greet us, a tall woman, slim with white hair that gleamed above blue eyes. She was handsome, her skin weather-tanned, though still taut on her facial bones. There was an air of suffering about Margaret which I always put down to her belief that in falling in love with Christopher, Kit's father, she considered that she had made a grave mistake.

Margaret's dog, released from the back of the car by Kit, ran barking to his mistress, jumping up at her legs.

'Down, Nobby, good boy,' Margaret said, slipping the dog a chocolate drop from a supply kept permanently about her. 'Kit dearest, and Isobel,' she said, looking up briefly from the delirious dog. 'And Josie, you're looking well. We see you too rarely down here these days.'

We all kissed her with the formality she liked, and then Kit, who was indulgent of his imperious mother, followed her in first, looking behind at Isobel and me, raising his eyebrows in question.

'Come, all of you, to the small sitting room and have tea,' Margaret said. 'Have you had a good walk?'

'Very good, Margaret,' Isobel said. 'But if you don't mind I'll just go upstairs and take a bath. I got a little cold and damp. You and Kit and Josie have tea without me.'

'Oh,' Margaret said. Her expression indicated that she thought this poor form, and I couldn't help but smile to myself at its predictability. 'Well, if you must. I'll ask Sutters to bring you up a cup.'

'No need, really,' Isobel insisted. The exchange was inevitable and I knew that nothing would offend Isobel more than the idea of poor Mrs Sutton waiting on her like some ancient flunkey. And why, Isobel would frequently ask her husband, couldn't Margaret dignify her house-keeper with a proper name? Kit would try to excuse his mother but his explanations would collapse in the ever deeper mire in which he found himself. All the same, since his marriage, Kit called Mrs Sutton by her first name, as I always did. It had been a small victory for Isobel, and one that Margaret still held against her.

In the small room to the left of the front entrance, a log fire was decomposing into a seductive glow. Margaret rarely used the larger drawing room these days, but she refused to move out of the house, as Kit often suggested, despite the absurd amount of money it cost her to keep it up. Its décor was generally in need of updating, but the structure of the house itself was well preserved and carefully maintained, rather as she was, I thought, as we followed her into the pretty front room. She had allowed this, I noticed, to be redecorated, but its pale green wallpaper was identical to that which had been there before. It was a feminine room, despite the clean Georgian lines. She had softened it with cushions and a tapestry frame, untouched since her eye-sight had deteriorated, a condition which she did her best to hide from anyone visiting her.

'Just the three of us then for tea, darlings, how nice,' she said as she sat on one of the small sofas in front of a low table that supported a tray.

Kit hovered, still standing, smiling but uncertain, as his mother settled herself.

'Let me do that,' he said, reaching for the silver teapot.

'Thank you,' Margaret replied, as carefully as if he were not her son but some visitor to whom she must be gracious. 'Josie dear, get yourself another cushion from the window seat; that chair is too deep. It's bad for the back.'

'It's fine,' I said. 'I'm very comfortable. How are you, Margaret?' I asked. Isobel had been right, the news would be a shock, but fortunately Margaret Haddeley looked quite robust. Not that she would tell us if it were otherwise.

'I'm very well for my age, Dr Goodwin keeps telling me,' she smiled. 'And all the better for seeing you both. Neither of you come often enough.' She took the cup Kit offered her and stared straight at him for a moment. 'And you've got something to tell me,' she said.

I was brought up short by Margaret's perceptiveness, or perhaps it was more her propensity to want to get straight to the point. I knew that Margaret was able to pick up on Kit's moods, but I hadn't expected it to happen so quickly. People had accused Margaret Haddeley of coldness, but not where Kit was concerned. He was her only child, and in him she had invested all the passion that she had decided early on to withhold from her husband, poor Christopher.

'Nothing gets past you, Ma.' Kit smiled, but only briefly. 'You're right, something has happened. Well, not happened . . . emerged, I suppose.' His voice dropped and he stopped briefly to take a drink from his cup, before pressing on. 'There's a boy, or rather a young man, who has come forward,' he said. His words seemed to me curiously stiff. 'He came to the house to see me. Josie was there.' He nodded towards me. 'He says,' Kit paused again, turning back to his mother. 'This will come as a shock, Ma. He says he is Alice's son. Well, he is in fact. We've been into it and it's true.' He stopped for a moment to see if there was any reaction from Margaret, but seeing none, he continued. His voice was a sort of monotone, uninflected. 'Alice had a baby. She was only just sixteen when he was born. We've no idea who the father was, or is, no way of knowing.' He had looked away as he uttered the last sentence, but now looked up again, into his mother's face. But it was impassive and she remained quite still.

'It's true, Margaret,' I said quietly. 'I met him too. And Kit's checked. It's hard to believe, I know.'

Margaret opened her mouth to speak, but Kit seemed not to see.

'How could it be, Ma?' He seemed to beg her to contest the information he knew to be true. 'I've been over and over it. I've asked myself, when? Well, I know when, but how? How could no one have known? People knew her. We knew her. People we knew, knew her. Someone must have known? Surely? And why . . .' He put his head in his hands and moved as if to rock himself, then thought better of it and pulled himself up straight to face her.

'You want to know why didn't she tell you.' Margaret finished his sentence.

'Yes, exactly,' he said, calm again but clearly upset,

ashamed, almost, of a momentary loss of control. 'Why couldn't she . . .'

I wished at that moment that I had not been there after all. I could not remember seeing Kit this distressed since the period after Alice's death. It felt indecent, my being present, witnessing the pain that Kit had brought home, like a small boy, to his mother. I picked up my handbag and stood up slowly, as if to creep away, but Margaret waved to me to sit down.

'Did you know about this child, Josie?' She turned her gaze directly on to me. It took me a moment to realise she was asking if I had known all along.

'Of course not.' I was shocked. 'How could you think that?' But Margaret's thoughts moved on.

'Anne must have known,' she said. 'But poor Anne is dead.' She was quiet again and we sat in a silence that neither Kit nor I felt we could interrupt. A moment later, she said, as if pronouncing finally on the matter, 'A boy,' and then to Kit's and my consternation, she smiled and her face was soft and rounded. 'Alice's boy. How wonderful.'

'Well,' Kit said, after a moment, 'that wasn't exactly the reaction I was expecting.'

His mother put her hands together in her lap. 'But a boy, darling. Don't you see how marvellous that is?'

I wondered if Margaret had heard precisely what Kit had said, or if she had misinterpreted it, or slipped in our absence into senility. Kit had clearly had the same thought.

'He's not mine, Ma, if that's what you're thinking,' he said.

'Put another log on the fire, would you, darling.'

He gazed at the grate where the wood lay red but tired, then pulled himself from his seat and dutifully placed a couple of logs on top. Margaret sat back; the blue of her eyes, faded with the years, seemed to have temporarily deepened.

'I realise that,' she said. 'I may be old, but I'm not yet silly. That's what you were thinking, isn't it?'

'No, no. Not at all,' Kit said.

'You were. I can see that. Both of you. You should know better, Josie. I just meant that Alice was one of us. Family. Any child of hers is family. She was almost a cousin after all, Kit.'

'Hardly a cousin, Ma. You'd have to go back generations to find a connection. I'm probably related to Isobel on that basis.'

'I doubt that very much.' Margaret's tone was cold.

Like Kit, I had often found myself trying to make excuses for Margaret but there was no way round the fact that she was a snob. The moment she had identified Isobel as not just outside her social circle but far beyond its parameters, she had done little to hide her disappointment in Kit's choice of a second wife. I too was regarded as being from a lower station, of course, but years of familiarity and a hint of subservience on my part had allowed her to make an exception.

'I loved Alice very much,' Margaret said. 'I loved her as my own. And any child of hers is welcome to me. She lives on.'

'She's gone, Ma.'

'But not forgotten. Not by me.'

I wished that Isobel would come downstairs, awkward as that might be. I wished she would come and stop Margaret. But stop her from what? I wasn't sure.

'We will need to welcome this boy,' Margaret went on. 'Does he look like her? Can you see her in him, darling?'

I watched Kit hesitate and I knew why. Neither of us had yet admitted to each other that even in that brief meeting in the Turkish café, a part of us had known at once that the boy might be honest. Luke did have a look of Alice, and rather more than a look in his distinctive, narrow eyes, once you knew the truth.

I had heard Isobel ask Kit the same question just a week or so before. It was the day after the solicitor had rung, and Isobel had called in to the gallery, ostensibly to borrow a small statue to include in a portrait. She had been careful with her words and warm in her general support, but I could see her confusion. And then, suddenly, she could no longer restrain herself.

'Couldn't you tell?' she had said to Kit, in front of me. 'Didn't this boy look like Alice? Surely you guessed the truth?' And Kit had lied. He said he hadn't known, couldn't have known. His words were convincing but I could see that Isobel didn't believe him and that she was angry.

'You only ever see what you want to see,' she said to him.

I was grateful that she hadn't asked me.

But later that same evening she had come to my flat, knocking quietly on my door and creeping in, an air of defeat hanging about her. She was wearing her pyjamas and a dressing gown, childlike and unhappy. I offered her a glass of warm malted milk which she drank as I sipped my whisky, and then, after a few complaints about Kit's coldness, his inability to talk about how he felt, and so on, she said a strange thing.

'Sometimes,' she said, 'when I come to the gallery and watch you and Kit handling those weird things, and everything you do, all that work with graves and tombs and stuff that belongs to the dead, it makes me think of her. And how you love your ghost. And then I think sometimes that you do what you do, maybe, to try and find her, to see if you can wake her up.'

It took me a moment to realise what she was saying, that she was talking about Alice. It was a curious idea she had got into her head and I found it disturbing.

'You're upset, Isobel,' I said. 'And you're having a baby. I'm not underestimating what has happened, but at the same time we must try not to let this get out of proportion.'

She laughed. 'Ever sensible, Josie. Well, tell me what would be in proportion? You can't get us out of this one so easily. You can't exactly sort this out.'

Sitting with Margaret, by her fire, I felt Isobel's absence now as an exclusion, as if the past were pushing her further and further away from us. Kit was staring into his cooling tea but at last he answered his mother's question.

'There is a resemblance to Alice, yes,' he said. 'And you thought so too, Josie, I think.'

'Yes,' I said, 'I thought I could see it.'

Margaret's face softened. It seemed almost sentimental.

'But we saw him so briefly,' Kit said, as if his answer were a betrayal. 'And really, at that moment I wasn't thinking . . .'

I didn't believe him. A part of his mind, like mine, must have been poring over the boy's features, looking for the echoes of his dead wife. But another part had not wanted to see what I had seen. Isobel had been right. He hadn't wanted to see Alice in the boy's face. But as I listened to him, I remembered it clearly, and for a brief, confusing moment I understood Margaret's joy.

I lay in the long bath, adding hot water as it cooled. I could see the sky through the window and watched the clouds grow dull as they lost the illumination of the April sun. I could feel alien here, in Margaret's house, even though, through circumstance and tragedy, we had become odd friends. Like Isobel, I would always be an outsider. I have wondered from time to time if she was foolish to marry Kit, if the cultural gap between them was too wide. Jack Whaley had certainly thought so. 'If my daughter marries that toff,' he had said when the two of them had got together, 'I'll never speak to you again for introducing them. It's bad enough that they got you, that lot, Josie.' But Isobel had married Kit, and I had known in any case that Jack was not entirely serious. But there was a point to his teasing.

I narrowed my eyes as I looked down at my body in the water. My limbs and torso felt separate from me as I lay there, like a bit of statuary in the gallery, only darker hued and with pubic hair of course. I liked my body still. It wasn't as firm as once it had been but it was still a fine shape, and pleasing in a good light. It could still give pleasure. We're all the same, silent and naked, I thought, and yet we still persist with our systems and castes to cover that fact. I reached for the large green bath sheet which hung on an old-fashioned towel rail. The bath was free-standing and deep, and it was quite a stretch to pull out the plug. As the water gurgled out and I wrapped the towel around me, I wondered how Isobel would take to Margaret's unexpected rapture over Alice's son.

I pulled a dress from the cupboard where I had hung it earlier. It was a wraparound, in fine maroon wool, which I had worn only twice since buying it with a rush of pleasure just before last Christmas. I would look smart for dinner, I decided. I have always used clothes to overcome any lurking nervousness. To be smartly turned out is the best plan of action, I find, when faced with uncertainty. Dinner with Margaret always had a certain formality, so the effort I had made would please her. The local vicar and his wife were coming, which was just as well in the circumstances. It would give us a respite, for I doubted that Margaret would want to talk about Alice's child in front of them. As I put on my make-up, I looked out of the window at the long expanse of lawn and flower borders that stretched out behind the house, a view interrupted by an avenue of trees, symmetrically planted at least fifty years previously by Margaret's father. They were still almost bare, of course, in this season but lopped to a matching perfection, their tiny unfurled buds stretching like fingertips at their extremities.

Kit and his mother, her arm resting in his, came into view by the side of the left-hand border. It was almost dark but the lights from the terrace allowed them to continue their inspection, and I watched as they moved at a very slow pace along the well-kept lawn, both wearing rubber boots. Margaret's were the old-fashioned kind, wrapover galoshes that she no doubt found easier to slip on these days. She was pointing, filling him in on her latest planting, soothing their excitement with nature and the seasonal rhythms.

'Josie.' Isobel knocked, then opened my bedroom door as I called her in. She walked across the room towards me smiling, and admiring my dress, anxious to talk, I could tell, but reluctant to start the conversation.

'So what did she say?' Isobel finally asked.

'Haven't you spoken to Kit?' I said.

'Briefly. But Margaret wanted a turn in the garden.'

'Yes, I saw.'

'He said it was strange, that she was strange. She was thrilled, he said. It was as if she already knew, not that she did. It was as if the baby was his.'

'He's not a baby,' I said. 'He's a grown man. Well, almost.'

'Well, Margaret is welcoming him into the family before we even know anything about him.' Her words spilled out. She sounded harsh, almost choked. 'That's what Kit said. He sounded worried. What did you think?'

'She was very close to Alice . . .' I said. I found myself faltering. I rarely used Alice's name in front of Isobel and it took both of us by surprise. 'I suppose she feels some obligation. I suppose we all do.'

Isobel shivered. She seemed to feel the room was cold, though the old radiator was scalding to the touch.

'I feel like I want to just get in the car and drive home,' she said. 'But I can't.'

I put my arm around her. 'The thing is,' I said, 'Margaret thought of her as a sort of daughter, I think. And I know how hard that is for you. It would be for anyone.'

She hugged me briefly then pulled away.

'I'll get through it,' she said. 'We'll get through it. We'll get through dinner and we'll get through it all and we'll come out the other side of this, won't we, Josie?'

I nodded. I wanted to reassure her. I wanted to help her, for Jack's sake as well as hers, and for Kit's. But this news had put something between us. She was harder to reach.

A week later, Isobel lost her baby. Kit rang through to the gallery, crying as he told me. He was in Oxfordshire at a sale and was on his way back to the hospital. I was to ring Jack, and go to the hospital myself, if I didn't mind. As I put the phone down, I had a sense of *déjà vu*. This had happened the last time, Jack and I at the hospital, waiting for Kit, the past repeating itself. But now the future contained a more robust new life, and one that poor Isobel might find ever harder to welcome.

Nine

For the three years that Anne Wearing had required cover for her affair, she liked to put about the story that Toby was a doting godfather, and that she was obliged to bring Alice to see him frequently. But in truth, it was me, of course, rather than Toby who spent most time with the little girl. It was true that Toby was very fond of Alice, and he was amused by her, but his patience with small children was limited and it suited him to encourage my affection for his pretty god-daughter. It brought him pleasure, too, I knew, as if my love for Alice confirmed him as a connoisseur. He saw it as a kind of appreciation of the many objects of beauty and desire with which he surrounded himself.

It was during the first months of Anne's arrangement that we were confronted with the news of Ilya's disappearance and probable death. Toby came round to my flat late one Sunday afternoon to tell me. He had brought a bottle of brandy, and he stayed in my bed, drunk, for two days, refusing food and my gift of Ilya's Tawaret, which rested now on my little dressing table. On the third day he emerged, and from then on he appeared to

126

make a quick and surprising recovery, with a succession of young men. I thought at first that his behaviour was unfeeling, then after a while I decided, generous as usual on Toby's behalf, that the ever-increasing promiscuity he appeared to pursue was just an expression of his grief. But as time went on, there were an increasing number of aspects of Toby's life which it became hard to justify and there were occasions when I would remember what Ilya had said about Toby, about his selfishness, that last afternoon, before the two of them had left for Dover.

The burst of sexual energy that Ilya's demise had precipitated seemed to engender a renewed enthusiasm for business. Right from the start of his dealings, even back in Camden Passage, Toby had seemed to have the Midas touch. The sums of money that changed hands for certain ancient fragments, however beautiful, were initially beyond my comprehension. There was a fevered and clandestine atmosphere around some of the exchanges that took place. Toby did the deals himself, keeping me out of anything shady, but even those with which I helped were sometimes borderline in their legality, and I felt bound to point it out to him.

'For God's sake, don't fuss, Josie,' was all he would say. 'Don't fuss. It's accepted. Everyone does it.'

He had a point. The trade was unclear and unregulated, and though the majority of Toby's deals were legitimate, the ambiguity was part of its appeal. He had explained to me once that most of our Greek objects had most likely been stolen by the Italian Mafia from major sites in Italy, then legitimised by reputable dealers who knowingly sold them back and forth to each other, laundering the stock, as it were. I was never sure how much to believe, but it made me anxious, though I managed, most of the time, to justify what Toby was up to. After all, he himself hadn't stolen anything. He paid for the objects. He might suspect that their provenance was murky but he couldn't prove it even had he wanted to. And over the years, he did make adjustments, if mostly cosmetic. Once we moved into the smart new premises, the seedy men with paper parcels who had come to the flat in Chelsea were banned, but Toby would still disappear in taxis to meet them in Bayswater cafés, buying the occasional piece, chasing the irresistible thrill of a dubious purchase.

Toby could make money but he had no idea how to hang on to it. I was more canny, and had backed us up with banks and accountants, but much of the time, like Toby, I behaved as if we were at some permanent party. We were younger, of course, with that sweet energy which can push through all but the worst effects of excess. But even early on I was conscious that things could get out of hand, especially for Toby.

We loved to go out drinking together, to go to parties given by the smart friends and clients we had by now acquired. Toby had always used drugs, and I liked a line or two of cocaine myself. But as the years passed I knew that whereas I usually knew my limit, Toby did not, and that although he liked to drink as much as I did, it was drugs and the chase for them, and for boys, that really seduced him. A bottle of alcohol drunk politely in a restaurant was no fun in comparison with a dark staircase or an alley where a deal could be done, often with men who might throw in extra for a blow job. Not that Toby needed either discount or incentive.

I found it difficult sometimes to tell where the business and the drugs diverged. Sometimes Toby would come back from a trip to the Edgware Road with a brown paper parcel under his arm. It might contain a Canopic jar, or a papyrus fragment but in his pocket there would also be a piece of white paper folded like origami and stuffed with cocaine, or a handful of pills, or a Thai stick to help the come-down from whatever had put him up in the first place.

I was never censorious, despite my anxiety that his use was heavier than it should be. I knew that it would be hopeless to try to control Toby, and, in truth, we were having too much fun. I wasn't averse to the chemical buzz, or the languid smoke which would set us both off into hysterical laughter. I couldn't imagine our life without these things. Sometimes, in the late afternoon as we sat in the old-fashioned splendour of the side room of the gallery, the little gas fire burning as Toby sobered up after a long client lunch, we would decide to start our evening early. Toby would produce his cocaine, which he would cut up with a razor blade on the back of one of the thick and learned periodicals to which I was now a keen subscriber. As five o'clock approached, we would open a bottle of wine and within minutes we were at our own fiesta, sometimes forgetting to close up for the day. The arrival of a late customer became part of the game, testing our ability to maintain equilibrium and, of course, Toby's powers of seduction.

There were other men in my life during those years, straight men who wanted me. But I never escaped from Toby. There was Richard, with whom I fell passionately in love, but only because I knew that he wasn't serious. He was a man like Toby's brother Christopher, in search of a woman who could keep him, and though Toby was getting rich at the gallery and was not ungenerous, I was still only the paid help.

There was a more likely candidate for the long term, Bob Ridley, a solid lawyer whom I saw for a couple of years, on and off, and who loved me and wanted to marry me and rescue me from Toby. I should, I think now, have said yes, but Toby sneered at him, and when I pictured myself lying in bed with Bob, decade after decade, with the little desire I felt for him having long ebbed away, I said no. Sometimes I would lie awake at night, muddle-headed from an evening out, and I would weep. It was my fate, I thought, to be pursued by good men who wished to save me from myself, but to whom I could not give what I wasted on Toby.

The days and nights that Alice came to stay with me were a steadying influence, but after the visits stopped, it was two or three years before I saw her regularly again. There was an occasional trip to London, but only for a musical, or to Hamley's toyshop before Christmas. Anne and Alice would stop off briefly at the gallery, at Alice's special request, and Anne would look bored and impatient. She could also be spiteful and her bile from time to time was aimed in my direction. I began to understand that Alice's affection for me, which had been so useful during the course of Anne's romance, was now a source of jealousy, especially in the wake of her miscarriage.

One night, or rather early morning, when Toby and I were still wide awake, at the end of a party, we decided to walk, in the absence of taxis, through the empty streets back to the flat in Victoria. Toby, in a way that he had when faced with a vacuum, began to make mischief, or at least that was how I chose to interpret the conversation, as the first streak of a summer dawn began to spread over London.

'Anne's definitely becoming a lush,' Toby said. He had been talking about a weekend he had just spent in the country.

'We all drink too much, though, Toby, don't we?' I said. I knew that Toby was right, but despite her brusqueness with me, I felt sorry for Anne who was clearly unhappy.

'You're too nice, Josie,' he said. 'Too nice for your own good. She's not nice about you.'

I wished now we had found a taxi. I suspected that something unpleasant was coming.

'She thinks you're creepy,' Toby said, and laughed. 'She's such a bitch.' He began to imitate Anne's affected upper-class drawl: '"All that creepy stuff, she likes, Toby, it's so unhealthy."' Toby sounded horribly like her to my ears. 'That's what she said, Josie,' he went on in his normal voice. 'She meant the gallery. That you're so clever about all the stock.' Toby caught his foot on the edge of the pavement and almost fell over, grabbing on to me for support. 'I defended you, darling. "Unhealthy," I said to her, "that's rich, Anne. The very air you breathe is unhealthy." That put her right. She thinks Alice is over-imaginative; she's worried about her and says it's all your fault. Too imaginative. What's wrong with that? She's a silly cow.'

I remember stopping in the middle of the street. I felt as if someone had slapped me. It seemed so unfair of Anne. I had been trying to help her out, after all. And I loved Alice. And now, this . . . accusation. Toby squeezed my arm but it was too late for comfort.

'You mustn't take it seriously, old girl. Anne's a lush. But let's indulge her. We'll have to find another way of keeping our eye on Alice.'

Over the years that followed I had cause from time to time to think about what Anne had said to Toby. I would veer between anger and feeling anxious. Of course Alice was imaginative, I would tell myself, but not overly so, what-ever that might mean. Toby was right, Anne was a stupid woman. But what he had told me brought back Alice's voices and I tried not to think that they might once more have made themselves heard.

I had thought they were long gone. Alice never men-tioned them in the little cards and stories she continued to send me about the animals in the gallery. I was surprised that Anne allowed our correspondence to continue. But writing, it seemed, was permissible. According to Toby, it was the fact that I had permitted Alice to touch the objects in the gallery to which Anne had taken exception, as if they were some kind of contagious fetish. Her logic was ridiculous, but still, I was relieved that I hadn't been banished altogether from Alice's colourful world. It was a world I knew I cherished because it took me away from the messy reality of my own.

Ten

It was the sale, at last, of the fine Egyptian head of which Kit was so fond, that had enabled us to expand. It was fortuitous that the floor above the Belgrave Square gallery had unexpectedly become vacant and we had snapped up the lease. We had talked of moving to larger premises in nearby Motcomb Street, earlier in the year, but the thought of so complete a change had faded as it became clear to Kit, indeed to all of us, that there were other more complex adjustments to life that we now had to make.

The business was doing well. Despite the events and upheaval in his private life, Kit had not lost any of his concentration. I had done a lot to set up the sale of the head, but it was undoubtedly Kit who closed the deal with his tight, military efficiency. There had been initial negotiations, then the secondary negotiations, the final decisions, the clearing of the provenance, the export licence, and a plethora of further bureaucracy to facilitate. Yet when the time came, we were both sad to say farewell to an object of such beauty. It was often that way. She had, after all, been with us for a couple of years. That was how long it could take to move a very good piece. That was how long we sometimes had to wait, for the right time, the correct legal procedures to be adhered to, and, of course, the right price, to allow us to move such treasures on.

Kit had been hankering to expand and change the business for some time; wanting to feel that, finally, he was emerging from behind Toby's shadow. There were still many people in the world of ancient objects who remembered his uncle with affection, but also with suspicion. In my weaker moments I worried that their doubts might extend to me, though most of them were well aware that it was I who had kept Toby straight enough to avoid major trouble.

All the same, I had wondered during the last month or so if Kit might like me to retire as part of the new changes he was making. But when I dropped a hint to this effect, I was met with a string of protests. I was invaluable to him, he said. He couldn't imagine working so closely with anyone else. I was as good as family and how could I think of such a thing at such a time?

I liked to regard myself as self-sufficient. I was a single woman who had made her own way, but still Kit's arguments were a reassurance that I secretly needed. The truth was that I enjoyed being 'family', and I would always prefer this odd situation in which I had ended up to finding myself outside it. It was good to feel that Kit seemed to need me again these days, now that our 'family', despite Isobel's miscarriage, appeared to be growing.

I had remained downstairs in the same office in the newly expanded gallery, while Kit had moved upstairs to a bigger one. I was happy to stay where I had always been, and it wasn't as if I was alone. I was now sharing the space with young Luke Tyler, as I had been for the last three months. He was sitting at Kit's old desk in the corner, in front of a large computer, his dark head bent towards the screen, his narrow body too long, somehow, for the chair that swivelled to and fro as he concentrated.

Watching him, I was, as usual, astonished that he could have become so much a part of our lives so quickly. I knew that I watched Luke at work more frequently than I should, trying to come to terms with an unexpected delight in his existence. He seemed not to notice. He displayed, I thought, an unusual concentration for someone so young, or perhaps it was simply that I didn't know anyone else of his age, and my own youth had been so much less focused.

The job Kit had offered him was intended as temporary. He had suggested that Luke might help us out during the move, but now it was almost autumn, and there seemed to be no wish on either side for him to leave. Luke had taken easily to the work we gave him. He had skills we could only dream of, able to track provenances and bills of sale through online archives we didn't know existed. He was a godsend, in more ways than one.

It seemed a shame to disturb him, but it was eleven o'clock and I was a creature of habit. It was time for me to make coffee and he looked over as I got up, and nodded.

'Yes,' he said, anticipating what I would say. 'Yes, please.'

'The usual?' I said.

He nodded again.

'I brought you something,' he said. He delved in a ruck-sack beside the desk and pulled out a packet of expensive chocolate biscuits. Frank, the dog, who was still housed in my office, scrambled sleepily out of his basket and waddled towards him.

'That's kind of you, Luke,' I said, taking the packet from him, 'and they're the ones I really like.'

'Not kind, just a thank-you,' he said, holding my wrist for a moment as I took them. 'Really, Josie,' he said. 'You've been brilliant.'

He was given to compliments. They were a sort of payback, I thought, for whatever had been offered to him, but at the same time they never felt insincere. He had charm, but it was a charm that appeared to be unself-conscious.

It was hard now to recall the awful tension of our first meeting in the Turkish café, or even the nervousness we had felt when we met Luke for the second time, soon after the confirmation of his adoption. It had been on a Saturday. Kit had decided that we should meet in a restaurant in Bayswater, a quiet place, yet still public. He hadn't wanted Luke to come round to the house, or not yet. Isobel didn't come with us. It was not her place, she said, and I thought she was right, though it was obvious, too, that she didn't much want to meet the young man. Instead, she made sympathetic noises of support for Kit and said that, if all went well, then perhaps next time Luke should come to Millbury Street for tea.

It was May, and the trees were in blossom as we walked

through the back streets of Bayswater, an area of hidden charm, not entirely gentrified, laburnum cascading down walls that were in need of shoring up. As we reached the main road, Luke was waiting for us. The doorway of the restaurant cast a half-shadow across his face. He spun round as we approached, and I heard myself actually draw in my breath, his sudden turn so sharply recalled the quick, vivacious movements of Alice. He smiled when he saw us, something he hadn't had much cause to do at our first meeting, I thought. It was a good smile and I found myself returning it. I looked round at Kit to see what effect it had on him. His features appeared to have softened, but he looked cautious.

Luke still seemed young for his age. Standing outside, leaning against the window, he could have passed for under twenty. But as we took our seats in the restaurant I was struck by a more mature sense of ease. I had thought him an unsophisticated boy, almost rough around the edges, and after the solicitor had confirmed his story I had begun to imagine how we would take him in hand, smooth him over, educate him, and so on. But the striking young man in front of us looked as if he would require little of that.

He was wearing jeans, but with a light jacket and a white soft-collared shirt. There were expensive-looking sunglasses peeping from a top pocket. It was quite a different image from the one he had previously presented, and it crossed my mind, briefly, that he knew the effect of both. In the weeks since we had first met Luke, I had thought about him a great deal. I had been trying to remember his features and whether he resembled Alice. In my imagination he had assumed her face, her softness even, and so I found myself surprised that though he did indeed have a look of her, certainly her eyes and dark colouring, in the flesh there was a sharp masculine edge. His face was boyish but worldly.

We knew little about him. He had told Kit that he had been adopted in Scotland, but we had already learnt that from his papers. He had grown up in Edinburgh, he said, but he had been living in London for more than three years now, that he was just completing a diploma in Business Studies at a private college in Acton. I supposed that was why any accent was all but eradicated, though I guessed, too, that he had been privately educated. As we took our seats in the light and open room, and a waiter brought our menus, I had a chance to observe him more closely.

He made a good first impression. His manners were excellent. Over the years, I had grown to be more conscious of such things, or rather, I could be worried by their absence. Luke was very attentive to us both. He was guarded, certainly, but polite, and he straight away thanked Kit for inviting him to lunch.

'Not at all,' said Kit. 'Josie and I were keen to meet you again. And we wanted to say, I think I speak for you too, Josie?' he turned to me, and I nodded, 'that we are very sorry that we probably caused offence the last time. It was the shock, the uncertainty . . . We had to be sure . . .'

There was a silence as we waited for him to reply.

'That's okay,' he said. 'It must have been a shock, finding out. And I did think about it before. Me barging into your life. I did think, maybe, I shouldn't have.'

'No, no,' said Kit. 'You were absolutely entitled to do so.'

'After all,' Luke went on, 'I'm nothing to do with you, Mr Haddeley, I know that. I'm sorry if it's upset things. I just wanted to know more . . .' He stopped and looked as if he thought he had said too much and as if he wanted to feel his way carefully.

'More about your mother?' I offered. He nodded and looked down at the table, fingering the menu. He seemed suddenly an insecure boy again.

'Yes,' Kit said. 'Well, that's understandable. Shall we order? Get it out of the way?' Kit looked uncomfortable and I tried to catch his eye but he avoided me.

'What would you like to eat, Luke?' I heard myself saying, as if he were a child. Then I tried to cover myself, afraid he might feel patronised. 'We'll ask the waiter about the specials.'

To know almost nothing about someone can be a discomfiting experience. We are so used to the idea of provenance, of background, to help us feel our way with strangers. Who do they know? we ask ourselves. What do they do? Where do they come from? These things are important to us, I thought, as we sat at the table, partly shielded from the other diners by a light modern screen, as important as the pieces of paper that mapped the journeys of the gallery's treasures. We knew next to nothing of Luke Tyler's provenance, but trying to discover it felt like an imposition.

'I would like to know more about my mother,' he said. 'But I suppose you want to know more about me?' He put down his menu and smiled. There was just enough nervousness on his part to keep a balance of reassurance between us. I was to learn quickly how attuned Luke could be to the nuances of atmosphere, how he could sense to an unusual degree what other people experienced.

'Only what you want to tell us, Luke,' Kit said. 'We don't want to pry.' He paused, and then said, 'My wife, Isobel, wants you to know that she would very much like to meet you. She's sorry not to be here. It's just that she's pregnant and it's early days. She's not feeling too bright.'

I thought I saw a flicker of something in Luke's eyes, a reaction I couldn't identify.

'I'm sorry she's not well,' he said. 'Isobel? She's called Isobel?'

'Yes.'

'Is that a Scots name?' he said. 'I know a couple of Isobels back home. My mum was a Scot – my adopted mother, that is. My dad is English though.'

Kit looked pleased at this bit of information.

'My wife's American, in fact,' Kit said. 'She's an artist.' He sounded proud of Isobel. 'But her father's British.'

'Jack's father was a Scot, I believe,' I said. 'That's Isobel's father, Jack Whaley.' I had forgotten this bit of biography. It had come rolling back from somewhere, another piece of provenance.

'She thought it best if we came along without her today,' Kit said. 'But you must come to the house, very soon.'

'I'd like to, Mr Haddeley, thank you.'

'Oh, Kit, for goodness' sake,' Kit said, smiling now. 'Please call me Kit.'

'All right, Kit, thank you,' said Luke. The ice seemed to have been broken. We were still nervous but there was an unspoken agreement that we could proceed.

Luke had ordered a hamburger but half of it lay uneaten on his plate as we plied him with questions. He was in his final term of a business studies course, he said. He was about to sit his exams. He'd not gone to a proper university because he had not been much good at school.

'Did you not like your school?' I asked.

'They didn't like me much,' he said. He looked sheepish, then laughed. 'They expelled me. They said I gave them a bad name. It was quite a posh school.'

'Oh,' I said. So I had been right. But I didn't like to ask why he had had to leave, and he didn't offer an explanation.

'What about college?' Kit said. 'Business studies. How's that been?'

Luke nodded. 'Good,' he said. 'It's been good. A lot of computer stuff, IT, you know. I like that.'

It explained, I thought, the un-student-like appearance that Luke now presented. Business studies was different from English or media studies, the sort of things my friends' children did at university. And yet, my first memory of Luke in the Turkish café would not go away. That boy had looked different, more vulnerable. Today's image was tougher, more calculated. And yet it was natural that a young man should try on different guises to see what felt right.

He had been adopted through an agency in Glasgow, he told us. He hadn't thought much about his birth, or not till recently, and he'd always assumed that his real mother must be Scots. His adopted mother had died of an aneurysm, eighteen months previously, and that was when he'd decided to look for his birth mother. He revealed these few facts to us, speaking slowly, in a low voice. He was almost matter of fact and he spoke without a hint of self-pity, giving nothing away. He had said little about his family life, just given the one indication that school had not gone well. There was clearly more to tell, I thought, but no doubt it would come in his own time.

'I did nothing about it to start with,' he was saying. 'I thought it over for a bit, well for nearly a year, and then I thought, well why not, it's worth just seeing, so I wrote to the agency in Glasgow.'

'Glasgow?' I heard myself say, though I knew already that that was where the adoption had taken place. 'Why Glasgow?'

I looked at Kit who shrugged. 'It's on the papers,' he said. 'A Catholic agency, I believe.'

'My mum and dad were Catholics,' Luke explained. 'Well, I suppose my dad still is.'

Alice had been staying in Scotland that summer, with her father, so I supposed that they must have kept her there for the duration of her pregnancy. But still, I couldn't fathom Glasgow. Perhaps because no one would think to find her there.

'I got hold of the name and found the address,' Luke said, 'and I came round to your house about six months ago, just to look really, and that was when I was told she was dead,' he said, 'your wife.' He turned to Kit. 'I asked someone in the street if they knew her and they said I'd got the wrong name, that Alice Haddeley was dead. So I checked.'

How sad for the boy, I thought. He had dared to look back into the past, only to discover that Alice was dead after all. It was a loss, but he couldn't know how much of one. And yet, when I thought of Alice now, it was hard not to think of what she had concealed, not just from me, but from Kit, her husband. The knowledge breathed some substance into what had often puzzled me: that as an adult she could be so generous and yet so secretive and febrile, so different from the child I had known.

Luke's posture had sunk a little into his chair.

'And maybe I should have left it there,' he said. 'Maybe I had no business bothering you again. But . . . And I'm sorry about the letters. I don't know what made me put her name on them. It was stupid. It was like I wanted her to be there. But I knew she wasn't.'

He really did seem like a child now, one in need of direction. We were back where we started, I thought.

'It's all right, Luke,' I said. 'Finish up your lunch. You need to eat. There's plenty of time to talk.' He looked at me with what seemed to be a sort of conspiratorial gratitude. There was a reticence about him that endeared him to me, combined, I was to register over the months to come, with a peculiar ability to make one feel chosen, selected for a special understanding.

Not long afterwards, he came round to Millbury Street for tea, invited by Kit. It was a warm afternoon and we sat in the garden. I could see that Luke was impressed by its size. Isobel was polite, if a little cool towards him, though she had dressed carefully, I noticed, in a very pretty, light grey wool dress, with a grey-and-white-striped trim. I hadn't seen it before but it was loosely cut and I supposed she had bought it for her pregnancy.

It was once again clear that Luke did not want to discuss his family or his background much, beyond divulging basic information, a point of view with which I could sympathise because I too had come to London to make a fresh start. Isobel, I could see, found it perplexing. She should know better, I thought, than to keep asking him questions. She was a foreigner after all, and from a country where background wasn't supposed to count. She should surely respect Luke's right to be reticent, to be out of step even, though when I tried to work out in what way he felt out of step I found it hard to quantify.

Isobel's presence seemed to inhibit him, and he asked nothing more about Alice. He was showing discretion, I told myself. It was Kit who eventually brought the subject up.

'Your mother never actually lived here,' he explained. 'Or not when we were married. Not with me. I didn't have the house then, it was my uncle's. My uncle was her godfather.'

'So you were related to her?' Luke said. 'I didn't know that. So you're related to me?' He looked excited.

'No,' Kit said. 'No, he was just her godfather. But our families knew each other, yes. And she used to come and stay here, didn't she, Josie?'

'Oh yes,' I said. It felt odd to talk about Alice in this way, about her being here, in the house. 'She loved it. She used to come and stay with us from time to time, when she was older and her mother was unwell.'

'So you lived here too?' he asked, looking puzzled, as well he might.

'Yes,' I said. 'I've lived here a long time. I was a great friend of Kit's uncle, Toby Haddeley. It was like a flat share, you know. Friends sharing.'

'That's nice,' he said. He sounded unsure. 'And my mother stayed with you?'

'Oh yes. We had great fun. Toby was terrific fun to be with.'

As I spoke, I sensed Isobel's eyes watching me. She too was absorbing the idea that Alice was part of the house's history.

After tea, Kit insisted on showing Luke around the house. Isobel and I opted to stay outside, sitting in the late-afternoon sun, until my need to be doing things caught up with me. I collected up the cups and plates, carrying them off into the kitchen, and after a moment or two, Isobel followed me inside.

'Do you think that's wise of Kit?' she said. 'Showing him round?'

'Why not?'

'Josie, we know nothing about him.'

'Yes we do. We know his name and who he is and who his mother was and where he comes from. And . . . '

'And . . .?'

'He seems a very nice boy.' I had been charmed again by Luke that afternoon. He seemed to me to carry some echo of Alice's curious allure.

She shook her head. 'I don't want to be the killjoy here but . . .'

'What do you think he's going to do? Come back in the night and rob us?'

'Maybe. He looked pretty impressed.'

'But you're not,' I said.

'I just think we need to know more about him. Kit's rushing things, don't you think?' She looked at me, her blue eyes implying that Kit was not alone.

'He is who he says he is,' I said. 'That's good enough for me.' My firmness of tone surprised me, but it seemed only natural that Isobel would resist the idea of Luke, and I thought it best to be straightforward in this matter from the start. I liked the boy. I wanted to help him and so did Kit.

'We'll all have to get used to it, Isobel,' I said. 'You're right to be cautious but facts are facts. We need to find a way to accommodate him. I grant you, it might not be easy.'

In the weeks that followed, Luke began to be a regular visitor to Millbury Street, calling in for coffee, coming over for supper from his bedsit which wasn't too far away. The more we met him the more we liked him, or at least Kit and I did. It was hard to read Isobel, who was always welcoming and polite but seemed, for the most part, to resist the flattering overtures that Luke made. We gleaned some more small bits of information. He didn't much like his father, but he had been fond of his mother. It had been a middle-class Catholic family, comfortably off but not wealthy. He mentioned, briefly, a younger brother but he seemed as reluctant to talk about him as he was about anything else.

He seemed happy enough, though I guessed he had been glad to leave home. He had made good friends in London, he said, and he certainly seemed familiar with the sort of bars and clubs where I knew that young people went to have a good time. He didn't seem short of money, which surprised me, given his age, but I presumed his father kept him well supplied, guilty perhaps that things were not better between them.

And so it seemed only natural that when his term finished, Luke should come and help us out at the gallery. But after just a very short time, the pleasure that Kit and I took in having him there was overcast by the sadness of Isobel losing her baby. Nothing was ever said, but I suspected that we had all asked ourselves if the shock of Luke's appearance had been a contributory factor. She was brave and stoic in public, but privately she seemed even more distressed than on the previous occasions and not long afterwards, when we sat together after supper one evening, she said to me, 'I feel even more of a failure this time, Josie. It's even harder to lose my own child now that Alice's child is here.'

༄

This fact of Alice's child had its own effect on each of us. For poor Isobel, Luke was a constant reminder of her own inability to carry a baby to term. For Kit, I presumed, Luke was the reincarnation of someone he had loved and lost. For me, he was . . . well, for me, too, he was a reminder of Alice, but also an echo of a past I had put behind me, a past I hadn't cared to look at too closely and that now pushed itself forward in those moments of intense recognition that Luke could inspire.

He had a way, for example, of walking, his shoulders hunched down a little. It was exactly as Alice had walked. I hadn't noticed how pronounced it was, at first, but one lunchtime, soon after he came to work at the gallery I found myself following him, quite by chance, into St James's Park, where I was going to sit and eat a sandwich. The weather was warm, or at least it was when the sun emerged from behind the partial cloud. It was mid-May and the trees were clean and fresh and snowy with blossom. As he swung left through the gate, I could see him walking down the path, as if he were heading for Trafalgar Square. It was then that I noticed it, the same slight sway as he held his shoulders a little forward. It was Alice's walk.

I increased my stride, not wanting to let him out of my sight, and by this time I was directly behind him with no other pedestrians between us. I was about to call to him, but I wanted to watch him for just a bit longer, to see if this physical inheritance was real or if it was something I merely wanted to find in him. But suddenly he turned to his right and stepped on to the grass and he raised his hand as if in greeting.

My gaze followed his gesture and it was then that I saw the woman sitting on a bench, her bag by her side, her hand acting as a shield against the sun as she watched Luke striding towards her. She must have been in her early forties, her light brown hair cut to her chin and highlighted with fair streaks. She was wearing a tailored blazer over pale blue jeans and over her shoulder was an expensive dark red shawl, cashmere, I was almost certain. She stood up as he approached and he kissed her on the cheek, although to my surprise he put his hand on the small of her back in a way that suggested something intimate. It was a gesture of possession, and the woman seemed to give way to it.

As I watched them, I became aware that standing still, as I was, in the middle of the path, I might attract their attention. Luke had his back to me but the woman was looking in my direction. Her interest, however, seemed to be entirely in Luke. It was impossible to decide what to do. If I went forward, he might turn and see me on the path. He might think I had been following him. If I retraced my steps towards the gate, and he saw, he would know that I had seen him and turned back. I decided to do as he had done and stride across the grass, but in the opposite direction, towards Birdcage Walk. If he were to see me there he might assume that I was, after all, just walking in the park at lunchtime on a pleasant day.

As I wove my way through the Victoria back streets I thought again about what I had seen. I was curious as to who the woman was, of course, though it was none of my business. Luke had been living in London for three years or so, we knew that. But it was difficult to get any further sense from him of how his life had been. He was a student, but, as he said, and I had observed, business students are a different breed. He had lived in various places, Bethnal Green, Spitalfields at one point, and about six months previously he had taken a bedsit quite near to us in Queensway.

Later that afternoon, back in the office, having eaten my sandwich and drunk a glass of wine as was my habit, I was able to make more sense of what I had seen. The woman was perhaps a tutor, I thought, or even a relative, though it was odd that he had not mentioned her if that were the case. He had told us he had no relatives outside Scotland, or none that he was aware of. And yet there had been something about his hand on her back. But then again, I might be reading too much into the gesture. Young men could take liberties with older women that they might not take with someone closer to their age, and such liberties were merely to be interpreted as affectionate flirtation. After all, Luke had once or twice put his arm around my waist as we walked, a gesture that had surprised but pleased me.

It seemed to me, sitting in the office after lunch, that I had simply been surprised to see Luke, now back at his desk in good time, out on his own. I was behaving as if I had taken ownership of him in some way, and he had allowed me to do so. I had almost believed him to have no existence outside the coterie of Millbury Street and the gallery, places where we had assumed that he belonged, because of Alice. But that was nonsense. He had another life, he was twenty-four years old and was entitled to his privacy. I would say nothing about what I had seen. I didn't want him to think I was spying.

At about four thirty, he looked up at me from his computer, and smiled, raising his eyebrows in expectation. He was particularly fond of the fruit cake that I sometimes produced at teatime. Frank, too, had raised himself from sleep and was now scratching his ear in preparation.

'I'll make tea,' I said.

'Yes,' Luke said. 'Yes, yes. And I've found something interesting, Josie. You might like this.'

'In a minute.' I disappeared into the tiny kitchenette which was tucked away at the back of the office and then put my head around Rita's door to ask if she would like some tea. It was a mere formality. Everyone had tea, every day, unless they were out, as Kit was this afternoon.

'Look.' Luke showed me a picture on his screen. It was of an alabaster bowl, very fine, its opalescence tinged with a hint of orange at the rim, probably Ptolemaic, I estimated, about 300 BC.

'How beautiful,' I said.

'Yes,' he paused. 'Do you think Kit could sell something like this if he got hold of one?'

'I'm sure he could.' I laughed.

'I think I might know someone who wants to sell one,' he said. 'Or I know someone who knows someone.' He looked up at me as I stood next to him, gazing at the image. There was almost a tease in his voice, a hint of conspiracy that reminded me of Toby. Knowing someone who knew someone had been the basis of Toby's operations.

'Really, Luke?' I said. 'Who?'

I had been taken aback by his declaration. I had hardly expected Luke to start seeking out deals so quickly. After all, he knew nothing of our trade yet, or only the little he had picked up in the few weeks he had been with us.

'Someone a friend knows,' he said.

'Are they bona fide?'

'Sorry?'

'Are they trustworthy?' I said. 'Bona fide. Good faith. We have to be very careful who we buy these things from, Luke. We have to know that they haven't been stolen, or smuggled, that sort of thing, you know.'

He was silent for a moment, digesting what I had said.

'I understand,' he said. 'It's cool, I think. The bloke who told me about it is straight.' He looked embarrassed for a moment, as if he were suggesting he might know people who weren't. 'I mean, he's an okay bloke. He just happened to mention to someone he knew that I was working here. But I'll check it out. For definite.'

'And this other person, the person your friend mentioned it to. Does he actually own the bowl?' I thought I saw a shadow of disappointment cross his face. 'Don't take this personally, Luke,' I said. 'I would ask anyone the same questions.'

'Would you?' he said. But he spoke the words as if not to me, but to himself. Then he seemed to recover and flicked a pen through his fingers as if twirling a miniature baton. 'Let me make a call.' He took out his phone and disappeared off into the old gallery, now used just for our smaller pieces. He returned looking pleased with himself.

'He's acting on behalf of the owner,' he said, looking up at me in a very worldly-wise manner, as if he had been in the business for ever. 'But the owner, who wishes to remain anonymous for the moment, has had it in his family for years.'

He had been well briefed, I thought. It was a classic line and I'd heard it used by both genuine and dodgy sellers. Owners did like to stay anonymous for as long as legally possible, for a variety of reasons, including taxes, inheritance and divorce.

'Well, the first thing to do is to have a look at it,' I said. 'We can certainly do that.'

'Okay,' he said. 'I'll fix it up for next week. Any good?'

I nodded but I was noncommittal. I didn't want to discourage him, but I was intrigued as to why such an approach to us (for that was what it was) had been made through Luke, rather than directly. But then ours was a strange business and much of it was done with a nod and a whisper, through mutual contacts.

I was really much more curious about the social circles that Luke was mixing in than about some chancer who was trying to broker a deal, and this new revelation, combined with what I had witnessed earlier, served to emphasise how little we knew about him. It seemed absurd that he should still be so secretive, and his talk of the bowl and his contacts seemed to give me licence to speak. How, after all, I told myself, would we ever get to know this boy if we didn't pursue the few lines of inquiry that offered themselves?

'I was in the park at lunchtime,' I said. 'I couldn't help but see you there. With your friend, the blonde lady.' Lady was not a word I would normally use, but a certain reticence obliged me to now. I could hardly call her a girl, and to say woman seemed louche somehow. Luke held my gaze for a moment, then he looked back at the bowl on the screen.

'She's the wife of one of my teachers,' he said. 'She's called Caroline.' He glanced up at me again, checking my expression. 'She was very good to me when I first came to London. And I help her with her son sometimes.'

'Oh?' I said. 'Her son?'

'Yes. He was getting into trouble at school, that sort of thing. Like me. She told me about him one day, and I told her a bit about me, how I used to be like that, and she asked me if I'd talk to him. I ended up teaching him computer stuff. She pays me. But he's a good kid.'

Luke looked up at me, almost shy at offering this small part of his story. I was enchanted by the confidence, elated that I had at last elicited something from his past. But I wanted more.

'So what sort of trouble did you get into?'

He swung round to look at me properly. 'I didn't want to tell you or Kit, that first day, when it came up. I thought you wouldn't understand, that if I told you, you might not want any more to do with me.'

'Go on,' I said. 'You'd better tell me now. What sort of trouble?'

'Oh, kids' stuff really. I stole a car once.'

'Oh?'

'It was only an old one.'

'Does that make a difference?' I knew what he meant. The image of an old car did seem to make the transgression less serious, or at least more juvenile, but I felt I should steer a moral line.

'I don't know,' he said. He was laughing now. 'It was ages ago. I was an idiot. I had to go to court. All that.' His face assumed a more serious expression. 'My dad wouldn't speak to me. I ran away for a bit but they brought me back and I was put in care for six months. I think he was glad. He doesn't like me much. He prefers my brother; my brother's his real son.'

'I'm sure that's not true,' I said. 'He's your father.'

'But he isn't, is he?' said Luke. 'Not really.'

I tried to picture Luke, just a boy, standing in the court-room, his father cold and rejecting, but I found it almost impossible to see him in any other way than as he was now. Suddenly I hated this man, this would-be father, who had taken Alice's child from us, stolen him away and then brought him up only to reject him. How could he have let him be put in care? And what of his mother? I wanted to ask more, but knew I would have to wait.

And then I thought of my own father who had been little better in some ways. He had brought me into the world then left me, and when, years later, my mother had told him about my pregnancy and abortion, in her continuing desire to punish him, he'd recoiled from me again. Fathers were there to judge. They were harsh and unforgiving and neglectful, and this shared understanding was part of the bond that existed now, I thought, between Luke Tyler and me.

❧

I wasn't alone in my growing feeling for Luke. Kit too, I could tell, was becoming more and more fond of the young man. I'd known all along that Kit would be generous to him, for that was his nature, that he would want to help Luke as much as he could. But I hadn't anticipated the closeness that now surfaced, almost as if latent, between them. I watched them each day in the office, heard the way they spoke to each other as they shared jokes and the sports news, exchanging the generalities that can conceal affection between grown men.

Kit seemed captivated by him. Luke was the secret, of course, that Alice had kept from Kit and that lent the boy, I presumed, an extra fascination. I guessed too that Kit felt betrayed in some way, and I wondered how that coloured his memories and his grief. I could only imagine what it felt like for this ghost to walk into Kit's life. For that was what Luke seemed to be, a sort of phantom inheritance from someone we had all thought long buried.

Even so, I was surprised when Kit asked me one morning over breakfast if I would consider having Luke to stay in my flat for a while.

'Just for a few weeks,' he said, 'while we all think about the next step. He's bound to want his own place soon, or to share with his friends. But I thought it might be nice for him to be with us at the house. Just for a bit? What do you think?'

I wondered which friends Kit was referring to, and if he knew any more about Luke's life than I did.

'And Isobel?' I asked. 'What does she think?' I pictured the four of us living cheek by jowl, Kit, Luke and I in a sort of domestic harmony, with the figure of Isobel, even further discomfited, in the background.

Kit looked away. 'I've talked to her about it,' he said. 'She thinks, on balance, it's a good idea. I admit she wasn't for it at first, but now she says it would be an opportunity to get to know Luke better. After all we spend so much more time with him than she does. She's hardly had the chance.'

He had a point. I still wasn't sure that this was the best way to bring them together. I guessed that Kit had suggested that Luke came to stay with them, in the big house, and I could just imagine how Isobel had responded. I felt for a moment imposed upon. I feared that I was once more merely a useful backstop for Kit and Isobel, someone to solve an awkward impasse. But my indignation gave way almost at once to something else.

'Do you really think he'd want to come and stay with me?' I said. 'I'm almost old enough to be his grandmother.'

'I think that's the point, don't you?' Kit said. 'Luke needs family, stability. He needs us. And I did mention the idea to him, I hope that wasn't premature. I have to say, Josie, that he jumped at it.'

The thought that Luke would like to come and stay; the idea of having him living in my flat, his presence in my every waking hour, caused something joyful to stir inside me. It was a feeling of life, a sort of quickening.

Eleven

In those hours when I find myself sitting in my pew in the cathedral, watching the old priests at their business, I often think of how the world turns without our consent, and how we like to believe we are steering the days through. But so often we discover ourselves in a life we never intended or foresaw. And we know that we were foolish to imagine that there ever existed such things as our moments of decision.

If such moments do exist, one passed me by on a warm June afternoon at the end of the seventies. I had just finished yet another unsatisfactory love affair, this time with a publisher's editor called Adam. I was lying on the chaise longue in the gallery, unable to concentrate on a monograph on early Assyrian bronzes, and considering the possibility of breaking away, finally, from Toby. I was sick of the curious life I had been leading during the past decade. It was time, I thought, to put an end to it. I wasn't built for long-term hedonism. And I was even tired, I had decided, of the morbid air of death cults and underworlds with which I was surrounded each day.

I was almost twenty-nine, and by now, if I had stayed

in the suburban town where I grew up, I would have been married to a solicitor with at least one child. I would not be running around London, taking drugs with promiscuous homosexuals and men who were too ambitious or feckless to settle for love. I couldn't see the wood for the trees, as my mother liked to tell me on the rare weekends I went home. I was throwing my life away, she said. All the decent men would disappear, picked off by women more sensible than me, or at least less demanding.

In this mood of disillusion, I began a systematic assessment of the possibilities open to me, all the alternative modes of being that life might offer. I could move back home or go to another city. I could enroll again for teacher training (my mother's favourite), but this idea induced such a leaden weight inside me that I quickly dismissed it. I then became more adventurous in my thinking. I could do Voluntary Service Overseas, or be a nanny in America, or teach English as a Foreign Language in Buenos Aires where handsome men on horseback called to me like the Sirens to Odysseus.

But as I stared around the gallery in search of inspiration, I knew that although I had stumbled into Toby's orbit by chance, I really loved the world in which I found myself, this close proximity to things not quite understood, the sheer beauty of the objects in the room, a beauty made more powerful for me by the millennia through which they had passed.

In between our hedonistic forays, I had thrown myself into antiquity. I was becoming almost a scholar myself. I should perhaps have applied to do a further degree, or offered myself as an assistant on a dig in Egypt or Iraq. It wouldn't have been difficult to find work with my background and contacts. I could have explained it to Toby as a sort of sabbatical, if he minded, which he probably would have done. But he would soon have adapted. I remembered how quickly he had seemed to forget poor Ilya. I still had Ilya's Tawaret, tucked away like some talisman against betrayal. I found myself wondering how much it would fetch at a sale. It would certainly pay for a stay in Buenos Aires, with some cash to spare.

But such dreams of escape presupposed a will to make them real, and a resistance to forces other than my own, and these particular fancies were disturbed by Toby's return from an extended lunch. I scrutinised him, as he came into the office, from my new perspective. I was a woman in charge of her destiny. I had known him now for seven years and in that time his appearance had changed from that of a perpetual boy to a striking man of thirty-three. He had taken to wearing smart suits with shirts from Jermyn Street and colourful but elegant ties. It was true that the look could go askew as his evenings wore on, but the consequent disarray was often artful.

'I have news,' he said. I could see he was excited and I wondered if he was already high. 'Are you ready?'

The phrase was a code between us for something momentous. I wasn't ready in fact. Today of all days I wasn't sure I wanted to hear something that might distract me from my plans, however diaphanous they might be.

'Yes,' I said. 'Shall I make tea first?'

'No, we'll have champagne.' He reached into the little

fridge that sat on the floor out of sight next to his desk and pulled out a bottle of Veuve Clicquot.

'Right,' he said. 'Glasses?'

He had brought with him an air of urgency and I rushed to get down the flutes from a corner cupboard. Champagne was usually reserved for a big sale but I couldn't think at the moment what that might be.

I set down the glasses in front of him and he paused before drawing the cork from the bottle. Then he could contain his news no longer, and like the stopper he was about to remove, it came bursting out.

'I've bought a house,' he said. 'A big, beautiful, magnificent house.'

Toby had never mentioned wanting to move. I had imagined him in the flat in Chelsea for years to come, perhaps for ever. It was big enough to suit his needs. He had decorated it since the early days and it was grand enough for his pretensions, or so I had thought.

'Well,' I said. 'This is . . . a surprise.' I couldn't think of anything clever or original to say. He'd bought a house. Good for him. I could even feel a smidgen of resentment creeping over me. In the light of my earlier reverie, this seemed further evidence of his selfishness. But I couldn't be cross with him. I wanted to be pleased and I threw myself into the game. 'So, where? What? How exciting. How marvellous,' I said. 'Why didn't you tell me?'

'I wanted it to be a surprise. It's huge, Josie. And I can't live there all alone. I want you to come and live there with me.'

So that was it. That was the real news, the nub of the

surprise. He was drawing me closer. It was as if he had suspected my thoughts of flight. I would never get away.

'But I live at the flat,' I heard myself say and it sounded absurd.

'Keep the flat,' Toby said. 'Of course you must keep the flat, but come and live with me. I can't think of anyone else I'd want to share with. You can let the flat out. You don't need to pay me rent, just a bit to cover bills and stuff. Then you can buy your flat if you want. See, I've thought about it. Come on, you'll be better off. Just think what fun it will be. Think of the parties we can have. Wait till you see it, Josie, I can't wait for you to see it. You'll love it.'

I was a pushover. His appeal worked on two counts. Most effective was this clear, fresh evidence of how important I was to him, but at the same time the practical aspects of this proposition appealed to my sense of self-preservation. My landlady had in fact recently offered to sell me the flat but I had been reluctant to take on a mortgage. If I let it out, as Toby was suggesting, I could buy it for my future security. Buenos Aires, the Valley of the Kings, even teaching, seemed foolish in comparison with the seeming good sense of Toby's offer.

Toby stood in front of me now, pouring champagne into my glass, confident that I would accept, toasting our new life, and as I drank it down he was already chopping up lines of cocaine on the back of a copy of *International Antiquity Review*.

'And also, Josie . . . ' He stopped. He seemed unsure of what sort of response he might get from what was to come.

'What?' I said.

'If you came to live with me, when you do, I hope . . . I thought . . . that sometimes we might have Alice to stay with us. In the school holidays.' He snorted a line through a rolled-up fiver and handed it to me.

'To stay with us?' I said. 'What about Anne?'

Toby rolled his eyes, though whether at the mention of Anne or because of the powder he had just put up his nose, I wasn't sure.

'Gordon's divorcing her, finally. It's no surprise, is it? But we're all worried about what will happen to Alice. Chris and Margaret will help out. But we could look after her some of the holidays. Anne won't object. She's in no fit state. She doesn't want Alice at home much at all if truth be known.'

As I watched him pressing his fingers to his nose, I thought that this new home he was contemplating for Alice might not be so much more regular. But I had to admit that Toby's idea did make some sense. Alice was now eleven and about to go away to school. For the last three years our meetings had been limited to the occasional London visit, though we still wrote to one another. I had guessed the divorce was looming. Gordon was a decent man who had stuck by Anne far longer than many men would have done. And he had been kind to his stepdaughter. But now it seemed that even this thin thread of stability had snapped. I would have to stay where I was, if only to help Toby hold things together for Alice. I suppose it was being needed that seduced me. This new idea of Toby's, this household – it would be a strange ménage, but perhaps Toby was right.

It was better than leaving Alice alone for too long with Anne whose life had turned ugly, and who spent too much time in bed with just a bottle of gin for company.

We finished the champagne, had one more line of cocaine and closed up the gallery. Toby, bored now and anxious for more excitement, insisted that we find a taxi to take us to Little Venice to see the house he had bought. When we reached our destination, Millbury Street, he told the driver to stop and we sat looking through the cab windows, unable to see a great deal, even though it was still light, because of the high wall and the house's secluded position. It wasn't possible to go inside that day, though Toby promised we could return at the weekend and he would give me a tour. He was high, of course, his voice chattering ahead of his brain, as he described the house room by room. All I could make out were the upper windows, the tops of several trees and the fact that the house was a large one, much too big for the two of us. It was a grand folly, in every sense, and it made me wonder how he would fill it up, for fill it up I knew he would.

I said nothing of any of this. I didn't want to spoil Toby's excitement, or mine, which was growing as I took in the sheer extravagance of his purchase. He grabbed my hand and ordered the taxi to drive further on and over the bridge to where we could stand at the canal's edge. From there, if we leant over, we could glimpse the end of the garden across the pretty, watery basin, and see the small mooring which he claimed was for the house's use.

'My very own house and my very own mooring,' he said. He sounded both gleeful and incredulous. He would buy a boat, he said. He began to sing, a camp rendition of 'The Owl and the Pussycat'. And as we climbed back into the cab, the driver winked at me.

The thought of Toby with access to a boat after a night out was scary and I knew I would have to make him promise not to have one. But that was all for the future, and as the evening progressed, it seemed that everything became possible, for both of us. Day became night, and Toby's friends, who these days were my friends too, were summoned to celebrate at a favourite restaurant. Not that anyone actually ate the dinner which Toby paid for. I hated waste, and even in my heightened state, I protested that they should all eat more, which just made Toby laugh.

By eleven, I had had enough. I felt myself withdraw, lose interest, and knew it was time for me to go home. Toby would go on, of course, with the rest of them, to some other nightspot. I slipped out of the restaurant as Toby tried to order a taxi for me, he was always solicitous in that way, telling him I would get one in the street. I wanted to walk home. It was only half a mile and I wanted to clear my head.

As I passed Victoria Station where the night buses pulled up to change drivers I noticed, as always, the ever-changing faces of the young boys who hung around its corners. I speculated, briefly, as to where they spent their nights, while I was about to live in a palace. But at least Toby and I were going to make a home for Alice, I thought, that at least was something unselfish.

As I rounded the corner, past the cathedral, my party mood dissipated further. I was seized by panic at what I might be entering into, and the fear that I might be making a terrible mistake, that I might be giving up the last chance of a life of my own. But it seemed as if I was helpless, or rather the part of me which tried to question my judgement. It wasn't just loyalty that bound me to Toby, it was the pull of a strange kind of love, and in his own strange way, I knew he returned it.

I poured myself the glass of whisky that had now become habitual before I went to bed and as I did so, I stopped to think for the first time about where the money had come from for Toby's new house. Although Toby was doing very well, I couldn't see that the deals we had done lately would cover it, and neither he nor Christopher had private money of their own, despite their grand ways. That night I asked myself, as I did less and less often, what Toby was up to. I had great faith in his entrepreneurial abilities but when they were literally unaccounted for I felt rather queasy.

Twelve

Once the decision had been taken that Luke should move to Millbury Street with us, there seemed little point in delaying, and to my great surprise, it was Isobel who offered to help him move his things. Just a few nights before, Luke had come to the house for supper, as he frequently did now. Isobel had invited her father and Helen along too, to meet Luke properly. They were keen, both of them, to get a closer look at the young man whom they had only so far met in passing.

Luke arrived early and offered to help me with supper which, as usual, I was in charge of. Isobel was still at the studio, and Kit rarely bothered with any cooking apart from scrambled eggs, which he would present from time to time as if it were a culinary triumph. Luke, in contrast, was clearly at home in a kitchen, which surprised me. I had given him some eggs to beat and it was obvious that he had done it more than once before.

'So,' I said, 'did you help your mother to cook when you were growing up?'

Luke laughed. 'No,' he said. 'Not really.'

'I'm surprised,' I said. 'What about at school? You handle food as if it's a pleasure.'

'My mum cooked,' he said. 'But it certainly wasn't a pleasure to eat what she made. It was okay though.'

'But you seem to know about food, Luke.'

'I worked in a kitchen for a bit.'

'Oh.' Another new piece of information had emerged to be fitted into my ever-growing picture. 'Where?'

'Just in the holidays, you know. In my first year. Here, let me cut that up for you.' He took the knife from my hand and examined the blade.

'Could be sharper,' he said, and proceeded to chop up the parsley with professional ease.

'That's amazing,' I said.

He laughed. 'I'm just showing off. I can't do much else. It's a party trick.'

'I expect it impresses your girlfriends,' I said.

He smiled at me, amused, knowing I was prying. 'I don't have a girlfriend,' he said, 'not a special one.'

'Ah.' I was relieved to know this. It was one less complication to deal with for the moment, I thought. One less tentacle of Alice's legacy.

I was enjoying this small intimacy with Luke when it was interrupted by the arrival of Jack Whaley, always a whirlwind event. This evening he appeared to be trailing Helen behind him like a braking parachute. They were irritable with one another before supper and I saw Isobel take her father aside at one point to scold him for bad behaviour. I would like to have done the same to the humourless Helen, though Luke's appearance in my life seemed, among other things, to have mellowed the petty jealousy of Jack's girlfriend that I customarily felt.

I had had some qualms about us exposing Luke to Jack who could never be relied on to tread softly, but to my surprise Luke seemed to warm to him, laughing at his jokes and quizzing him about his Scottish roots. I found it intriguing that he should respond so well to the older man. By the time we reached the pudding stage, Jack was on to his old war stories about being arrested, usually for behaving badly on demonstrations, but once for attempting to shoplift a parrot from a pet shop in Camden when he was drunk. I had heard it several times before, but it was an amusing story, and Luke seemed to find it hilarious.

'I was done for shoplifting,' Luke said, when he finally stopped laughing. 'In Dixons in Glasgow. I only nicked a Palm Pilot though.'

Whether it was the wine, or the oneupmanship, or whether Jack Whaley really did have some professional gift for eliciting secrets, we were all astonished at this sudden confession. I had been careful to say nothing to the others about the car-stealing he had told me about, and I had naïvely thought that it must have been an isolated event.

After a notable pause, Jack came back in. 'Well done, lad,' he said. 'All property is theft.'

'Dad, for Christ's sake,' said Isobel. 'That's so out of order. But what made you do that, Luke?'

Kit stepped in. 'That's not helpful, Jack,' he said, then turned to Luke. 'You were young, I take it?'

'Fourteen.'

'Well then,' I said. 'Too young to know better.'

Luke smiled across at me.

'The kids I hung around with nicked stuff all the time,' he said.

'Your schoolfriends?' Helen asked. She had been sitting quietly all evening, not sulking exactly but keeping out of Jack's way. It was almost a surprise to hear her speak. I remembered that she had a son about Luke's age.

'No.' Luke seemed to be enjoying our attention. 'I didn't hang out with the kids from school. I hung out with the village boys. It really annoyed my mum and dad. They spent all that money on my posh school and I ended up fighting, same as the local kids. They were always fighting, and I liked that. They were always getting arrested.'

'An excellent way to annoy your parents,' Jack said to him.

Luke laughed. 'I once told my dad that I was going to be a hairdresser. You should have seen him. He wanted me to be an engineer.'

'What's wrong with a hairdresser?' Isobel said. 'It's a great skill. You can earn lots of money if you're good.'

Luke shook his head as if she didn't get the point.

'I really did want to be a hairdresser,' he paused, then his eyes gleamed, 'but only because I thought it meant you got to sleep with lots of girls.' He laughed again and we all joined in, if a bit nervously.

Jack had been watching him closely. 'Makes sense to me, boy,' he said. 'All those lovely women. What could be more logical for a young man?'

Luke looked grateful, and relaxed again, addressing his next words to Jack.

'My dad didn't get it. He thought it meant I was gay. He was so angry he . . . he nearly hit me.'

'A true liberal then,' Jack said. 'Never mind, Luke. The question is, have you escaped?'

Luke looked confused. The struggle to make sense of what Jack had said seemed to make him almost cross.

'How do you mean?' he said, looking over at me as if for help.

'Leave Luke alone now, Dad,' Isobel said. 'You can analyse him later if he'll let you. He hasn't had a chance to finish his pudding.'

'So when exactly are you planning to move in to Josie's, Luke?' Isobel said, after supper. She was clearing the plates from the table and Luke had jumped up at once to help.

'I thought on Saturday,' he said, 'if that's all right with you, Josie?' He turned back to me. 'That's what we said, isn't it?' I nodded.

'Damn,' Kit said, 'I've got to go up to see Ma. It's just for the day, to sort out some papers for her. She can't read numbers properly any more. But it means I won't be able to help you out, Luke. Can you hire a van?'

'A van?' It was Isobel who chipped in. 'He surely doesn't have enough for a van. I'll do it. I'll bring the car,' she said. 'I expect I can park up right outside if you're ready, Luke, and if we're quick. You don't have a lot of stuff, do you?'

'No, a couple of cases and a computer. That would be cool of you, Isobel.' Luke beamed at her.

I felt a sudden desire to be included in this approbation myself.

'If Isobel has to wait in the car, you'll need someone else,' I said. 'I'll come too. If you want me to?'

'Yes,' he said. 'Yes.' He expelled the word as if he'd won a game. If Kit had volunteered to change his mind and come along as well, I thought, Luke's triumph would have been complete.

❧

Luke's move to Millbury Street inevitably made me think back to the times that Alice had spent with us, and how thrilled she was to be allowed, finally, to come to stay. The house was a refuge for her, but also a kind of fantasy castle, and every time she visited, the pleasure she took in Millbury Street renewed its attractions for Toby and me. Sometimes I would go and collect her from the station, or sometimes Toby would fetch her, and as she got older, she liked to take a taxi by herself. On her arrival, I would open the door and let her in, and each time I would see the house through her eyes, always as if for the first time.

She would run up to the front door and then into the hallway and up the staircase, exclaiming at the beauty of the Moroccan glass and brass lamps that hung on chains from the ceiling, and the blues and pinks of the exquisite flowers on the Persian runner that covered the stairs. Many of the furnishings and textiles in the house had been chosen by me, but it was Toby who had decided on the big pieces. He had bought most of them from Robert Townley, a dealer and an early mentor of his, a man who regarded his trade as an art form in itself, and who had encouraged Toby to see his business through similar eyes.

I would follow Alice up the stairs where she would run into the large drawing room, throwing herself on the newly upholstered bergère sofa, laughing with pleasure at being back, then up another flight to her room – the one we had given her on the top floor, at the other end of the landing from mine.

For her twelfth birthday, Toby had decided to take the refurnishing of Alice's bedroom with new seriousness. They had gone together to Robert's emporium to select a bed and other furniture, which Toby saw as part of her aesthetic education. He was thrilled to report to me that Alice had fine taste, that he had hardly had to instruct her at all. They had returned with a carved French bed with curved mahogany whorls that swooped together to make the head. A few days later I took her to Portobello Road, and together we chose a Victorian velvet bedcover, azure blue with little tassels and gold binding. To Alice's delight we also discovered two matching rolled cushions. She was enraptured.

'It looks so beautiful, Josie,' she said when we got home and laid them out on the bed. 'Like something draped on an Egyptian barque, one to take the dead to the afterworld.'

'I'm not sure that they had velvet then, darling,' I said. 'And this is Victorian, you can tell by the quality of the nap.'

I had begun to discourage all but an academic interest in antiquity. It was important, I felt, that Alice should clothe her enthusiasm for the ancient world in fact and history. Toby agreed with me. He was anxious to keep the unpredictable Anne reassured that he was caring for Alice properly, and was keen that nothing should provoke a ban on her coming to Millbury Street. In her sad state of mind, Anne could be capricious, and Toby wanted Alice to have a home with us, to have some semblance of love in her curious world.

Alice had asked Toby if she could have something from the gallery, on loan, in her bedroom but he had refused her. No antiquities in the house, he said; it was asking for trouble. But I sometimes wondered what sort of trouble he meant. I had imagined that this rule of his was born of practicality, to avoid theft or breakages, given the sort of people who sometimes drifted in and out, but then again, perhaps he was more superstitious than he liked to admit. The artefacts were not trinkets for decoration, he would say, but objects of reverence, a link with the dead. It was an admirable view, I often thought, though one that sat oddly with his casual disposal of them. But I had never challenged him on this, with one exception.

Sitting in a small locked box in my bedroom was the Tawaret that Ilya had left with me. I had always felt unable to sell it on, and I had grown fond of the little statue. It was far too valuable, really, to have in the house, but now, on a whim, I offered it to Alice. I said that she could have it in her room when she came to stay, though she could not take it home with her. I told her that it had sentimental value for us, not only because it had belonged to a friend of Toby's but also because it had been a favourite of hers when she was small.

And so it stood, whenever Alice was in residence, on the

small mahogany chest which Toby had bought to match her fine bed. I liked to see it there, as a reminder of the first day we had spent together, since despite any worries we might have had about Alice's early obsessions, or of what we might have exposed her to at Millbury Street, there seemed to be little evidence of anything that might worry her mother, or us. She was still a unique personality, charismatic and self-contained, but her interests were turning outwards like those of other young girls of her age. She was developing nicely, we told ourselves, and breathed a sigh of relief.

Thirteen

Luke's bedsit was above a barber's shop and on the day of his move, I followed him up the narrow stairs, noticing a slight smell of coriander and lemon, not at all unpleasant, which seemed to seep through the walls. Isobel was somewhere below, circling to avoid predatory wardens. Luke's room was on the second floor; it was very small and now quite bare, stripped of everything that belonged to him, his possessions packed into a smart black suitcase and scruffy battered holdall. There was also a box, carefully packaged with tape, which I presumed contained his computer. The window looked down over Queensway and I wondered how he had managed to sleep through the endless traffic, the lights, and the late-night café life.

I picked up the holdall but he stopped me.

'I'll carry the box down,' he said, 'then I'll come back for the bags. You can bring my suit if you like.' He nodded towards a plastic zip-up bag hanging on the back of the door. 'But wait till I come back so I don't need to lock up.'

'But no one could get out of here, surely?' I said. 'I mean if they were to steal anything?' He looked at me as if I were a naïve creature from another life, and I shrugged.

Within what seemed like seconds of his footsteps disappearing down the stairs, there was a small knock on the half-open door to his room and the face of another young man appeared. He was thin and small and Asian-looking, and his black hair was dirty and streaked with green.

'Where's Luke then?' the face said. His accent was pure South London.

'Who are you?' I countered.

'Jimmy. I live in the next room. Is he off then?' He looked around the room and took in its emptiness.

'Yes,' I said.

'Are you his mum?'

I hesitated. I didn't want to pretend to be Luke's mother, but I didn't want to enter into a precise explanation of who I was.

'I'm a friend of his,' I said.

'He has a lot of friends.' Jimmy followed this observation with a laugh that was more of a sneer. 'He's always staying with his friends. I could tell you some things about his friends, if you wanted.' He emphasised the word with a sort of envy mixed with contempt. 'Have you got a few quid I could have? I'm broke.'

I was taken aback by the directness of his approach. I could hear Luke coming back up the stairs and felt guilty at having been unable to prevent this intrusion, which I could see now that I had been left to guard against. Jimmy turned in the doorway as Luke reached the landing.

'Fuck off, Jimmy,' I heard Luke say. 'Just fuck off.' His tone was resigned rather than aggressive.

'Okay, man, where you going then?'

'None of your business.'

'Lend us a few quid.'

Luke pushed past Jimmy into the room and stood between me and him. He fished in his pocket and handed him a ten-pound note.

'Now, get lost,' he said to Jimmy, then, 'Sorry, Josie.'

Jimmy put the money in his pocket, looked around and waved at me. 'Cheers, Mrs,' he said, then disappeared across the landing into his room and closed the door. Within a few seconds, it opened again and he ran down the stairs.

'That'll keep him quiet for the afternoon,' Luke said.

'What do you mean?' I said, though I had a good idea of the answer.

'He's gone to score,' Luke said. 'You know, heroin.'

'Yes, I do know,' I said.

I was surprised by how little Luke brought with him to my flat. The clothes he hung in the old French wardrobe which had come with me from Victoria, seemed even fewer than those I had so far seen him wearing, and I couldn't help but wonder what he had done with the surplus. But he proved to be a model lodger, courteous, tidy and discreet, washing up after himself, most of the time, and he rarely finished the milk without replacing the carton.

Isobel had been generous and said that he must have the use of one of the bathrooms in the main house, so that I would not be inconvenienced. And so, in the mornings, I would hear him creep out of the flat and through the

179

connecting door, to the landing beyond. I would be up myself by the time he returned in his new dressing gown of dark brown towelling with a taupe stripe, which I had found for him in Liberty's, and which suited his colouring well, as I had known it would when I bought it.

It struck me that perhaps it was unnatural in a young man, a student at that, to be so self-sufficient, so careful of others, so fastidious, but I reminded myself that he had been thrown back on his own resources for some considerable time. His gratitude to me for giving him a home, however temporary, was effusive, and it moved me in a way I found perplexing.

I could see that there was a poignancy in the pleasure I took in having him to stay and it embarrassed me to think that others might observe it. I tried my best to hide what I felt. The comfort he brought me seemed to emphasise how narrow my life had become in the years since Toby's death, and now the thought of returning to it was something I didn't want to think of. I was devoted to Kit and Isobel, and grateful that they had included me as a part of their daily existence, but still, after all these years and despite Kit's kindness, there was a feeling that they took me for granted, and that I could only ever be peripheral to their lives.

Luke, in contrast, seemed to thrive on my attention. He could be both serious and teasing but he was always sincere. He noticed what I wore, praised my cleverness, and asked me to teach him what I knew about the business, and, to my delight, not just the commercial side of it. He seemed to share my passion for antiquity, and at the gallery nothing was ever too much trouble for him to document, or find out.

Now that he was living with me, I hoped that he would confide in me still further. He liked to ask questions about Alice and I liked nothing more than to talk of her. I had told him what I remembered, how lovely she had been as a child, how precocious and curious as an adolescent, how unusual and inventive. But although he had begun to talk more freely about his past, his own present still appeared to be off-limits, and I wondered more and more why he needed to keep it so separate. I had phoned Jack to ask for his view soon after the evening he had been to supper, but he was cranky and unhelpful, too concerned with his own domestic difficulties.

'I expect the lad is sick of women on his back,' Jack said. 'Leave him alone.'

'Are we being a bit subjective here?' I said.

'That may be,' he said. 'But it doesn't make it any less true.'

From time to time, Luke asked me about Alice's grown-up life, when she was married to Kit. I told him what I could, but said that he should ask Kit himself. I had known her best as a child, I explained, and that was the truth. I had loved the grown-up Alice, and enjoyed her, especially her company in the gallery, but she was somehow less real to me than her younger self. It was as if something of the person I had known before had been left behind. And now it made more sense to me. There were the bouts of illness she had suffered and hidden for one thing, and then there was Luke himself, the biggest secret of all, which she had kept from everyone and which had distanced her from us.

༄

I had found it curious from the start that Luke did not pursue the question of who his father might be. I assumed that as time went on, he would do so, that he would want to know more of what had happened, but he never raised it after his first inquiries. He seemed concerned entirely with Alice, and with us, and to have taken at face value what Kit and I had said, that we simply didn't know, other than a casual holiday boyfriend, just as we had not known of his own existence.

And why should he not accept the truth? It was me, rather than Luke, who now wanted to know more. It was me who could not forget that when Kit had stood in the office, white-faced and stunned after the solicitor's confirmation, I had felt a flicker of *déjà vu*. It was as if this news was a knowledge I already possessed, and a small, cramping fear had made itself felt, then been pushed away quickly to some recess of my mind.

It was only now, months later, that my brain, accustomed to sifting for information, was beginning to have the courage to forage in its files. *It all makes sense when you think about it,* Margaret Haddeley had said, the weekend that we had broken the news to her. *It must have happened that summer, when Anne told us Alice had had her first breakdown, you remember, Josie? Alice was up in Scotland, with her father, with Roddy. And really, that man must bear some responsibility, buggering off like that. He hardly ever bothered to see the poor child. We can't blame poor Anne for everything.*

But I knew that couldn't be quite right. Alice could not have got pregnant in Scotland. Margaret was muddled. Luke had been born at the end of January, according to his adoption papers. His conception must have been earlier than she had thought. I had managed to recall that there had been a boy around, a sort of boyfriend even. Alice had met him at home in Norfolk. He had come to work on Anne's house with his uncle, a local builder. Alice had told me a little bit about him, though not too much since I supposed she thought that I, like her mother, might disapprove on class grounds. It was a crush, that was clear, and I had the impression that he was older than Alice and that it wasn't serious. She had met him at spring half-term. I remembered that because, for the first time, Alice had been keen to spend some of the Easter holiday at home with Anne, and I had guessed that the boy must be the reason.

But by the time she came to stay at the end of that holiday, just before she went back to school, the friendship was over, she said. She had cried on my shoulder as she told me that he had confessed to having another girlfriend, at home in Great Yarmouth. But Alice had soon recovered, excited as always at the prospect of staying with Toby. Her mood, which had begun to swing in an adolescent fashion, quickly picked up and she was once more vibrant, full of energy and humour.

Fourteen

The summer had been dry and hot and the leaves were already beginning to turn. Nothing had been settled about Luke's future, but I was hoping that Kit, who had just returned from a late holiday, might be thinking of offering him a permanent job. Luke had proved himself a fast learner. He was extremely good with our customers, and what he lacked in knowledge, he made up for with a deference that the clients enjoyed, making sure that, where he could, he had a flattering acquaintance with the stuff of their lives.

The mysterious affair of the alabaster bowl had come to nothing. There had been a couple of calls that I had overheard, and one day, when I answered the phone, a man who said his name was Michael asked, rather brusquely, to speak to Luke. The voice was distant, foreign, the English almost fluent and clearly learnt in America. It was unfamiliar and yet I wondered if he was someone I might have met in our small world of antiquities. It was unlikely, but if that were the case, it was all the ruder of him, I thought, not to acknowledge an acquaintance with me.

When he put down the phone Luke seemed excited. He asked me if Kit or I might be available to see the bowl the following week, and I said I was sure something could be arranged. But the appointment was never confirmed, and when I inquired about it a fortnight later, Luke shrugged and said he thought that the owner had had an offer from the Middle East, an offer over the odds.

'Did Michael tell you that?' I asked, curious to find out more.

'Michael?' Luke said. He spoke as if surprised that I should mention the name. 'You know Michael?'

'No. I don't know him. I mean your friend Michael, the one who rang up. Is he the one who was the intermediary?'

'Yes,' Luke said. 'Sorry, yes. Michael, of course. I'd forgotten he rang here. Yes, he told me that. He said he was sorry if I had put you to any trouble.'

'I did wonder,' I said, 'if I might ever have met him. Ours is a small world.'

Luke looked over at me, a little wary. Perhaps I had overstepped the mark.

'I don't think so. He's never said so. But I'm sorry about it now. I wish I'd never mentioned it. I feel an idiot.'

'It happens all the time,' I said. 'But it might be interesting to meet him, if he has dealings in our world, I mean.'

'Yes,' said Luke. 'I'll talk to him.'

I wanted to ask more. I wanted to ask Luke how he had met Michael, and if he was a friend, but on balance I decided it was best to wait. Luke seemed to have a pattern of disclosing what I wanted to know when it suited him, as if the timing were of consequence to him and he couldn't be rushed.

I heard nothing more about Michael, and forgot about him myself, until he rang again one morning in late October, when Luke was upstairs with Kit. It was clear that whoever he was, he knew Luke well. When I asked him if I could say what his call was about, he just said, 'I'm a friend, he'll know who I am.' He said it in such a way that I felt that there was a world to which both he and Luke belonged, one to which I was not privy. He asked me to tell Luke he would call back, but Luke walked in at that moment and I put the call through.

Luke had given me just enough information about his social life to allow me to imagine a world of young people who lived, I suspected, rather as Toby and I had done, all those years before. From time to time, he would mention names. There was a Sam, whom he went off to meet in bars, and a young woman called Tessa and one called Amy. There was also Caroline, the woman he had met in St James's Park, whose son he continued to mentor, he told me. I said that any of them would be welcome at Millbury Street, he just had to say, and he thanked me. But no one ever came.

Throughout the summer there had been a number of nights when Luke had stayed away from the flat altogether. When I mentioned it to Kit, he just laughed and said young men came and went, and that was just the way things were. There was no need for me to worry, he said; I should assume that he had been to a party, or that a girl had taken him home. It would have been surprising, I told myself, if that had not been the case. He was, after all, a most attractive boy and one who clearly enjoyed, albeit discreetly, the effect he could have on those around him.

But I couldn't help being curious about what he got up to. His centre of social operations was his mobile phone on which he received a large number of calls and messages. I had often been tempted to look, on the odd occasion that he left it lying around, but I only once succumbed. He had cleared all but the last three, one from Caroline, one from a 'Tim', and, of course, one from Michael.

And now here was Michael again on the end of the telephone at the gallery. I wondered why he hadn't used Luke's mobile. And I wondered if it meant that he had some new artefact up his sleeve to try to sell us. As I watched Luke conduct a subdued and inaudible conversation with him, I had a picture of Michael in my mind, a man in his thirties or early forties, smooth and clever, a man perhaps a bit like Toby had been. They were a type, some of these dealers, men who were skilled at trading, barrow boys with a polished veneer. They might have been trading in bonds or futures, livestock or gems, or just off the back of a lorry; it was merely circumstantial that their trade was in relics of the ancient past. And now Luke was one of them, I suspected, enjoying the arcana of antiquity but eager to master the skilled and profitable process of turning a major sale. I couldn't help but be anxious for Luke. It was Kit he should stick with, I thought. It was Kit who was the honourable example. There were still a few shady folk around and I was worried that this Michael might be one of them.

∾

It was later that day that Kit, arriving back in the gallery fresh from lunch at Green's Oyster Bar, put his head around our door and smiled at us both as Frank the dog struggled out of his basket in the eternal hope of a walk.

'You two should be going to Christie's soon, if you're going to catch the viewing before it shuts,' he said. 'I'll hold the fort as planned.'

Luke looked round, excited.

'Can't we all go?' he said.

'I can stay, if you want to go with Luke, Kit,' I said, though I hoped that he would keep to the agreement we had made the previous day.

'No, no. You go. I have to make calls to New York. I went this morning as planned.'

'And?'

'The Fayoum tomb painting is quite beautiful but its reserve is too high in my opinion,' Kit said. 'Or too high for the trade.'

'They think they might sell that direct to a buyer.' I addressed this to Luke who was looking puzzled.

'What's a Fayoum tomb painting?' When Luke spoke, it was to ask a question more often than not, I thought. His own answers were less forthcoming. He pushed back his chair and stood up, stretching himself like a cat in front of us. I found myself, as so often, surprised that we had felt even a moment's doubt that morning in the Turkish café . . . the narrow eyes, the curly hair, he was so very . . . *familiar* . . . even though he was as tall as Kit. And for a moment it was as if Alice was here in the room, smiling at us, as if to say, you can't forget me after all, because this boy, this child, is mine.

As I watched the two of them chatting together, I couldn't help but think how different things might have been if Luke had been Kit's son. It was possible, in theory. Kit had known Alice at the time. He had even been to Millbury Street while she was staying with us; I could remember at least a couple of occasions. But Luke wasn't Kit's son. Alice had been too young for Kit. He had been at university and about to take up his Army commission. Kit would never have taken advantage of so young a girl.

The more I thought about Alice's pregnancy, the more I thought it was almost a bigger mystery as to why she had had the baby at all, rather than how and with whom she had conceived it. Why had she not had an abortion like everyone else? Anne Wearing's instinct, I was sure, would have been to rush her straight off to a clinic. Perhaps it had simply been too late. I found myself wondering if Mrs Durden, that good Catholic figure who had instructed Alice in the ways of the Virgin Mary, had become involved. Or if Alice herself had protested. It was a mystery, but also a miracle, I thought, looking up at Luke who was restless and ready to go, stretching his arms above his head once again, too tall for the low-ceilinged room.

'I'm all yours,' Luke said to me, then turned to Rita who had heard the three of us talking and come through to see what was happening.

'Don't feed the dog all the biscuits while we're out.' He winked at her and I could see that she too had been won over.

'As if I would,' she said, smiling and looking at the floor, flustered beneath a cropped helmet of mousy hair.

'You're kind-hearted, Rita. You'd give him your last biscuit.' Luke beamed at her and she glowed. As I watched, I felt a small nip of jealousy and also, perhaps, the potential for trouble in Luke's charm.

Kit waved at us from the big upstairs window as we walked away from the gallery before turning into the street that led to Hyde Park Corner. We took the underpass to Piccadilly, and with time to spare, walked up and through the Burlington Arcade, a small detour on our way to St James's. It was almost dark now, but the arcade was lit like a Christmas grotto by the sumptuous window displays, a tunnel of luxury and status. I sneaked a glance at Luke in the reflective glass as we passed by. He took a keen interest in what was on sale, commenting on the styles and cuts of the clothes. He had learnt quickly that I knew about such things and despite our age difference he seemed keen to seek out my judgement.

Luke was now on our payroll. He was officially Kit's and my assistant. He had a small salary and, of course, a home, for he was living with me for the moment. Despite his fondness for window shopping, he had shown no obvious signs of greed, or any envy of Kit's wealth. There seemed to be an understanding between them that, until Luke knew what he wanted to do, where he wanted to be, Kit would help him. But it was difficult for any of us to know what

Luke wanted. He didn't appear to want anything much, except a family.

We were walking now through Christie's pillared hall, up the staircase, stopping to speak to one or two familiar faces, before entering the Aladdin's cave of antiquities in the North Gallery. I had studied the catalogue, of course, and already shown Luke the items of interest. The sale was to be the next morning and it was both my and Kit's habit to wait until the day before to see the objects in reality. It was a trick taught to us by Toby who had always trusted the quasi-mystical connection he felt with an artefact as it stood in the saleroom, one that could not be trusted to last more than a day or two. Something, he said, might interrupt the current. We knew it was irrational, but more often than not it worked for him, and Kit had followed suit, seeing no reason to change the routine.

Luke was standing in front of the Fayoum tomb painting that Kit had mentioned. It was hanging on the wall in a frame. It was the frame, I thought, that added to the startling modernity of the thing, a quality which was absent from the rest of the objects in the room. Here was a man one might have known, a face staring back at us with the intensity of a Dutch portrait.

'They're extraordinary, these pictures, aren't they,' I said, though in fact there was only one in the sale. 'Like nothing else. When Kit goes to Cairo next, he should take you. They have the best collection.'

Luke seemed mesmerised by the picture. He continued to stare at it, but didn't respond to my chatter.

'He looks a bit like you,' I went on, 'don't you think? The dark eyes and curly hair?'

'He's young.' Luke spoke now. He sounded surprised.

'Yes. Well, I don't suppose life expectancy was very great.' I was delighted by Luke's absorption, by the fact that he was giving it thought. 'They're from the Greek period. When the Greeks took over Egypt, that is. Relatively late in the day but still a hell of a long time ago. I'll find you a good book on them.'

'It's different from all this other stuff.' Luke waved his hand towards the glass cases that filled the long room.

'Yes. Different for all sorts of reasons. It feels like the work of a much later period, I always think. It's the surface it's painted on, the texture of the paints. Advances in brushes.' I was enjoying my mentor's role. 'That's why they seem so much closer to us.'

'How much is it?' he said.

'One went the other day for a hundred thousand,' I said, 'though this one won't fetch so much as that – maybe fifteen thousand or so. But the thing I've never understood is that this will sell for a small sum compared to a piece of later art by a second-rate artist's pupil, or compared to some rather poor contemporary work.'

'But you wouldn't buy it?' he asked. He looked puzzled.

'No. But it will bring a good price here. So for us, there's no profit to be made.'

'But you could buy it for yourself?'

I was taken by surprise at this suggestion.

'I couldn't afford it, Luke. I'm not rich, you know.'

'Well, Kit then. Couldn't he buy it?'

'If he started doing that he'd go out of business,' I said, though Luke had a point. Kit could buy the picture for himself, but he wouldn't.

'You can't really be a collector and a dealer,' I explained. 'Or Kit can't. He has to keep those two ideas separate.'

Luke shrugged his shoulders. 'But he's got stuff in the house, I've seen it.'

'Little pieces. But he'd be in trouble if he started buying seriously. He'd never want to part with anything.'

Luke seemed about to argue, but then to change his mind. His features settled into agreement.

'You're right,' he said. 'He's a smart bloke. Keep your distance. Don't make it personal.'

'Is that what they taught you at college?' I was curious as to where this streetwise counsel had come from.

'No. I just picked it up. You're smart, too, Josie. I want you to teach me.' He squeezed my arm and the gesture made me jubilant. I felt as if I had just been promoted.

'Take your time, have a look around at whatever catches your eye,' I said. 'I've got some things marked to see.'

'Then I'll come with you,' Luke said.

It had become clear to both Kit and me that though Luke had not taken an academic route, he was clever, and up to a point had had a sound education. And he was literate in ways that eluded us. We had recently let him take over the gallery's website and now it seemed a miracle of modernity to us, whose technical knowledge and skill were minimal.

'What's that?' Luke asked. We were peering down

through the glass counter, on to a crowded shelf, as if we were in a shop. I had been inspecting a job lot of early Classical pottery bowls, the sort of thing I knew Kit could shift quite quickly to balance the slower turnover of more expensive objects, which could take so long to sell.

'What?'

'That thing.' Luke was pointing at a tiny blue-green figure which lay on its back a few inches from the vessels, among the exquisite small combs and rings which made up so much of this sort of sale. 'I've seen one like it at home, at Millbury Street,' he said.

'It's a Tawaret,' I replied. 'It's quite a good one by the look of it. I'll get them to pull it out in a moment. But do have look at these.' I pointed at the group of bowls, one of which was alabaster. 'These are good, and that's almost a smaller version of the one you showed me.'

'What was it for?' he asked.

'Who knows,' I said. 'It might have been a domestic utensil or it might have been used in a temple for offerings. Or for purification on entrance – but only for VIPs, not the hoi-polloi, they weren't allowed in.'

'Like holy water in church, you mean?' Luke said.

I was surprised by this. A reference of this sort to his Catholic background was something that Luke usually sidestepped.

'Yes,' I said, 'I suppose like that. It seems to have been a common enough religious practice through the ages. I suppose it's some sort of purification. Cleanse yourself before communicating with the gods, that sort of thing.' I hesitated a moment, wondering if what I had said might have offended him. 'Or God,' I said. 'Whatever you happen to believe in. I sort of gave it all up is the truth. I suppose you must have gone to church a lot, growing up?'

Luke was silent. I thought for a moment he hadn't heard me. It was as if he were remembering something, but then he said, 'Yeah, yeah, lots. But a long time ago. And I haven't been in a church since Mum died. She was the religious one.' He turned to me. 'You go to church though, don't you, Josie?'

I looked at him, taken aback by this observation.

'I saw you a few weeks ago,' he said. 'I was walking up Victoria Street. You went into the cathedral, the Catholic cathedral. You never told me you were a Catholic.'

'Well I'm not, not any more,' I said. I had never mentioned my Catholicism to him. I suppose it was something I might have done, given his upbringing, but I had thought that he might hold it against me, that he might not want this link between me and his former life.

I found myself disconcerted by the idea that he had seen me in a private moment, but without my knowledge, just as I had seen him in St James's Park a few weeks earlier. I wondered why he hadn't told me before.

'You never mentioned it,' I said. 'As I say, I don't practise my faith but I pop into the cathedral sometimes. I used to live just round the corner. It's more just to have a think. I don't really believe it these days.'

'I know what you mean,' he said. 'It's good to have a think sometimes, isn't it?' He nudged me gently, and it felt soothing, but all the same, I was uneasy to realise that he had watched me; uneasy, too, that he might feel I had kept my shared religion from him, as if it were something to be ashamed of.

'I'll be back in a minute,' he said. 'I need to find the gents.'

I had been wandering through a small avenue of statuary on the right-hand side of the saleroom, waiting for Luke to come back. He had been gone a little longer than I expected and I walked over towards the doorway to see if his attention had been caught by the numerous other artefacts in the room below which had nothing to do with the sale in hand. And then I saw him, standing at the bottom of the stairs, and he appeared to be talking to someone who was just out of my vision, obscured by a pillar. Luke was smiling and as I watched, he extended his hand. As he did so, a portly man came briefly into view. I saw him only for a moment, but I at once had the feeling that this man must be Michael. I tried to pin down the features, see him properly, but he stepped back again and Luke turned as if to start up towards the saleroom. I pulled back quickly before he could see me and moments later he was at my side.

We had returned to the small objects counter where I now made a detailed survey. These were the bread and butter of the trade, some more valuable than others, easily transportable, collectable, and unthreatening to the novice buyer. The auction assistant had laid out before us the vessels I had requested, and also the tiny Tawaret, and he was waiting, ready to turn them over and around, as we wished.

'I sort of like that,' Luke said, pointing at the Tawaret. 'What's it worth?'

'A few hundred pounds. What do you like about it particularly?' I asked.

'Don't know, it's a weird thing.'

I laughed. 'The one at Millbury Street is Isobel's,' I said. 'Kit gave it to her for her birthday.'

'But it's bigger than this,' Luke said.

'Bigger and better,' I replied.

I looked closely at the little hippo-faced figurine in front of me. 'That's a nice example,' I said, squinting. 'But, yes, I do think Isobel's is better, and not just because of its size – the tiny ones can be even more valuable depending on what they're made from.' It occurred to me that I had not seen Isobel's Tawaret since the night of her birthday. I wondered where she kept it. It was hidden from public view, that was certain.

'What's it for?' said Luke. 'They're always for something.'

'It protects pregnant women, and it's a sort of fertility symbol.'

'It didn't work then,' he said, looking at me.

'No,' I said. 'Not this time.'

Although Isobel appeared to have recovered from the miscarriage, sometimes I would look at her and see the flatness of her belly and its contours, or rather lack of them, and they would feel like a rebuke, as if it were our fault, mine and Kit's and Luke's. Since the end of the summer it had become harder and harder for her to conceal her mixed feelings about Luke. She was disappointed, I suspected, when Kit offered him a more permanent position at the gallery, though Kit reassured her that it was just a way of getting Luke up on his feet. She seemed confused by Luke; she found his easy self-deprecation engaging, just as we did, but there were times when it was clear that she felt threatened by his presence.

I had to admit, too, that I had begun to experience a guilty pleasure in her discomfort, and the feeling unsettled me. I was disturbed to sense this small rift opening between us because I liked Isobel, or I had always thought I did. And I liked her father even more. But fond of her as I was, I couldn't help but fret that sometimes her kindness to me, so far, had more to do with pity than with liking, and I could not bear to be pitied. Under this new dispensation, our positions were reversed. Luke was Alice's son, Alice who had belonged to Kit and to me. It was now Isobel who was envious of an intimacy to which she was not admitted. Isobel was the one left out.

As I stood with Luke at the Christie's counter, looking at the Tawaret, I thought that if I were Isobel, I would be worried. I would think that the bond between Kit and Luke Tyler might make a future child, especially one that was not biologically his, less important to him. And if that were the case, would it mean that Isobel might also matter to him less? I pushed the thought away, it was cruel and corroding, and I turned back to Luke who was watching the small wiry man on the other side of the counter display a Bactrian comb to the customer next to us, waving his white-gloved hands like some old-fashioned minstrel.

'You still haven't told me why the Tawaret caught your eye,' I said to Luke, pointing to the amulet in front of us. 'It's important to notice what draws you. It's how you refine your taste, how you start knowing what you're looking for.'

Luke stared down at the little creature and touched it with his finger while the assistant continued to be distracted by a customer at the next case.

'Well, partly because I saw the one at Millbury Street,' he said. 'But I like that it's more than one thing. It's like something stuck together. Different animals. It's like the strongest bits.'

'Potent might be more appropriate,' I said, remembering Jack's insinuations.

'Potent?'

'Powerful,' I interpreted. 'It's a symbol of all sorts of power.'

'I suppose that's what I like then,' Luke said.

Fifteen

'I was thinking this afternoon,' said Isobel, a few days later, 'about Luke.' There was an effort in her voice, as if she had been taking her time, considering what she was about to say.

'Yes? What have you been thinking?' I asked. She was sitting on the terrace, wrapped in a coat, watching as I cut back the vigorous, woody geraniums that were threatening to topple the terracotta pots they sat in. The gardener was away, on his annual holiday in Goa, renting a small palace no doubt on the proceeds of what the joint residents of Millbury Street paid him. Perhaps, I thought, I should make that my new career. I had a feel for it after all. The plants in front of me seemed to stand firmer after my tending and snipping.

We were waiting for Jack who was on his way over in a taxi to join us for supper. Kit was entertaining a client and wouldn't be back till later, and Luke too was out, absent in the mysterious manner to which I had become accustomed. I treated it now as a sign of his feeling at home, and was pleased that he felt no need to explain his comings and goings, not that he had ever done so.

It was warm for the time of year, though too cold to be outside for long if not walking. It was dark and the terrace was lit by small lamps as well as the light from the kitchen. We could just about see the water at the grass's edge. It looked sluggish, the usual ripples barely perceptible, while the small ducks and moorhens rested on top of the water, enervated and still.

'I've been thinking about Luke a lot lately,' Isobel continued. Her voice implied that we were about to have a serious conversation and there was a new insistence in her tone. I was surprised for it had seemed, recently, that she had stopped mentioning Luke at all, unless Kit or I brought him up. Her daily manner towards him was pleasant enough and she had dropped the edge of hostility that had occasionally crept in.

'I was sitting at my table in the studio today,' she said, as she cradled a cup of coffee, 'looking at some sketches for the Reddaway portrait, and I found myself doodling, and thinking about Luke and you and Kit, and then I wrote down a list of words that were dancing in my head.'

There was something in her tone that made me unsure that I wished to hear what was coming next.

'I wrote a list of words that came to mind when I thought about Luke.' She drank from her cup, all the time keeping her gaze on me. I took off my gardening gloves and fished in my pocket for a bar of chocolate. I offered her a piece but she refused, and I bit into it myself, dark and bitter. I sucked on it slowly, knowing she was waiting for me to give her permission to go on.

'And what were they?' I felt I had to answer, or rather ask the expected question.

'Seductive,' she said, and smiled at me, 'that was the first word, followed by reticent, knowing, chameleon, handsome, and . . . damaged – but I did find myself putting a question mark after that last one.'

'Goodness,' I said. 'Quite a few words.' I was surprised to feel as affronted as if she had been talking about me. I wanted to ignore the last of what she'd said, but it was impossible.

'Damaged, Isobel? That's rather strong.'

There had been times in the past when we had sat here discussing other people in our lives, as women will do from time to time, always with the others' best interests at heart, speculating as to how they might improve themselves and their lot if only they could see things as we did. But I found it made me queasy to start such a conversation around Luke, and I could not collude with Isobel, from whom I was feeling increasingly distant.

Isobel, however, appeared to be unaware of any change in me, unaware and perhaps uninterested, I thought; I was after all just a part of the comfortable, well-supported fabric of the life with which she had been provided. I might be there, as far as she was concerned, just to listen to her, to make her supper, to keep the wheels well oiled.

'Yes, it is strong, isn't it?' she went on. 'And I guess I don't really think that. It just came to mind. But then, it's not like he's had it easy, is it? He's more complicated than he looks. He has to be. I know Dad thinks so.'

'Really?' I said. Jack had said nothing to me, but then

there had been little opportunity. Still, I thought, it was clear that Isobel had some sympathy for Luke, at least, and I felt I shouldn't be quite so provoked by the implications of what she was saying.

'I'm not sure that I would want to describe anyone as damaged,' I said, 'and certainly not Luke. It sounds like damaged goods or something, as if someone were beyond the pale.'

'I'm sorry,' she said. 'I didn't intend for it to sound like that.'

'I'm sure you didn't,' I said. I wondered how, precisely, she had intended it to sound. 'But what did your father say?'

'You can ask him when he comes. But it wasn't Dad's word, not "damaged".'

'Perhaps you should ask him why you wrote it down.'

Isobel laughed. 'Or perhaps we had better not mention it to him. The D-word, I mean.' She hesitated. 'But I do sort of like Luke, Josie, you know. I do really. I just don't get him.'

It was true. She had been trying to make the best of this curious set-up she found herself in, but I knew she had begun to wonder if Luke would ever leave. For her, he would always be a stranger, and a reminder of a woman she had thought long dead. But for Kit, Luke might have been the child they couldn't have, and he was reclaiming something precious, something that he had given up hope of existing.

'I'm jealous of him, Josie,' Isobel said suddenly, standing up. 'That's the truth.'

I followed her back into the house where she took off her coat. She was wearing a pale green wool cardigan over a T-shirt and had pushed up the sleeves to reveal a dark brown paint splash on her forearm.

'I don't mind admitting it, or at least not to you,' she went on. 'I'm ashamed of myself.'

I was disarmed by this unexpected admission. There was a part of me that wanted to push Isobel away, as if to make more room for Luke, but now she was asking me to help her. She was asking me to stay close. I felt at that moment that it was physical comfort she wanted but I couldn't bring myself to put my arms around her, it seemed awkward, so I patted her hand instead.

'It was bound to be difficult, Isobel,' I said. The words sounded useless and empty.

'The thing is,' she said, 'I've tried to think about it. In different ways. I mean if Luke had been Kit's long-lost son, I mean his actual son, I could understand this attachment he has for him. But then Alice would never have had Kit's son adopted. That's the point.'

Was it the point? I thought. I was unable to follow her logic.

'If Luke were Kit's son,' she went on, 'then I would be obliged to love him, to mother him even, if he would let me. As it is, I don't know what's expected of me. I've tried to explain this to Kit but he doesn't understand. We had an argument this morning, Josie. We hardly ever argue.' She looked at me as if begging me to make things right.

'I'm sorry to hear that, Isobel,' I said. 'I'm sure Kit

wouldn't want to hurt you, or to make you feel awkward.'

'He said I should leave it alone, that we should leave things alone. That they would find their own level.'

'That sounds quite sensible to me,' I said.

'But I have been leaving it alone, and it just gets worse,' she said. Her face was angry now, frustrated like a small child. The doorbell rang and we looked at each other. It was almost certainly Jack.

'Have you talked about any of this to your father?' I said.

'Yes,' she said, getting ready to let him in. 'Yes, I have.'

It was a relief to hear that she had someone else to confide in, though I was also a little surprised. Isobel and her father were close, but I had thought that her marriage, or certainly any marital difficulties, might be something she would hesitate to share with him.

'I'll come upstairs with you,' I called to her. I didn't want to be alone in the garden brooding on what she had said, especially now that Jack had arrived. He would pick up on any tension between us straight away. His political sense was acute. I followed her into the house and together we climbed the wooden stairs to open the door.

'I'll tell you one thing,' she said. 'Dad says that which-ever way I look at it, it will always come back to the same thing. Luke is Alice's son.'

The sight of Jack Whaley was even more welcome than usual. He stood just outside the front door, a small bunch of flowers for each of us in his hands. It was an incongruous but touching gesture from a man whose presence was rarely reassuring, though this evening it felt so. I was pleased, too, that he had come without Helen who was visiting her daughter in Monmouth.

'Good thing too,' he said. 'We're fed up with each other.'

'You don't mean that, Dad.'

'Yes I do,' he said. 'It's a sad fact, but I don't know if we can really rub along much further.' He seemed to look over at me as he said this, and in spite of myself, I felt a small but unaccustomed yearning. Jack was a flirt, I told myself. There was no point in making myself appear foolish.

'I'm sure you'll sort things out between you,' I said. I didn't like Helen much, but part of me suspected she was good for Jack. Or rather, she was capable of the necessary patience that being attached to him required. 'She suits you,' I continued.

'In some ways she does,' he agreed. 'Perhaps that's the problem. Being suited can be dull.'

Isobel took his coat and quickly changed the subject. I sensed that neither she nor I were in the mood tonight to pursue Jack's line of thinking.

'How hungry are you, Dad?'

'Very,' he said.

Jack retained a student's appetite. He was rounder in the middle than he had once been but his body was still straight and strong. I was glad to notice that he had stopped the winter coughing that had bothered him earlier in the year and seemed his old self again. We sat together at the big kitchen table as he ate two plates of pasta followed by a bowl of sticky toffee pudding and cream which I had made specially for him, knowing that Helen would not be there to disapprove.

We didn't talk at first about Luke but about Isobel's work, about paintings and portraits and an exhibition of contemporary art which Jack had been to, and whose excesses he defended loudly against what he still called the bourgeoisie. It felt comfortable, sitting there in the warm kitchen, untroubled for now by the past or the future, and I thought how pleasant life would be if this were our permanent world, containing just the three of us, a world without Luke Tyler or Kit, or Margaret Haddeley or Helen; especially, perhaps, without Helen. And for the moment I forgot about Luke, and I forgot to be cross with Isobel, and life seemed simple once more.

But as the evening wore on, Isobel could not resist bringing up the subject of Luke. I watched her as she recounted, to her father, the words she had ascribed to him. Jack's face gave little away, but he was listening now with intent and I wondered if that was how he looked to his analytical patients and whether I would want him to look at me in that way.

'The thing is,' Isobel was saying, 'there are no precedents. I can't be a stepmother, wicked or otherwise, since Kit's not his father. I'm nothing to Luke. Why should I be of any interest to him? It sometimes feels to me as if I don't exist for him, or that he would prefer it if I didn't.'

This was a new complaint, and it seemed harsh. As far as I could see, Luke had always acknowledged Isobel. There had even been a few occasions when I had seen him flirting with her, and she, to my surprise, had responded. I had been taken aback, even a little shocked, but I had told myself that if it disarmed Isobel's hostility, I couldn't blame Luke. Isobel was an attractive woman, not so much older than him; he would not be immune to her physical charms. But it was true that sometimes Luke did behave as if Isobel were superfluous. Sometimes he did appear to forget her, and then make a deliberate, almost clumsy, effort to include her. At such moments it was possible to feel that he too had a picture of a parallel life, one in which the three of us existed, him and Kit and me, one in which she played no part.

Jack was still listening patiently to his daughter's grievances. He waited till she stopped and I could see that she was anxious for his response.

'Isobel,' he said at last. 'For once that husband of yours is right. It's going to take time for this to resolve itself.' His tone was appeasing, apologetic for the banality of his words. It had an air of repetition, as if he had soothed her on this matter several times before. Isobel started to talk again, seeming to be beyond his comfort. The sound of her voice grew sharper as she vented further frustrations. It seemed to echo over the garden and down to the water which now looked viscous in the thick dusk. She was angry with Kit, she was angry with Luke, and she veiled her fury under a torrent of self-justification. As I sat quietly between them, not wishing to be part of their argument, I could only suppose that she was also angry with me.

*

'Think about where this boy has come from, Izzy,' Jack was saying to her. 'He's just a child, for God's sake, a child with no bearings.'

Isobel was silent at last. She looked at her father, both surprised and annoyed at this sympathy for the source of her anxiety.

'So he's got to you too, Dad,' she said. 'I rest my case.'

Jack got up from the table and went to the fridge to help himself to another beer.

'Listen to yourself, woman,' he said, banging the bottle on the table. 'You're making Luke sound like a demon child. Like a changeling. You have no evidence for these difficulties you anticipate, do you?'

'No,' Isobel admitted. 'Not really. It's just a feeling.'

Jack turned to me, raising his eyebrows. 'Any whisky, Josie?' he said.

He looked tired, I thought, and even a bit troubled. Perhaps his relationship with Helen really was under strain. There was a bottle of whisky on standby in the kitchen cupboard and I fetched two glasses, pouring him a good measure with a dash of water. By the time I sat down again he was expanding on his point of view.

'Kit feels guilty,' he was saying, 'and he can hardly compound his guilt by ignoring the woman's child.' It felt harsh to hear poor Alice referred to as 'the woman', though I knew he didn't mean to wound.

'Why, Dad? Why should Kit feel guilty?' Isobel protested.

'It's his default position,' Jack said.

'Oh, Dad. That's just shrink talk.'

Jack shrugged and took a large slug of his drink.

'He's taking the only reasonable route open to him,' he said, 'and if you want to hang on to him I suggest that you go along too, my girl. And that's a father's advice, not a shrink's.'

I was embarrassed by the baldness of Jack's approach. It felt too honest for my consumption.

'And what if he wants to keep me?' Isobel sounded angry as she lifted her glass to her lips. 'Where do I fit in all this? Am I just supposed to put up with it?'

'Oh, Isobel,' I said. I wanted them to stop. I wanted it all to stop. Alice would have hated this, I found myself thinking. It's not what she would have wanted.

'Kit didn't have to invite him to live with us,' Isobel said. She looked at me for corroboration. 'I know that strictly speaking he lives with you, Josie, but you know what I mean. And after all, it's a terrible imposition.'

'He's no trouble,' I said. I wanted to say more. I wanted to say that I adored having Luke staying with me, that the presence of this young man had brought a new vitality into my life.

'There's something in the boy that Kit needs.' Jack's voice was more gentle. 'You have to accept that.'

'What?' she said.

He looked pained, knowing what he said would hurt her.

'A part of his first wife,' he said. 'A part he hasn't mourned. They don't just go away, the dead. You can't just make them history.'

Jack raised his empty glass to me, by way of a question,

and I nodded. He grabbed my glass along with his, and got up from the table, his whole body suggesting a slight impatience with his daughter. He strode towards the whisky bottle which stood on the counter and poured two more generous measures. As he turned back and smiled, bearing the glasses aloft, I thought of all the many others who had drunk and slept in this house over the years, especially the Toby years, and despite my earlier tenderness of heart towards Jack, I felt an unexpected weariness.

On the odd occasion that Alice's mother Anne had visited Millbury Street she too would sit in the kitchen, just as we all continued to do. She would drink until Toby helped her to the sofa at the far end of the room where she usually fell asleep. By the time Alice was eleven, Anne had deteriorated to such a point that Christopher and Margaret had arranged for the long-suffering daily, Mrs Durden, to move into a cottage close to Anne's Norfolk home to keep an eye on things. It was an arrangement that suited everyone, including Mrs Durden, now a widow.

Alice still spent part of the longer holidays with Anne in Norfolk and she saw her father, Roddy, when he returned from Rome to Scotland for a month each summer. But now, increasingly, she spent much of the holidays, and most of her half-terms, with Toby and me.

The time we had spent together in her childhood had laid the foundations of a fond relationship, and I sometimes felt she was more my god-daughter than Toby's. Not that Toby didn't adore her, but his attention span was short, and however fond he was of anyone or any thing, there was always the next person or drug or party to distract him. He admired Alice too; she had grown into a very pretty girl, extremely slim and with no sign of any adolescent gaucheness. Her hair was long, very dark and glossy with a slight curl, and she had retained her air of intriguing eccentricity, now combined with a flirtatious gaiety in her feline eyes.

There was also an independence about her. She seemed uninfluenced by her contemporaries, and she would talk about the girls at school that she knew in a way that suggested she was indifferent to their opinions. I had once wondered if she held herself apart because she might have been bullied, or through some difference of view, but having taken her to a couple of schoolgirl parties in London, I came to the conclusion that this was not the case. Alice was popular, it was obvious. She just didn't seem to require a best friend, or to share confidences in the way that most girls of her own age did. She liked instead to talk to me and to Toby and our friends. All traces of childhood seemed to have disappeared early on. She was already, and perhaps too quickly, an adult.

I had tried to keep evidence of the sometimes dissolute life we led at Millbury Street away from Alice, but it had proved futile. She was far too intelligent not to take in the landscape that Toby, particularly, inhabited, and he was far less concerned than me about leaving traces of its existence. She was also, I came to understand, very much more sophisticated than I had been at a similar age, and I wondered where her knowledge came from. I could only presume that she and her schoolfriends had shared the secrets they had gleaned from their individual grown-up worlds.

But there were moments that had begun to worry me. She liked to spend time alone, reading in her bedroom, something I encouraged. But then she would put the books aside, complaining that the words could not keep up with her thinking. Her mood might become heightened and she would have sudden enthusiasms which were engaging, but the energy that accompanied them was draining. I tried to remind myself that she was entering adolescence, that she was a young girl, beset by the usual changes in body and mind, especially when she came back from shopping with several bags of expensive clothing which I had to make her return the next day.

Sometimes she would still be up at 2 a.m., long after I thought she had gone to sleep. I would see her bedroom light on, and go in to find her pasting together bits from magazines, making collages, often of family groups, I noticed. It was an art project for school, she told me, which I knew was true, but it made me uneasy. I felt ill qualified, however, and too exhausted myself to do anything but make her get into bed and turn off the lamp. I promised myself I would mention it to Anne or to Alice's house-mistress the next time an opportunity arose.

My misgivings sometimes led me to ask if Anne had been right in accusing me of telling Alice too many stories. I would dwell on this conundrum, sitting in the gallery, staring around at the figures and silent fragments, nursing a cup of coffee or, depending on the time of day, a glass of scotch. And from time to time, when I went to sit in the cathedral, I would pass by the statue that had so caught her attention. It was then, especially, that I would fear that perhaps there was something in what Anne had said; that I had allowed a child, too young and vulnerable, to handle the dead.

Sixteen

There was, of course, at least one person still alive to whom Luke Tyler was actually related, his grandfather, Roddy Wearing, who was now almost eighty and suffering from partial dementia. Roddy had never really been a part of my life, though I had met him once or twice since our first meeting all those years ago in the Sombrero nightclub. He belonged to an earlier time. He had been a friend of Margaret's from childhood, and later became close to Toby, a friendship based, I assumed, on their shared homosexuality.

Roddy was old school. He was a man who, despite gay liberation and the relaxing of the homosexuality laws, had chosen to live a semi-secret life devoted to his pleasures. According to Toby, he had found it easier to do so away from his class and his country. He should never have married, of course, and after his early divorce from Alice's mother, he had gone to Rome where he still lived, cared for by his long-term lover, Domenico, in a splendid rented apartment overlooking the Tiber.

With Luke's permission, Kit had contacted Roddy, or rather he had contacted Domenico, soon after we had learnt about Luke's existence. It was difficult to know how much Roddy understood of what had happened. Domenico told us that sometimes he seemed to remember that there had been a child, and in those moments he knew that the child had been adopted, but nothing more. A visit had been arranged, but then Roddy had become quite unwell and it had had to be postponed. Now, however, Roddy was asking to see Luke, or so Domenico thought. It was hard to tell, he said, but we all agreed that Luke should go, and soon, our unspoken thought being that it would be horribly unfortunate if death were to deprive Luke of family contact yet again.

He was booked on an early flight from Heathrow and I offered to drive him there. I had intended just to drop him off but, anxious that we shouldn't be late, we arrived far too early. Despite his protestations, I insisted that I should park the car, come in with him and buy him breakfast. Luke was almost silent as we ate, sitting at the Formica-topped table. He had ordered scrambled eggs and sausages, brought by a waitress who spoke no English at all as far as I could see and who was wearing a checked apron with an old coffee stain on it, which offended me. Surely at least she could start the day clean.

He ate with a strange concentration, looking neither to right nor left. I wondered if it was because he wanted to avoid further conversation with me. It was perhaps too early in the day for him to be sociable, and I had foisted myself on him before he was ready. But this explanation didn't make sense. I knew that Luke was the type of person who entered his day on first waking. We were similar in

216

that way, I liked to think. Even with a hangover, I too tried to grab the morning and not waste it hiding behind the cornflakes packet. We had been good breakfast companions. Not like with Toby, I'd often thought, who had resented my morning cheerfulness and had learnt to hide until he had fought his way out of the melancholy fog which beset him each day.

'Are you nervous about meeting your grandfather?' I said, finally, reduced to the obvious.

Luke looked up at me and put down the toast which he had been carefully focusing on.

'Sorry, Josie,' he said. 'I was just thinking.'

'That's all right. It would be odd not to be nervous.'

'Oh, I'm not nervous,' he said. I waited. 'I was just wondering . . .' He hesitated, then said, 'Is he rich, my grandfather?'

I was taken aback by his question though it was reasonable. Luke never really talked about money. Kit paid him a small wage and he paid no rent to me, though Kit gave me something for his food and keep.

'I don't think so,' I said, thinking of the run-down house where Anne had lived and the complaints from Alice's school that the fees were late again. 'I think he might have been, once, but Toby told me that Roddy was hopeless with money. He tried to persuade Roddy to invest in the business, early on, but Roddy never thought that Toby would make a success of it.'

'But he lives in Rome?'

'Rome is cheaper than London, Luke.'

'He doesn't work.'

'He lives on his dwindling capital.' I knew that Domenico had told Kit that he feared the money would run out, and that soon Roddy would need greater care.

'What about his flat?'

'It's rented, I believe.'

I was beginning to feel uncomfortable, but why should Luke not entertain the idea of an inheritance? For the first time it occurred to me that he might feel he was due one, but from whom? He had been adopted. I assumed he had no legal claim on Roddy, or Kit, or anyone else, though I wasn't sure. But he might, I thought, have a moral one.

There was a further silence between us, and again Luke stared into space as he took a large bite of a second piece of toast. He had slicked back his dark curls with some product or other and was wearing a blue jacket over his jeans. He looked, in fact, Italian and I was struck by the self-consciousness of this and reminded of Isobel's list of words. She was right about that too. There was something of the chameleon in Luke, a need to blend in, which given what had happened to him was unsurprising.

Luke's glance wandered for the first time beyond the food and the table. I followed his gaze and he looked back quickly and smiled at me.

'I'm not after his money,' he said. 'I just wondered.'

'Why shouldn't you wonder?' I said. 'He's got no children, after all. You're his nearest relative.'

'He knew about me, though, didn't he?'

'You mean he knew that you had been born, yes. That's my understanding now.'

Luke's face was clear of emotion, as if he had erased all

traces of feeling. I could not imagine what it must mean to know that someone had allowed you to be given away, someone adult and responsible. Luke might just forgive Alice who had been almost a child, but how much harder it must be to forgive Roddy, a man, a grandfather, who had had the means to provide for him.

'He's old now,' I said, by way of appeasement. 'And ill. You might not get much sense out of him.'

'I'm not expecting to,' Luke said. 'I'm just going for the ride.'

'Aren't you curious?'

'A bit. But in the end it makes no difference, does it?'

'Difference to what?'

'He didn't want me around. None of them did.'

'I don't expect it was like that, Luke.' I could hear anger just below the calculated flippancy. He was usually so guarded. I felt apprehensive, but also excited at being privy to his inner world, even if it was a dark one.

'I think it was,' he said. 'I think it was just like that.' He finished his coffee and began to collect his things together. 'I'd better go through now. Thanks for coming, Josie, and for coming in. I really appreciate it.' He kissed me on the cheek and all his warmth was back. He turned and smiled as he crossed the concourse and I waved at him.

'I'll pick you up,' I called.

'No need,' he said and blew me a kiss.

As I turned back towards the exit I caught sight of a figure crossing to my right and heading towards Departures, a man carrying a briefcase, wearing a blazer and smart well-cut linen trousers. He was quite portly, and his bald head and something in his bearing made me think of the man I had glimpsed so briefly at Christie's. I watched the figure move towards the security gates. I couldn't be sure they were one and the same person, in fact, it seemed most unlikely. But as I turned to leave I couldn't resist another backward glance. He was standing in line and there was something elusive about him, about the way the man blended into the crowd. He disappeared suddenly, swallowed up in the queue to go through the doors. As I turned to leave, I felt an absolute conviction that I was right, and that this was no coincidence. It was the man, Michael, and he was going to Rome with Luke, I was sure of it.

❧

During the week of Luke's visit, I had plenty of time to reflect on whether or not I was imagining what I had seen at the airport. I had to acknowledge that I had no real evidence that the man I had spotted was the same person that Luke knew. But I couldn't stop asking myself, if it was him, then why was he going to Rome? He might have business there, I told myself, and had chosen to go at the same time as Luke. The obvious implication was that Luke was gay, and that Michael was his friend, but I was unconvinced. I liked to think that sexual preference was something I could tell about men, I had had enough experience, but Luke was a new generation and it might be that now there were different signals to which I wasn't privy.

But I had seen Luke flirting with women, with Isobel, even with me. I found myself wondering if he were one of those young men who are, let us say, adaptable, seductively ambidextrous for their own purposes. I had come across men like that. It saddened me to think that Luke might feel the need to use himself in such a way, but his circumstances had been such that he had a tendency to want to please everyone. I couldn't have cared less if he were gay, but I did wonder how the others would react to such a revelation and I smiled to myself as I thought about Margaret. Margaret Haddeley, it had to be said, would be very disappointed.

To my surprise, on the third day of Luke's absence, Isobel asked me out to lunch, a rare invitation when she was working hard on a portrait. I wondered if she had detected my low mood, but it was more likely, I thought, that she had something to ask me, or to say to me, that she considered important, and that she felt should be aired properly between the two of us.

The restaurant was just a short walk from the house and we emerged from the quiet tree-lined streets of Little Venice on to the surprising bustle of Edgware Road, an area which I liked to regard, in an over-romantic fashion, as London's Arab quarter. As we walked along, people were skirting around us, hurrying to buy their lunch or aiming for the bus stop or the cafés further down the road, where they could sit outside and smoke a pipe with friends.

Persepolis was a small Persian restaurant, with about six tables for four, each laid with a plain white cloth, and no attempt, I was relieved to see, to provide any spurious heritage décor. We were greeted by a grey-haired man who served as manager and waiter and was quite likely, from his air of authority, to be the owner as well. Isobel handed him the bottle of wine she had brought with her and he whisked it away, returning quickly to pour us each a glass, and speaking to us in perfect if inflected English.

'We have applied for a licence for alcohol,' he said. 'It is not a religious observance like the Arab restaurants here. It is just the licence.'

The two of us looked at each other.

'That felt a bit racist,' Isobel whispered after he had taken our order and disappeared.

'He might just be distinguishing himself from the Arab community,' I said. 'Persians aren't Arabs,' I added.

'I know that.' Isobel looked after the man to check that he wasn't in earshot. 'But most of them are Muslims.'

'Perhaps he's a Zoroastrian,' I said.

Isobel looked suddenly interested. 'There was a boy at my school in Chappaqua who was Zoroastrian,' she said, by way of explanation.

I tried to imagine Isobel at an American high school, but she seemed too self-composed to have fitted into the sort of thing I had seen only in films.

'But I never knew what it was about,' she went on, 'the Zoroaster thing.'

'Well, I could tell you,' I replied, 'but I don't think that's why we're here, is it?' I was aware that my voice might sound rather sharp. I hadn't intended it to, so I smiled at Isobel and raised my glass. 'No lectures today,' I laughed. 'Unless, of course, you really want to know.'

She looked like someone caught out. 'You always get straight to it, Josie,' she said.

'You want to talk about Luke?' I asked.

'No,' she said. 'Well, partly. But what I really want to talk about is Alice.'

The directness of her statement took me by surprise. She had gained the advantage.

'I see,' I said. To my relief, a large tray of food was now making its way towards us. I was hungry. 'Well, now we both know why we are here,' I said, 'first we can eat.'

Isobel hardly touched her food, and she drank even less. Instead she talked, avoiding the subject she had put up for discussion. She spoke fast, telling me about the picture she was working on, about how much she disliked the man she was painting, and then, almost without pausing, she said, 'We've never talked much about Alice, you and I. Not really.'

I put down my fork and swallowed the mouthful of rice I was savouring. It occurred to me to stall for time, to side-step the issue, but I decided instead to reciprocate her directness.

'You could always have asked me,' I said. 'You could have asked before if you'd wanted to.'

'It wasn't a question of want,' Isobel said. 'Kit told me enough. But with you, I thought it was a subject best left alone. I didn't want to press in on your memories. I didn't think it was for me to share them. Perhaps I didn't want to share them.'

'But now, you think differently, because of Luke.' I hoped I had said this in a matter-of-fact way and not accusingly. I tried to seem encouraging as I looked across at her, though I didn't feel so in the least. 'This is very good,' I said, 'would you like to try some?' I pushed my dish towards her but she shook her head.

'No, thank you. I've still got plenty,' she said, waving in the direction of the plate in front of her. She took a sip of water before continuing.

'It's just that now I really need to know more,' she said. 'Now Luke's with us.'

'Yes,' I said. I forked up the last few grains in front of me. I wished that we were not having this conversation here, at Persepolis. I wanted to relish the food. I wanted to be greedy and indulgent and talk of abstract things or gossip about people who didn't matter to me.

'Is it something specific you want to know, Isobel? Do you mean Alice's illness?'

'I need to know everything,' she said. 'I'd like to know all about her.'

'Everything? I'm not sure I know everything.'

'I think you know what I mean.'

'Have you talked to Kit? About Alice? Recently, I mean.'

Isobel looked away. 'I've tried,' she said. 'But he says it's difficult, now. He says he doesn't want to hurt me.'

'I'm sure he doesn't,' I said.

'But he's hurting me more by keeping me outside it all,' she said. 'You could at least tell me more about the old man, Roddy, her father. Is he really senile?'

'He is,' I said. 'And it sounds as though he's got worse. It's such a shame for Luke. Very bad luck.' And for us, I thought, or for me. I wanted to know everything, too.

'Bad luck?' Isobel said. 'That's an understatement. The boy's a walking tragedy.'

'Well, that's what very bad luck is, isn't it?' I said. 'Tragedy. That's how the Ancient Greeks explained it.'

Isobel shrugged. 'I don't know,' she said. 'That's your department. Will he leave Luke any money, do you think?'

I was intrigued that Isobel, like Luke, was concerned with this question.

'I don't think there is any,' I said. 'Or not much.'

'He must have some, surely? He's never worked for a living, has he?' There was a censoriousness in her tone which, I thought, her father would be proud of. 'He doesn't sound like he was much of a father,' she went on. 'Kit said he hardly ever saw Alice. So why would he be interested in Luke?'

'Roddy was never interested in children, not really,' I said. 'But Luke's not a child. And then Roddy has always enjoyed the company of handsome young men.'

'I see,' Isobel said, raising her eyebrows. But I shook my head. I had spoken foolishly. I had meant it lightly but I wondered what had possessed me to say such an inappropriate thing.

'I wonder if you do,' I said. 'I don't mean to be rude, Isobel, but you've grown up in a world where everything is tolerated. It was different for men like Roddy, and even for Toby, though he was that bit younger. It was far more complicated, being a gay man then.'

'I do know that, Josie,' she said. She seemed deflated by my scolding.

'Yes, of course you do. I'm sorry.' I filled up my glass and drank, and I could feel the wine softening my resistance to

225

her questions. 'It was all just such a mess,' I said. 'Poor Alice and her hopeless parents. Such a mess. At least Toby had the good sense not to get married. And she was such a lovely child,' I found myself saying, as if I were about to embark upon something, but then I stopped myself.

'Oh, go on, Josie,' said Isobel. 'Please. Tell me what she was like.'

I put my glass down directly in front of me, a barrier between me and any pain that the memories might bring.

'As a child,' I began, 'she was very sweet. She was vivacious and intelligent, and she remained like that throughout her life – her short life.' Isobel was listening to me with a sort of transfixed expression, as if I were the source of some sort of revelation. 'She was a thoughtful little girl too,' I went on, 'but there was something else about her, a sort of lightness. It was very engaging, except, of course, later on when it got out of hand and sometimes it was as if she floated away, and felt unreachable.'

Isobel nodded but said nothing, and I wondered if I had already betrayed Alice. I hadn't said much, but I had made her sound other-worldly, ethereal, I thought. The Alice I remembered had been flesh and blood, full of laughter, her enthusiasm infectious and tangible.

The waiter hovered by our table, silencing the past with his offer of sweets and pastries. I had been clutching on to the menu, a sort of handle on the here-and-now.

'Isobel, won't you have something?' I said.

'I'll have a mango sorbet, please.'

'Only a sorbet? You are a delicate flower,' I said. 'But

then you look so lovely, I can see it would be a shame to get fat.'

The statement was blunter than I was given to, and I surprised myself, but Isobel laughed.

'Or only for the right reasons,' she said.

'Alice was very slim.' It was a crude return to the subject, but I was unable to resist it. I now wanted to talk about her, it felt like a compulsion. 'She didn't eat much, either,' I went on. 'Toby and I could never educate her about food. She just wasn't interested. Like you in that respect, at least, Isobel.' She flinched and I felt guilty. Why had I added that 'at least' to my observation? There was something diminishing about it. And I had meant to be unkind. But Isobel brushed it aside, and nodded for me to continue.

'I wonder now sometimes if she wasn't anorexic,' I said, 'but we didn't know so much about that sort of thing then. I suppose it was all part of it.'

'She was diagnosed as bipolar, wasn't she?' Isobel said.

I wasn't sure how to reply. I hated hearing Alice described in cold psychiatric terms, none of which seemed to fit her brief flights from reality.

'Well, that's what they call it now,' I said. 'It was manic depression then. But that never seemed right to me, and I don't remember her being depressed. There were some low moods, yes, but not really depressed.'

I picked up my spoon as soon as the waiter set down a plate of sticky sweetness in front of me.

'This looks good,' I said, taking a bite. Isobel watched me, waiting for me to go on.

'I never minded the manic bits,' I said. 'There could be something almost wonderful in them, though they had to be held in check. But I couldn't bear to see Alice sad afterwards and she was only sad, I think, because she felt she had let us down.'

'Poor Alice,' Isobel said.

'Yes. Poor Alice,' I echoed. 'But you have to remember that the episodes weren't frequent. They began, seriously, when she was sixteen, or at least I think so. That was when she was supposed to have had the first breakdown. Then they were every couple of years, though I've gathered from Margaret that there were two bad ones that she hid from Kit for a while, after they were married.'

'But what about before that?' Isobel interrupted. 'What do you think really happened? How did she get pregnant?'

'I don't know,' I said. 'I've tried to remember as much as I can.' I had almost finished the cake. One sad mouthful lay in a sticky pool in front of me. 'If I'd known or suspected, it's not something I would have kept quiet about. Or rather, I can see that I might have done. I might have considered it better to keep Alice's secret. But I can assure you, I simply had no idea.'

'But she was so young. Don't you remember anything from when she used to stay with you at Millbury Street?'

It would be impossible to convey to Isobel, I knew, the chaos of Millbury Street, to explain just how erratic and curious our lives had been.

'Anne, her mother, was very inconsistent,' I said, by way of justification. 'Sometimes she wanted to have Alice to herself, sometimes she sent her to us. I can't remember exact dates. They were complex times.'

'Well, what was she like when she came back? Can you remember?'

'We didn't see her for about ten months. They said she was in a hospital outside Norwich, and not allowed visitors. I suppose it should have seemed odd, but we didn't question it. You have to remember we'd been told she'd had a breakdown. And I think she may have done, in addition to the pregnancy. She certainly seemed fragile when she got back, removed, as if nothing touched her. We assumed it was the medication she was on.'

I wiped the corner of my mouth with my napkin. A dribble of honey was making its way down my chin.

'The time all slides into one,' I said. 'She didn't go back to school, I remember. She had a tutor for a while, and then she stayed with us in London, getting ready to do her history of art course, and seeing Kit, who had come on the scene by then. She should have gone to Oxford or Cambridge really, but Anne never encouraged her. She seemed fine again, more or less. She seemed happy and stable, and then she and Kit got engaged. I remember the party they had, at Fleet. She had such a stillness about her for almost the first time. It was wonderful to see, and I suppose we all hoped the illness was in the past.'

I saw Isobel's gaze move towards my hands, which were resting on the table, and that I had begun to squeeze the still-wrapped sugar twist I was holding.

'I really have given it a great deal of thought, you know,' I said. 'I've thought about Alice a lot, especially recently, and whether we did the right thing at any given time.'

'But what could you have done, Josie?'

'I wish I knew,' I said. 'I feel there was something, or that there should have been something. I feel we failed her.'

'No, Josie,' Isobel's voice was firm.

I smiled up at her. 'That's why we can't fail Luke.'

Isobel closed her eyes for a moment. 'There's another reason,' she said, 'that I want to understand it all. An important one.'

'Oh?' I said. 'What's that?'

'I'm pregnant again.'

I was astonished. In my constant preoccupation with Luke I had somehow regarded Kit and Isobel's life as being on hold, and I felt an odd twinge of indignation that somehow this had come about without my involvement or knowledge. After all, the previous pregnancies had entailed trips to clinics and so on. I had known. I had had to cover for Kit at the gallery.

'Pregnant?' was all I could say. 'How?'

Isobel laughed. 'Yes,' she said. 'You might well ask how. The normal way. Nature's way. Isn't that fantastic? The baby is Kit's.'

'What?'

'Yes. After all that. They told us at the clinic that it wasn't unknown, just very unlikely in our case. But it's happened.'

'Oh, Isobel,' I said. I heard myself whisper and I had no idea why. And then I heard myself say, 'I wonder what Luke will think?' As soon as I had spoken, I regretted it.

'Quite,' said Isobel. She smiled as if to herself. I could see that the thought of what Luke might think gave her satisfaction.

It was the best of all possible news for Kit and for Isobel. And however ungracious my astonishment had made me, I was pleased for them. As I drank my mint tea, I made a decision that I would put all my petty concerns and jealousies to one side. I would make an effort now to bring this family together. I enumerated to myself the benefits Isobel's pregnancy would bring. She would feel more secure. She would be happy to have Luke around. I experienced none of the misgivings I had felt on previous occasions. Isobel would bring the pregnancy to term, I was sure. This child would make it through.

It was odd not having Luke be around the flat and the gallery, even just for the week. He rang home a couple of times and like an anxious mother, I found myself elated, warmed to the core by the contact. I said nothing to him, of course, of my fixation about the man Michael, which had already begun to fade, though the night Luke had left for Rome, I had a dream in which he told me he was homosexual, and that his father had rejected him. I had gathered him up into my arms to comfort and reassure him, but he had laughed in my face and he was no longer Luke, but Toby.

The first time Luke rang from Rome, he was also laughing. The situation in which he now found himself was surreal, he told me.

'He can't remember who I am,' he said, speaking of Roddy, his grandfather. 'He can't remember who he is either most of the time.'

'How awful,' I said. 'Poor Roddy. And poor you, it must be awful for you. Your only real relative and he's . . .'

'Not the full shilling,' said Luke.

'What?'

'A Glasgow expression,' he said, his voice light.

'It must feel a bit much,' I said, but I could feel myself starting to smile too.

'Well,' he went on, 'I wasn't expecting much.' I heard him laugh again, but this time it was with someone at the other end of the line.

'Luke?' I said. 'Are you there?'

'Josie? Sorry. I was just talking to Domenico. He's been fantastic. And he's a laugh. He treats the old boy well too.'

'Good,' I said. 'That's a relief.' As I said it I wondered why I should care, but the thought of any old person alone with no family to look after them, at the mercy of a paid companion, filled me with intimations of my own lonely future. 'Are you managing to see anything? You must get to the Pantheon at the very least.'

'Not yet. I will. I've been walking around the place though. And Domenico's taken me out a couple of times, in the evening. He gets a friend in to babysit Roddy.'

I found myself wondering if Domenico's haunts were entirely suitable for Luke, but then reminded myself that he was a grown man, and possibly a gay one at that, in which case it would be home from home.

'Domenico says I look like Roddy used to look, like my . . . grandfather. But I don't think so. He showed me a picture of him when he was younger.'

'I think it must be true,' I said. 'Toby always said that Alice, your mother, looked like Roddy.'

'There are pictures of her here too,' he said. 'And Domenico knew my mother, he met her once or twice.' Luke's voice was almost wistful for a moment. 'Though he says he can't remember much about her.'

It was odd, I thought, to think that there was another person in the world who had known Alice in a family sort of a way, someone I had never met. 'Yes,' I said, 'I suppose he must have met her from time to time.' I recalled that Alice and Kit had gone out to visit Roddy on two or three occasions, after they married, but that they had never been to stay with him in Scotland, as Alice had done as a girl. Or perhaps it was simply that Roddy had given up the house. I couldn't remember.

Luke rang a second time, the night before he was coming home, but this time he seemed less relaxed. His voice was clipped as he gave me the time of his flight though he didn't protest when I volunteered once more to fetch him.

'Is there anything the matter?' I asked.

'No, why?'

'You sound a bit . . . on edge.'

I heard a man's voice speaking in the background, and I was fairly sure that it wasn't Domenico, whose voice, like his name, had a musical lilt I had come to recognise.

'I told you, I'm not doing that.' Luke's voice was sharp.

'Sorry?' I said.

'Sorry, Josie, I wasn't talking to you. I'm trying to pack and there's someone here. A friend of Roddy's, that's all.' It was strange to hear him refer to Alice's father as Roddy. It felt wrong.

'Oh,' I said, thinking again of the man at the airport, but I could hardly ask Luke to explain himself on the basis of a far-fetched whim of my own.

'I'll see you tomorrow then,' I said.

'Yes, thanks, Josie. I'm looking forward to coming home,' he said, sounding more cheerful, and I put the phone down, reassured.

❧

When Luke got back from Rome, I saw that there was a change in him. His mood was more mercurial, he seemed less able to sustain his concentration, and a certain bitterness crept into his conversation. Whenever I asked him about the trip to Rome, he insisted that it had been a good one, and that although Roddy had been unable to acknowledge him most of the time, there had been an odd moment, he said, when the old man had seemed to understand who he was. There had even been a point when Roddy had cried and shouted out Luke's name, and had seemed in such despair that Domenico had had to give him an injection to calm him down.

'How sad, Luke,' I said.

Luke nodded but he didn't look as if he cared. In the weeks since his return, he hadn't looked as though he cared about much, and I wondered if it was the disappointment of meeting Roddy which had upset him, or perhaps the news that Isobel was having a baby.

I had told him about the pregnancy the night he came back. We were in my small sitting room, drinking whisky. His flight had been late and we were both tired as it was almost midnight. I knew that he had heard what I said, but the news seemed barely to register. He found the grace, however, at least to acknowledge what had happened.

'I'm pleased for Isobel,' he said, eventually. 'It's what she wanted.' The words were perfunctory, uninterested, as if Isobel were someone he hardly knew.

'Yes,' I said, but I couldn't resist asking, 'Aren't you pleased for Kit too?'

He had appeared distracted, as if his mind was far away, but now he seemed to concentrate and his voice was challenging, almost petulant.

'It's not Kit's baby, is it?' he said.

'What?' I said.

I felt a wave of fear at his reply. I had no idea how Luke could have known such a private thing. He was wrong in this instance, of course, but I had thought that only Margaret and I had known Kit and Isobel's secret.

'How could you know about . . . that?' I said.

'You told me,' he said.

'No, I didn't.'

He shrugged. 'I thought you told me. That the babies were someone else's, someone else's sperm.' His emphasis on this last word was contemptuous. It was as if I had brought home an unpredictable stranger.

'It's only like adopting, Luke,' I said.

'It's wrong,' he said. 'It's wrong and unnatural.'

At another moment, in another context, I might have been inclined in some small way to sympathise with this feeling, though not with its expression, but I was not going to be disloyal now.

'Well, this time the baby is Kit's,' I said. 'And conception happened naturally.'

He seemed to struggle with this idea and although he tried to cover what I assumed was his distaste, I could tell that the adjustment he was making was profound. He was still holding the glass of whisky I had given him, and now he raised his glass.

'To the son and heir then,' he said and stood up. 'I'm going to bed.'

~

In the days following, Luke was quiet, but I was reassured to see that he seemed like his old self. He took great care to congratulate Kit and Isobel and express his happiness for them, but I guessed he was anxious as to what it might mean for him and the place he had begun to carve out. He was careful to conceal his moods from Kit and from the clients, but with me he began to show something darker that I found hard to pin down, though for much of the time he was still the friendly, if complex boy we had come to know. I had asked myself if Luke's moods might be affected by the time of year. We were approaching Christmas now, a season that I too found difficult, and this year, for the first time in their marriage, Kit and Isobel were going to spend the holiday with Isobel's mother and stepfather, in Florida.

I had not liked to ask Luke too soon what he was planning. It was even possible that he might go home to Scotland, though that seemed unlikely. But Christmas was a time for patching things up, after all, and there had been one or two phone calls with his father, Philip, which I had overheard in the office. They had sounded a little chilly but at least his father had rung, and I hoped for Luke's sake that relations were improving, and that perhaps their differences were just the legacy of a difficult adolescence.

One afternoon in early December, however, there was another phone call from Philip Tyler. There were just the two of us in the office plus Frank, of course, who was breathing heavily in his basket while his mistress, Rita, had taken a couple of hours off to do her Christmas shopping. I tried not to listen in on the conversation but it was clear to me that Luke seemed put out about something. 'Do what you like,' I heard him say at one point. 'You always have till now.' When at last he put the phone down he looked tense.

'It was my dad,' he said.

'I know,' I said. I had, after all, transferred the call to him, curious about the voice that I had now heard once or twice but couldn't put a face to.

'He and his girlfriend, and my brother, are going to Sri Lanka for Christmas.'

'Oh,' I said. 'I didn't know he had a girlfriend.'

'He met her at the church,' said Luke.

'Did he want you to go with them?' I asked.

Luke laughed. 'No, Josie. He didn't. He definitely didn't want me to go with them.'

'Would you have liked to go?'

'No. It wasn't them going that I was pissed off about. It was that he said I couldn't stay in the house.'

'Couldn't go home?'

'No. And that's what I'd thought I might do. You know. Go back. Stay at home. See some people. But he thinks I'll nick stuff.'

'Really?'

'I wouldn't though. But some of the stuff there is mine anyway. My mum wanted me to have it.'

'I see. That seems a bit harsh,' I said. I didn't know whether to be pleased or alarmed at his admission. 'Well, I don't know what you want to do for Christmas, Luke, but you are welcome to spend it with me. Though it might be a bit boring for you.'

'Aren't you going to your family then?' he said.

'Not if I can help it,' I said. 'Not if I can find a good reason why not.' We smiled at one another, conspirators in our orphan state. I rarely went to relatives for Christmas; it made me feel too much like a maiden aunt among the cousins and in-laws to whom I felt little connection. My family had given up on me long ago.

'It would be just you and me, at Millbury Street?' he said.

'I expect we could go up to Fleet and stay with Margaret, if you felt like it,' I said. 'I'm sure she'd like the company, with Kit and Isobel away.'

'Whatever,' he said, moody again now. 'I don't like Christmas much.'

'Not even when you were younger?' I asked. 'Surely things were better then, with your father?'

'You don't get it, do you?' he said, sounding irritated. 'He never much wanted me around.'

'But he adopted you, Luke,' I said.

'So?'

'I mean, he must have wanted you.'

Luke was petulant. 'Not really,' he said. 'It was my mum who wanted me. He just went along with it. And then I got into trouble, and Mum died, and he only keeps in touch because the priest tells him to. He's glad I'm out of the way.' Luke pushed away from the desk, his face angry. This self-pity was definitely new, I thought.

'Feeling sorry for yourself won't help,' I said. 'It never does.'

'You and your sort don't know much, do you?' he said. He seemed both defiant and ashamed at what he was saying.

'Our sort?' I asked.

'People with no troubles and stacks of money,' Luke said.

'There are no such people, Luke,' I said. 'We all have troubles. And I don't have money. Well, not much.'

'What about my grandfather?' he said. 'Never done a day's work and spent all his money on himself. Not a pot left to piss in.'

'Well, that may be true,' I said. 'But Kit is nothing like Roddy Wearing.'

'Maybe,' he said. 'Sorry. I didn't mean anything by it. Sorry.'

There had been real fury in his tone. It scared me, but I was determined to confront his mood.

'You're right in one way,' I heard myself say. 'We don't know what it was like for you, or what your parents were really like, or anything much. But that's not our fault. You don't tell us a lot, young man. You don't bring your friends home, you don't talk about where you go or what you do. You're a mystery, Luke.'

Luke brushed his hair back from his face. He looked, I thought, hunted, and I was already regretting saying too much.

'Look,' he said, 'I shouldn't have said that stuff. My dad and me, we just don't get on. He makes me angry. There's not much to say.'

'And that's your prerogative,' I said. 'You don't have to tell me anything. But don't expect me to read your mind.'

❧

The weeks up to Christmas were always busy at the gallery and we stayed open longer hours to accommodate our clients. Some of our rich customers would come in to buy smaller items, the jewellery and combs and exquisite little dishes that could be given as presents. It was just as it once had been, I liked to think, just as they had been offered long ago to their ghostly owners.

Luke had begun to talk about finding a flat of his own after Christmas. He remained entirely mysterious in his comings and goings, despite what I had said to him, but I suspected that the strain of compartmentalising his life was beginning to tell.

'I can't live with you for ever, Josie,' he said to me one morning as I made him porridge, which I liked to think made him feel at home. 'You've put up with me long enough. And I'm making enough money now to get a place of my own.'

He certainly didn't seem to be short of money. He would often produce a new item of clothing which he would tell me he had bought in a warehouse sale. Sometimes he just passed them off as cheap but my eye was too good. It wasn't just the cut. Anyone surely could tell a fine cut from a poor one, but I could see the weave of cotton, feel the sheep in the wool. I wasn't fooled. They were expensive and I wondered how he managed to afford such clothes on the salary Kit paid him.

It amused me sometimes to think that he might have inherited this peacock streak. I had to admit that the dreadful Anne, his grandmother, had always been beautifully dressed. There had been a particular pale green Ossie Clark party frock that I remembered. It was low cut and dropped into fine crêpe folds from below her small bra-less breasts. I had envied her the dress beyond reason, and when Toby told me one day that she had fallen over drunk and ripped it from waist to thigh the previous night, I had felt torn myself, between a fury at her carelessness and a guilty pleasure at its destruction.

Luke could not stay with me indefinitely. I knew that, but I was going to miss him very much when he finally left the flat. Life, however, could not continue as it had been.

Isobel's baby was due in the late spring, and Luke would move on. And now Kit was starting to talk about him going to New York, to work with one of our affiliated galleries. At first I was cross. Isobel, I was sure, had put Kit up to this, but how could I deny Luke such a good opportunity?

Whatever the family reasons behind such a plan, Luke was delighted, and in public, at least, fully restored to his former self. He would huddle now with Isobel each evening to talk about America, and this sharing of excitement appeared to bring them closer. I told myself that I could visit Luke if he went away, that it would be wonderful to have a trip to New York. I would take him to the Frick and the Met, but I felt apprehensive for him too. He would be all alone in an alien city and in his current erratic state of mind I wondered if that was for the best. But I couldn't share my misgivings with Kit. I couldn't betray Luke's trust.

Seventeen

There were some days, after moving into the big house with
Toby Haddeley, when I regretted ever having done so.
There were mornings, especially, when I wished I was
waking up, safe in my little flat in Victoria, safe at the top of
the stairs, behind the red-brick façade overlooking the
cathedral. Those were the hangover days. The days when I
felt quite ill from the late-night excesses of the evening
before, the days when I would come down the stairs to the
beautiful first-floor drawing room and look at the sordid
mess left behind, the ashtrays, the Rizla papers, the pipes,
the strewn albums and cassettes. I would see the takeaway
foil trays, soiled, brown and crusty, and the sight and
memory of food, ordered and eaten at some point in the
night, long after I had stumbled into bed, made my stomach
heave. There were glasses everywhere, and empty bottles.
The smell of stale alcohol and smoke lingered, and sometimes there was even a body or two, alive just, and breathing
heavily, stretched out on Toby's expensive sofas.

It was the contrast between the splendour of the house
and the squalid revelation of daylight. There was something masochistic in my ritual revisiting of the night's

detritus on my way down to the kitchen. I would hover in the doorway of the drawing room, indulging some need to imprint its image on my mind, to register my self-disgust, not at the idea of an occasional wild evening but at the frequency with which I took part. I did try each day to be up by nine. I liked to make sure that the gallery was open by eleven. Toby rarely appeared before lunch, except sometimes briefly, to show a client an object before taking him off to a restaurant to negotiate a price.

Coming downstairs one morning from my top-floor bedroom, I noticed as I stood outside the drawing room, peering in, hesitant at what I might find, that the arm of one of Godfrey Marr's statues had been broken off. I felt an acute stab of despair at the sight. I was sentimental about this piece of Marr's work, the only one that Toby owned. It reminded me of the first night we had met in Elgin Square, and how I had wondered about the mysterious Godfrey and his ethereal creatures who seemed to reach out in their sadness, and how Toby had seemed to take notice of me when I said so. I had met Marr once or twice over the years, when he had flown into London. He was as short and round as his creatures were thin, but he lived now in New York and rarely came to England. I lifted up the withered arm from the floor and wrapped it as tenderly as I could, as if it were a wounded bird, in the towel I was carrying. It was a miracle, I thought, that more things didn't get broken.

I had been living at Millbury Street now for almost five years, but I suppose I still felt that in some way it was only a temporary arrangement. Just as Toby had suggested, I had bought the Victoria flat and installed a tenant, a quiet man who worked as a book-keeper in the cathedral office. I thought of its peace and isolation as I cleared one of Toby's Persian cats from an armchair and sat down in the middle of the mess, allowing myself to feel the headache and the wrung-out feeling that followed a night like the previous one. There was, at least, no one here today, I thought, no one left behind, though I suspected there might be a young man upstairs in Toby's bed.

Elena, the cleaning lady, wouldn't be here for another hour or so, by which time I would have scrubbed myself free of the party smells, put on clean clothes, eaten, with deliberation, a good breakfast, and left for work. I had made it my job to pick up anything incriminating, such as the more obvious signs of drug-taking, before Elena's arrival, in case her sensibilities should be offended or she should ever feel vindictive. It was a laughable exercise, just as it was with Alice. No one could spend time in this house without having a sense of the way life was lived, and Elena had been with us for two years. She was a small, round, Portuguese who had married a Scotsman, and her home in the suburbs, to which I had once been invited, was the cleanest place I had ever visited. She would clear away the debris, restoring Millbury Street to her idea of what it should be in a very short time. I did sometimes wonder what she thought about what she saw, but considering how much Toby paid her, it was far more likely that she chose not to see or think about what she encountered.

As I made my way down a further two sets of stairs to the kitchen, my brain began to engage with the day. Alice was coming later that afternoon for summer half-term.

Anne had rung Toby just a couple of days before to ask if we would have her, as we knew she would. This time she claimed she was having some sort of alternative treatment for her spine, but it was more likely that she had begun one of her drinking jags which lasted, these days, for about three weeks. Toby had winced when I told him the excuse she had given.

'We used to have fun once, she and I,' he said. 'But not any more. Not like the fun you and I have now, Josie.'

I was no longer sure that I was having fun. I was thirty-three after all, still young, but perhaps not young enough for the life that Toby was leading, despite his being older than me. But it seemed I had missed my moment for change, and if that was what I had really wanted, I told myself, I should not have moved to Millbury Street. After all, what could be better than my life in this marvellous house, filled by Toby with remarkable people?

In the gallery world, Toby's world, business overlapped with friendship. There were rich foreigners and ageing pop stars and businessmen who enjoyed collecting. There were academics and the would-be artists who helped us or came to look at the beautiful pieces we were known for. Some were homosexual, but by no means all. Some of them seemed to accept my presence in Toby's life as the surrogate wife I had become, and those of them who were seriously interested in the ancient world were delighted to find that I had the detailed knowledge which Toby had no time for.

Still carrying the broken piece of statue, I told myself that I was straying into self-pity, a state of mind I had always regarded as unhelpful. I pulled myself out of my reverie and considered my position. I wasn't trapped. I was still having a good time. I could stay at the party for as long as I wanted to, and when things got too much I could walk away, though not today of course. Today, Alice was coming to stay.

I pushed open the kitchen door, hoping to find the room clean, untouched by the previous evening's guests. Last night had been just a few people coming back after dinner, and though Toby and I had fetched glasses to take upstairs, no one else had been down here, as far as I knew. To my relief, as I came through the doorway, all appeared to be undisturbed as I expected, but then I realised with a sudden shock that there was a figure, a man with his back to me, sitting at the breakfast table. At first it seemed impossible. I was always the first one up in the house. But, yes, there was someone in the kitchen, someone who appeared not to have heard me come in. The radio was playing quietly; I wondered that I hadn't heard it myself as I came down the stairs. Whoever it was sat very still, reading a morning newspaper.

I could hear the birds through the French windows, close to the water beyond. Just for a moment I was immobilised by the still composition of the image before me, and then I felt brave, and spoke into the silence.

'Hello.'

I pulled my dressing gown closer around me as if it might protect me. Even in that scary moment I registered how pleasing its fine pale blue wool felt to me, how reassuring its Liberty's quality. As I did so, the newspaper was lowered slowly, for effect, I thought, and then the figure turned around, smiling. I heard rather than felt my own quick intake of breath.

'Hello, Josie.' The silence in the kitchen was absolute. Even the geese now seemed to have gone quiet. 'It's me,' the man said. 'Back from the dead.'

'Ilya!'

'Yes. Back from the dead, as you see. Do you have coffee? I could not find it.'

'Yes,' I said. 'Hello, Ilya. Coffee. Of course.'

I went that same afternoon to King's Cross to meet Alice. There had been a bomb scare. Someone had left their brief-case in one of the station cafés, and it had been taken for an IRA device, a common enough occurrence in those years. The train was over an hour late by the time the terminal had filled up again with weary passengers, and as I stood near the platform, waiting to collect Alice, my thoughts reverted to what had been preoccupying me all day: the unforeseen resurrection of Toby's friend.

Seeing Ilya in the kitchen that morning, I had been thrown completely off-balance. I had made his coffee like a speechless automaton, while he laughed and joked over the stories that had circulated about his disappearance. What shocked me most was the implication that Toby too had known. Not at first, Ilya hinted, but soon afterwards. Ilya had sworn him to secrecy. I was almost more aston-ished by Toby's ability to keep this secret from me, if it were true, than I was by a man come back to life whom I had thought long dead. I knew Toby could be tight-lipped about business, but about his love affairs he was usually incontinent.

Watching the train approach, keeping clear of the crowd who were now impatient to board, I had a moment of shattering clarity. I had been foolish and naïve. This had been, in part, about business; Ilya had been far more involved in our business than I had ever realised. He was a thief, there was no other word for it, and it had suited him to disappear, to make people think he was dead. He'd been in trouble and had very likely been about to drag Toby with him. He was a looter, a grave-robber, and probably a spy to boot, some low-rent, low-life courier for whoever would pay him.

As the train pulled in and its doors began to open, I found myself wanting to laugh, though I wasn't sure what exactly was amusing. The incipient laughter was more of a panic reaction. Our business was based on illegality, far more so than I had been prepared to acknowledge. The house, the money – I had known there was something amiss, but I had refused to look closely. Our books were clean after all. Clearly there were artefacts passing through Toby's hands that never saw the gallery. Stolen, obtained, or brokered by Ilya under whatever guise he had adopted. And now he was here, which meant what? As I saw Alice stepping out on to the platform in her grey uniform, her regulation suitcase in front of her, I put the thoughts aside. It would have to wait.

When we got home, I followed her upstairs, then, leaving her to unpack her things, I went down a flight. I hadn't seen or been able to contact Toby all day and reaching the landing, I put my head around the door of his bedroom. Ilya was asleep on top of the four-poster bed, fully clothed. He had arrived at Millbury Street in the middle of the night, he had told me that morning. Toby had let him in and he had gone straight to bed but had woken at dawn, unable to go back to sleep. That was why I had found him sitting alone in the kitchen.

Toby had known that he was coming, Ilya said, but he hadn't known precisely when. Ilya was sure that Toby had intended to tell me, to warn me in advance. It was just, he explained, that his plans had changed, as they so often did, and he had arrived a month or so early. He had wanted to visit England again sooner, he said, but there had been complications. But now, any problems had at last been smoothed over. He was full of charming apology. It was nine or ten years since I had seen him and he was precisely as I remembered.

'I was going to tell you, darling. Of course I was.' Toby had arrived back from acquiring a statue of Apollo from an aristocratic friend forced to sell under pressure of death duties. 'I tried phoning you at the gallery but it was engaged.'

'All day?' I said. We were sitting at the kitchen table together as we often did, but it was rare for the atmosphere to be so tense. I felt I could no longer keep my temper. Alice was upstairs watching an Australian soap opera, a favourite forbidden at school. I had thirty minutes to vent my fury in the spotless room, scrubbed and bleached earlier in the day by Elena.

'Well, I could hardly keep asking to use their phone, could I?' Toby said. 'And poor Johnny was in a bad way. His father's death has hit him hard.'

In the bank balance, I thought, but didn't say so.

'No doubt,' I said. 'But Toby, you let me think Ilya was dead all these years. That's a dreadful thing to do.'

'I thought he was dead, too, sweetie, for a bit at least,' Toby said. 'And I loved him. You never liked him much.'

'That's not true.'

Toby stretched back in his chair and folded his arms. I knew the look. He wasn't going to be chastised.

'When did you know?' I said.

'About three months after he left.'

'So for all these years you've kept this to yourself?' I was so astonished I almost forgot to be angry.

'It was all hush-hush, you know. Ilya's . . . I can keep a secret, you know. He's a friend now, nothing else. I've seen him a few times, on trips. He had to disappear.'

'Oh, for God's sake.'

'No, seriously, Josie. His life was in danger. And he's called Ivan now, you'd better remember that.'

'What about all the other people who knew him?'

'He won't be here for long.'

'What's he brought?'

'What do you mean?'

'You know what I mean.'

Toby shook his head. 'Don't ask me that, Josie. I've kept you out of it.'

'I want to know.'

'No. It's enough that you know what you do. Leave it.'

As I sat there, I was aware that my fists were clenched under the table, and that I was shaking in an odd, involuntary way. I started to cry. It was like wanting to laugh at the train station, it seemed to come from nowhere.

'Oh no, Josie. Don't cry.' Toby got out his handkerchief and handed it to me, putting his arm around my shoulder. 'Look, this is the last one. Okay? I've told Ilya, Ivan, that that's it. We can't go on doing this stuff. I want the business to be strictly legitimate. The authorities are really cracking down and the museums are becoming paranoid. And the market's good. We can still make a great living. I might have to work a bit harder I suppose.' He laughed. 'I promise, Josie. That's it. Please don't cry.'

I was sobbing now. I had contained my anger and shock all day but the tears and shaking felt as though this was an outpouring of a far longer and greater frustration. I took his hand and tried to catch my breath.

'It was such a shock,' I said, 'this morning, to see him. He . . . just sitting there . . . here. I really thought he was dead.'

Toby hugged me to him. It was a rare physical gesture these days.

'I'm so sorry, Josie. I should have told you. And I certainly would have warned you he was coming. If I'd known. I was going to. Before that . . . to be honest it didn't seem to matter. I thought it was best if you thought he was dead.'

I took a deep breath and began to calm myself down.

'How long is he staying?' I asked eventually.

'Not long, just a day or two. Then he'll disappear.'

'Why's he come back now?'

'I don't know. He doesn't tell me everything. And I don't want to know.'

'Do you think he's a spy?' I said. I had never asked directly before.

Toby laughed. 'I'm sure he is. But he's hardly James Bond, is he? I expect he's a courier.'

'Yes, that's what I thought.'

'Still dangerous for him though,' Toby said.

'What about Alice? Should he be here when she's here?'

'I don't think there's any cloak-and-dagger stuff here. He's hardly going to be poisoned with an umbrella tip. I think it's more when he's cruising round the Baltic or the Middle East.'

'Oh, I see. Picking up antiquities as he goes.'

'A bit of that, yes. Look, let's have a drink, eh? That terrible programme Alice is watching must be nearly finished.'

'What about Ilya?'

'Ivan. He's fine. I'll see him later on. He'll sleep for a while yet. Where shall we take Alice for dinner?'

❧

I had been looking forward to the week with Alice. Now fifteen, she was a wonderful companion most of the time, original in her thinking, curious and full of fun. She still seemed uninterested in discussing her school life or her friends but she always answered my questions about them in a good-natured way. School was something she tolerated, allowing others to buzz around her while her own mind was pursuing its independent groove.

She planned to study archaeology when the time came, she had told us, and she liked to spend time with me at Belgrave Square in the mornings, before touring the shops and museums and cinemas with one of us, or with her friends, in the afternoon. I liked to watch her in the gallery, prowling round the airy space where each month Toby and I changed the layout of our exhibits.

That year she had taken to wearing the new short skirts or cropped coloured cotton trousers with small-heeled shoes and ruffled tops, a fashionable look of which I approved. She would make little notes on a smart leather pad which I had put in her Christmas stocking and swoop on Toby's newer acquisitions. Her latest passion was for Hellenistic jewellery, she claimed, but she could still be seduced by the sight of a new Egyptian cat or ibis and I was always secretly pleased to see that the child I had known was still present.

Toby, on the contrary, was thrilled to think that Alice was grown up. When she was a child, he had been happy enough to hand her over to me after an hour or so, but now it was different and he would encourage her to stay up late with us in the evenings, letting her drink a little wine, despite my protests. I would watch nervously, wondering what was enough, where a line should be drawn. He had even allowed her a small puff on a joint ('No worse than the glass in her hand,' he would say). I agreed in theory, but the reality of seeing Alice sitting on the chaise longue, smoking, dressed in her tiny, full skirt, her hair tumbling down her shoulders, troubled me.

And yet, as Toby pointed out again, these were things she was almost certainly trying out with her friends. And Alice was not my child, but then nor was she Toby's. Her mother Anne was useless, there was no point in discussing it with her. I had once asked Alice what she thought that her father, Roddy, would make of her staying up late with us, but Alice just laughed and said he was unlikely to mind much and anyway he had been letting her drink wine for the last three summers.

It seemed to me that there was little I could do to slow down Alice's precociousness. It was hard to know where to look for advice. My own female friends, of whom I had few, had children who were younger, and they hadn't yet faced what it was like to be confronted with a more knowing generation.

And there was a further difficulty with Alice, the difficulty of judging what behaviour was normal for a girl of her age and class, and what belonged to that ethereal energy which sometimes seemed to propel her even faster towards adulthood. She seemed untrammelled by the usual rules and constraints, and always appeared to know what she was doing. Her assurance often wrong-footed me, made me timid in the face of her certainty. It made me almost gauche and childlike myself.

Eighteen

Margaret Haddeley was thrilled at the idea of having Luke and me for Christmas.

'I had almost decided to go over to the Hardings',' she said on the telephone. 'I won't hear of you not coming. It will be marvellous. I can't think why Kit and Isobel want to go to America. It's far too hot and full of ghastly hippies, isn't it? We shall have a proper Christmas.'

The prospect of Margaret on her own, without Kit to soften her, was a little alarming, but I agreed that we would arrive on Christmas Eve and stay until Boxing Day evening, then I would have to return to open the gallery. The period just after Christmas was always quiet but it was a fine opportunity to sort things through.

It would be Luke's third visit to Fleet Farm and he seemed pleased that we were going to see Margaret. Each time so far, Kit had told me, he had been received by Margaret as a prodigal son, and I wondered if this time, with a grandchild of her own on the way, something might have changed. But there was no lessening of her delight when we arrived in the late afternoon, me dragging across the gravel my large wheelie case full of carefully wrapped Christmas presents.

'You look like a bagwoman, Josie,' Margaret said. 'You usually have more style.' Thus was I dismissed while Luke was swept up into her embrace. 'Come and have tea, darling. You too, Josie.' Margaret led the way through to the small sitting room. 'Or perhaps you would like to go to your rooms first?' We made a strange trio, I thought, two women, one old, one middle-aged, and a young man related to neither by blood but doted on by both for the sake of a dead woman.

'No, that's fine,' Luke replied. But I needed a moment to put myself back together. 'I'll just use the downstairs loo, Margaret,' I said. 'I'll be with you in a moment.'

On the back of the cloakroom door I looked, as I always did, at the photograph of Kit's father, Christopher, together with Toby and me, standing outside the British Museum, next to a poster of the famous Tutankhamun exhibition. It was unmistakably the seventies; our hair and our clothes, and something about the ironic insouciance of the three of us, shouted out that decade. I had often wondered why this photograph had been selected as suitable for people to contemplate as they sat on the lavatory, and I had come to the conclusion that Margaret regarded the esoteric world that her husband and brother-in-law, and I by extension, had loved, as somehow not quite the thing. Either that, or the fact that she didn't share our interests, made it of little consequence to her.

I was struck by the slightly decadent air that Toby, in particular, exhibited in the picture. He had a flowing scarf around his neck, and though the picture was in black and white, I could remember the vibrant Indian colours beneath his dark, layered hair. Christopher was more conservative, in a suit and tie, while I, petite between them, my arms linked with them both, was beautifully dressed in a dark green, as I knew it to be, silk frock that I had found in a King's Road shop, and my black suede boots. I was beaming at the camera, my expression suggesting an excitement with the way my life was unfolding.

Sitting on the loo that December afternoon I realised that it had never occurred to me before to wonder who had taken the photograph. I pictured Alice for a moment, holding Toby's old Nikon, asking us to smile. But it wasn't possible. Alice would have been far too young. As I washed my hands at the ancient porcelain basin with its pretty blue-and-white tiled surround, I remembered that the girl Clara, whom I had met on my first evening with Toby, had been with us, the girl with the tinkling laugh and the large breasts. She must have taken it. She had been Christopher's mistress for a while, one of many over the years whom Margaret chose to overlook.

'Now, darlings. Let's make the most of this, it just being us.' Margaret had poured our tea and was sitting back in her chair. Luke sat back too, in imitation of her. 'Now, Luke,' Margaret continued, 'how are you getting on?' She turned to me and smiled, and I had a sense of some mischief on its way. 'What do you think of this new baby?' Margaret added, stressing the 'you', as she turned once more to Luke. 'I expect Isobel is very pleased with herself.'

I had wondered if Margaret might want to get through

tea without this question. I was cross with myself, too. I had stupidly mentioned to Margaret, on the telephone, that Isobel was rather lording it over Luke now that she was safely through the first three months of her pregnancy.

'It's good,' Luke replied. 'Isobel really wants a baby, so it's good.'

'You mustn't take any notice of Isobel, Luke,' Margaret said.

'What?' Luke was puzzled, as was I, at this non sequitur.

'Pregnant women can be excused a lot of things,' Margaret went on. 'And she is American, you must remember. They fuss too much about matters medical – and psychological. I don't go in for that stuff, though that might be her father's influence . . . terrible man . . . Josie knew him years ago, I believe, didn't you, Josie?'

'Yes,' I said. 'So did Christopher, Margaret, if you remember. We all knew him, and we all liked him. He taught at the school for a bit, you know, the language school.'

'Oh, the school,' she said. Her expression became contemptuous. 'He was a dreadful leftie, as I recall. And now he's a psychiatrist I believe.'

'A psychologist, Margaret. It's quite different.'

'Whatever he is, I don't have time for it.' She turned her attention back to Luke who was listening carefully to what she was saying.

'Isobel and I are okay,' was all he said. 'If that's what you're worried about.'

I thought I detected a slight disdain for Margaret. He

259

seemed a little less willing to please than on previous occasions. But if Margaret was aware of the little sting in his words, she didn't show it.

'You are so very like your mother, darling,' she said, holding the teapot up to offer us a refill. 'I hope neither of you mind me saying so. We should be able to speak about these things now, don't you think?'

Luke was sitting up, his attention fully engaged.

'Please,' he said. 'I wish you would talk about her. Everyone seems to have stopped talking about her. Since the baby.'

'Oh, Luke,' I said, 'that's not fair. We've talked about her, you and I.'

'Such a shame poor Anne isn't still with us,' Margaret said, ignoring this exchange. 'What a joy you would have been to her.' She picked up a plate of biscuits and offered them first to me and then to Luke. 'They were like family to us, the Wearings, Luke. Well, of course, after Alice and Kit's marriage, they *were* family.'

I had certainly heard this before. We all had. Margaret hadn't entirely avoided the subject of Alice over the years. It had been known to make its way into her conversation, especially if Isobel were present.

'But Anne was quite incapable of family ties, Margaret,' I said, feeling compelled to inject some reality into this conversation, for Luke's sake, if not for Margaret's. 'Especially latterly,' I continued. 'She was unwell. She would have been no more use to Luke than she was to Alice.'

Glossing over the truth was a Haddeley trait which I

found infuriating. When I had first encountered it in Toby I had put it down to the necessary hypocrisy that being a homosexual entailed, at least in his youth, but I had come to understand that it was a family characteristic. They preferred to deflect anything hurtful or anything that might disturb their sense of their place in the world. In many ways this outlook was effective and logical. Why should Luke be told about Anne's shocking decline? Wasn't it bad enough that neither his birth mother nor his adoptive mother were still alive, and that a part of his life had been spent in care? It was surely all the more important that he should know that there had been no gilded world from which he had been excluded. Sadness and trouble had existed here too.

'Sorry,' Luke said, standing up suddenly, 'I've spilt my tea.'

We were both surprised by his interruption. It was as if for a moment we had forgotten he was there. But now I could see a stain expanding across the crotch of his jeans.

'No need to fuss. Down the left-hand corridor,' Margaret called after him. 'Oh dear,' she said, 'you were a bit harsh on Anne. I think he's upset.'

'He's not upset. He wants to know,' I said. 'And what I said about Anne is the truth.'

Margaret pulled herself up then leant over to pick up the brass poker, stirring the glowing embers and coaxing the little yellow flames to flare prettily in the grate. I was mesmerised by their dance, their flickering up and down in an hypnotic cycle. I couldn't speak even if I had wanted to. I felt silenced by the force of Margaret's will.

'You think I don't know about people, don't you,' she

said suddenly. 'You and Isobel. But you would be surprised. It was I, after all, who looked after Alice. The doctors and the psychiatrists, they were useless. And as you say, Anne was hopeless. And Kit was away. I never told him all of it.' She sat down again, her movements slow. 'So Luke's existence is less of a surprise to me than to you,' she went on. 'Because I saw Alice at times when she wasn't quite who any of you thought she was.' Margaret's voice was steady and matter of fact, and she leant forward to reach for the teapot.

'More tea?' she asked.

'Let me, Margaret,' I said.

'I'll do it.' Luke had slipped back into the room and I wondered how much he had heard. Margaret's ancient body seemed to sink a little and her rod-straight back sagged in an uncharacteristic pose.

'I feel rather tired, darlings,' she said. 'It just comes on these days. If you don't mind, I think I might have a rest.'

Dinner at Fleet that night was informal, which was a sort of formality in itself. For once I would have welcomed a vicar or two, or a dull neighbour to distract me from the sight of Margaret doting on Luke who seemed to take it as his due. I was out of sorts that evening. I could see too much of myself in Margaret's fawning, and it brought me up short. I had indulged in it myself. I was almost jealous of Margaret. I had become much too attached to this young man who had no ties to me at all. I would have to encourage Kit in the New York business, hard as it might be. Isobel was right, it was for the best. I took comfort in the excellent wine that accompanied our dinner. Margaret Haddeley had never been stingy with drink, in fact she encouraged it, though I had noted over the years that she was careful never to lose control herself.

Luke had also drunk more than usual and by the time we were having coffee and whisky in the library, he seemed determined to get Margaret to talk again.

'I'm not sure if this is the time,' Margaret said when he began the conversation.

'I want to know,' he said. His voice was insistent. 'About my mother, about when she was ill,' he said. 'No one will really tell me. You should tell me. She was my mother.'

Margaret frowned, then seemed to take a decision. She plumped up a cushion and placed it with some deliberation behind her back.

'Very well,' she said. 'I will tell you.' She sat very still as if bracing herself. 'It would blow up,' she said. 'Just like a storm at sea, as if poor Alice was a little boat, tossed about until it ran its course. She always knew what was happening to her when it was starting – and if Kit was away, which he almost always was, she would telephone us, and we would drive up to Fulham to fetch her. Then she would be up all night, talking to people we couldn't hear. Christopher would sit with her. We tried to keep her inside the house, though once or twice she got out and we had to collect her from the local hospital. They wanted to section her, but I wouldn't let them. It wasn't necessary. The doctor came each morning and evening, and gave her a sedative. Then afterwards, I'm talking about mere days, she was Alice again, though she was very frightened and exhausted.'

Margaret took a sip of camomile tea from her china cup. 'And so were we,' she added.

'So she was really out there then,' Luke said. 'Psychotic.'

The word sounded shocking in his mouth. I didn't think that Kit or I had ever used the term. It hadn't come from us.

'What does that mean, precisely?' Margaret said. She sounded disdainful.

'Seeing stuff, hearing things, I think,' he said.

'Yes, I'm afraid so,' Margaret replied. 'Sometimes. She certainly heard things. But only when it was at its absolute peak, and never for long. I don't know when it started, but it got worse. Puberty, probably, the doctors said.'

I said nothing. I had never told anyone about the voices. I could feel Margaret looking at me, but it had been our secret, Alice's and mine.

'She wasn't mad,' Margaret said. 'Just disturbed, briefly. It just had to be managed and we managed.'

'It must have been hard for you, Margaret,' I said.

'I did my best.' She pulled back her bony shoulders once again. 'But one's best isn't always good enough.' To my amazement, a tear crept down her cheek. Except briefly, after Alice's death, I had never before seen her weep. Not even at her husband Christopher's funeral. I watched her put down her cup and pull a small white handkerchief from the handbag which sat next to her on the sofa. She dabbed her face with deliberate movements.

'Your mother seemed to be growing out of it, that was the saddest thing.' She spoke directly to Luke as if I wasn't present. 'The doctors said she might.' Margaret folded the handkerchief, put it back in the bag, and snapped shut its old-fashioned clasp.

'I think perhaps I should go to bed,' she said. 'If you'll excuse me.'

We stood up, watching as she pulled herself up from the sofa. Her bag over her arm, she walked slowly to the door, then turned to face me.

'The voices,' Margaret said. She seemed not to address me directly but to speak into a void. 'The psychiatrist said they were quite usual, but I didn't think so, not in Alice's case. Anne and I always thought that it was your fault, Josie. I know Anne blamed you. She told me how you filled poor Alice's head with nonsense when she was a child. You were a very foolish woman.'

I felt momentarily cold against the heat from the fire, stunned at this onslaught and fearing more. Luke looked from me to Margaret and back again, gripped by the turn the conversation had taken, and anxious to follow its thread. But Margaret turned away and disappeared in one sudden movement, through the doorway, then I heard her call back into the room, 'Help me up the stairs, Luke darling.' And I was left alone.

The full impact of Margaret's words had not yet fully made its way through the warm defences of the wine and the two large whiskies, and as I heard Luke and Margaret shuffling up the main staircase I helped myself to another. I tried to be firm with myself. I would not take Margaret seriously. It was one of her gambits. But I could feel an involuntary spasm of grief rising up in me and I felt myself begin to cry, distant tears that rolled down my cheeks, seeming to belong to someone else. I sat on the sofa, hunched over, clutching my glass, and waited for the first wave to stop, and for Margaret to be safely in her room. Then I crept upstairs to bed.

I woke an hour later, fully clothed, stretched out on top of the covers. It was a moment or so before the words came rushing back to me. *A foolish woman*, Margaret had called me. *Filling her head with that nonsense*. I made myself get off the bed, undress and clean my teeth, and then I fell into a half-sleep filled with images of Margaret and Luke and Isobel, and the shadowy figure of Alice enveloping them all. Luke appeared to be laughing, or perhaps crying, and then the sound seemed to regress to a baby's cry, until I woke up with a jolt, still able to hear the sound, the baby's cry, or rather a bird, screeching outside in the moonlight.

'Josie,' a voice whispered to me and I froze. 'Josie. Are you awake? It's me, Luke.'

'Luke?' I looked towards the door and there he was. He was closing it quietly behind him.

'I couldn't sleep,' he said. 'Do you mind?'

'No,' I said, though I wasn't sure what it was I didn't mind. He sat himself down on the end of the bed and I sat up. He was wearing the dressing gown I had bought him over a pair of dark blue flannel pyjamas, a present from Isobel. His feet were bare and there was enough light to see that he was smiling at me in a curious way which seemed to be both anxious and hopeful.

'I was worried about you,' he said. 'I was going to come before, but she kept me there, showing me old photographs and stuff. And when I came to bed your light was off. But then I couldn't sleep and I had to come and ask you. What did she mean? She wouldn't tell me. What was she talking about?'

'Oh, Luke,' I said. My voice must have sounded pained because he immediately reached over and took my hand.

'What was it you did?' he said. He squeezed my hand tightly as if to extract the information he wanted.

'I didn't do anything,' I said and my tone was sharp. I pulled my hand away. 'All I tried to do was be good to your mother when everyone else was busy being selfish. Your grandmother wasn't much of a mother. I'm sorry, Luke, but that's the truth. She was no better than your father – your adopted father, I mean. Worse probably. At least he hasn't drunk himself to death.'

Luke reached for my hand once more and shuffled further up the bed.

'Sorry, Josie, sorry,' he said. His voice was soothing. 'I didn't mean to upset you. I would never upset you. You've been so good to me. Better than anyone.'

The tone of his voice was intended to calm me, but the guilty feeling that I might have pushed Alice over some imaginative edge would not leave me. Having Luke so near intensified the idea. His presence seemed to resurrect that childish voice across the decades, with its chatter of babies and stars and gods.

I wanted to explain to him that I hadn't made his mother mad, or ill, or whatever term he cared to use; that it wasn't possible to make someone ill, or not in the way that Alice's mother had implied. And surely if any one person was responsible for Alice's instability, it was Anne Wearing herself, with her drunkenness and self-obsession. I was crying again now, my head on my knees, and Luke had moved to sit beside me, his arm around me.

'Let's try to go to sleep,' he said, as if I were a child myself. 'I'll lie down here beside you. I'll get under the blankets though, if you don't mind. My feet are freezing.'

I lifted my head and shook it. 'I don't think that's a good idea,' I said, imagining the possibility of Barbara Sutton finding him there beside me in the morning.

'Oh, go on. It's Christmas Eve. And I used to do this with my mum,' he said. 'When I couldn't sleep. Please, Josie.'

I was too befuddled by lack of rest and no doubt by all the drink I had put away the previous evening, to protest. I moved over to let him in and almost immediately I fell asleep. And when I woke up briefly, an hour or so later, there we were, curled up, my back to him, like two spoons. It was a curious feeling, a halfway house between childhood and maturity, not wholly right, I knew that, but wholly innocent. Two lost creatures needing comfort in the night.

When I woke up again, it was light. It was Christmas morning and I could feel Luke fast asleep against me, his flesh warm and comforting. His arm was still around me and, to my embarrassment, I realised that his hand was curled around my breast. I felt myself grow hot, and for a moment I was too shy to wake him up, or to move it. A moment later, the solution was obvious. I simply removed myself, pulling on a dressing gown and making my way across the landing to the wide staircase. I would make some tea, I thought, and bring it up. The hand, I was sure, had been a simple reflex of which he was quite unaware. Luke would have his tea, then go back to his room before Margaret was up and about. And that would be the end of it.

I had a pounding headache which was no surprise, but still I felt easier than when I had gone to bed. Luke's presence had comforted me. I looked back as I left the room. He was half in, half out of the bedclothes, still wearing the dressing gown. The offending hand was now tucked under his cheek like a small boy. One foot hung over the end of the bed and I could just see the other sticking out from under the sheet. He moved his position and his foot stretched itself out as if in reaction to cramp. As the long toes flexed, I saw that there was a thin piece of skin connecting each one, a hint of webbing just half a centimetre high. It was a small accident of birth, though one more suggestive of a cat than a water bird or a frog, and its imperfection seemed to endear him to me even more.

~

'What would you like to do today, Luke?' I said. It was Boxing Day, Margaret was having her breakfast in bed, and I was feeling almost cheerful. We had got through Christmas, given presents, including a large cheque for Luke from Margaret which particularly pleased him. We were due to leave after tea, which I was looking forward to. The sun shone weakly through the window of the breakfast room but the morning was just as a Boxing Day morning should be, blue and crisp. The temperature had dropped in the night to well below zero, and the lawns and trees were still covered in a glistening frost.

I watched Luke's hands as he buttered his toast. They were elegant hands and I felt for a moment their imprint on my body. The previous night he had come again to my room and crept into bed and fallen asleep against my back, and I hadn't had the heart to send him away as I should have done. I was aware that we were travelling in dangerous waters, and it was a relief to think that, once back in London, this odd little episode would be at an end.

'Well, if it's okay with you,' he said, 'what I'd really like to do is go and see the house again where Alice lived.' He had visited Pindock, Alice's childhood home, with Kit on a previous weekend. He had told me all about it, and about its owners, the Gibsons, whom he seemed to like. 'I could go on my own, Josie, if you'll lend me the car? But I'd love you to come with me. And meet Molly.' He managed somehow to make me feel that this was important to him. He was back on form, I thought.

'There's the point-to-point,' I said. 'That's what we sometimes do. We could leave Pindock till next time.' I meant we could leave it until a time when he could legitimately go alone, or go again with Kit. I wasn't sure I wanted to be in the house where Alice had lived with Anne. But then I heard myself say, 'All right, why not?'

'Pindock it is then,' Luke said, looking pleased with himself.

*

It was a pretty house, not as big as Fleet but standing in at least an acre of land with views across the valley. It stood just outside the village of Aston Novers and had presumably been one of the 'big' houses, as indeed it still was in comparison with the pretty cottages which made up most of the place. It was owned now by a family who had moved here to live a life away from the city. Judging by the bikes in the drive and the three or four cars that stood outside, it had been a busy Christmas, and now the door opened and a small round woman with short curly hair was smiling at us and ushering us inside.

I could hear the sound of a television and also some sort of electronic game. The Gibsons had four children of their own, and there were clearly more staying. There was a definite air of mayhem, but Molly Gibson seemed to have survived the season on her obvious good humour.

'Coffee? A drink? John and his brother have gone to the point-to-point with the eldest two. The rest are here, as you can no doubt tell.'

'Didn't you want to go?' I said.

'No, can't stand that sort of thing,' she said, endearing herself to me immediately.

'Me neither,' I said in a low voice. 'Did you have a good Christmas?'

'Oh yes. No one killed anyone. Not much broken. Pretty good.' She turned to Luke.

'You can look round again if you like. Feel free to wander.'

'Thanks,' said Luke, but he didn't move. I wondered if

his reluctance was just good manners or if he too was drawn to this motherly woman.

'Come on, then,' she said. 'I'll take you. Just let me put the coffee on.'

'I'll make it,' I said, reluctant suddenly to take on the house.

Alone now, I walked to the window and stared out at the view. It was a big country kitchen and I could imagine that Alice might have spent a lot of time in here, perhaps with Mrs Durden, I thought, discussing the Virgin Mary. I could see an outbuilding at the back with a stable door and I seemed to remember that they had kept at least one pony. I had once seen a picture of Alice, sitting on top of a small brown creature.

I filled the cafetière from the boiling kettle and stirred it. Leaving it to settle and feeling braver, I wandered into the large, deserted drawing room, comfortable with battered sofas and a dog basket. As I looked at the books on the shelves, I heard exclamations from upstairs, competing with the television noise coming from a room off the kitchen.

'Josie,' it was Luke's voice, 'Josie. Come and look at this.'

I hesitated, then curiosity won out and I climbed the staircase and followed the sound of their voices.

As I entered the room, I saw Molly holding a sheaf of papers. On top, I could see a child's drawing.

'We found them the other day,' she said. 'We were clearing out the attic, and they were in one of a number of cardboard shoeboxes we'd managed to shove behind some rubbish of ours. They were full of old papers. I got the local solicitor to come and pick through them but I kept this for Luke. It was the only interesting thing.'

She held it up. The pieces of paper were stitched together with black thread to make a little book. On its front page, I could see Alice's name – Alice Wearing – in very big, childish handwriting. The rest of the paper seemed to be painted blue, a pattern or a picture of some sort but I couldn't make out what.

'Look,' Luke said. He sounded excited. 'She must have done it after she'd been to the gallery.'

'What is it?' I asked.

'She's written a little story and drawn pictures,' Molly said.

'It's a Tuareg, like Isobel's got,' Luke said. 'On the front.'

'Not a Tuareg,' I said, taking the pages from him, 'that's a North African nomadic tribe, Luke.' I turned the pages carefully, as if I were handling an ancient papyrus. My hands were trembling but I tried to keep my voice steady. 'A Tawaret. Look, there's the eye. It's side-on. And the hippo jaw, and the lion's feet. She's even got the breast in here, hanging.' She had coloured it a deep blue. It was Ilya's Tawaret, my Tawaret.

'I wonder how old she was,' said Luke.

Molly took the pictures from him, scrutinising the large half-formed letters written in red crayon.

'Judging by the handwriting, I'd say, about six or seven? What did you say it was?'

'A Tawaret,' Luke said. 'It's an Egyptian amulet. That's right, isn't it, Josie? Josie's the one who knows, she knows everything.' I had never seen him so animated. His breath pushed out his words in short squeaky sentences. 'Kit's got one. Or Isobel has. At home, their home I mean, haven't they, Josie? Only theirs is greener.'

'The one Alice has drawn was made from lapis lazuli,' I said. 'Very sought after. The Egyptians imported it from Badakhshan.'

'Where?' said Molly.

'It's in Afghanistan now,' I said. I hadn't meant to embark on a lecture. 'I must go down and rescue the coffee.'

'I'll come with you,' Molly said. 'Stay here for a bit if you like, Luke. Take your time.' She followed me down the stairs, like a faithful dog in pursuit.

'Sit down,' she said when we reached the kitchen. 'You don't look well.'

'I'm fine,' I said. 'The pictures, they took me by surprise, that's all.'

'Funny thing to draw,' Molly said.

'She used to come to our gallery,' I said. 'Antiquities. It was Toby's.'

'Oh, I see. I didn't know they'd had the place that long.'

'You were right, she was six,' I said. 'When she did those pictures. I remember.'

'You knew her then, when she was a child?'

'Yes.'

'I hadn't realised, I'm sorry. I'd no idea.'

'That's all right,' I said. 'It's wonderful to have them. They belong to Luke now, of course.'

She reached out and took my hand and the small gesture was enough to make me start crying again.

'I used to work with Toby Haddeley,' I said. 'Kit's uncle. Alice was his god-daughter. We spent a lot of time together.'

'Oh, I see,' Molly said. 'Complicated. So she was a sort of childhood sweetheart for Kit Haddeley?' She turned to get cups from the cupboard and said, almost under her breath, 'That must be difficult for the second Mrs Haddeley.' There was something in her muttering that made me smile, in spite of myself.

'Yes,' I said. 'I think it is.' She heard the humour in my voice and turned to me and pulled a face.

'It's a minefield,' she said. 'I can assure you. Not that my husband was widowered, if that's the right word, just divorced, and there were no children, but, you know, it's still baggage as they say.'

'Baggage,' I said. I wasn't sure I liked that word. It was an ugly word for the accumulated sorrow of our lives, an ugly word for Luke.

'We don't see her, thank God,' Molly said. 'The first wife.'

'Well, we don't see Alice, either,' I said, 'but for someone who is dead she's remarkably visible.'

Molly looked at me as if ready to pay close attention to what was coming next but then we heard Luke's footsteps coming down the stairs.

'Another time perhaps,' she said, and I nodded, grateful

to her for these few moments of closeness with a stranger.

Luke was very quiet as we drove back to London that evening. I tried to get him to talk but he gave short replies to any attempt to get our usual banter going. I gave up, thinking that the excitement of the morning had worn him out. I put some Rachmaninoff on the CD player. To my surprise he seemed to like it. It reminded him, he said, of a teacher he'd liked at school.

'I learnt the piano for a bit,' he said.

'I suppose you gave it up,' I said.

'Yes.'

'Most people do,' I said. 'It's a shame.'

'I want to tell you about something, Josie.'

I felt at once on edge, anxious but also excited at the prospect of a confidence. I waited but he said nothing.

'Are you worried about something?' I said, impatient.

'Not exactly. But you might hate me when I tell you.'

'That's very unlikely,' I said.

'How do you know?'

I looked over at him. 'Well,' I said, 'I've got to know you, a bit at least, and I know that you mean well. So whatever it is, it's either nothing to be ashamed of or, if it is, you'll be sorry about it, which makes it all right.' I wasn't sure this was strictly true, but it felt reasonable.

He settled further down in his seat as if trying to hide himself.

'I've been to prison,' he said.

'Oh.' This was unexpected.

'I was in care, I told you, and then I was in and out of Young Offenders a couple of years,' he went on, 'and then I got sent down for nine months.'

'What sort of prison was it?' I said. And what sort of a question? I thought. I heard Luke laugh.

'Prison sort of prison, Josie. Strangeways, in Manchester.'

It was impossible to comprehend the idea of Luke in Strangeways, not that I had the faintest notion of what Strangeways might be like. Just its name made it alien.

'It's all right, Luke,' I said with a conviction I didn't feel. 'It's a good thing that you've told me.' What on earth would Isobel say? was my first thought. And did she need to know? my second. 'What were you in prison for?' There, I'd asked it. That was surely the important bit.

'Car theft,' he said. 'I told you a bit about that.'

I felt relieved. Stealing cars wasn't armed robbery or drug dealing. But a moment later, I wasn't sure I believed him.

'Can you play the piano?' he said, as if the prison conversation hadn't happened.

'No,' I said quickly. 'I'm hopeless at anything musical. Toby used to say it was the one area where I had no taste.'

'But you like this,' he said. 'This is good.' The Rachmaninoff was still playing.

'No, this is regarded as a bit naff, Luke.'

'Really?'

'Really.'

'That's a shame,' he said and we both laughed. We could

afford to leave the subject for now, surely, I thought; we could come back to it. We would get through the rest of Christmas and New Year and then I would have to get to the bottom of Luke Tyler. There surely couldn't be very much more to discover.

Almost as soon as we arrived back at Millbury Street, Luke was on his mobile phone and then announced that he was going out. I was pleased for him. He'd had a dull Christmas with two old ladies. He deserved some fun.

'Don't wait up for me,' he said. 'It's a party. Not that you would, wait up, I mean. You're not my mum.' And then he winked at me, which I didn't much like. It felt out of character, the gesture of someone cruder than I had thought him to be.

Nineteen

For the next three days and nights he disappeared. There was no note, or phone call or message. I felt desolate, almost abandoned. I told myself that he would come back. He was simply taking a sort of holiday. Kit had given him the time off between Christmas and New Year and I was alone, both at the house and at Belgrave Square, the streets and the buildings dead and dull. Even Rita and Frank the dog were absent, eating themselves silly with chocolate somewhere in South London.

I tried without success not to be anxious. I tried not to think of Luke in hospital, or at a police station. He was a young and independent man. He had no need to explain himself. But I found myself, on the second morning of his absence, putting on the answering machine at work, locking up and wandering through the Bond Street sales to avoid my own thoughts. By the third afternoon, I was angry with him. I walked through Victoria, wrapped up in the grey alpaca coat that only came out on the coldest of days, and went up the steps and into the comfort of the cathedral. It was surprisingly warm and I thought, as always, how expensive it must be for the Church to keep it so. I sat in my usual pew and tried to think things through clearly.

Luke owed me the courtesy of letting me know he was safe, I was right to expect it, but he had not done so. It wasn't the negligence of a careless boy, he was far too knowing for that. It was consciously done, to worry or to hurt me. Then there was the small matter of what he had told me in the car on the way home from Fleet. He had dropped his bombshell and then absconded before I was able to discuss it with him further. We had been much too cautious with him. He needed us to be firmer. He had tried, in his way, to tell us what we wanted to know, but through our misguided respect for his privacy, we had made it more difficult for him. We might, I thought, have appeared not to care.

And now I was left alone to shade in the faint, if rather shocking, outline he had begun to provide. My mind ran on what he might have suffered in prison, in care, what damage might have been done to him, the sort of damage that Isobel could not have anticipated when she was making her list. I wasn't naïve. I knew that the prison system harmed people, that it could harm young men and corrupt them. As the light outside the cathedral changed to the darkness of a winter afternoon, and the little candle flames of memory became ever more visible, I convinced myself that he would not come back.

But on the third morning after his disappearance, I heard Luke's key in the lock. I waited, thinking he might call out my name, but I heard him go into the bedroom and then leave the flat via the connecting door, presumably to take a shower. He appeared ten minutes later in the kitchen, newly shaven and in clean clothes, looking at me expectantly as I made coffee.

'Hello, stranger,' I said. My voice sounded false to me. I was biting my tongue, waiting to hear what he would say.

He took the cup that I offered and sat at the table seemingly without a trace of embarrassment or concern.

'How have you been, Josie?' he said.

'Well, thank you.'

'Are Kit and Isobel back yet?'

'No,' I said. 'They're due back tomorrow night.' I was surprised at how welcome the idea of their return had become. The house was cold and empty without their presence.

'Everything okay at the gallery?'

'Yes, thank you.'

'What's the matter?' he said. I was astonished. This, from the boy whose ability to read people had so impressed me in these past months.

'I think it might have been courteous of you, Luke, to let me know that you would be away for a few days.'

He put his cup down on the table and looked at me, surprised, it seemed, at my reaction.

'I was just out and about,' he said. 'And I did come back a couple of times but you weren't here.'

'Oh.' My resentment was briefly de-railed by this odd justification. 'Couldn't you have left a note or something? A phone message?' I was beginning to feel that I was getting this wrong.

'I never thought that you . . .' A moment of impatience crossed his face but he hid it quickly. 'I'm sorry, Josie,' he said. He lowered his head and his tone became formal, humble almost. 'Next time I'll let you know.' Then he looked up and said, in a slightly mysterious voice, 'I got involved in . . . something.'

I was afraid to ask what.

'Would you like some breakfast? Scrambled eggs? With the eggs I brought from Fleet?'

'Yes please,' he said, grabbing at my gesture, his voice eager now to make amends. 'I'm really sorry, Josie, if I upset you. I wasn't thinking.'

'No,' I said, cracking the eggs in a bowl. The yokes were a vivid yellow colour from the corn that Margaret's hens were fed on. 'Just a phone call would have done. I think, while you still live here, if you are away for more than one night, I would appreciate that.'

'Done,' he said and smiled. 'Are we friends again?'

'We'll always be friends,' I said. 'Just because I can be pissed off with you doesn't mean we're not friends.'

He shrugged. 'Not where I come from,' he said.

'I want to talk to you about that,' I said.

He frowned.

'What you told me about – on the way back from Fleet,' I said. 'I'd like to know more.'

'What's to tell? It was shit.'

The word surprised me. It wasn't one he used. Not that he never swore, there was the odd fucking or bollocks, but not shit. And the tone when he said it suggested it was reserved for darker moments.

'When did you first go to juvenile detention or whatever it's called? How old were you?'

'I was in care some of the time. But you mean a detention order. Fourteen,' he said.

'Fourteen!'

'It was no worse than being at home.'

'Really, Luke? You said home was all right while your mother was alive.'

I was confused. I had thought I had some small grip on Luke's story, but apparently not; it was shifting and changing as we spoke.

'I've told you before. My dad wanted me out. He said they'd made a mistake. He called me a pig in a poke.'

'A what?'

'A pig in a poke. When he testified against me in court. He said to the judge that you didn't know what you were getting when you adopted children. It was like buying a pig in a poke, he said.'

The absurdity as well as the vileness of this account made it impossible to doubt that what Luke said was true. And in that case, Philip Tyler should never have been allowed to be a father. I wanted to rant and rave on Luke's behalf. Nothing Luke had done could be worse than such a betrayal.

'You should have told us, Luke. We had no idea. What about your mother in all this?'

'She was okay. I've told you. But she couldn't stand up to him. Sometimes it was easier if she just went along with him. The worse he was, the worse I was.'

'Did he hit you?'

Luke wouldn't look at me.

'Did he hit your mother? Or your brother?'

'Not my brother. Never. I told you. He liked him best. But he hit me. So like I said, I was glad to be out of it.'

The eggs had congealed in the pan.

'I'll make some more,' I said. 'Or something else?'

'No, don't bother. I'm not hungry.' He stood up. 'I've got to go.'

'Will you be back tonight?' I regretted asking at once, but to my surprise his voice was soft as he turned round to me.

'Not tonight, no, but tomorrow. I'll be back tomorrow evening.'

But he did come back that night, or rather the next morning at about 3 a.m. I had gone to bed early, a little nervous for once at being all alone in the vastness of Millbury Street. I woke suddenly and heard him whispering my name, just as he had done on Christmas Eve at Fleet.

'Josie?'

'Luke?'

'Can I come in?'

'Yes.' I reached for the bedside light. It threw his face into relief as he sat on the edge of the bed and I could see a red mark and the start of dark bruising around his left eye and cheek.

'Oh, Luke,' I said. 'Whatever happened?'

'I got mugged,' he said. 'It's okay.'

'Where?'

'Pimlico.'

'Pimlico?'

'People do get mugged in Pimlico.' He laughed as he said it, then put his hand to his face and winced.

'Let me get you something to put on it.'

'It's fine. The skin's not broken.'

'Arnica, at least,' I said. 'I've got some somewhere.'

'What's that?'

'Homoeopathic cream.'

I got out of bed and went to the bathroom to rummage in a cupboard. 'Did you phone the police?' I called out as I did so.

'No,' he said. 'What's the point?'

'Well, you need to in case they find your wallet. I presume he – they – took your wallet?'

'No. I think something must have scared them off. They hit me then they ran.'

'That was lucky,' I said. At last I found the old tube of cream, and when I returned, he had taken off his jeans and belt and was sitting in his T-shirt and pants, under the bedclothes.

'I can stay here tonight, can't I?' he asked. 'Just for tonight?'

I hesitated. He looked vulnerable sitting in my bed, a pale, thin creature, hungry for human warmth. I could not throw him out.

'Just tonight, Luke,' I heard myself say, 'then it's back to normal, okay?'

I climbed back into bed beside him slowly and lay down, all too alert to my body's response to him as he lay next to

285

me. He reached for me and pulled me close. His evident need of my comfort was more seductive to me than any charm or flattery.

'Josie,' he said. 'Keep me warm.'

He began to kiss me gently on my lips, cheeks, forehead. I could feel the delicate brush of his mouth. He touched my breast with his fingers through my nightdress and the feel of someone else touching my flesh after too many years alone was strange and marvellous. He made me feel as if my breast was something precious and vital to him.

'No, Luke,' I heard myself saying. 'No, this is not right.' I was unconvincing to myself and he was over me now, smiling down, and I felt both present and removed from what was happening. It wasn't that I couldn't have stopped him, or that I couldn't help myself, or any of the clichés. I could have stopped him and I didn't want to.

~

I hardly slept. I could hear Luke breathing steadily against my naked back, feel the warmth of him. I wanted to turn and cuddle him, to hold him like a child, but I could not allow myself to do so. When I drifted off into sleep, my dreams were of Alice and Luke together at the house at Pindock. In another, I saw Toby and Luke embracing in the gallery among the statuary and the two of them turned to look at me and Toby said, 'Josie is a very foolish woman.'

I woke up feeling hot, although the room was quite cool. Luke was lying on his back, his breathing quiet and regular. It was dark outside though I thought I had heard the sound of morning traffic. I closed my eyes and felt a wave of deep sleep engulf me, and then I was awake again, or rather I was being woken by the sound of my bedroom door opening. As I turned over, only half afraid, in my stupor, to see who was there, I saw Isobel standing in the doorway, just for a moment, before she turned and disappeared.

As quickly as I could, I got out of bed, grabbed my dressing gown and followed her out through the connecting door. I couldn't see her but I guessed that she had gone downstairs to the kitchen. I could not begin to imagine what I was going to say to her. I told myself it was none of her business and that she should not have come into my bedroom. It was true that she had done so before, often at my request, to wake me up after a convivial night. It was a family joke that I could sleep through any alarm. But she wasn't supposed to have done so today. She wasn't supposed to be here at all.

She was leaning against the Aga, her head bowed. She looked up as I came in and we stared at one another for a moment.

Then I heard myself say, 'It's not what you think.' The absurdity of my words might have made me smile in another context, but I was awake and nervous enough of my position to know that this would not be wise. 'Luke was mugged last night, Isobel. He came home distressed and . . .'

'And so he slept with you?' she said. The incredulity, not to say distaste, in her expression was not flattering. Was it really such a terrible thing to have happened? Still, I could see it looked very wrong.

'It's not . . . an affair,' I said.

'Well, that's a relief at least,' she said, and for a moment I felt indignant. It was not so grotesque an idea. But then again, perhaps it was.

'Whatever do you think you're doing, Josie?' she said, finally.

'I thought you were coming back tonight?' I said.

'We had to change our flight. Kit's got a meeting. He sent you a text. You haven't answered my question.'

I decided to go on the attack. It was easy enough. Her disapproval was close to being offensive.

'Don't be so starchy, Isobel. Have you never had a spur-of-the-moment night with a friend?' I said. 'I could think that you're jealous.'

Isobel's mouth opened and then shut and I felt a moment of triumph. I had trumped her.

'So it hasn't happened before?' she asked.

'No,' I said, 'and it won't happen again.' I didn't see why she should know the whole story. It was between Luke and me.

'He's got to go,' Isobel said. 'This confirms it. He's got to leave. It's not healthy.'

'What do you mean?'

'I've seen you, Josie,' she said. 'The way you look at him. And Kit's not much better, or he wasn't. All both of you can see in him is Alice. It's as if you're trying to get her back through him.'

'Don't be ridiculous,' I said. She was wrong. Last night had not been about Alice, it had been about me. I had wanted what Luke had to give me, even if it was fleeting. He had offered me love of a sort and I had taken it. I looked

Isobel in the eye. 'The only true thing you've implied is that Luke is Alice's son. He's also an attractive young man in his own right.' I waited a moment, then continued, 'And I thought you thought so too.'

'You know what I think, Josie. You just choose not to acknowledge it.'

'What's that?'

'That he's charming, yes, but he's manipulative and I don't trust him, not really.'

'Why do you fawn all over him then?' I said.

'I don't.'

'You do. Before Christmas you were thick as thieves with him. You were all over him at the Wilsons' party. I remember thinking that it was a good job that Kit wasn't there.'

Isobel's cheeks were red, but whether with anger or embarrassment, it was hard to tell. Her reaction confirmed what I had known already. She could be as susceptible to Luke as the rest of us; she just disliked herself for it more.

Isobel and I were watching each other carefully.

'You know what?' she said. She turned away from me, reaching up to a cupboard for a glass. 'I think that maybe we should chill out and try and get things in perspective.' She sat herself down at the table and waved at me to do the same. 'I wasn't going to tell you this, Josie, not yet, but while we were away we decided to move. We're finally going to sell the house.'

'Sell Millbury Street?'

'Yes. You knew we would, eventually.'

'Yes.' I just hadn't expected it to be now. I had thought with the baby coming that they would wait a year or two, or even more.

'I want to start afresh, in a new house, away from all this.' She spread her hands, indicating what appeared to be the kitchen fittings, but I knew that she meant the rest of the house, the over-decorated Tobyness of the place, and all its past associations.

'I see.'

'So we'll all have to find somewhere else to live, us, you, Luke. It will do us all good. And we'll all see one another but it won't be so . . .'

'Claustrophobic?' I offered.

'Worse than that,' she said. 'There's something sticky and rotting and unwholesome here, though I don't know what exactly. And now coming back and finding you and him . . .'

'It's really nothing to make such a fuss about,' I said.

'He was in your bed, Josie. In your bed. He's twenty-four, you're well over fifty. Can't you see how weird that is?' Her words smashed the tenuous justifications I had gathered about me, and I sat down suddenly on one of the wooden kitchen chairs and felt myself begin to sob. This was twice in a week I had wept and I knew I would have to acknowledge that my life was not held together as tightly as I had liked to imagine.

Isobel filled the glass she had been holding with water and came over to me. She sat down beside me, gently, and put her arm around my shoulder.

'Dear Josie,' she said. 'I know you meant no harm. And I don't blame you. I think that Luke is taking advantage. I only wish I knew why. Don't misunderstand, I do believe he's fond of you.' She pulled me to her again, but I shrank back and she let me go. 'Have a good cry,' she said. 'You'll feel better.'

'I'm not crying,' I said.

'I think you are,' she said. 'I think we should tell Luke that you're not well, and that you need to rest. Kit will put him in a hotel or a B & B for a few nights till we find him somewhere else.'

'There's no need for that,' I said. I couldn't bear the thought of Luke being sent away, and it being all my fault.

'I'll talk to Kit,' she said. 'We're going off tomorrow for New Year, just for two nights, you know that, but I'm not leaving him here alone with just you and that's that.'

'There's no need,' I said. 'I'm going away too.'

She knew so little about me and my life, I thought. She didn't know, or care, that this year I had booked myself into a health farm just to avoid the holiday. They had arranged, I knew, to go to Dorset for New Year, to stay with an old Army friend of Kit's, and even before Luke's recent comings and goings, I hadn't really thought that he would be around. It was a time, after all, when the young stuck together, a time for those who were excited at the idea of the future. I stood up to leave, and Isobel took my arm.

'I'm serious, Josie,' she said, facing me now. 'I'll say nothing to Kit but I want Luke out of this house. Whatever it takes. I'll leave it to you, if you like, but if you won't address the situation, then I will.'

❧

Luke was up and dressed when I returned to the flat. He was cooking himself bacon and tomato on the stove.

'Hey, Josie, do you want some breakfast?' He beamed at me, his eyes shining although the bruise across his face was now prominent, blue and purple. I shook my head.

'Kit and Isobel are back,' I said. 'They got an earlier flight.'

'Great,' he said. 'I'll go and say hello.'

'I think they've gone to bed for an hour or so,' I said. 'I wouldn't go yet.' I went towards him and picked up the loaf which was sitting on the kitchen surface. 'I'll just have toast,' I said, and put a slice in the toaster. 'Have you put some more arnica on your face?' I could hardly bring myself to look at him.

He shook his head. 'It's fine,' he said. He looked almost proud. He came over and kissed me on the cheek.

'What are you doing for New Year, Luke?' I said.

He looked surprised at the question. 'I don't know. There are a couple of parties. You're away, aren't you?'

'Yes,' I said. 'But I don't have to go. Not if you need . . .' The expression on his face was that of someone who looked suddenly trapped, and I felt silly. 'I didn't mean that,' I said. 'Last night, I . . . it was just the once. It shouldn't have happened. It was very nice, of course.' I had imagined myself to be worldly-wise but here I was blushing and calling sex 'nice'.

'You have a good break,' he said. 'You deserve it.'

I pictured myself at the spa, wrapped in my towelling dressing gown on New Year's Eve, pampered, a little hungry, and desperate for the night to be over.

'Yes,' I said. 'I shall enjoy it.' I took my toast and sat down at the table, watching him as he loaded bacon on to a plate. He had completely ignored my reference to the night before. I would have hoped he might at least have said something.

'There's another thing I should mention, Luke. It's important.'

'Uh oh,' he said. 'Sounds like trouble.' I could tell that he didn't really think so. His mood was upbeat and I was loath to upset it, but it was perhaps best to broach the subject while he was clearly so robust.

'Kit and Isobel have decided to sell the house.'

He said nothing, hardly paused in what he was doing. He carried his plate over to the table, pulled out a chair and sat down. He didn't pick up the knife and fork he had brought but sat looking at me, waiting for more.

'I think that they may want to do that quite quickly. I can move back into the Victoria flat next month. My tenant is leaving.'

'So she wants me to go too,' he said. His tone was neutral but his face had gone pale and the bruising now stood out against the white of his skin. 'Fine. I'll go. No problem.'

'The timing is perfect in some ways, for me,' I said. 'I'm more concerned about you, Luke. I'd have you to stay in my flat, but it's just too small.'

'I was looking for somewhere anyway. I can look after myself.'

'I know you can. And you'll find somewhere quickly. And Isobel was talking about what they could do. Kit will put you in a B & B for a bit if that would help.'

'She is keen, isn't she,' he said.

'It's not like that, Luke.'

'No?' he asked. 'I think it is.' He still hadn't touched his food and I could see small globules of bacon fat beginning to solidify on the matt white plate. 'They don't want me around because they've got a kid of their own coming. Why would they?' he said. 'I wouldn't. I knew, as soon as she got pregnant, or when you told me it was his. I knew they would want me out.' The words were flat, dead, and I feared for what was beneath them that bred so much anger and defeat. 'But still,' he went on, his voice sarcastic, 'better get on and get looking.'

'Eat your breakfast,' I replied. 'Don't be rash, Luke. We can talk about it again later.'

He pushed his plate away. 'I'm not hungry any more,' he said.

Towards noon, I was sitting in the gallery, trying to avoid my own thoughts, especially the thought of what I had allowed to happen the night before, of the compromised intimacy between Luke and me. I had promised myself a walk across the park at lunchtime. I might even have time, I thought, to go down to the cathedral. I could look up at my flat and contemplate the future. It might be small compared with what I was used to, but it was at least mine. It would hold me together and keep me sane until I could find out what I thought and what I wanted, if such a thing were possible, and of course the likelihood was that I would simply never move again.

I was interrupted by Kit who appeared at the door of my office, looking tanned from his holiday, if a little thinner. He also looked worried as he approached me and kissed me on both cheeks.

'A belated Happy Christmas, Josie,' he said. 'So you survived Ma?'

'Happy Christmas to you too,' I replied. 'Margaret was fine. You must be exhausted,' I said. 'I thought you were asleep.'

'Not for long, that would be fatal,' he said. 'I'd never sleep tonight. And I wanted to come into the gallery.' He began to fidget with the newspaper he held in his hand, then thinking better of it, put it on my desk.

'I'm very cross with Isobel,' he said. 'I should have been the one to talk to you, Josie, about us selling up . . . After all these years. I'm very cross with her.'

'It's all right, Kit,' I said. 'I knew it would happen one day. And you're right, both of you, this is a good time. I'm ready to go, too.'

I could see the relief in his face. 'You've lost weight,' I said. 'Despite Christmas.'

He patted his stomach.

'Yes. Stress, I suppose they'd say. It's been an odd year, Josie, don't you think? What with Luke, and now this baby coming after everything . . .'

'It certainly has,' I said.

'This business, about Luke going,' Kit said. 'I've tried to get Isobel not to be so rushed but she's got a bee in her bonnet. Must be the pregnancy.'

'Yes,' I said.

'Isobel said you would talk to him?'

'I've already mentioned it.'

'What did he say?'

'He was a bit surprised, at the suddenness.'

'Yes,' he said. 'It is a bit sudden. But we were always going to move him in the New Year. This American option looks likely, if he's still interested.'

'I'm sure he will be,' I said.

The conversation was feeling a bit stiff. It was hard to know how much Isobel had told him. It had always been difficult for Kit to be emotional, but now he seemed genuinely upset and he took hold of my hand.

'We'll miss him, of course, but it will be good for him. It's you I'm concerned about, Josie,' he said.

'You don't have to worry about me.'

'Don't say that. I shall always be concerned about you. I don't mean to be patronising but I regard you as a member of my family, you know that. I feel I have obligations.'

'Now you are patronising me.'

'Sorry. That was pompous. I apologise.' He pulled out his old chair, the chair in which Luke usually sat.

'I think,' he said, 'that where Luke is concerned we all got rather . . . I can't think of the right word.'

'Dazzled,' I offered.

Kit laughed. 'I'm not sure that's the word I would have chosen,' he said. 'But I know what you mean.'

'It was almost as if Alice had come back,' I said.

'That's silly, Josie. That's a dangerous way to think.'

'But you thought it too.'

'No, not like that. I admit that for a while I was, well, overcome in some way by how much he reminded me of her.'

'Yes.'

'But now I can stand back a bit. And he's terrific, a young man with great potential and it's up to us to send him on his way, Josie.'

'Yes.' I could hear the words he was saying but I felt I didn't really understand him.

'I thought you might like a trip to New York too,' he went on, 'at the end of next month. I thought perhaps you might like to take on the Armory Show this year, and then you could check out Lendlemans, and see if you think it's the right place for Luke?'

I had been preparing for the Armory winter show on Kit's behalf throughout the autumn. It was a highly prestigious event in our calendar. We were one of only a handful of specialists who took part. But I was usually left behind in London while Kit oversaw the coveted stand, and dined the clients and experts who came to see what we had to offer. It was a highlight of the sale year, and he relished it. For him to suggest that I should be in charge was a big concession. I felt suddenly excited at the idea and, even better, a sense that there might be some juice left in life after all.

'I'll come over for a couple of days,' he went on. 'But you'll be in charge. It will be your show. And then we might think about you looking after just the foreign sales side. You said you might enjoy being more part time? You're always talking about doing a second degree. If you wanted to do one, I think the business could fund that. It might be tax-deductible. Think about it. Think about it all.'

It was only later when I began to walk across St James's Park that I understood that Kit was buying me off. We were all carrying guilt. Mine was about Alice. His was about me, as well as about Luke. Luke had been right after all. Kit had made his decision. He was putting his family first and I was being let go. Whatever he said, however much he protested that I would remain a part of them, I knew that at last I was being let go, like the employee I was. The realisation was an odd one, of surprise, freedom and loneliness. I sat down on the nearest bench and knew that what I wanted more than anything was to have someone to talk to, and the thought that I had no one was overwhelmingly sad. And then I thought of Jack Whaley and I knew that he would listen to me. I might not like what he would say, but he would listen and he might even make sense of it all.

Forty-five minutes later I walked through the door of Penton College, an affiliate of the University of London, which specialised in psychology, and where Jack taught a weekly seminar on the history of psychoanalysis. I could see him coming to meet me from down the corridor and I tried to speed towards him, but as I did so, a man in uniform stood in front of me and asked me where I was going.

'To see Dr Whaley,' I said, waving in Jack's direction.

'Do you have a pass?' the man said.

'No,' I said. 'No, I'm sorry. But I . . .'

'It's all right. She's come to see me.' Jack had now reached us. He pulled me to him and kissed my cheek with determination, then stood back. He seemed smaller in the shadow cast by the other man's bulk.

'She needs a pass, Doctor,' the man said.

'I'll vouch for her.'

'I'm sorry, sir, she must have a pass.'

'Oh really,' I said. 'Isn't that a bit unnecessary?'

'We'll go back to reception and get one,' Jack said, in an unusual display of patience. 'It's the health and safety people,' he explained as we made our way back. 'And security, of course.'

'What's that got to do with it?' I said.

'Well, you might catch a deadly disease, or bring one in. Or you might be an animal rights terrorist.'

'But there aren't any animals here, are there?'

'No. They're long gone. But some people might not know that.'

I didn't pursue the idea. I was in no state to dwell on the thought of unpredictable people intent on possible harm.

'So,' he said. 'What's this all about?'

We were sitting in the canteen, which appeared to have been designed to lend an upbeat unconventionality to the business of feeding. The tables came in a variety of different shapes and sizes, and were coated in pink or purple Formica. It was quite horrible to my aesthetic sense, and seemed like a sort of madness. It was hardly an aid to

299

digestion, but then I supposed that most academics were indifferent to food, or too poor to take a serious interest. I had suggested we went out, to the patisserie across the street, where I could at least have bought Jack a decent cake, but Jack was having none of that.

'Why go and pay a fortune,' he said, 'when we can get a perfectly good cup of tea cheaply here.'

'Because it tastes better,' I said. 'And you could have a cake with proper cream, not that artificial muck you've got in there.' I pointed to the mass-produced cream cake he was finishing up.

'Says who?'

'I do.'

He laughed. 'Thank God you're not Helen. She wouldn't let me have the cake at all. You are good to indulge an old man, Josie,' he said.

'How is Helen?' I hadn't liked to ask.

'Gone for good. Before Christmas. It's been a long time coming.'

'Really?'

'Yes. This time, really.' His voice was just a little forlorn as he scraped the crumbs from his plate.

I looked round the room, a modern refectory, filling up now with hungry foreign students, too far from home to leave the college for Christmas. Some of them were hooded like ancient monks, pursuing their legitimate afternoon break from whatever was preoccupying them.

'Now we're here, I feel rather foolish,' I said.

Jack said nothing but waited.

'I think perhaps I might have been rather foolish,' I said.

'Margaret said that to me at Christmas. She said I was a foolish woman.'

'Margaret is a bitch,' Jack said. His words were so categorical, so full of feeling, that for the first time in days I felt I wasn't alone. I felt my eyes well up. He reached across the table and took my hand. 'There, there,' he said.

'I feel like one of your patients,' I said.

'If you were one of my patients, I wouldn't be holding your hand. I would just sit here and let you cry.'

'But I'm not crying,' I said.

'Come on,' he said. 'Let's find somewhere more private.'

He led me through the dingy corridors with their peeling paint and old noticeboards. The limp that had bothered him earlier in the year seemed to have vanished and as I walked behind him I thought how much more vigorous he seemed and that perhaps Helen's departure had been a tonic. Reaching a small door, he let us into a square room with three or four armchairs and a small sofa. There was also a desk on which stood an antiquated computer.

'Good, no one here,' he said. 'The Fellows' common room. They're not back from Christmas yet.' There was a key on the inside of the door and he turned it. 'That will keep anyone out,' he said. 'It's often locked during the holidays.'

'Not from the inside, though,' I said.

He patted the seat beside him on the sofa and I sat down.

Twenty

The week of Alice's half-term, Toby had planned a party. He had made a major sale to a museum and was determined that everyone should know how clever he had been. It might have been wiser, I thought, to be more discreet, but then if the museum was happy with the provenance provided, why should Toby worry? It was me who fretted about such things. What if someone came forward to make a prior claim? What if the government of the country of origin were to file a case for the object's return? Things were getting tougher, restrictions tighter. Business could not be done as it had once been done, by a gentleman's word, or a blind eye turned. Finder's Keepers had been the old watchwords, but no longer.

Millbury Street had been decorated for the occasion. It was the sale of a magnificent Roman krater that was financing the celebrations, and we were to have a Roman feast. Low tables had been brought in. Fake busts, plates, cups and so on had been hired from a theatrical warehouse, and everyone was to come appropriately dressed. I found the idea tiresome, though I had, of course, spent more time than I wished on its organisation. I would have preferred to run away and hide somewhere, and I might even have done so, taken myself off for a night on the pretext of visiting one of my cousins, but Alice was staying with us and she was in a state of high excitement.

I had arranged for a dressmaker friend to make us something suitable to wear and the day before, we took the train to Cricklewood to try on our costumes. It was warm and the tube was hot. Alice was wearing her short full skirt and her long legs were tanned. Her dark eyes were intense as she looked around the half-empty carriage.

'Why do we believe things?' she said. It was the sort of odd, all-encompassing question that she was prone to asking. She gave me no time to respond before pushing on, as if I had objected. 'Go on, why do you think we believe things?'

'We believe evidence, I suppose,' I said, trying to get into the spirit of philosophical inquiry. 'We believe what is demonstrated to be true, or I do.'

'But I don't think that's true of most people,' she said. 'Do you?'

I raised my eyebrows. 'Then they're fools,' I said.

'But they're not, Josie,' she said. 'And you know it, and that's what makes the question interesting. And you believe things that can't be proved, too, don't you?'

'What do you believe?' I said. It was she who had moved the terms of the argument, I thought.

'I believe in trying to be good,' she said. 'Trying to love people.'

I found her words immensely touching but I didn't want to appear sentimental.

'Is it hard then, to love people?' I said.

'Sometimes. Not you, Josie. I love you, and Toby.'

'So who do you have to try so hard to love?'

'All sorts of people. Mummy. I mean I do love Mummy, but sometimes it's very difficult.' She said this with the resigned air of someone much older.

'Yes,' I said, 'I can see that it might be difficult sometimes.'

'Do you remember,' she said, 'when I was little, I told you that I sometimes heard things?'

'Yes,' I said. 'I remember.' I waited for a moment, then I forced myself to ask her, 'Have you ever heard them since?'

She went quiet and I wondered whether I should prompt her.

'Not really,' she said. 'Only slightly, once or twice. But I thought I might be dreaming.'

I wasn't sure whether this explanation entitled me to feel relieved or not.

'What did you dream?' I said.

'That someone was telling me to try to love people better,' she said. 'But it wasn't at night, or at least I was in bed but I don't think I was asleep.'

'Who?' I said.

'I told you. Mummy.'

'No, who do you think was telling you, in the dream?'

'You don't believe me.'

'Yes I do, darling, I believe you.' The train was pulling into Cricklewood Station. 'I just think it was probably a dream.'

'I don't know who it was.'

Alice was too bright for me to humour, but I didn't want to give the story too much credence. She was highly intelligent, but she had also always told stories; not lies exactly, but she liked to embellish and dramatise. As we climbed off the train she spun away from me and pirouetted across the platform as if she were very much younger. She looked so graceful, her tanned arms stretched, her little skirt flaring above her slim legs. At that moment she looked a truly ethereal creature, and it seemed only natural that she should inhabit a world of wonder and disembodied voices. She came to a halt and then bowed, laughing. A couple of men had stopped to stare at her, mesmerised by her youth and unusual beauty. I felt proud of her, but a little afraid too.

It was a magnificent party. We had hired young men to carry flaming torches to usher in our guests. And there were still more young men, and women, whose dress seemed closer to Greece than to Rome in my eyes, who brought in trays of food and drink. There was a small boat, whose driver was forbidden to allow a drop of alcohol to pass his lips, which cruised around the canal basin and landed guests from time to time so that they could enjoy the hospitality of a marquee set up on the little island in its centre.

Toby was everywhere, rushing around, talking fast and loud, too much cocaine bursting through his system. There were friends from every part of his life. Toby's brother,

Christopher, had come down specially from Norfolk, though Margaret had made some excuse not to be there. She disliked what she regarded as Toby's 'flamboyance', by which she meant his public homosexuality. She would have preferred him to be more discreet.

I had based myself in the kitchen, always a good vantage point at a party, and at about ten thirty, I found myself face to face with Christopher Haddeley. I rarely saw Christopher these days, except at the occasional social event, and I had always regretted losing the closeness we had had when we first met. He had been my first real bridge into a life that I had thought I wanted. He had always been fond of me, but when I went to work for Toby, I think he felt that I had made a choice and that it wasn't possible to have both of them. Embarrassed now to face each other, we turned to watch Alice, deep in conversation with a pretty young man dressed as a Roman centurion.

'She looks lovely, doesn't she?' I said.

'Yes,' he said. 'A shame my son isn't here. I think he's getting a bit of a soft spot for Alice.'

'Kit?' I said. This was news to me. 'Really? When?'

'She came to the house with Anne, to a party last year,' he said. 'Of course she's still much too young. But I saw the way he looked at her.'

'I'm surprised Anne bothered to get out of bed to go to a party,' I said, regretting my bitterness at once. Christopher laughed.

'Free drink, I suppose. Dreadful woman.' He leant down

to me and whispered in my ear, 'Do you have a lover, Josie?'

His question felt so intimate that I felt myself redden. The truth was I hadn't had a lover for some time, and had begun to wonder if I ever would again.

'Not at the moment,' I said. 'How's Margaret?'

'What a waste,' Christopher said, ignoring my attempt to change the subject. He meant well, meant to be kind even, but the word 'waste' hit me like a truck. My wasted life, I thought, the constant nagging worry I had myself, that it was all just one big waste. I tried to laugh it off. He was just trying it on as usual. Everyone knew that Christopher was predatory, that he would take sex, discreetly, where he could get it. He relied on the numbers principle, I thought. If he tried enough women, some would oblige. But not me.

'She's a very pretty girl,' he said. He raised his glass in the direction of Alice. 'I hope you are keeping an eye on her.' I felt rebuked, though I knew he hadn't meant it in that way. I had wondered if Alice should really be here, but what was the harm? Toby and I were present to keep an eye on her, or I was, at least. Toby had decamped to the island marquee where he was holding court. I hoped he wasn't taking drugs there. It was far too public.

I had said that Alice could stay at the party until after the fireworks, which were to be just before midnight, and after that she must go bed. Looking at her now, I could see she was very animated. There was a glass in her hand and I suspected that it was champagne rather than the sparkling apple juice I had ordered for her specially. Her cheeks were a little flushed and I made my excuses to Christopher and went over to her.

'Are you both enjoying yourselves?' I asked her and her companion.

'Oh yes,' she said. 'It's a brilliant party, Josie. This is Neil by the way.'

'Hello, Neil.' I could hear my voice raised above its usual level. The chatter around us was enough to make it a slight strain for me to hear. 'Are you a friend of Toby's?' A silly question. If I didn't know him, he must be.

'Not really. Ivan invited me.'

'Ivan?'

'Toby's friend.'

He meant Ilya of course. It was difficult to get used to this alias, if that was what it was.

'Ivan, yes of course, sorry.'

He looked at me as if not to know Ivan was a social solecism.

'Would you like to dance?' he said, turning to Alice.

'Yes please,' she said. He took her hand and she waved goodbye to me as he led her upstairs. I had no fears about Neil. He was definitely what Margaret would term one of Toby's special friends.

It was four in the morning when I woke up suddenly. I had gone to bed only a couple of hours before. I had enjoyed the party, in spite of my earlier misgivings, helped by having drunk a great deal. I had even given in to a line of coke, though drugs were something I tried to avoid. As far as I knew, no one had drowned or overdosed or even been sick, though I had seen Christopher Haddeley go off into the night in a taxi with a woman who looked far from well.

I was thirsty, and had forgotten to bring water with me to bed. I got up and put on my dressing gown and hoped that I had a glass lurking around the bedroom somewhere so that I wouldn't have to go all the way downstairs, but I couldn't find one. I remembered that I had seen a couple in Alice's room the previous afternoon and thought it probable they were still there. If I crept in, she would be unlikely to wake up at this hour.

To my surprise, as I tiptoed across the landing, her light was on and music was playing softly on her little cassette player. I could hear voices, kept low deliberately, and stifled laughter. The door was very slightly ajar and if I crept to the hinged side I thought it likely I would be able to see in. I hesitated to do so. It was a violation of her privacy. But then she was still a child, and my responsibility.

I moved towards the door as silently as I could, though my discretion was unnecessary as my movements were masked by the music. I tried to angle myself so as to be able to see in and as I did so I suddenly saw the back of Toby's head as he sat on her bed. My initial reaction was relief that it was Toby, but this was followed by a sort of fury that he should wake her and keep her up this late. I assumed he must have woken her because when I had put my head round her door on the way to bed, she had been fast asleep. I was about to go in and protest when I heard a third voice. It was Ilya's. I craned my neck a little further and then I saw him, sitting beside Alice on the bed, stroking her hair.

Like a snake with a snake charmer, I was held in upright suspension. I was wide awake and anxious, and yet now I could not burst in on them. Ilya's presence held me back. It would seem petty and I would be thought a killjoy. It was Toby's party. It was Alice's holiday. She was grown up. She had stayed up late with Toby before, though never this late.

She was laughing now, I could hear her, and I wondered if Toby had let her smoke some of his hash. If I twisted my head yet another way I could see her half sitting, half sprawled on the brocade bedcover which we had bought together, the long legs that the men on Cricklewood Station had admired stretched out under a fine lawn nightdress that I had found for her.

There was something in Ilya's face that I had not seen before. Something sensuous and greedy. But he was Toby's lover. Toby was there, sitting on the end of the bed. There was nothing really to worry about, other than the fact that Alice would no doubt be exhausted for a day or two. I turned round and went back to my room.

It was my recollection of that evening that I now poured out to Jack Whaley, sitting on the old green velour sofa in the Fellows' common room, or rather it was this that he elicited from me. I told him what I had seen, plucking at a bald patch on the cushion between us as I did so. He was still holding my other hand, patting it gently.

'I went back to my room, Jack,' I said. 'I should have gone in and sent them both away.'

He waited for me to go on, as he had all through my account, wanting me, I knew, to tell him what I feared, but I couldn't bring myself to say it.

'All I could think,' I said, 'was that I would be mocked for being prim, that Alice would laugh along with them and for some reason, that night, I found the idea unbearable.'

'You didn't want Alice to think you were spoiling her fun?' he said. 'You didn't want to seem a spoilsport.'

'Yes. Exactly that. I didn't want to be the one who always did the telling-off. They were all like children. Alice, Toby, Ilya. I was tired of them, even of Alice when she was in that mood.'

'What mood was that?'

'Overexcited. That's how she used to get. Of course, we know now where that led. But none of us knew that at the time. But I should have known. Just the day before she had told me that all wasn't well. Not in so many words, but with hindsight . . . but then with the arrangements for the party and the business . . . still, there can be no excuses. I have to accept responsibility.'

'For what, Josie?'

'For whatever happened.'

'What do you think happened?'

'I don't know. I can't possibly know. I just . . . something . . .'

'They were just two fairies, weren't they?'

Even in my misery this made me smile. Jack's political incorrectness had always been resolute, and his antiquated terminology was comical.

'Yes,' I said. 'But still I fear we – I include myself,

we – the life we led – it may have been corrupting, and I wondered if after that she . . . with someone . . . It was madness, all of it. What were we doing, Jack? What was I doing?'

My breath had begun to shorten, and I dreaded the incipient sobs that now swelled up in my chest. In over twenty years I had never acknowledged that this memory had taken up residence inside me, squatting like a dormant virus, pushing me further and further into a kind of isolation. It had marked me, I saw now. It had left me unfit for the love and care of others.

Jack pulled me to him and pressed his cheek against mine.

'You were always too good for them, Josie,' he said. 'I always said so.'

We sat for a moment or two until my breathing had subsided to some semblance of its usual pattern.

'Now,' he said. 'What can we do to cheer you up? How are you spending New Year?'

'I'm booked into a health spa,' I said. 'I hate New Year. Even more than Christmas.'

Jack laughed, then looked straight at me, pleased with himself.

'Then we shall spend it together, you and I,' he said. 'You will come to Chiswick and I'll give you some dinner of sorts, and we'll get very drunk on malt whisky and then maybe . . .' He kissed my cheek again but said no more. I squeezed his hand, unable in my upset state to make full sense of what he was saying.

'But I've booked the spa.'

'Well, unbook it, woman,' he said. 'Life's short enough without starving the New Year in.'

I thought for a moment, collecting my scattered wits. I was disinclined to abandon my plan altogether, having paid for my room, but I knew that I wanted to agree to Jack's proposal.

'I'll go for one night instead of two,' I said. 'I'll go tomorrow and come back on Thursday, on New Year's Eve. That way I'll get nearly the two days. I'll drive straight to you, to Chiswick. About nine thirty? How about that?'

It had already been dark for a couple of hours by the time I got back to Millbury Street that evening. There were no lights on in the flat and those in the main house I recognised as security measures. There was no one at home. I let myself in through the side gate and the exterior lights immediately flooded the small courtyard.

I sensed, even as I climbed the stairs to the apartment, that Luke had gone. When I looked in his room, it had an empty air. He hadn't taken everything, but the cupboard had been half cleared and his big suitcase was no longer above the wardrobe. He had made his bed, which I found rather a touching gesture, but he had left no note of any sort.

After the emotion of the afternoon I felt calm, resigned even, to his departure. After all, he would have to return at some point, if only to collect the rest of his things. I told myself that he would telephone, or if not, that within a few days he would reappear. He was due back at work the following week and surely he would not abandon the gallery and the potential for his future. But Luke was not the type of person who built his life block by block, he was someone who reacted, who would pick off whatever came to him by chance, forgetting what had been there before.

I walked around the flat and into the kitchen. There was little evidence that he had ever lived there. I didn't feel his absence so much as wonder if he had ever existed, as if the ghostly presence of Alice which he had seemed to embody had taken flight. There was a sadness, but I felt lighter than I had done for some time, excited even. I had been invited to spend New Year's Eve with Jack, I was going to New York in January, and a part of me was almost happy.

I poured myself a drink and sat on the plump little sofa which I had had re-upholstered only last month in a blue and cream *toile de jouy*, and on which I did now find one sign of Luke: a small pink smudge from an accident with a bowl of strawberries quite soon after he had arrived. I put my finger on it and it made me think that I had not told Jack Whaley everything. I had not told him about the nights that Luke had spent in my bed. Isobel might tell him herself, of course. I sipped from my glass and felt the comforting fire of the liquid hit my throat. I reflected that perhaps I would tell him myself. I didn't know what he would make of it, but I no longer cared to keep secrets.

Twenty-One

We were dancing together when the phone rang, or perhaps holding on to each other as the music played would be a more accurate description. It was about one in the morning and we had drunk the New Year in. The evening had been a success. Jack and I had reminisced, argued, laughed and argued again. And now we were dancing, saying little, the warmth of our bodies protesting at the passing of the years.

And then my mobile rang. I didn't hear it at first. The music wasn't loud but it was enough to disguise its tone, and when I finally picked it up, I saw that there had been two calls already from a number I did not recognise.

'Hello?'

'Ms Price?'

'Yes.'

'This is Detective Sergeant Neville, Metropolitan Police.'

The words cut through the intimate whisky haze in which Jack and I were enveloped. He had been holding one hand as I groped in my bag for my phone with the other, and he still held it now. He was smiling at me, oblivious of the crude intrusion. I pulled my hand from him and turned away slightly.

'Yes. The Metropolitan Police,' I repeated for Jack's benefit.

'I understand you live at number nine Millbury Street?'

'Yes.' There must have been a burglary, or worse, a fire.

'And where are you now, Ms Price?'

I gave Jack's Chiswick address.

'I'll send a car,' he said. 'I would be grateful, Ms Price, if you would return home. We need to ask you some questions. In the meantime do you know the whereabouts of Mr Kit Haddeley?'

'Yes, Mr Haddeley's in Dorset, with his wife. Why? What's this all about?'

'I'll explain when you get here, Ms Price. Do you have an address where he is staying?'

'I have his mobile number.'

'We've tried that. There is no response.'

'I don't have the address. I believe it's in Abbotsbury. Some people called Pringle. They own a house there.'

'Thank you, that's very helpful. I'd be grateful if you would stay where you are until the car comes.'

'Yes, yes of course.'

I sat down on the sofa and looked up at Jack who had quickly understood that something was wrong.

'Isobel?' he said. 'Are they all right, Kit and Isobel?'

'I think so,' I said. 'It's something at the house. It can't be Kit and Isobel because they're trying to find them.

They're sending a car for me. They want to ask me questions.'

'I'll come with you,' he said. He reached for my hand again and squeezed it. 'This is one way of sobering up,' he said. He began to check his pockets for his wallet and his keys, an attempt to revert to his usual routine. I felt cold with fear under the numbing of the drinks we had consumed.

'Do you think this might be something to do with Luke?' I asked.

'I think it may be,' he replied.

As we turned the corner to approach Millbury Street I was astonished at what I saw. White tape had been pulled across the end of the road to close it off. There seemed to be police everywhere. Neighbours were milling about on the pavement. Some appeared to be being interviewed by police officers in uniform; others were talking to one another, anxious and curious. They turned to stare as our car was ushered through, the tape temporarily set aside.

We pulled up outside the house and an officer came to open the car door. I could see that there were arc lights planted somewhere in the garden, sending up beams, and I had the absurd image of myself stepping on to some red carpet, as if I were royalty attending a film première.

A man came forward to meet us and I knew at once it was Detective Sergeant Neville. He was wearing a dark overcoat and gloves and I could see his breath in the early-morning air. I found myself smiling at him, as if meeting an old friend, but my smile was not returned. I followed him through the gates and into the house, Jack walking behind me like an attentive consort. I looked around and the reality of what was happening began to make itself felt. I had lived here for three decades. But the house no longer belonged to us, it had been taken over.

There were men, mostly men, everywhere I looked. Men making phone calls, men coming in and out of the front door and the side door, some dressed in white forensic suits, some in casual clothes who didn't look like policemen at all. I saw two women being put into a police car. They were dressed as if for a party and I assumed they were witnesses to whatever had happened. They must have been at one of the neighbouring houses, I thought. I looked up to the upper floors. I found myself moving automatically towards the staircase but at once DS Neville stopped me.

'I'm afraid you can't go up there at the moment, Ms Price. Would you like to come in here and sit down?' He was standing at the door of the ground-floor dining room, a room which Kit and Isobel rarely used. He turned to Jack. 'I think it might be better, Mr Whaley, if you waited out here. WPC Simpson will look after you.' He hesitated for a moment, then appeared to register that Jack was, if not old, then an older man. 'You could sit in one of our cars if you like?'

'I'm not sitting in one of your bloody cars,' Jack said.

'Mr Whaley is Mrs Haddeley's father,' I said quickly. 'Couldn't he stay with me?'

Detective Sergeant Neville looked at a tall man with light brown receding hair who had appeared in the dining-room doorway. 'That's all right, Don,' he said. 'Mr Whaley can stay for now.' He made a gesture indicating that Jack and I should follow him. He placed us opposite him at the table and beckoned DS Neville to join him on his side. He shook both our hands and introduced himself as Detective Chief Inspector John Carver.

'This is an informal chat, Ms Price,' he said. 'Don't worry.'

'I'd like you to tell me what on earth is going on,' I said.

'All in good time,' he said. 'Where did you spend this evening?'

I told him.

'So you didn't attend the party here at Millbury Street?'

I looked at Jack.

'What party?' I said, my heart sinking.

'We understand a party took place here this evening, a party given by a Mr Luke Tyler. Mr Tyler tells us he has been living here, is that correct?'

'Yes,' I said. 'Is he all right?' DCI Carver didn't answer. It must be drugs, I thought. But why so many policemen for drugs at a party?

'And Mr Kit Haddeley and Mrs Isobel Haddeley, as far as you know they were not present at this party?'

'No. I told your colleague, they're away.'

'Yes,' he said. 'You were very helpful. We've managed to locate them; I believe they are on their way back.'

Then why ask me if they were at the party? I thought, but I knew better than to say it out loud. They no doubt had their reasons.

'My daughter is all right?' Jack said.

'Yes, sir,' said DCI Carver. 'Quite all right as far as we understand.'

'Has Luke done something wrong?' I asked.

He looked up at me, then down again at the notes in front of him.

'Do you know a Mr Michael Kovalchuk?'

'No.'

'Are you sure?'

'Yes. I mean I think Luke knows him.'

'He seems to know you,' said DCI Carver. I turned to Jack and shrugged.

'Was he at this party?' Jack asked.

'It's not possible at this point in the investigation to give you answers to all the questions you ask, sir. I hope you understand,' said DCI Carver. He was very polite, I thought, but Jack frowned.

'What investigation?' I said.

'There has been a fatality,' said Carver.

'Someone's died,' Jack interpreted.

'Yes, sir.'

'How?' I said. 'Who? Not Luke. Oh please, not Luke.'

'No, not Luke Tyler. We haven't yet formally identified the body.'

'How did they die, Chief Inspector?' Jack's tone was mollifying, respectful, which surprised me, but then he had learnt to get what he wanted from people by more subtle methods than those of his youth.

'Drowned,' said Carver. 'He was only a boy. And he drowned.' I had imagined that a policeman in this situation would be impassive, unemotional, but DCI Carver seemed upset. He was sad, I thought, for a stranger who had died at my home.

It was a moment or two before I was able to respond to him.

'Drowned in the canal?' I asked.

'It would appear so.'

'Where is Luke, Chief Inspector?'

'Mr Tyler is at the police station, helping with our inquiries.'

'He's been arrested?' I asked.

'No. As I say, he has gone voluntarily to answer questions.'

'Does he need a lawyer?' Jack asked.

'I believe one has been arranged for him.'

'A police solicitor?' Jack continued.

'No. Mr Kovalchuk arranged for his representation. I don't think you need to worry on that score.' There was touch of sarcasm in his voice, which made me angry.

'I don't know Mr Kovalchuk, I told you,' I said. But I was beginning to think that I might. I was beginning to piece things together, though it was impossible to make the picture cohere. As I sat waiting to see what would happen next, DCI Carver stood up and walked to the other end of the room where he murmured inaudible instructions into his mobile phone. He then dispatched DS Neville, after a whispered exchange, through the dining-room door.

'How long have you lived here, Ms Price?' Carver said, now that the three of us were alone.

'Nearly thirty years.'

'And Luke Tyler is the child of Kit Haddeley's first wife?'

'Alice, yes, that's right. But we had no idea of his existence. He was adopted. Alice was very young when she got pregnant. None of us knew.'

'So you took him in. He was no relation to any of you. Why did you do that?'

I looked up at him. He was staring at me, his light blue eyes blinking, intermittently, like a lizard, I thought.

'He was Alice's son,' I said. 'He was working for us, or with us, I should say. Kit gave him a job. We all got on very well. Why wouldn't we help him?'

'And what about Mrs Haddeley?'

'You mean Isobel?' I said. I felt Jack stiffen next to me and I put a hand on his arm.

'Yes. Was she happy with him being here?'

I sighed. I had no quarrel with the police. I wanted to be co-operative but he was, it seemed to me, being unnecessarily provocative.

'I think so,' I said. 'But if, as you say, she is on her way back you will be able to ask her that yourself.'

'My daughter is a generous woman, Inspector,' Jack added. 'She was very good to this young man. Too good by the sound of it.'

I said nothing, but I thought it wrong of Jack to sound a note of doubt in front of the police. I reminded myself of the amount he had drunk and what time of night it was. We were not at our best, either of us. My head had begun to ache though at the same time it felt quite clear now. There was a knock on the door and DCI Carver stood up.

'That will be all for now, Ms Price, Mr Whaley. We may want to talk to you again in the morning. Is there somewhere you can go, Ms Price? Do you need to find a hotel? I'm afraid you can't stay here tonight.'

'She can stay with me,' Jack said. I nodded.

'It was an accident.' I said the words as a statement but I meant it as a question.

'I can't tell you anything more at the moment, I'm afraid.' Carver sounded stern but it was as if it were a pose to distract from a basic humanity. 'A car will take you back. Thank you.'

It was clear that the interview was over and we turned to go. He opened the door for us and followed us out watching as we left. I had expected whoever had knocked to be waiting outside, but there was no one there. We walked to the front door and towards the gates, under the glare of the security lights. At that moment, I saw Neville walking towards us followed by a small, smartly dressed, rounded figure. I found myself face to face with the man, who smiled at me sadly, shaking his head.

'Josie,' he said. 'You don't recognise me?'

But I did. Now, I did. It was the man I had seen at the airport and almost certainly at Christie's. It was Michael. Only it wasn't Michael as far as I was concerned. It was Ilya. He was considerably fatter than I remembered, soft and almost bald, but I could see now that the person I had been struggling to recall all these weeks was still present.

Our reunion, however, was both brief and bitter.

'I'm sorry, Josie,' was all he said to me in his oddly familiar way. DS Neville was manoeuvring him gently towards another car and it occurred to me that he might have been arrested.

'Luke?' was all I could say at first.

'He's okay,' said Ilya. 'He will be okay. He has a good lawyer. Go now.'

'What has he done?'

'Nothing, nothing. It's just a formality. I will ring you tomorrow, Josie, I promise. I am so sorry.' I recognised the voice now, too, despite its American overlay.

'My number,' I said. I began to open my bag for a pen.

'I have it.' I must have looked surprised and he nodded as if to reassure me. 'I have it. Don't worry. This will be explained. It will be explained to the police. It is a tragedy but it is an accident.'

His words left me more afraid than reassured. Jack put an arm around me.

'Come on, Josie,' he said. 'Time to go. We can't do anything tonight.'

'What are you doing here, Ilya?' I said as we turned to go. I had whispered the words, though DS Neville could hear me, I was sure. 'What were you doing here, with Luke?'

'Tomorrow, Josie. Tomorrow I will tell you. All will be well.' I wanted to slap him. I wanted to pummel him and shriek and shout.

'Come on, Josie.' Jack's voice was firmer this time. 'We're going home. I've tried to ring Isobel but there's no answer. I've left a message. She'll ring when they can. That's the best we can do.'

*

324

It was impossible to sleep. Returning to the Chiswick flat, I sat with Jack on the sofa, both of us nursing a glass but for once I was unable to drink. I found it difficult to speak, and when Jack asked me to explain more about Ilya, about 'Michael Kovalchuk', I was at a loss as to how to begin to portray him, let alone to offer any possible explanation of how he had come to be involved with Luke.

'We always thought he was a spy,' I said. It sounded odd to say it out loud, after all this time. 'We joked about it, but I think he sort of was. Did a bit of this and that on his travels, you know. More than a bit.'

'It's plausible enough,' Jack said, 'if what you say about him is true.'

'I haven't seen him since long before Toby died,' I continued. 'They fell out, over the business, I think. I know he contacted Kit a few years back, claiming Toby owed him money. He was always well connected,' I said. 'Friends in strange high places. I have no doubt at all that if he says he has a good lawyer for Luke, that will be so.'

We had very little idea as to why Luke needed a lawyer. Jack thought that he might be charged with negligence of some kind, and I wondered if Kit might be liable too, in some indirect way, though surely any fault of Kit's would not be criminal.

'It's so awful,' I said, 'and I'm so very tired that I don't think I'm going to even begin to try to think about it. I might just close my eyes for a bit if you don't mind.'

Jack moved himself closer to me.

'Poor Josie,' he said. 'Those bloody Haddeleys. Always

trouble.' He put his arm around me and I laid my head on his shoulder.

My phone was ringing in my ear. I woke up, still next to Jack who was fast asleep, undisturbed by the tone.

'Hello,' I said, trying to sound as if I had been awake for ages.

'Josie? It's Kit.'

'Kit, thank God. Where are you?'

'At the Fairfax.'

It was a small hotel around the corner from the house.

'They very kindly let us in, even though it was so late.'

It was typical, I thought, of Kit to be speaking graciously about hotel staff, instead of rushing to the nub of our nightmare.

'What have the police told you?' I said. 'We couldn't get hold of you last night to let you know what was happening.'

'They asked us not to make or receive calls on the way back to London,' Kit said. 'I mean they were very polite but we were sitting in the back of their car, so we were hardly going to disobey. Someone's drowned, in the canal, but the body was found on the bank at the edge of the garden. There was a party – Luke – but you must know that. It seems they're trying to establish what happened. There might have been some sort of fight.'

'A fight?'

'Well, something happened. He didn't just fall in drunk. Or they don't think so.'

'How do they know?'

'I've no idea.'

'And they think Luke was part of this . . . fight?'

'I don't think it's as clear cut as that. They've got five of them in custody.'

'Five?' I was astonished. Who were these five people? Who were these people who had come to our house and allowed death and all its consequences back in, when we had worked so hard to turn it out? 'How's Isobel?' I asked. Jack was still snoring beside me, quietly.

Kit sighed. 'Not good, not happy. I think she's physically okay. She's in the bath. I'm glad Jack was there with you, Josie. I'm very glad you weren't on your own.' He sounded genuinely relieved that I should have been looked after, and his words touched me. 'How could this have happened, Josie?' he was saying now. 'Have we been very foolish? Should we have seen it coming?'

There was that word again, 'foolish'. It was the word that I had been trying to avoid, but now Kit had said it.

'Perhaps,' I said. 'But we've got to deal with this now. What do you want to do?'

'I'm going to the police station,' he said.

'I'll come with you.'

'No. Stay there. I'm going to send Isobel round to Jack's. Stay there with her, Josie, till I ring you, I think that's best. When I find out what's going on, I'll let you know. What about this Kovalchuk man?'

I hesitated. I didn't know how much Kit knew. He would have to know, of course, but it was such a complicated story and one that only led to more unanswered questions.

'What about him?' I said, stalling.

'He seems to be a friend of Luke's, a good one to have. He arranged the lawyer – a smart one, I've checked.'

'Yes. Did you meet him last night?'

'No. I spoke to him on the phone. He said he knew you.'

'Yes,' I said. 'But I didn't recognise him. He was an acquaintance of Toby's from a long time ago.'

'And he knows Luke. How odd. Why didn't Luke tell us about him?'

'Indeed,' I said.

I felt hung over and dirty. Jack had tried to persuade me to lie down for an hour or two to try to get some more sleep, but it was beyond me. I made myself coffee in his tiny kitchen, then I rang DS Neville, whose last gesture had been to give me his card, to ask if I could at least collect some clean clothes from the flat. He put me on hold and then returned, pleased with himself, to tell me that yes, it would be possible, and that I could go back to the flat now. It was no longer under investigation, although I must confine myself to that part of the house.

'You can lock the connecting door, if you like,' I said. 'There's a key in the landing bureau.'

'Good idea,' he said. 'For your own benefit, Ms Price.' I couldn't imagine what benefit would accrue to me, but I said nothing. I ordered a taxi and was about to leave a note for Jack when he emerged from the doze into which he had fallen.

'I won't be long,' I said. 'Just a couple of hours.'

'If you're not back, I'll ring the police,' he called as I left.

'Ha ha,' I said, pulling the door behind me.

The flat appeared to be as I had left it just two days before. There was nothing to suggest that Luke might have spent a night there. I ran a bath and filled up the tub, washing myself vigorously as if I had something to atone for. I had just pulled on my big towelling robe, always a comfort, when the doorbell rang. I thought immediately that it might be Luke. He might have been let out of the police station and have come straight here. But he would have a key still. And then he might be more likely to go to see Ilya rather than me. It was Ilya who was looking after him now.

'Miss Price?' It was a woman's voice on the intercom.

'Yes?'

'My name is Raven, Caroline Raven. I very much need to speak to you. May I come in?' Her voice was cultured and middle class. Her tone, however, sounded strained, as if she were holding something back.

'What about?' I said.

'Last night,' she said. 'Please let me in. I think the police will send me away if they see me. And I do need to talk to you.'

I buzzed her in, pulling my towelling robe around me. I felt awkward admitting a total stranger into my flat, my hair dripping wet and no time to dress.

She walked through the door and I recognised her at once. It was the woman I had seen with Luke in St James's

Park, the same groomed blonde hair, though now it looked dull and artificial. Her skin was paler than I remembered, but it was her eyes that struck me. They looked huge and yet they had retreated into their sockets. They were dark and sunken, the whites bloodshot. There was something terrible in her face that precluded questions and I turned to lead the way into my small sitting room.

'Do sit down,' I said. I hadn't meant to invite her in. I'd intended to stand with her in the hallway to find out what she wanted, but it was clear that if she didn't sit down she might collapse.

'Can I get you some water, some coffee?'

She nodded. 'Thank you. Both, if it's no trouble.'

I turned to leave her and go into the kitchen but she followed me, as if she couldn't bear to let me out of her sight. She almost tripped over the kitchen threshold and I moved quickly to support her.

'Sit here,' I said. 'Sit here for now.'

She sat at the head of the wooden table with her back to the window. She twisted to look out of it, then turned back, seeming disappointed. I put on the kettle and took cups and coffee from the cupboard.

'You're a friend of Luke's,' I began. 'I saw you with him once. I . . .' I moved round to face her. She was crying silently, almost without movement. And then she spoke.

'My son is dead,' she said. 'It was my son. He drowned here last night.'

For a moment I felt nothing. I found myself thinking instead that it was strange that her mascara hadn't run, and that perhaps she had had her eyelashes tinted. Then I thought of the Ancient Greek figures I had seen through the years, on vases and fragments, the tragic mothers bewailing their dead boys, and here was something real, and I wished very much that I wasn't alone with her.

'I'm so very sorry, Mrs Raven,' I said, finally. 'I really am. But I wonder if you should really be here. You need to be with your family or a friend. Can I ring someone for you?' I spoke from experience. I knew what it was like to be suddenly bereaved, the shock, the numbness. But at least she could shed tears, I thought, as I looked at her, and I wondered if she was aware of them.

She seemed to be trying to steady herself. Her breathing was deep and self-conscious. I handed her a glass of water which she sipped slowly.

'Don't call me Mrs Raven,' she said. 'It's Caroline. I know who you are. You're Josie. Luke told me about you.' Her words were careful, kindly almost. 'My name is Caroline and I've come to tell you . . . I should have come before.' She lifted her face to mine. 'I had to go to the morgue,' she said. 'I had to see him lying there. He's sixteen, and he's lying there dead.'

I sat down beside her. Part of me wanted her to go away. I didn't want to deal with such awful grief but there seemed little choice, and then I had to know what she could tell me. I wanted to know what had happened. About what had happened to Luke.

After a moment or two, she began to speak again. Her tears had ceased and her voice was steady.

'I know Michael,' she said. 'It was him I met first.'

'Michael Kovalchuk.' I repeated the name, less by way

of encouragement than as an acknowledgement of his inevitable involvement.

'Yes. I met him at a party at an auction house. I had gone there with a girlfriend. I wasn't terribly interested in the art world, to be honest. But my friend had invited me and she knew him and we all went out to dinner. I liked Michael. He was very charming, cosmopolitan. Well, I expect you know.'

She looked at me as if seeking permission to continue, and I nodded.

'My friend was staying with me,' she said. 'We had had quite a lot to drink that evening and when we got home, we drank some more and she confided in me that Michael had introduced her to a young man. I wasn't sure what she meant at first, but then I realised that this boy she was speaking of was a sort of prostitute. Not that she would have called him that. A companion was how she described him.'

'Luke?' I asked.

She nodded.

I felt sick and yet it made sense. It made sense of things I had not yet even begun to examine. I had an instinctual knowledge that she was telling the truth.

'I knew she was drawing me in,' Caroline said. 'My so-called friend, and I suspected that this Michael man had put her up to it, though perhaps she really did want me to have some fun – to cheer me up, that's what she said.' She took a Kleenex from her jacket pocket and blew her nose. 'I'm very ashamed. I haven't told the police. I know I'm going to have to. I think I thought if I told you, if I told someone else first, it might be easier. And I'd been going to come here. I was trying to find the courage to come and tell you. I needed you to help me. And now it's too late.' She stared ahead of her, retreating once more into a private vacuum.

'I'll make us some coffee,' I said. I got up, turning away to fuss around the worktop, waiting for her to collect herself and find the strength to go on.

'So,' she said, pushing out the words that followed, 'I met him, Luke, I liked him, and I paid him for sex.' She looked at me, willing me to flinch on her behalf, but instead I found myself inclining my head gently to acknowledge that I had absorbed what she said. The truth was I had no judgement at that moment. It was information I wanted, however unpalatable. I set down a cup in front of her.

'Tell me, Caroline,' I said. 'Tell me everything. I think that's best for us all.'

She took the cup in her hand, but she didn't drink.

'I was lonely, that's my only excuse,' she said. 'My husband, Mark, has a mistress. He travels. He's hardly ever at home. And Tim,' her voice stumbled, 'Tim, my son, doesn't, or rather he didn't, get on with Mark. Tim is – was – gay. I'd suspected it for some time though we never talked about it. Mark knew it too and he couldn't come to terms with the idea. But Tim would never have met Luke if it hadn't been for me.' She paused and I thought she was going to break down and cry, but apart from a brief catch in her voice, a hoarseness that hinted at the pain she was concealing, she moved on almost without faltering.

'The truth is that I became fond of Luke. Despite the fact that I paid him, he was so warm and affectionate and his affection seemed so genuine, and the money seemed almost irrelevant, like an allowance or something.' She looked down, away from me, attempting, perhaps, to lessen her shame. 'Yes,' she went on, 'I know it was absurd. And I hadn't intended for him to meet my son, but I honestly thought he might be able to help Tim. Luke had had problems with his own father . . . Ah, I see he told you too.'

I must have nodded again, or perhaps shaken, my head. I had begun to register my growing sense of recognition. This account she was giving, of her susceptibility to Luke, to his increasing affection, to the distressing story of his childhood and adolescence, it could have been my own and I too felt ashamed.

'I had not thought for one moment,' she said, 'that Tim would become infatuated with Luke, but he did, and Luke took advantage of it. As soon as I found out they were lovers, I stopped seeing Luke and I tried to stop him from seeing Tim. There were all sorts of odd people around, drugs too, I'm sure. I suspected that Tim was stealing things from me, and from other people too, to give to Luke. Luke was too clever to steal them himself. When I tried to get Luke to leave Tim alone, he threatened to tell Mark about me and him.'

Caroline drank now from the small china coffee cup I had given her, small delicate sips, her hand shaking as she did so.

'I had decided,' she said, putting the cup down carefully

on its saucer, 'that, whatever the consequences, I had to do something. I'd found out about you and your gallery. He hadn't told me at first, but then Tim told me, and it became more and more obvious you should know what you were dealing with. I thought you might be able to stop him. And now it's too late . . .'

Caroline Raven was crying again but her face was quite still.

'Luke killed Tim,' she said. 'Whatever he did or didn't do last night, he killed Tim in one way or another. The drugs, the sex . . .' her voice became almost inaudible. 'He'd been sexually assaulted, the police told me.'

For the first time, the real horror of what she was telling me began to make its way into my consciousness. Was she saying that the boy had been raped? But if Luke was this boy's lover, how could it be him? I began to feel a sense of panic. This was information that the police needed to have. Luke came out of this sordid story very badly, but whatever else he might have done, he was surely not guilty of such an assault.

'Caroline,' I said, as gently as I could. 'You will have to tell the police. You said so yourself.' She nodded. 'Shall I call someone?'

She sighed and shifted in her chair. Tears began to roll silently down her cheeks again and she nodded. I looked in my bag for DS Neville's card. He was probably still here, somewhere in the house, though I supposed he might be resting for a while. He answered my call sounding sleepy, as if I had woken him, but when I told him who was with me and that she had information for him, he was instantly alert. On no account, he said, should either of us leave the flat until he or someone else arrived.

I stayed with Caroline Raven until a Woman Police Constable came to lead her off, no doubt to some small grey room where she would tell her tale again. I felt profoundly sad for her. She had not yet even begun to anticipate the pain that would consume her. As I sat alone at my kitchen table, I wondered if it would be possible to carry on living with knowledge such as hers. She would continue to blame Luke but I also knew from listening to her that she would blame herself more. Her fury would turn inwards, until it destroyed her.

I was still in my dressing gown, my wet hair almost dry. I changed quickly and pulled myself together. I washed up the cups and glasses we had used, wanting no reminders of Caroline's presence. It was strange how life outmanoeuvred plans, I thought. Just days ago, the idea of leaving Millbury Street was a sad one, and yet now the old life was suddenly and categorically over. I had no doubt that Kit and Isobel would feel the same way. What pleasure could there be to look out on to the garden now, down to the watery basin where a young man's body had lain in disarray?

I walked out through the side gate which was quiet, unlike the main gate further up, which was still manned by two uniformed policemen. There was a marked police car outside, and an air of people coming and going. I walked quickly up the street hoping to avoid eye contact with any neighbours, most of whom, thank God, I didn't know. My phone was telling me they were all trying to reach me, Kit,

Isobel, Jack, but I didn't return the calls. I sent text messages instead, stalling for some time, some air to breathe. I should at least have rung Kit who was waiting at the police station, but I didn't want to know what was happening to Luke. I had heard enough.

I caught my usual bus. There is a comfort in familiarity, and I let it take me down to Victoria. I wished I could get into my little flat now, straight away, but it wasn't yet empty. I would walk around, I thought, acclimatise myself to the changes I had half observed over the years and which now I would need to absorb. Many of the old shops had gone, replaced by familiar high street names. I couldn't be nostalgic, for much of the area had been dull and depressing, but I did regret the passing of some of the smaller eccentricities like the bespoke bag maker, and the pet shop that had once been hidden in a side street.

I went into the cathedral and, as I had intended all along, I lit my candle for the dead. At the top of my list I put the name of Tim Raven, a boy I had never met. For the first time in many years, I crossed myself, knelt down and crossed myself again, saying a prayer for Caroline Raven as well as for her son. Then I walked up the nave, hardly aware of the visitors who were few at this time of year and sat in a pew, not my usual seat but one right in the centre of the building, while I tried to take in what had happened to me.

I felt frightened, more afraid than I could remember having been ever before. I was afraid for Luke, afraid of what he might have done, afraid of who he really was. I was afraid for Kit and Isobel, for their happiness. But it was myself I was most afraid for, afraid for my future, for my judgement, for my conscience. I gazed down the aisle at the statue of Mary and her homunculus child, the one which had so attracted the young Alice. Well, she had had her baby too, just as I had predicted she would. But what a sad and sorry story it had turned out to be.

I knelt down and said a final prayer. Everything I had thought solid had given way in the last few weeks. And there hadn't been much to start with. I had been living from day to day, offering to those who knew me an illusion of stability, a sense that I had made the best of an awkward life. And now the enormity of my loneliness swept in on me, forcing me to accept, if only briefly, the consolations of a religion that I had thought extinct, consolations that pushed me to salvage what redemption I could, for myself, and for Luke.

As I walked down the steps outside into the tiny square in front of the cathedral, I became aware of a figure moving towards me, as if it had been waiting for me to emerge.

'Josie.'

'Ilya.' I wasn't surprised to see him. I wanted to say, 'What are you doing here?' but there seemed no point. 'I thought the police might have detained you,' I said instead.

'No. Why should they? I was not at the party.' He smiled.

'Did you follow me?' I said.

'I wait for you to leave Millbury Street.' I was aware again of the American slant to his accent. But his English seemed to have partly reverted to its former usage. 'Then you took bus.'

'So you did follow me?'

He inclined his head. 'There was no rush,' he said. 'I saw Caroline leave your place. I wanted you to have time.'

It seemed an odd thing for him to say but I understood what he meant. It was all coming to an end in some way. There was almost a sense of not wanting to hurry things. Or rather wanting to slow down, to have time to take things in.

'I don't suppose I should be talking to you,' I said.

'Why not?'

'I don't understand you,' I said, 'but what you've done, it's very wrong.'

'Now I don't understand you,' he said.

'You're a pimp, Ilya. At the very least. And the only reason I'm still standing here is because I expect little else of you. You were always crooked.'

He looked hurt at my words, then shrugged.

'We see things differently,' he said. 'Perhaps if you came from where I come from . . .'

'And where is that exactly?' I asked.

He smiled. 'Easier for me if you don't know.'

'No doubt.' I waited a moment, and then I asked him the question that had been forming in my mind. 'You knew, didn't you? You knew about Luke?' That was as far as I had got. It was beyond my powers of reasoning to ask how, or why, or when.

'Yes,' he said. 'And no.' He took my arm and dropped it as I flinched.

'I am not the devil, Josie. You will see. Let's go somewhere inside. It's cold for you, standing here.'

He was right. It was cold but I had hardly noticed. Now I began to shiver. He led the way across Victoria Street and through a back road to a small Polish café which could have been there since the fifties. I remembered it as Italian, so it must have changed hands, a new wave of immigrants had taken it over. Where once there had been bottles of grappa and Fernet Branca, now there were vodkas of various kinds.

The man behind the counter greeted Ilya with excitement, speaking to him in rapid Polish which Ilya clearly understood. The language was no shock, but I was taken aback by the familiarity.

'You've been here before?' I said, as we sat down in a small back room.

'No. But I know him a little,' Ilya said. 'I know his family.'

Vodka was set down in front of us and I raised my eyebrows.

'You would like coffee?' Ilya said. 'Don't worry, it's coming. Vodka and coffee, yes?'

I became aware for the first time that morning, of feeling hung over. I was running on adrenalin, exhausted but wide awake. A shot of vodka was appealing, and I lifted the small glass to my lips and drank half of it.

'*Na zdrowie!*' he said, and drained his glass. We were sitting in the far corner of the room, furthest from the public part of the café, but still he lowered his voice.

'You are very patient, Josie. I feel you are waiting.'

'Yes. Waiting for you to tell me what you know.'

I wanted to add 'you bastard', but I felt quite calm. Somewhere in the past fifteen minutes since I'd met him I had taken the decision to elicit what I could by complicity. In my moment of acceptance in the cathedral, I had known that whatever Luke had done, I must try to help him face up to the truth. But to do that I would need to know what it was.

'First of all, Josie,' Ilya said, 'I want you to know it was an accident, this death. I am sure of it. That is what they will say, the police. I am hoping that Luke will be free soon. He just found the boy dead. He telephoned me to help him. I made him phone police straight away. I arrive after police.'

'There are so many questions,' I said. I picked up my glass and finished the measure of vodka. It slipped down my throat, cold and burning at the same time, clearing my head and helping to focus my thoughts. 'I don't care about Luke's sordid party,' I went on. 'I do care that this boy is dead, of course I do. I care that Luke is in trouble, that he deceived us and lied to us, but the immediate question for me, Ilya, is how long have you known, about Luke?'

He sighed and poured himself another shot from the bottle between us.

'Toby knew,' he said.

My heart began to pound, not helped, I thought, by the vodka I had inflicted on it. Toby had known and had not told me. I had been closer to Alice than any of them and they had not seen fit to tell me. Because I was not one of them.

'How could that be?' I said. I was aware that my voice was barely audible.

'He promised Anne that no one, no one would know.'

'But he told you?' The pain of knowing that Toby had confided such a thing in Ilya and kept it from me was hard to bear.

'No, no. You do not understand, Josie. I did not know. I only know because the old man, Roddy, told me, many many years later. After Toby died.'

'After Alice died too,' I said. 'More to the point.'

'Yes. This is true. I was in Rome. I was . . . passing through. I went to see Roddy for old times' sake, to talk of Toby. We drink, a lot, and he tells me. He thinks I am able to find out about this boy. So I do. And I tell him the boy is okay. He has family. But when I try to tell him what I find later, he does not remember telling me, or seem to remember the boy. He was not well. He is not well now.'

'No.' That at least was true. 'So what did he tell you, Ilya, the first time?'

'That Alice was pregnant. That it was he who realised. That Anne was a stupid bitch – he said that – not me. It was too late to have abortion. He arranged it, the adoption. And then afterwards, Alice was not right, in the head. They had to put her in a hospital.'

'Yes, that's what Toby told me,' I said. 'About the hospital, not the pregnancy.'

'That's what Roddy said. I think it is true.'

'Yes,' I said. 'I think so too. It makes sense. But who was the father?'

'She would not speak of it, Roddy said. His wife think it

some boy she knew. In the end, Roddy said, perhaps better not to know.'

I looked at the vulpine, duplicitous face opposite me. I could see beneath the plumpness the remnants of what had once been so attractive to Toby, and I remembered how struck I had been that morning all those years ago when I had seen him almost naked. But both our lives had moved on, we were well past our prime, and we both carried in the folds of our ageing flesh our dirty little stories.

'So you contacted Luke? Did Roddy ask you to do that?'

'No. I didn't contact him. Not at first. I located him. Not difficult.'

Not difficult, I thought, if you were Ilya.

'He had been in trouble, but he was back home. Where I come from, fifteen is grown, for boys and for girls. He was fed, housed. I am not sentimental, Josie. These things we should not take for granted. Compared to some he was fortunate,' Ilya said. 'So I think he is okay. I think no more about the boy,' he went on, 'but then I hear about him, from the friend who find him for me.'

'The friend?' I said.

'Yes. Don't pretend, Josie, that you don't know what.'

I shrugged. 'I suppose I will never know,' I said.

'He tells me that Luke is in London. He has Luke's name in connection with something they are watching. He was escort, you know, rent-boy . . . just out of prison.'

I heard myself moan, a sort of wail of comprehension.

'Not on the street,' Ilya's voice was tight. 'He was too smart. He was with agency that my friend was

343

watching – they had interest – political. Once I knew this, I had to take action, no? What to do? Should I come to you and Kit, and say there is this boy, you know nothing about him, and he is a prostitute?'

Yes, I thought, *that is what you should have done.* But would we have believed Ilya? We might have thought he was trying to extort money as he had after Toby's death. Ilya was observing me now, testing me to see my reaction to what he was telling me, seeing how far he could go.

'I decide to approach Luke,' he said. 'To help him maybe. But by this time, he had moved on from agency. He was doing okay, he was at the college. He was still prostitute, but not so much, and for women, older women, of course, and more for clothes and for presents, cash too, but it was not so . . . sordid.'

'Not to you, perhaps,' I said. 'You were his pimp.'

'No. Never.'

'But you introduced him to Caroline,' I said.

'Yes, but not for that. I was, how you say, keeping an eye for him. I thought she was good business contact. Her husband was rich. I did not think that he . . . Luke . . . he had other woman, I thought . . . but then the son . . . my God.'

I listened to him, unsure whether all of what he said was true. I believed that Roddy had told him about Luke. I believed his dubious friends might have located him. I believed that Luke had been a rent-boy and a prostitute. I didn't believe that Ilya was not somehow involved with this last business, or that he was not guilty by implication in some way.

'I knew,' Ilya said, 'that Luke had found out about his mother. I waited for him to tell me. I did not tell him at first that I knew family.'

'It seems odd,' I said, 'that he should confide such a thing in you, Ilya, so soon.' But I knew it was not odd at all. Ilya, like Luke, was someone who could elicit intimacy when he chose to. Ilya smiled at me.

'I encouraged it, of course,' he said. 'And when he tells me I tell him that I know of the Haddeleys, that I knew Toby Haddeley, though I do not tell him all.' Ilya gave a sort of sad laugh, which for an instant made him almost human to me. 'I tell him I think it best to contact Kit,' he went on. 'But he tells me Kit has sent him a letter saying do not contact again.'

I remembered sitting at the table at Millbury Street with Isobel, not even ten months ago although it seemed an eternity, looking at the letter addressed to Alice Haddeley. That letter must have been a second one from Luke.

'Really,' I said, 'that sounds unlike Kit.'

'Why? The boy is not his.'

I could not explain to Ilya that Kit was a man who had been prepared to bring up a child with another man's DNA. But perhaps even Kit had felt that one was enough.

'Men protect the family,' Ilya said. 'That is what they do.' I was startled to hear him saying what I too had concluded. 'But you are right, Josie,' he went on. 'Kit is a good man so I tell Luke to write again.'

'He knew that Alice was dead.'

'Yes.'

'But he still addressed the letter to Alice.'

'Yes.'

I wondered if Ilya had told him to do it. He knew it would get under Kit's skin. I found myself wondering if, after all, this was some elaborate scam on Ilya's part, something to lever money out of Kit, out of Haddeley Antiquities. He would if he could, I was sure.

'I still don't understand why you hid yourself from us,' I said.

'I tell him not to say,' Ilya said. 'I am always this way, you know that.' I pulled a face but I had to admit the truth of what he said. 'And I was not sure you would welcome me,' he went on. 'You would disapprove.'

I pushed back my chair. Our friend, the patron, brought a second pot of coffee for us, talking and gesticulating to Ilya who shook his head and waved him away.

'Time to go,' he said. 'So do not worry. Lawyer says they will release Luke later today, he thinks.'

'What?' I said. 'You've known that all this time and didn't tell me.'

It was his turn to shrug. 'You did not ask,' he said.

'So he's cleared?'

'I did not say that,' he said. 'There may be more . . . formalities. They are waiting. I will tell you what I know, Josie, I promise.'

'Yes,' I said. 'You owe us that. One thing . . .'

'Yes.'

'The son, Caroline Raven's son. Is it true that he was Luke's lover?'

Ilya sighed. 'Lover, friend, man, woman, it is all same to

Luke. Sex means little. It is just a game, or exchange.'

'So what did he want from Tim Raven? He was just a boy.'

Ilya seemed to think about this carefully, and I was surprised to sense something other than cynicism emanating from him, some genuine emotional response that I had not seen before.

'I do not know,' he said. He sounded suddenly tired. 'To tease the mother maybe, to make her afraid?'

'How sad,' I said. 'How very very sad.'

He raised his vodka glass to his lips to steady himself. It was as if he too was about to lose heart.

'You think,' he said, 'that I manipulate Luke. But it is not so. Perhaps I tried to, for a while, but . . .' He seemed to be holding himself in, afraid of what he felt, and a thought that had been struggling to articulate itself in my mind for weeks now, saw its opportunity.

'Ilya,' I said. 'I need to ask you this. Don't be angry.' My heart was pounding but I had to go on. 'I have to know this. Is it possible that Luke is your child?'

His face showed no expression, and I very much wished that I had let him pour me another shot of vodka.

'Why do you ask me this?' he said.

'Your interest in Luke,' I said. I could not bring myself to tell him how I had spied on him, how I had lurked on the landing, too timid to enter a fifteen-year-old's room. I shrugged. 'You traced him,' I went on. 'You watched over him in your odd way. If it's true, you have an odd way of showing fatherly concern, I grant you, but . . .'

'But?'

'You're unlike anyone else I have ever met.'

'How could this be true, Josie? It's not possible.'

I scrutinised Ilya's features, comparing them with Luke's. I could see nothing to substantiate my hunch.

'It is possible,' I said. 'You were there.'

'Many people were there. Many people. And what about this boy they all talked of?'

I shook my head.

'Take a test,' I said. He smiled.

'Maybe,' he said. 'Maybe, for you. But this is not the time, Josie.'

He was humouring me, playing with me. But he was right that this was not the time.

'Don't say anything to Luke about this,' I said, 'will you?'

It was a stupid thing to ask and it made him smile again.

'I will say nothing, certainly,' he said.

We parted on the pavement outside the café, barely able to hear one another for the sound of drilling nearby. He was impatient to be off. There had always been something in Ilya's manner that suggested he felt he should be somewhere else, that another life awaited him. He offered his hand to me and to my surprise I took it. I needed him now. I needed to keep him on side, to tell me more, for there was more to come. There had to be.

I walked from the café to St James's Park. It was deserted. Even the birds seemed to be hiding in the thickets, waiting for the year to begin in earnest. I sat down on a bench, pulling up the collar of my coat against the wind which had begun to increase, and returned Kit's call. He sounded strained, and anxious.

'Where have you been, Josie?' he said. 'We've all been worried about you.'

I was about to tell him, to say that I had been with the man he thought of as Michael Kovalchuk, but then I thought better of it. Not yet, I decided.

'I'm just out and about. I wanted a walk, Kit, to think a bit. Where are you?'

'We're at home. The police have let us back in. There's still a bit of the garden that's out of bounds, but they seem to have finished with the inside of the house, thank God. We can get it cleaned up. Mrs Andrews is coming in and her daughter is going to help out too. It's not too bad. There's no real damage.' There was a silence as we both realised the absurdity of what he had said.

'To the fabric of the house, I meant,' he said. 'Of course there's damage of another kind.'

'I thought you might decide to stay at the hotel for a bit,' I said.

'No, no need for that,' he said. 'We have to face these things.'

These things? They were hardly commonplace, I thought.

'Did you see Luke?'

'No. They're still questioning him. But they will probably release him later on. They're unlikely to charge him, it seems, according to the lawyer.'

'That's a relief.'

'Yes. It seems as if it was an accident.'

'That shouldn't make it better,' I said, 'but it does.'

'Yes,' he said. 'I know.' He paused and I knew that he was about to say something he found difficult. 'I have to ask you this, Josie. You didn't know about this party, did you?'

'Of course not.'

'Sorry, I had to ask. I knew you wouldn't have but . . .'

'Does Isobel think I knew?'

'No, not really.'

So she did. She really did think I was an idiot. Well, perhaps I deserved her scorn.

'I'll come home in a while,' I said.

'Would you like some lunch?' Kit asked.

I thought of the night's drinking I had done, and of Caroline Raven, and the coffee and vodka. All I had eaten was some smoked salmon, this morning at Jack's, left over from last night, and a piece of baguette. I was hungry, but even so, the notion of returning to a normal routine, of sitting down to lunch in the kitchen at Millbury Street with Kit and Isobel felt impossible.

'No thanks,' I said. 'I'll get a sandwich on the way.'

He rang me at about five o' clock. I had returned once again to the gallery. I needed contact with what was left of my real life, my old life, and I was leafing through a catalogue proof which had arrived that morning, ready for the New York fair.

I was half-expecting Luke's call. And when I heard his voice at the end of the phone, I found that my stomach was churning as if he really were a lover, though my feelings towards him were closer to hatred for what he had done to us all. He asked if he could come and see me, and said that he would prefer it if we were alone. Kit had arranged for him to stay in a hotel. It was clear, he said, that Isobel did not want to see him, let alone have him in the house.

I had gone back to Millbury Street, briefly, where an air of brisk activity, the sound of hoovering and the smell of disinfectant was overwhelming. Isobel had said little to me and as the three of us gathered, drinking tea as if to ward off the spirits, her eyes, when they met mine, were angry. I noticed that every now and then her fists would clench and unclench as Kit fussed around her. He had persuaded her to visit her doctor that morning, to be checked over, but all was well, at least with the baby. She had closed the shutters in the kitchen where we were sitting in semi-darkness, so as not to be able to see out to the water's edge.

'I'm so very sorry, Isobel,' I said, finally, when Kit had gone upstairs to supervise the cleaning of his office, and check that all his papers were intact.

'It's not your fault,' she said.

'I feel as though it is.'

'No.' She was emphatic. 'Look, I admit I'm furious with you in one way, but it's myself I'm really pissed at. Dad's right. I should have followed my gut feeling.'

'What could you have done?' I said, just as she had once said to me.

'Made an effort to find out more. It wouldn't have been that difficult. Why were we all so hands-off?'

'He's a grown man,' I said. 'We were respecting his privacy. We thought he needed time – all those things, I suppose.'

'We were crazy.'

'Yes.'

Luke appeared in the gallery unshaven, wearing the clothes he had worn the night before, though I knew that Kit had taken clean things of his own to the police station for Luke to change into. The black suit Luke was wearing looked, as always, expensive, but the knees of the trousers were stained with earth and grass and there was a smear on the thigh. Seeing the marks I felt sick. What were they – vomit, semen? And I wondered what sort of torment, or pretext, had obliged Luke to continue to wear them, a man who was usually so fastidious.

I gestured to the chair in which he habitually sat, but he chose to remain standing. It was just as well. If he had sat down within my reach, I might have hit him.

'I'm going to have a whisky now,' I said instead. 'If you want one, get your own.' He shook his head.

I sat in my chair, clutching my glass, and he perched on the edge of his desk but he would not look at me. He couldn't face my fury.

'It was an accident,' he said, eventually. 'Tim, I . . . he shouldn't even have been there.'

'Caroline Raven came to see me this morning,' I said. I was surprised to find my voice even and rather cool, despite the anger I felt. 'She had been to identify her son. The boy's mother . . . why did you . . . What were you . . .?' I turned away from him. 'I don't know why I'm even asking you. I clearly know so little about you.'

He raised his head.

'She told me about you, Luke,' I went on, 'about what you . . . are.'

'I was stopping,' he said. 'Did she tell you that? Did she tell you how she begged me to go on seeing her?'

'Don't,' I said. 'It doesn't matter. Her son is dead.'

Neither of us could speak. We sat almost motionless, each waiting for the other to say something.

'How could you do this to Kit?' I said. 'How could you arrange to hold a party in his house, in his absence, in my absence, like a teenager?'

He looked up again briefly. 'It was just to make some money. I thought if I just put some cash together. I owed a bit. Then I could stop. Go to America.'

'I don't understand.'

'I charged them, the people who came. Like a club. You know.'

'No, I don't.'

'A sex club, they came for sex. We usually do it at this other place, but I thought if we used Millbury Street for once, I'd make more money.'

'I see. Do the police know that?'

'Probably. But all I did was charge an entry fee to a load of swingers.'

353

'Drugs?' I said.

'A bit of that too.'

I had thought that my years with Toby at Millbury Street had been dissolute, but Luke's account was so tawdry and the poor boy's death such a terrible consequence that it was like some fag-end of our collusion with decadence, a vulgar, if tragic, repercussion of an earlier life.

'Tell me what happened,' I said. 'With the boy.'

Luke put his hands in his pockets. He sighed before he spoke and all I could think was that it was likely to be for effect.

'Tim was drunk,' he began. 'He'd been taking drugs. He was upset. He was obsessed with me, practically stalking me. He'd heard about the party and someone let him in. He was being a pain and there was a fight. Someone hit him. But everyone said he was okay, walking about afterwards. But then he must have collapsed, too close to the water. And he drowned.'

It was a possible explanation, plausible even, and it tallied with what Caroline Raven had said about her son's infatuation. Why should I not believe him? But nothing about Luke had substance now. Much of what he had been to me was a fantasy spun by him, a fantasy I had willingly entered.

'What are you going to do now then?' I asked.

He took a deep breath. 'I'm on bail,' he said. 'I've got to report to the police station each evening,' he added. 'They know it was an accident, but I don't think it's finished yet, Josie, I think they want someone sent down for it.'

I thought this was a far-fetched interpretation of events, but what did I know?

'I expect they're just trying to establish the truth,' I said.

'I was nowhere near Tim when the fight happened. I was hacked off with him for coming, it's true, but I hardly spoke to him.'

'You're all right then, aren't you?' I said. His self-justification repelled me. He seemed concerned only for himself. There was little regret for what had happened, no sense of shame or guilt. He was someone else, sitting there in his dirty suit. He was not the boy I had taken in and loved.

'So what will you do now?' I asked. 'Where are you staying?'

'At a hotel, near my lawyer's house.' He shrugged and looked almost puzzled, as if these strange events had little to do with him.

'Your lawyer,' I said. 'This is the one "Michael" procured for you?' I was no longer prepared to keep silent. 'His real name is Ilya, you know.' As soon as I said it, I realised that this name by which I had known him was as unlikely to be real as any other.

Luke shrugged. 'He sometimes uses different names. We call him Michael.'

'We?'

'People I know – the lawyer – he's a friend of Michael's.'

'Did you know Michael was a friend of Kit's uncle Toby, your mother's godfather?'

'I know he met my mother, that he knew Toby.'

'He and Toby were lovers.'

He was silent. 'I didn't know that,' he said.

'Are you gay, Luke?' I had felt, suddenly, that I had to ask.

He laughed. 'No,' he said. 'But I do what I have to do. Don't be a prude, Josie. I never had you down for a prude.'

I had liked to think I wasn't, that all those years with Toby had left me unshockable. I knew about boys that were paid for, and it would be true to say that Luke would not be the first to have set foot in Millbury Street. I knew about drugs; indeed I had had my own flirtation with them. But this life of Luke's was different again. It was the casual treachery that I couldn't accommodate, let alone the anatomical indifference to whichever sex he encountered.

When I recalled the recent nights he had spent in my bed, I shuddered. I had tried to think of them as just a natural hunger for human warmth, innocent in their intent, despite the final consummation. But now I was forced to see that on Luke's part it must have been more calculated. I felt dirty and ugly, and wondered what it was, precisely, that he had intended I should do for him in return.

'You've been good to me,' Luke said. 'And I'm sorry.'

I couldn't bear to look at him. His attempt at contrition made me hate him.

'For what, exactly?' I said.

He shook his head. 'Not being what you wanted. Not being like my mother.'

'No,' I said, 'and it breaks my heart. You have broken

my heart, Luke. But for her sake, I wish I could help you. She would have wanted me to.'

And then he had gone, and the gallery was empty again. I sat on the old chaise longue where Alice had once taken her naps, and I closed my eyes and half dozed, unable to sleep despite an overwhelming exhaustion. Pictures of the garden at Millbury Street played on the back of my eyelids. Alice was dancing across them as she had at Cricklewood Station the day before the Roman party, whirling about, both innocent and knowing. And then she was lying on the lawn, gasping, her clothes soaked with water and her skirt pulled up around her waist. It was a shocking image and I opened my eyes at once to try to erase it.

∽

The day after Toby's party, Alice and I had gone to Fortnum & Mason for a late lunch. It was one of her favourite places. She liked to order Welsh rarebit and seldom strayed from her choice. Toby and Ilya had still been asleep when we left, as far as I was aware. Alice, to my surprise, had knocked on my door, still in her dressing gown, just before noon.

She was unusually quiet over lunch, but she had been up till almost dawn and it was something of a relief to me that the heightened mood of the previous few days appeared to have subsided. I had already decided that I would write a confidential letter to the school doctor, with a copy to Anne, stating my concern, limited as it was, about Alice's swift changes of mood. I would, of course, have to tell

Alice, before she went back, and I was not looking forward to the conversation.

'You must be tired, darling,' I began after we had ordered. 'You were up very late last night.'

'Oh,' she said. 'Not really.'

'I got up to go to the loo,' I said. 'I heard Toby in your room. It was very naughty of him to keep you up like that. I thought you'd gone to bed.'

She shook her head. 'I did, sort of. But he came to say goodnight and I wasn't really asleep. So they came and told me stories about the party. They said that one man had almost set fire to the little boat, trying to light a spliff.'

Very amusing, I thought. And just the sort of thing we should not be exposing her to. But I was as much to blame.

'I'm just concerned that you get enough sleep,' I said. 'We can't have you going back to do exams looking like a heroin addict.'

'Thanks a lot, Josie.'

'Circles round the eyes, I meant. So Ilya was there too, last night?'

'Yes. They were both there. They were stoned I think, or something.' She took a bite of rarebit, signalling the end of this post mortem as far as she was concerned.

'I expect they'd had too much to drink,' I said. 'How much did you have to drink, young lady?'

'Only a bit.'

'Did you smoke anything?' I asked. She pulled a face and shrugged.

'Can we go to the cinema this afternoon?' she said.

'Good idea,' I said. 'Toby can mind the shop.'

'The shop?'

'It's just an expression,' I said. But the word reminded me of her mother, and a further pricking of responsibility made itself felt.

'Toby didn't leave you on your own with Ilya, did he?' I asked.

She looked at me, startled, and blushed. 'No. What do you mean? No.'

'I didn't mean anything,' I said.

She wouldn't look at me.

'I know what you meant,' she said. Her words surprised me. Did she know? I supposed she probably did. She and her friends were so much more worldly than I had ever been. And Alice in particular was so very much her own person, almost eccentrically adult, in her way.

'I'm just fussing,' I said.

'There's nothing to fuss about,' she said. 'Eat up your lunch. It will get cold.'

When we got back to the house in the early evening, we found Toby in the drawing room all by himself, looking ill and gloomy but nursing a large gin and tonic.

'Ilya's gone again,' he said.

'Oh,' I said. 'But I thought you knew that was going to happen. You said he was only here for a few days.' He had already been at Millbury Street longer than I cared to have him.

'Yes, but . . . you know, Josie. He's always been special. And I've no idea when he will be back, and he barely keeps in touch. By the way, Alice, I let him take the Tawaret, he needs to sell it, and it's worth quite a lot of money now. It certainly shouldn't be hanging around the house. It was his after all. You don't mind, do you?'

I looked at Alice. She was staring at Toby with what almost seemed like hatred. She turned without saying anything, and I heard her run up the stairs.

❧

I was still immersed in the past on the old chaise longue when Kit let himself into Belgrave Square. It had been dark outside for what seemed like hours. I knew he had been trying to reach me. Perhaps I had wanted him to come and find me. And now he had.

'You've heard from Luke, I presume?' he said.

'Yes. He came here, briefly.'

He sat down where Luke had sat just an hour ago. He looked exhausted and there were lines I had not noticed before running from his mouth to his chin. He must, I thought, be very angry, but there was no evidence of it.

'You look terrible,' I said.

He tried to smile. 'It's the betrayal,' he said, 'that I hate more than anything.'

'Yes,' I said. 'I know. But I should have . . .'

'You mustn't blame yourself, Josie.' Kit stopped me. 'No one thinks you're to blame. None of us are. We all thought we were doing what was right.'

I stood up and walked across the room and back, my arms folded, then sat down again.

'You're right,' I said. 'I do blame myself, but it's a waste of time. We must decide what to do, what to do for the best.'

'That's more like you,' he said. 'Pragmatic and sensible.'

But not entirely, I thought. I had my own wings of fantasy. Alice had known that.

'Come home with me,' he said. 'Isobel is worried about you. So is Jack.'

'Jack?' I repeated. But I wasn't sure if I wanted to see Jack. He had heard too much from me. I was too raw. But what else could I do but go back with Kit. Where else would I go? Millbury Street was still my home.

Twenty-Two

There is an advantage to age. There is the knowledge that life will continue, and that although the residue of any unpleasantness will hang around, the shock will recede soon enough and most likely be replaced by a more robust response. By the Monday after New Year, I felt better. I had almost shaken myself free, and although it was impossible to contemplate the death of a young man in our garden without horror and sadness, I could begin to see beyond Luke and look to the future with something approaching optimism.

I was to move back into the Victoria flat at the end of the month, and I had spent most of Sunday planning a complete revamping of its tiny interior. I would make it a perfect gem. Kit had persuaded me to take a morning off, and I had spent it sorting through my cupboards, filling bags with rubbish and clothes and objects for charity. My life was to start anew and I wanted nothing but essentials to accompany me.

The gallery was still ghostly and silent when I reached it after lunch. Business never picked up till mid-January. But Kit had assured me he would be back towards the end of the afternoon and life was starting to resume some semblance of normality. Isobel had gone to her studio. The police had packed up and now there was almost nothing to suggest they had ever been at Millbury Street, just the marks on the lawn from their shoes, and the holes where they had erected their sad white tent. Rita had gone to the bank and left Frank beside me in his basket. I watched him, quivering and twitching, envying him his dog's dream world, untroubled by mortality or love.

I heard someone put their key in the lock and assumed it must be Rita or Kit. Frank sprang up and barked briefly but quickly began to wag his tail. A moment later, Luke appeared in the office doorway. His face looked relaxed, more as it once had been.

'Hello, Josie,' he said. 'How's business?'

His tone contained all his easy charm. It was almost as if nothing had happened and this attitude threw me into an irritable confusion.

'What are you doing here?' I said.

'I came to see Kit,' he said. 'Is he upstairs?'

'No, Luke. There's only me.'

We looked at each other, waiting.

'I'm glad it's just you,' he said. He perched once again on the desk in front of me and now he was suddenly confidential, a supplicant. 'I've been thinking, a lot. I just sat in the hotel room all weekend and I thought about everything, about what you said, and I really want to start again. No, I'm serious,' he said, as I raised my eyebrows in disbelief. 'The thing is, I told you already,' he lowered his voice, 'all the sex stuff, I really was stopping.'

I felt distant from him now. It was all too late, I thought. It had all gone too far. The only thing I wanted from him was information, to know what he knew, and what he didn't.

'Then tell me this,' I said. 'I have to ask you. Was Ilya – Michael – was he involved with the prostitution? Was he involved in that?'

Luke looked down at the floor, saying nothing.

'Was he?' I insisted.

'He tried to get me out of the escort business, doing men that is. And he did. But I'd threatened to go back, so he fixed me up with a couple of women. He said it was less dangerous.'

I put my head in my hands.

'I'm sorry,' he said. 'I know you don't get it.'

I looked up at him. 'No,' I said. 'I don't.'

'He was a friend. He looked out for me,' Luke said.

'Did you never wonder why? Did you never think it was odd, that he knew us? It was a bit of a coincidence, wasn't it?'

Luke stared off into space. 'Sometimes,' he said.

'What did you think?'

'That he was using me. But I was using him. That's how it is.'

'What do you mean?'

He sat down finally on the chair at the desk and swivelled backwards and forwards for a moment.

'I'd found out who I was by then, and I told him. He said he knew you. He knows a lot of things, Michael, or he finds them out. It was him who encouraged me. He said you would probably come across. You'd feel guilty.'

'Well, he was right about that,' I said. 'What about the bowl he was trying to sell us. I assume that was him?'

'He said Kit owed him money, or rather Toby Haddeley did, and if I could help him get it he'd give me a share.'

'How?'

'I was going to get you to buy his stuff, but without you knowing it was him, that was the plan. I don't know where he got the stuff from.'

'That sounds a bit naïve for Ilya,' I said.

'It was me that was naïve,' Luke said. 'It was supposed to be a long-term plan. He was pissed off with me for telling you about the bowl. He said it was much too soon, you would be suspicious, but I didn't want to wait. And he was right. He's usually right.' Luke sat down suddenly in his old chair and began to examine his fingers. 'It was wrong, Josie. I know that. But Michael . . . he's okay, Michael, in other ways. He says we're like each other. We're the same sort.'

'He said that?'

'Yes.'

I was tired of being careful with Luke, tired of protecting him.

'I've sometimes wondered if he could be your father,' I said. The words were out before I had the chance to consider whether or not they should be spoken aloud.

Luke looked up and stared at me as if I had threatened to hit him. 'But you said he was . . .'

'Gay? I would have thought you should know that there

are plenty of people who can go either way if and when it suits them,' I said.

'No, I didn't mean that. You said he was Toby Haddeley's boy?'

'So?'

'It's not true,' he said.

'It may not be,' I said. 'But whatever he says, I think it's possible.'

He had turned white. I could see from his face that he was thinking about Michael, or Ilya, or whoever we were talking about, thinking back to details, conversations, conspiracies, lies. He pulled his phone from his pocket and pressed a number.

'Don't,' I said. He shook his head and turned away from me.

'Michael,' I heard him say. To my surprise there was no trace, as he spoke, of the shock and fierce emotion of just a moment before. I heard him ask if they could meet up and it was arranged for within the hour. He said nothing to Ilya about our exchange. I even heard him laugh.

But he was not laughing when he turned to me, clearly about to leave. He was tense, and his mood was quite different from the one he had brought in with him. When he spoke to me his voice was soft.

'It can't be true,' he said. 'But I have to ask him.'

'Feel free,' I said. 'He knows what I think.'

'Why didn't you tell me before?'

'I didn't know that you knew him till Friday night, Luke. Or I wasn't sure. I thought I saw him at the airport, when you went to Rome.'

Luke nodded. 'He came too.'

'Why?'

'He wanted to. It suited me, he knew Roddy and Domenico. And he wanted me to smuggle something back for him, a painting, a small one, but I wouldn't.'

'That's something, at least,' I said.

'Only because I thought I might get caught, Josie. I'm sorry, but that's the truth. That's what you want isn't it, the truth?'

After he had gone, I began to consider his sudden, final, directness. I wanted to feel cold towards Luke, or at least indifferent, but there was still the matter of what was owed to Alice, and perhaps, despite everything, to him. For a moment he had allowed me, once again, to think that there might be something worthwhile in him, something we should struggle to save. Within minutes of Luke leaving Belgrave Square, however, Ilya rang.

'Josie?'

'Yes.'

'Something is wrong.'

'Everything is wrong, Ilya.'

'With Luke. Just this minute.'

'I told him,' I said. 'I told him I thought you might be his father.'

There was silence at the other end. Then he said, 'That was not wise, Josie.'

'Maybe not,' I said. 'But this way you can rule it out.'

'I told you,' he said. 'This is not the most important thing.'

'I think it is to him,' I said.

'No. Not now. It seems the police will charge Luke now.'

Each time I had a grip on this peculiar reality in which I was swimming, events shifted.

'Why? How do you know?'

'I pay lawyer to know. Police have evidence now. Forensic, witnesses, Caroline Raven. First it looked okay. Now it does not look good.'

'Are you saying you think Luke may have caused the boy's death?'

'It is possible. Maybe accident. Maybe problem between them. I have known many like Luke. It is possible. Whatever, he did not tell police the truth.'

I felt as if I was going to faint.

'The truth,' I said. 'An elusive commodity. I think maybe, Ilya, that you too have not told the police all you should. I think perhaps it is time that I spoke to the police and then maybe we will get to know what is the truth.'

There was a pause on the other end of the line and then he said, 'You want to know?' He sounded flat, almost sorrowful. 'I will tell you. But you will be sorry for knowing. I will meet you. I will bring Luke to you, to your flat, in two hours. And I will tell you what you already know, I think. Then we will all go to the police. Yes? But say nothing, please, till then. Better to stay where you are now, then come.'

I sat at my desk, waiting for the moment when I could set off for home. I had no idea why I was obeying Ilya in this way, but I did not, in any case, want to sit alone in my flat waiting for them. When Rita returned to the office, wanting to tell me about offsetting and VAT and spreadsheets, I pretended to show some interest, then followed our usual ritual, making tea, slipping the dog a biscuit, and all the time watching the clock.

❧

As I walked down Millbury Street, towards the house, my heartbeat increased and I heard the blood rush in my ears, a surreal soundtrack to the pictures of my curious life which now played out in front of me, as they say they do when one is drowning. I put my key in the side door and stepped through into the courtyard. It was silent. Kit was still out and would no doubt once again come looking for me at the gallery. Isobel was at the studio, painting her scientist. I opened the door of my apartment and as I climbed the narrow stairs, I could hear the noise of the geese calling somewhere in the distance.

As I passed through the hallway to the kitchen I noticed that the door to Luke's bedroom was open, although I had closed it myself that morning. I pushed it further, half afraid, and saw at once that the room had been stripped. I felt the dull chill of defeat as I turned to go to the kitchen. On the table there was a note and on top was a small ball of carefully folded newspaper. I knew at once what it was. I sat down on a chair and picked up the little parcel, slowly unwrapping its leaves to reveal the little lapis lazuli Tawaret. Ilya had kept it after all, and now here it was, once again in the palm of my hand. I picked up the note and read it. '*Keep safe for us both – Ilya*', it said. So he still trusted me with his money, though not with his plans. They had gone. And they would soon, I had no doubt, be far away. Ilya had arranged it all.

I wondered when I would see them again, if ever. Or if Luke would ever know the truth about Alice. We had failed her, I above all. I should have understood everything long ago, even worse, perhaps I had. But as I sat at my table with a large glass of whisky, burning the note Ilya had left in an ashtray, I felt a sense of profound relief that at last Luke had gone, and Alice with him. And I was glad that he was not alone, but with Ilya, who understood him best. We would all be gone soon, after all. It was over.

Twenty-Three

I light candles now for the living as well as the dead. I light them for Luke and even for Ilya on occasion, when I am feeling generous. I come into the cathedral almost every day now that I live so close by. I'm enjoying life alone more than I thought I might. There is time to read and to think, and to see those friends that I have who are not part of the Haddeley life. There is an increasing number since I started my art class and my part-time MA, as Kit suggested. I work at the gallery two days a week, though I also go to the bigger trade fairs to help out Kit and young James, a great-nephew of Margaret's who has come to learn the business and to bring youth to our moribund world.

I rarely see Jack Whaley these days. We could not sustain our New Year moment of closeness, or perhaps I could not, though we both remember it fondly, and when Doctor Helen reappeared once again, he took her back. They are happy enough, certainly well suited. It's my fate, it seems, to be alone, but Kit and Isobel live quite near by, in Pimlico. They have made me godmother to their daughter Stella. She's a beautiful girl, born this summer, and I'm grateful to them for giving me this chance to get to know her.

As I sit in my old pew, here in my side chapel, and watch all the people walk slowly past, lost in their thoughts or gazing at the statues and pictures, the crucifixes and hangings, I think how many secrets they must carry. We wish to value truth, and yet I have come to think that, after all, it is not always best expressed. It carries too much power to hurt and shatter. I had known the truth about Luke before I could bring myself to admit it. I had wanted to believe his father was Ilya. But I had noticed the evidence at Christmas. I had noticed those strange webbed toes, a small birth defect I had seen before.

I have asked myself if I had known the truth for far longer as Ilya had implied. If I had seen or heard anything else in those months or years. And I am sure that I did not. I am sure that it must just have been that one strange night, unforgivable as it was. Toby was full of drugs, I keep telling myself; he was corrupted, by Ilya, by all of them. Toby loved Alice and she loved him. She would have forgiven him, even if she understood that what was happening was wrong. For him, I have no doubt, it was part of an endless search for something he would never find. But whatever I tell myself, the truth of what happened colours everything I have known and loved. I loved Toby. I loved a man capable of such a thing. I failed to protect Alice. Her mother had been right about me in her muddled way, but the failure was not in Alice's imaginative world, but in mine and Toby's. We had made our own fairy tales. We had built our castles in the air. And our legacy was a prince whose shining countenance had turned ugly.

I go to Mass now, twice a week, and to confession. I do

Good Works. I am told I am forgiven but it is difficult to accept. I think of Luke and I pray for him and that is all I can do. But like Alice, he is in some ways still with us, and there is always hope. When I see Kit, I see the best of Luke, for Kit is, of course, his cousin. When I see my innocent god-daughter, Stella, I see Luke, and when I see the hint of extra skin between Stella's small toes, I ask myself if it's possible that I see Luke there too. Could it be that Isobel sought him out, desperate to give Kit the child he wanted? I will never know, and either way this baby is a miracle of conception. But if it were to be true, and I were to know it, I would keep a father's secret.

Acknowledgements

I would like to thank Kate Morris, Deborah Susman, Kathleen Tessaro, my agent Judith Murray and editor Kate Parkin, and all at John Murray, for their help and support. I would also like especially to thank Rupert Wace for his invaluable guidance through antiquities – should there be any errors over pricing or practice, past or present, they are mine and not his. Finally I would like to thank Tony Wells for his close reading and his forbearance.

Read more . . .

Belinda Seaward

HOTEL JULIET

A love story

Memory Cougan, beautiful, black and in her twenties, has a successful career and a boyfriend who adores her. But on the eve of her engagement party, she panics. Brought to London and adopted at the age of five, she has no recollection of her childhood in Africa or why she left. Leaving her life in London behind, she returns to the country she no longer recognises – and to Max, the reclusive coffee planter who may just have the answers she needs.

Moving from Scotland and London to Africa and back again over twenty years, *Hotel Juliet* tells the poignant story of four people whose lives play out against the endless skies and wild beauty of the African landscape. An exquisitely written novel with at its heart a passionate love triangle that resonates down to the present day, it combines pathos and tragedy with the possibility of glorious redemption.

'A thrillingly observant writer and crafter of highly sensual prose, Seaward employs the language and lore of the skies to considerable metaphorical effect . . . its richly descriptive escapism is seductive'
Daily Mail

Order your copy now by calling Bookpoint on 01235 827716 or visit your local bookshop quoting ISBN 978-0-7195-2450-9 www.johnmurray.co.uk